Blood Red,
Sister Rose

Blood Red, Sister Rose

Thomas Keneally

HODDER AND STOUGHTON
LONDON SYDNEY AUCKLAND TORONTO

British Library Cataloguing in Publication Data
Keneally, Thomas
 Blood red, sister rose.
 I. Title
 823[F]   PR9619.3.K46

ISBN 0 340 35449 6

Hodder and Stoughton Editorial Office: 47 Bedford Square, London WC1B 3DP.

BOOK ONE

Shadow Kings

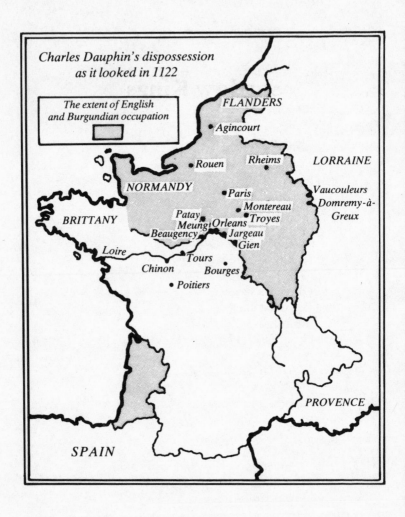

Charles Dauphin's dispossession
as it looked in 1122

The extent of English
and Burgundian occupation

FLANDERS

Agincourt

Rouen

Rheims

LORRAINE

NORMANDY

Paris

Vaucouleurs
Domremy-à-
Greux

Patay

Montereau

Meung

Orleans

Troyes

BRITTANY

Beaugency

Jargeau

Gien

Loire

Tours

Chinon

Bourges

Poitiers

PROVENCE

SPAIN

When young Charles was seven he lived in his own suite of apartments at the Hotel Barbette in the capital. His mother lived on other floors at the Barbette and sometimes visited him. Since she would bring with her a leopard on a leash or a baboon with smelly breath, Charles never liked her visits.

His mind was already subject to priest tutors, Dominican theologians from the University of Paris. They began to teach him that he would be king under God, that France and the Pope were consanguineous through God.

The head nurse at the Barbette, a fat Breton, twenty-eight years old, was a woman called Madeleine. It is important to consider what she taught him.

Madeleine: A king is god.

Charles: There is but one God almighty, *Deus Omnipotens* . . .

He'd already begun learning Latin.

Madeleine: Oh, but there's small gods. Kings and saints are small gods. Now a king needs a pair, a brother-king who's king secretly. And the brother-king has to be sacrificed and the brother-king's blood feels the power of the king himself.

Madeleine showed him her two index fingers.

Madeleine: This king is king openly.

She waggled her right index finger potently.

Madeleine: He wears the crown and people make oaths to him and sing *Noël*.

Her left index finger shifted subtly.

Madeleine: This king is the king who has to be sacrificed. Like Jesus died for us and made all of us wonderful. This king never wears a crown. His blood makes the king a firm long-reigning king.

7

Charles: Who's the king that's dying for Papa?

Madeleine: Duckling, your father hasn't got a shadow king.

Charles: Maybe Uncle Louis was Papa's shadow king . . . ? Uncle Louis bled . . .

Uncle Louis had been murdered three years ago outside the Barbette. Madeleine and Charles had heard the screams. The murderers had certainly made a copious sacrifice of Uncle Louis.

Madeleine: Duckling, your Uncle Louis was a nice man, but a witch.

She was able to say whatever she wanted to Charles, because when Queen Isabeau came visiting her son she had enough trouble stopping her wildcats from savaging the servants. And therefore no time to see whether her boy was being taught the right things.

Madeleine: It's because your father's had no shadow king to die for him that he's mad.

Charles: Will I have one?

Madeleine: You're a good boy. God will provide . . .

But the boy felt all the blood run from his chest into his belly. There it boiled about hopelessly. He knew it wouldn't happen: no shadow or brother king for him.

Unaided kingship, Madeleine implied on most days of all his years till he was ten and she was dismissed, unaided kingship was a terrible onus—it invited assassins, it bred wars inside and outside the king.

His father the king had wars inside him. He lived in locked apartments in the Louvre. He was incontinent in the clothes he wore. He beat up his attendants.

The little boy was very thin. He thought, I'll be like that. But I won't even be strong enough to bully the servants.

Madeleine: Now there's just you. You're the darling of the Armagnacs.

The Armagnac party was the party that upheld him.

Earlier that winter, in the Royal Castellany of Vaucouleurs, the girl-child of two peasants called Zabillet and Jacques had her baptismal day. She had two brothers and a sister. She was baptized Jehanne but the brothers and sister called her

Jehannette. The village they lived in was called Domremy-à-Greux. It had an interesting location, speaking politically. Only to say for now that the forests there were dark green and the Meuse wide and sombre.

To my honoured principal, the Esteemed Francesco Maglia-Gondisi, of the Bank of the Family Gondisi of Florence, from his newly appointed agent in Poitou and the Loire region, Bernardo Massimo.

Dated 23 July 1419

You must forgive me if other agents of the bank in other areas have already given you some of the information contained in this letter.

The fact is that since I came here I have found it difficult to acquire much real information at all. The dauphin's Armagnac Council and his foster-mother Queen Yolande of Sicily let go of news reluctantly. One of the reasons must surely be that the news is so consistently bad. They certainly want capital, they want bankers to underwrite their armies, they seek mortgage and credit arrangements. But they will not tell me the simple business facts and probabilities that any client seeking finance is usually anxious to detail. I have discussed this with other bankers, who are all treated in this same way. We can only conclude that with the English in Normandy and the south-west and the Burgundians in control of the north and of Paris, our Armagnac clients' dependence on us is so strong that they resent it.

Two most important items I have learned.

In the first place, the Duke of Burgundy, Jean (called sans Peur) has managed to introduce the dauphin's sister Catherine to King Hal Monmouth of England. There are a number of speculations on the subject of why he arranged the meeting, in fact it was simply one item on the agenda of a long conference Jean and the English king held west of Paris. What else happened at the conference few seem to know: only that King Hal met the dauphin's elder sister. Besides seeing the political merit in marrying her he is said to have actually fallen in love with her. I do not know when the marriage will be celebrated. But I am sure you understand how it will affect the dauphin. He

9

will have one sister queen of England and another, Michelle, duchess of Burgundy. If my honoured principal would permit a sketch map.

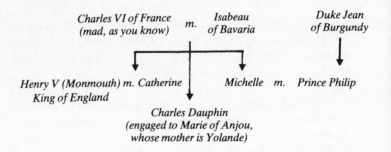

Charles VI of France
(mad, as you know)   m.   Isabeau
of Bavaria   Duke Jean
of Burgundy

Henry V (Monmouth) m. Catherine
King of England

Michelle   m.   Prince Philip

Charles Dauphin
(engaged to Marie of Anjou,
whose mother is Yolande)

You can see how the Armagnacs are not only outflanked but out-married.

In the second place, I have discovered that Duke Jean of Burgundy and the dauphin intend to meet again somewhere south of Paris, perhaps at Montereau, in September. There is a danger to our interests in that Jean will put heavy pressure on the boy, attempting to talk him into going north to visit his father and mother. In this way Jean hopes to absorb the boy the way he has absorbed the father (whom he keeps a raving prisoner in the Louvre) and the mother (who is said to be his mistress).

If Jean succeeds in this purpose there will no longer be an Armagnac party. The Royal Chamberlain, Monsieur Tanguy, is so concerned about the coming meeting that he fears the Duke might even consider assassinating the boy if he refuses to go north. Tanguy is taking a very vigilant attitude towards this possibility.

In view of these prospects I cannot see any profit for the Bank of the Family Gondisi in pursuing business with the dauphin, Queen Yolande, and the Armagnac Council. I shall therefore postpone final approval on all business pending until I receive your instructions . . .

Bernardo Massimo

One hot September day when Jehannette was nine she woke early. She twitched all morning, even in church. Her eyes stared. After Sunday dinner—bacon and bean broth—she had a convulsion, spilt very hot soup on herself. Jacques beat her on the face till her breath came back and she was put in the high family bed. Though she wanted to sleep her eyes kept snapping open and looked to the steamy light lying across the kitchen floor.

In that daylight she could read it: something would happen to put her at a distance from Jacques and Zabillet, to lock her into a solitary future. To cut her out of the thick musk of her family as a vealer is cut, mourning, out of the herd. She didn't want that. She was sure she wanted to grow up to be like Zabillet, ironic and fertile towards some warm oaf. That seemed enviable. A priceless direction to take.

About seven o'clock she thought, well, it's done now, the fat's in the fire. She was able to rest soundly.

That day (it was autumn 1419) there were to have been talks between Duke Jean of Burgundy and young dauphin Charles at the walled town of Montereau. Both parties to the talks were letting the fine Sunday go by. They were nervous about assassination and other possibilities.

Dauphin Charles had apartments inside Montereau. There he heard three Masses that morning. Perhaps he attempted by all these devotions to build up his royalty, which had diminished since Madeleine's day. He had lost Paris and his father was a prisoner there—yet another layer of imprisonment for a mad king.

On a wet afternoon four years before, the English King Hal had butchered the loyalist army. Agincourt was the place's bad name. Charles could tell in his blood that other tragedies would grow out of a name like that. Hal, Henry Monmouth, had spent the years of Charles's puberty in re-acquiring Normandy and courting Charles's sister Catherine. Successfully.

Maman Isabeau, the boy's mother, lived in Troyes with all her crazy, ravening or grotesque beasts. Exotic birds left droppings on the candelabra, monkeys ran along the tapestry rails and carnivores stalked around the partitioned rooms. Frequently she slept with little Duke Jean of Burgundy, cleaving her eighteen stone to his eight. No wonder (a political joke ran) they called him Jean sans Peur.

The meeting between Charles and Jean that Sunday was

11

to be at two o'clock. Charles had a plain buffed suit of armour put on his body and stood sweating into it.

On the hour delegates from Duke Jean begged a postponement. When his attendants took Charles's armour off, he was found to have a heat-rash.

Across the river Duke Jean himself had lunched very light and drank only water. Penitentially. He was saying, God, prince-to-prince, statesman-to-statesman, notice this little courtesy of mine. If there is danger this afternoon, remember my little abstinence at lunch. His family was distinguished in Europe for buttering up all sides in any dispute. He wasn't afraid. He was depressed, which wasn't often, and he had diarrhoea.

At two o'clock, while he was resting, the Count of Navailles came in. It was Navailles's idea to keep putting off the talks all day: he felt it would make the dauphin's party nervous, throw into chaos any plans for violence they might have. He was large in his armour beside the thin duke who lay in a shirt and drawers, bare-legged, bare-footed, on the bed.

Navailles: How are the bowels, Jean?

Duke: No problem.

Navailles: We had a carrier pigeon from our man over in the town. He says the houses by the river haven't any soldiers in them. They're occupied by the people who ought to occupy them. Meals are cooking. Kids getting put on the breast. All that.

Duke: Good.

Navailles: If they'd let you talk to the little prick. Alone, just the two of you.

Duke: It's not a perfect world.

Navailles: Would five o'clock suit you?

About ten past four, Navailles and eight other lords went downstairs straight on to the Yonne bridge. The tower in which they and the duke were billeted gave directly on to the carriageway. A trumpeter blew a parley call and the nine lords strode out over the bridge, one standard-bearer ahead of them but no escorts at all. From a tower over in Montereau an Armagnac trumpeter blew an acknowledgment.

The bridge was partitioned crosswise with walls, so that it displayed three compartments, an ante-room at each end of the bridge—one for the use of Duke Jean's party, one for the use of the Dauphin Charles's aides. The centre room was the meeting place. It had no furniture, but was hung with drapes, blue, white, red, green. A golden sun and golden lilies showed up on the blue, and the St Andrew's cross of Burgundy stood out on the red.

Navailles and the others waited ten minutes in their ante-room while the dauphin's advisers got their armour on and came out of town on to their end of the bridge and into the meeting hall. The protocol was that the French were to invite the Burgundians into the meeting place. The Duke of Burgundy was a vassal of France, according to feudal theories already laughable.

Someone unlatched the meeting-place door at last, but no one called out for the Burgundians to come in.

Sulky, said Navailles, and his colleagues tittered, moving in pairs into the meeting chamber.

To simplify the complex story of what happened that germane afternoon only Navailles is mentioned by name amongst the Burgundy lords. On the French side all the lords would fall or diminish because of what would soon happen on the bridge. Just the same, a few must be mentioned.

When Navailles went through into the meeting chamber he saw thirty yards off, against drapes of blue and gold, Tanguy Duchâtel with seven other Armagnac monsters.

Navailles saw, for example, Monsieur Brabazon, a real killer, who had once raped an abbess to death in Touraine. Just for the sake of saying he'd done it. He saw Pierre de Giac, Charles's bedmate. Burgundian spies said he was a Satanist and used witchcraft and poison for results. But his face was sensitive, he sat through all the Masses with which poor Charles tried to fortify his failing majesty.

Navailles thought, that pitiful little sod Charles. No mind of his own, and only murderers to talk to.

And Tanguy Duchâtel, the boy's most darling mouthpiece.

Tanguy: Are you serious this time? Or still farting around?

Navailles: Does five o'clock suit the dauphin?

Tanguy: Five o'clock. You've had all bloody day.

Navailles: Five's the best we can offer now. You'd better go and dress Charlie.

By this time the lords on both sides were catcalling and barracking each other. Burgundy's Monsieur Antoine Vergy and Brabazon were enjoying themselves. They were comradely about it, both being genuine pirates.

Navailles mistrusted Monsieur Tanguy Duchâtel. Earlier in the year, when Jean's troops entered Paris, Tanguy Duchâtel, Provost of the city, had woken young Charles the Dauphin at the Hotel Neuf des Tourelles, carried the whimpering boy in his arms out the Temple Gate to the Bastille where horses were gathered for flight south. Navailles knew how to deal with Tanguy's power-lust and homicidal intent. It was his new vanity as saviour of a prince that made him uneasy. The Tanguy of earlier days could be expected to act inside the limits of his cool, hard purpose. But some crazy bond, some father-son thing burgeoning in Tanguy's guts as he carried the sobbing boy across town and led his horse south—*that* was a thing whose consequences Navailles couldn't predict.

Correctly, he thought it dangerous.

De Giac knew Charles's soft frightened flesh. He kept pleading for everyone to be gentle with the boy.

De Giac: Remember the boy's mother. If anyone hurts Charles she won't ever let Jean back into bed. She prides herself on being a good mother. And none of this catcalling. He's likely to bolt.

He and Tanguy were jealous of their status as men who knew what made Charles nervous.

Before they all left, Navailles pointed to the riverside houses by the Montereau wall and wanted to know did the French have archers there.

Tanguy: If I want to hurt the duke I'll do it myself. I won't get some peasant to do it from two hundred metres off. He'll know it's me, his friend Tanguy. That's what chivalry's about.

Strangely, Navailles was satisfied. He left the chamber and the bridge with other members of the delegation.

Duke Jean's *overt* position towards the boy Charles would be this. The English have all of Normandy now. King Henry is living in Rouen and met your own sister at Meulan in May and eyed her up and wants her . . . It's sad, but there you are. Your father is ill in the Louvre, your mother's down in Troyes with her pets. It's you and me now. Let's forget the old, old issues, let's call the Estates General, at any town you name, let's raise a big levy, buy ourselves a big army, keep the English out of Paris. Come back to your mother. Come back to your poor father.

Duke Jean's *secret* position was this: he had an under-the-table alliance with Henry. So secret was it that he'd let the people at Rouen hold out against Henry, let them think he'd send relief. By the end of the siege the townspeople were sitting in the ditches outside the city. No one would feed them. Not the garrison. Not besieging Hal or his little brother Clarence. An English soldier said he saw babies sucking at the teats of dead mothers in those ditches. Duke Jean was said to be coming.

Hal had known Duke Jean wasn't coming. But didn't pass the word on to the ditches. Or the garrison. That was politics.

What Duke Jean wanted from the boy Charles was: submission. Jean had the schizophrenic father in the Louvre. He could have the queen in bed whenever it was apt to politics or concupiscence. He wanted the boy for his pocket.

But to the boy, Jean was a figure from mythology. When Charles was four, Jean had had Charles's Uncle Louis killed. In those days Jean and Louis had fought each other for control of the sick king. One night in November Uncle Louis had been at the Barbette, in Maman Isabeau's apartments, drinking with her. A happy scene: all the animals were placid when Uncle Louis was about. Unexpectedly the king's valet knocked at the queen's door. Papa was supposed to be having a clear-headed phase and wanted to see Uncle Louis. Downstairs the valet had a donkey and a small escort of armed servants on foot. Louis sat the donkey. Just beyond the Barbette gate, in rue Vielle-du-Temple, a legion of killers jumped out of the doorways. They strewed his brains, ran him through, pounded him to offal. They cut off an arm. The day after the funeral Jean admitted in the royal council that he had ordered the event. A necessary killing, he said, even if a bloody one.

Those mutilations recurred still, twelve years later, in the boy's dreams. His waking eyes cringed from his cousin of Burgundy.

Before the meeting Jean was sick and felt better for it, but not well enough to dress in armour. It was arranged that a servant would carry his armour before him across the bridge and retain it in the ante-room. So he had his britches laced on and slung over his head an orange tunic with Golden Fleeces. He was a careless dresser.

At five o'clock Navailles and the others came for him. The duke's secretary Père Sequinat went along too. As if the sanctions of canon law weren't likely to save him, he wore a cuirass under his Augustinian habit. One of the lords rat-tat-tatted on the heavy serge of the monk's chest. The sound was metallic.

Lord: Expecting trouble?

Twelve lords marched in front of Jean sans Peur to the ante-room on the bridge. There was little waiting. Very soon Tanguy opened the meeting-room door impassively, without any word or flourish.

Navailles went through first, and the others flanked him, on either side, like clerics peeling off either side of the sanctuary at the start of solemn high Mass. Tanguy remained holding the door. So that he was in their rear.

Sequinat stood back to let the duke through but when it was his time to step across the threshold, and there was only himself and Tanguy peering at each other through narrow eyes, a seizure of fear stopped him on the doorstep. Tanguy took him by the arm and pulled him through, feeling the metal under the sleeve of the habit of St Augustine.

Round the flank of the Burgundian lords, Tanguy moved back to his own side of the room.

Dauphin Charles stood close to the door there. He wore his white armour. It was splendid, a gift from his foster-mother Yolande, the Queen of Sicily. On most other sixteen-year-olds it would have been breathtaking.

Charles's thin Valois head stuck up inappositely out of its nest of steel. The pendulous end of the nose hung close to the lips.

When Jean, earlier in the year, had presented Charles's sister to the English King Hal Monmouth, it had been feared that the family nose (from which Jean himself also suffered through a common grandfather) would be the feature to disenchant the Englishman. Jean and the whore-queen Isabeau feared it. But Henry had been infatuated.

Charles had bulbous eyes too. Expectant of witchcraft and severing of limbs. He stood by the door on the Montereau side, and his lords stood V-ed towards him. Because he couldn't be expected to stand bareheaded to his cousin, he wore a blue turban. Either side of his nose, his face was greased with sweat.

Jean sans Peur walked straight up to the boy and curtsied to him and kissed his hand. The boy felt reassured that the kiss was painless and not demonically cold. The large lips made a painful smile.

Charles Dauphin: Put your hat back on, Jean. It's a hot day.

Tanguy was whispering to de Giac.

Tanguy: Even their pig's-arse secretary has armour on.

De Giac looked at the priest's habit and frowned.

Tanguy: Underneath! Underneath! If they make a movement push Charlie out through the door.

They couldn't afford the loss of Charles. Charles was their mandate for being what they were, executives in the Armagnac enclave, which was still a going business.

Jean: Your mother sends her best love.

Charles: Oh yes.

Jean: Don't say it like that. She thinks a lot of you.

Charles: How are all her animals?

Jean: Have you ever seen a black and white bear from China?

Charles: She's got one?

Jean: It's devoted to her. One day it reached out and sliced the ham out of a servant's leg. It wears pads now.

Charles: I see.

It wasn't that he hated his mother. You could somehow tell, even in the tremulous way he carried his head when her name was mentioned, that he yearned to be himself her pet monkey. Her little bear.

Since Madeleine died, his *de facto* mother had been Yolande, Queen of Sicily, whose present of armour he was wearing. He was engaged to Yolande's daughter and for the past two years Yolande minded daughter and son-in-law together.

Jean: Don't believe that Spanish lady when it comes to forming an opinion of your own mother.

Charles: Very well.

Jean: It's time you were all together again.

He spoke with authentic pity.

Jean: You and your father and mother. I mean, your father can't be moved. Have you thought how it would look if the English took Paris off me? Your father with it?

Charles: What about my sister? Does the English king want her?

Jean: I think it's going to be a good thing for everyone.

The dauphin began trembling. There was a little anger in it, but largely loss.

Charles: If they have a baby boy it'll be a good thing for the baby boy. He'll be made king of both countries, won't he? That's what it's all about, isn't it? To make a baby in place of me?

Jean: Please! You're not made for any of this. Let me look after things for you. You call the Estates General and I'll levy an army for you, thirty or forty companies. We'll hit the Commons for half a million.

The boy raised both thin hands and vibrated them in front of his face. The numbers Jean conjured up did that to him.

Charles: Nothing can happen unless you do public penance for killing Uncle Louis.

Tanguy: Hear, hear!

Jean: Listen Tanguy, it's between my cousin and me.

Charles: I want you to do public penance at the Cathedral of Bourges now and at Uncle Louis's grave in Paris at a time I'll nominate.

Jean: I won't do penance. Charles, it was a service to this country.

Charles: Don't say it, don't say it.

Jean: Come with me to your father. If he says do penance I'll do penance.

Charles: No, no, no. I know what you did. You bought Uncle Louis's servants and my father's valet. You cut his dear left hand off and poured out his brains in the mud.

The duke sighed and gestured a little with his left hand.

Jean: It's always like that when people get killed, it's sad but true. Did they tell you, Charles, that he was persecuting your mother that night?

Charles: Persecuting?

Jean: Charles, the poor woman had just had a child still-born! A brother of yours! I don't want to hurt you with these things. But your uncle was insatiable . . .

Tanguy: Listen, the boy knows his mother's a whore. Let's begin on that basis.

Jean: If you call the Commons, and come to your father with me, I'll beg public pardon at the man's grave. Not in Bourges though. At the man's grave. If you come with me.

Tanguy: You can't make counter-demands. First do your penance at Bourges. That's an absolute condition. Then we talk about other things.

Jean: Charles, I can't damn well do any penance at Bourges. Bourges is a sort of joke. The very name.

Charles: Is it?

Jean: Well in Paris they call you the King of Bourges. It's a nickname. The word Bourges has overtones . . . I've got nothing against the town, but I won't do penance there. I'll do penance in Paris. If you come with me back to your father.

Charles: You can't tell *me* when to go to *my* father.

Jean: Perhaps I have that much power.

The boy began squealing.

Charles: Under God have you? Under God's mandate?

Jean: Power in fact. It's from God too. And it works well enough.

Charles: The authority has to come from God.

Don't tell me God is changing (the boy was trying to say). Don't tell me God is giving you some special power underhand, contrary to contract.

The boy knew he had a chance only if God kept to the accepted forms.

Jean: Listen Charles, don't let's get theological. You're sixteen and you know what's happening in this country and who has the power.

Jean saw his poor cousin had closed his eyes again.

Charles: I have scholars to tell me the power is mine. That you're sinning . . .

19

Jean: Oh Christ. I have the faculty of Paris in my pocket. I can get *them* to tell *me* anything I like.

Charles: I have the chancellor of the University of Paris. You threw him out. He says . . .

Jean: And you believe him, Charles?

Charles: Yes.

Jean: He's a liar.

You were never meant to tell a dauphin that sort of thing. When a number of lords on both sides of the room spoke at once, Jean silenced his.

Jean: I'm giving you the lie, Charles. I intend to. Because what you have to see if you want to have a sane life is that I can make you come with me in the end.

Tanguy, Brabazon, de Giac were screaming in the dauphin's ear as if it was the poor boy who had said the scandalous thing.

Navailles came up to Charles, reaching for his elbow in an avuncular, child-fetching way. His face had a sort of self-conscious good intent in it. Benevolence for the boy.

Tanguy rammed him. Steel hip against steel hip, a dissonant impact. The blood of all those twenty-six men leapt and squirmed. *That's the sound*, the blood told its owners.

Tottering Navailles was drawing his sword. Some thought he had the thing by the handle as he tripped about and it was slipping out, not being drawn with intent.

Monk Sequinat was already dancing sideways for the door and so was the dauphin for his door, on his side of the peace-chamber.

The Burgundy lords saw that the Armagnac lords had their swords drawn. It won't happen, they thought. It's such bad politics. Even Tanguy can see what bad politics it would be.

Already Navailles had been gashed beneath the jawline and knelt streaming blood on to his hat, which had fallen from his head on to the stonework.

The Burgundy lords saw Jean, who was himself watching Navailles detachedly, hit on the head with a small axe. One of the Armagnacs, against law and reason, must have been carrying it in his belt, under his huke.

The boy knew that his Uncle Louis, twelve years ago, had been killed with an axe. The sense of awful re-enactment moved through him and he shambled out the door and performed the crooked action that passed for running in that knock-kneed family.

The watchers on the walls of Montereau saw the running prince. Terror made his gait uneven, he dragged one leg. His confessor met him at the gate and held him, comforting him through the white armour in which he was sweating.

He was no fool, that boy.

Charles: They'll blame me for this.

Confessor: For what, Dauphin?

Charles: They're killing Cousin Jean.

Jean stood on his knees, split to the nose. His brains fell out of his forehead. Brabazon was kneeling by Navailles unbuckling his cuirass.

Navailles: Oh Saviour Jesus.

Brabazon: How does this damn thing come undone?

Tanguy, who remembered Uncle Louis's mutilations in 1407, cut off the duke's left arm. Louis's assassins had understood that many of these royal people had made pacts with Satan, contracting a limb to Beelzebub in return for political influence. For Satan was strong in the lobbies and potent in council-rooms. But a man could not see God's face in paradise unless the limb was in fact paid.

Louis's assassins had done it for Louis, now Tanguy did it for the duke, cutting cleanly at the elbow.

Brabazon killed Navailles terribly, running a sword upwards under the waistline. Navailles' last scream was heard at the Provins Gate of Montereau. Sobs creaked out of the boy.

Charles: Won't they ever stop this sort of thing?

Two of the French lords left the peace-chamber and went, crazily leisured, to join the dauphin.

All the rest hacked at the duke's body. All they cared about for the moment was the electric resistance of his muscles and organs.

Once he was dead no message came to them along the blades. They sobered. Their ears began to prickle. They'd committed the crime of the age. They knew it was a fountain of murders they'd uncovered with their delving swords. It would take long wars in Champagne and Anjou and the south to settle what they'd done.

Already the axe lay dropped on the carriageway. Anonymous.

De Giac and Brabazon began to fight about who'd dropped it there.

De Giac: I could see it in your belt when you walked in.

Brabazon: Who'd believe a fucking wife-murderer.

De Giac was said to have given his wife poison at dinner and then rode with her all night in the forest of Issoudin. Given that she was pregnant, it was a wonder she lasted so long in the saddle with a stomachful of toxin.

Now Giac wanted to kill Brabazon: the inhuman meat of a duke and a general on the stonework slipped their minds. Except that they were sheepish about going back to town and facing the boy. They would rather keep their tempers up than do that.

Tanguy lifted the axe. He threw the thing two-handed right across the room, where it resounded against the partition and tore a hole in one of the Burgundian draperies.

Coming back across the bridge they tried to look bored. They carried their bloodied tunics folded on their arms or crumpled up in one hand. They did not hurry. They didn't fear the boy, the boy feared them. But they knew the sight of him would waken them to the subtleties of what they had done to Duke Jean.

Many of Charles's officers, down from the walls, ran out to ask them what had happened. Tanguy had a story.

Tanguy: Navailles tried to kill Charles.

Brabazon: They had an axe with them.

They felt better now that they had articulated what must become the Armagnac version; and it seemed robust enough by the afternoon light.

But the boy, with his priest, overheard.

Charles: Everyone will blame me. Maman Isabeau, Maman Yolande. What about my sister Catherine? What about Philip?

Philip was Jean's son, capable, full-grown, not backward at taking moral advantage.

Charles: Philip will make war on me. Maman Yolande will want to know why I didn't control you.

Tanguy: We acted from as much love as Maman Yolande.

22

Charles: Monsieur Duchâtel, you are never to touch me again.

Charles wiped his nose and turned back to his lords. He called for someone to come and start unbuckling him.

Charles: I will be nothing soon.

He didn't have a high sense of his own reality. No one ever told him he was a nice boy, that he spoke well or his manners were charming. He saw himself as a vapid presence affixed to the idea of kingship. Around his consecrated vacancy harsh friends gestured and performed atrocities he didn't understand. Now there would be so much disapproval that he *was* frantic he might vanish under it, shrink to nothing.

When his horse was brought, he rode to the Hôtel St Pierre where apartments had been set aside for him. The Provins Gate was closed when lookouts reported that seven hundred soldiers Jean had in the vineyards behind the tower were forming up. But nothing developed—they knew they'd be paid off next morning, so didn't want to do anything excessive this afternoon. A party of Burgundian knights went on foot to see the bodies, and came through on to the Armagnac side to shout threats. They called Charles a bastard and a whore-son. A few crossbow bolts were let fly at them but they went on screaming as if they knew what they were doing was worth a military risk. For their imputations filled the air and Charles, being dosed with hypocras and fondled by Giac, took them in at the pores. It would go a long way to putting meat on the spectre he was if he *knew* he would be called a king whenever his crazy dad should die. If people could say, without amazement, just with level acceptance, 'That's the king.' But it wouldn't happen: those Burgundian knights were screaming their certainty that he was outside genealogies, a putative being.

He groaned and Giac hugged him and kissed his forehead, greasy as it was from the afternoon's terror.

Charles: Maman Yolande. Send for her.

In Domremy-à-Greux young Jehanne went into a coma and they sent for the midwife. The midwife rubbed her closed eyes with belladonna in a chicken-fat base. Later the priest was sent for. But she woke normally next morning, and was up by noon.

When Jean's son Philip heard what had been done to his father he fell over in a genuine fit on the parquet floor of the great hall in his home in Ghent. His wife, Michelle, who was young Charles's sister and could not be expected to be quite so demented at her father-in-law's death, fell down too in reasonable mime of what her husband was at.

Despite his fit, Philip Charolaise was no hysteric. He did not rush into open alliance with the English, but even sent ambassadors to the frightened boy Charles. Philip wanted reparation and some lands south of the Loire. The boy felt once more that if any more earth was yielded up of that south land there mightn't be enough dirt left to sustain him in existence. He would vanish with a scarcely perceptible explosion. Besides, Yolande and the others wouldn't have allowed it.

Philip sent armies into Champagne. It was a savage invasion.

In the new year at the trade-fair city of Troyes, Henry Monmouth who was King of England, and Philip who was Duke now, made a strange treaty with the insane French king and with Queen Isabeau. Isabeau had been living some time in Troyes, with her leopard and bears, her exotic birds and sables.

They all assented that Henry would be the next French king and would be regent till the mad king died. Isabeau and mad Charles called Henry *son* continually. He was in love with Catherine. Isabeau and mad Charles emphatically called young Charles a bastard. He's not my husband's boy, said Isabeau. That's right, King Charles said. To get *his* affirmation to the treaty, the King of England and the Duke of Burgundy had to watch the lice moving in his clotted hair: the fug of all the body's secretions was heavy on him, because he couldn't tolerate being washed and clothed and tried to stab or strangle those who came up to him with clean linen. You think I'm dirty, he'd yell at them.

Hence Philip and Henry-in-love held their heads sideways and winced as King Charles signed denunciations of his boy with a hand scabbed from jigger bites.

Fat Isabeau, mightily fertile, mother of squadrons of infants, signed too. The documents said Charles had done an outrageous murder, talked of him as the so-called Dauphin from Vienne. And misbegotten as well.

When the boy was told that both his mother and father had signed him away as a bastard, he uttered a long grunt like someone winded.

Yolande, a big dark woman back from her Provence estates, told him that it was a shock, yes, but it was all so obscene a treaty that people would react against it in the end. But here was the day he had foretold: now he barely existed at all.

To my honoured principal, the Esteemed Francesco Maglia-Gondisi, of the Bank of the Family Gondisi of Florence etc.   Dated 22 June 1420

By now you would be aware that Charles Dauphin has been disinherited at Troyes. I am therefore both amazed and delighted that you have increased my domestic and office allowances. We have taken over an entire townhouse in rue St Euphrosyne. Might I be frank, sir? I understand perfectly that you must have excellent business arrangements with members of the English and Burgundian parties, but I am a little anxious that even these may not offset the losses we may incur as the Armagnac cause fades.

I have nevertheless, as you instructed, given sympathetic consideration to Queen Yolande's request for a credit note of 150,000 pounds tournois. She offers as collateral the following properties . . .

[Here follows a list of estates and châteaux.]

I have sent my good assistant Dumeo south to Provence to value these properties and shall forward his report to you on his return. I must say however that it is likely that by the time you receive the report the Dauphin may have abdicated all claim to the throne. Only Yolande, his confessor, and such friends as Monsieur de Giac have prevented this from already occurring . . .

Bernardo Massimo

On the borders of Lorraine, they held no effete doubts about their own existence. Life could have pungency there.

It wasn't as bad as places where they'd simply stopped work, closed the seasons down more or less, despaired that seed would ever germinate again. It was nearly as bad though. It could easily get as bad.

When the girl Jehannette lay down east-west at night she had a war to either side of her and one at her feet. At her feet for example, over the chalk cliffs, there was an Armagnac army vandalising the towns of the Barrois. Its general's name was simply la Hire—The Anger. That was the sort of nomenclature to make seed shrivel in the pod! That was where they'd given up—over where The Anger was.

And in the Vaucouleurs area, in the southern corner of which she slept, there were free companies from Burgundy and even some English and Welsh. Vaucouleurs was a region of France, but there was no real line between the free companies and the French. La Hire wouldn't go up into Vaucouleurs to seek and destroy the Burgundians, nor the Burgundians go west after la Hire. The subject-matter of war was the cows and stores and crops and flesh of the people. The line of battle lay at the peasant who wouldn't tell a free-lance where the horses were hidden, or at the peasant's wife or daughter screaming no.

Bertrand was in garrison at Vaucouleurs and sometimes stayed with Jehannette's family. He told what the war had done a little way to the north and west.

Bertrand: You remember last Easter when I was escort to Verdun for the Cardinal's secretary. We got to a little place where there were four or five childless couples, nothing else. All the people with children had gone. God knows where. In the fields an old man had hitched his wife to the plough. She was naked—you know the custom. Her breasts were like flaps. She didn't have teeth.

Jacques: Not like Mauvrillette.

Mauvrillette was the whore they used at Domremy each spring to pull the plough. The shadow of her good breasts and her belly fertilised the Meuse mudflats for the year.

But Bertrand didn't talk easily about village whores. For a soldier he was full of mysterious restraint. He got around with a lot of the priests from the collegiate church in Vaucouleurs.

Bertrand: It was sad. The Cardinal's secretary didn't like

26

that sort of thing, he thought it was superstition, the old religion. One of the clerics in the party called out to the old man. He said, do you think that's really going to help you grow corn?

Jacques: Superior bastard!

Bertrand: The sad part was the old man said they weren't going to plant. That they were going to let themselves die. And the priest said why are you doing this then, putting a naked woman on the plough, why are you doing it when you don't even mean to plant? The old man just blinked. His poor old lady was bent over in the traces, out of breath. He just said he was doing it for luck.

Jacques understood in spite of his flippancy about Mauvrillette. Everywhere people were doing the old rites but the old rites had no basis any more: at Agincourt the knights doing the inane rite of knighthood; in a paddock on the Meuse two old people doing the futile rites of luck before dying. Jacques and Zabillet knew they could be reduced to that insanity themselves.

Jacques was on the village watch council, himself as doyen, and the mayor and the sheriff. They made out no roster for the middle of the day, expecting that travellers on the road would tell them who was coming on behind. If the news was bad they kept their livestock hidden away on the slopes and brought them to water at night. They dug pits a good half mile from the town and left their bacon there, fetching it when it was needed. For the mercenary companies asked travellers that sort of question: are there towns along the road where you saw lots of cows in pasture, where they hang their bacon in the kitchen?

The watch was kept from late afternoon until the next mid-morning. The highway yielded up its daily visitors, equerries and businessmen, and lawyers going to Avignon and visionary refugees who had seen the apocalypse down the road.

Even nine-year-olds knew it was a bad year. In Champagne the peasants ate snails, in Touraine grass-roots. Acorns and horse-chestnuts were a staple food up and down the country. Stories of a thousand different ways of dying washed through Domremy, Greux, Burey-le-Petit. In these places however, there was still flour, beans, bacon.

Jehannette, at nine, saw her first battle. She was expecting something more vicious, less leisurely. She saw it all from the bluffs above Greux: her big sister Catherine took her. She twitched because over in Maxey, in what could be called a French force, Madame de Vittel, one of her godmothers, had a husband. The Lorrainers who were to fight the French had camped the night by the side of the Greux-Maxey bridge. The idea was this: the Lorrainers were allies of Burgundy and the English. The French over there were *in* Lorraine (Lorraine began at the river). Their generals were two brothers, Didier and Durand St-Dié. A nine-year-old girl might expect to see the state of the country encapsulated and displayed in the fight at Maxey. She might expect too to see there a sort of summation of the wounds and bereavements all the refugees carried up and down the Verdun road.

In fact it was a game with the Lorrainers and Didier and Durand. The St-Dié brothers put their forces on the slope outside Maxey, dismounted troopers in the middle. They spent the morning drinking while fatigue parties put up a sparse screen of stakes along their front. The unsporting Lorrainers attacked at one o'clock, from one side, across open fields and vegetable gardens. It made the morning's work futile. All the French ran to the church, a few of their pikers got gored and trampled. But the nine-year-old couldn't see that from over the Meuse. She got the impression that the men in Maxey were enjoying themselves. The French stayed in church all afternoon and shot bolts out of the church tower. Then you could hear culverins or mortars. Holes were knocked in the church door. The brothers surrendered.

That night a party of Lorrainers rode into Madame de Vittel's yard, assessed her property and told her how much she had to pay to get her husband back. Five pounds tournois, they assessed her at, nearly thirty Paris pounds. She raised it from the bankers at Neufchâteau but when Jehannette left home years later the Vittels were still paying off the interest.

From watching the little battle of Maxey, and other phenomena to be related at another stage of this account, Jehannette came to see that the process of battle was indecent.

Because it failed to imitate what happened to ordinary people when troops came to town. The etiquette and enterprise of ransoming was an insane business in France's hectic graveyard.

Not long after being decreed bastard, while he was at La Rochelle, Charles had an upper floor collapse beneath him.

His bed, his chamber pot, his chests and wardrobe and two servants with broken hips and internal lesions lay splintered all around him. His host, the military governor there, wouldn't forgive himself. But it seemed to Charles that structures refused to hold him up. Creatures that prided themselves for their solidity—planks and mortar—fled him. He began to favour small rooms then and slept in closets when he could and kept old familiar clothes too long. He wanted time, like masonry and flooring, to learn some quiescence. So he encouraged it to sleep by wearing last year's stockings. The gold thread of the royal lilies on his gown began to unravel. Fresh lilies would bring fresh shocks he was sure. The old lilies and the digested shocks of yesterday were enough for him. So he sent his doublets out to the mender.

Yolande feared this refusal of fresh clothing—it reminded her of his crazy father. Also it encouraged jokes about him being hard-up.

Certainly, that year, there was lack of ready cash. The Estates were slow paying up their subsidies. Direct tax was hard to raise from people who were already paying out to local lords of war.

The boy moved about a great deal after the floor fell under him. His phobia of big houses kept the court shifting from city to city. That was expensive: local businessmen expected top price for serving the court.

Tanguy had been ambiguously rejected by Charles. The boy never wanted to be carried out of falling cities by him again. But he was still a member of Charles's council. With all the contracting and letting of tenders that went on at each move Tanguy made entrepreneurial fortunes, took commissions at both ends of each transaction. The boy had to mortgage properties both to Tanguy and de Giac to borrow that sort of money back.

This was the pitiful nature of Charles's finances in the years after the murder of Jean. Maman Yolande anyhow thought it pitiful and did as much preventive book-keeping as she could. Yet she knew that if she told the boy how much his friends were cheating him the disillusion would send him mad. For the moment he had an infinity of nice land to mortgage. He could mortgage till he was eighty and still have good houses and river meadows to hock.

Bertrand was Sir Bertrand de Poulengy. Jacques liked to think a knight wanted to spend time with him, and Bertrand was some sort of knight, local and barely, and belonged to the provost office in the Vaucouleurs garrison. Jacques's father had been a freehold tenant, so had Bertrand's. There was a right balance of affinity and distance in the relationship. Both men felt flattered. Jacques always brought out wine for him.

Sir Bertrand acted up to it.

He already liked the little girl Jehannette.

She had large brown judgmental eyes more appropriate to a five- than a ten-year-old. Jacques thought she was lazy—she didn't like field-labour, she liked kitchen-work better but not well enough to be enthusiastic.

Bertrand: Jehannette, would you like to become my lady on your fifteenth birthday?

Jacques: You'll be sorry, Bertrand. She won't take your cattle out of pasture.

Jehannette: A knight's lady doesn't have to mess around with cows.

The girl said things in a detached way—they didn't sound like cheek.

Jacques cracked her ear for being a little bitch and cool as well.

For a year she had daydreams of being Bertrand's lady. But there was a pallor about him she couldn't get used to.

About the time she stopped dreaming of Bertrand she began on Madame Aubrit. Madame Aubrit wasn't really an aristocrat. Her husband was secretary to the local aristocrats, the de Bourlémonts. She owned a house outside Domremy-à-Greux and a town house in Neufchâteau up river. She had a large face, sensuous—though at eleven

Jehannette didn't know that's what its quality was. She dressed in velvet and brocade and wore silks in the summer. The house outside Domremy had Flemish tapestries on the wall. In church she had a seat and prayed frantically, like a real sinner.

Jehannette dreamt of sharing a bed with her, of being her lady companion, sewing for her, bringing her jonquils.

In fact Jehannette would dream of being child or bride or sister to anyone who dressed well, spoke more softly than Jacques, didn't fart so loudly, and looked at her eyes when talking.

So she made fantasies also about Madame Hélène de Bourlémont, spinster relict of the great family. Madame Hélène had a white, soft face. She always visited the sick, even in high winter, when her high blood didn't stop frost-bite sores on her nose and both cheekpoints. She was short but always put her hand on top of children's heads, even on children taller than she. She said the same to everyone.

Madame de Bourlémont: The king is frail and the kingdom is frail. Weep for the king.

But Jehannette didn't weep. Only sometimes internally, when she knew all at once and for ten seconds or so at a time, she was part of the king, the same way she was part of God.

So Sir Bertrand, Madame Aubrit, Madame Hélène took turns as Jehannette's secret passions in the last years of her childhood. Yet by the time she was twelve she'd grown out of them.

Yolande worked to rid Charles of de Giac and Tanguy. De Giac still often slept with the boy. Driving his gross member at Charles's thighs he actually implied this is all you have to fear, the friendly, good-hearted, coarse-grained but not too painful surprises you've already had for your own good.

Père Machet, the boy's confessor and Yolande's theologian, kept her informed about these sodomies. What Maman Yolande feared was that since the boy lived by obsessions, he might become as devoted to the love of men as he was to last year's jackets. Then her daughter Marie might not get a child from him.

31

To my honoured principal etc. Dated 25 January 1422

This, the coldest month of the year, must be doubly cold for the Armagnacs and poor Charles Dauphin must be shivering more than most. For his sister Catherine has had a son by Hal Monmouth. The birth occurred at Windsor in England. The baby is said to be flawless and to take his milk well. He has been christened Henry of course . . .

Bernardo Massimo

One day de Giac felt sure enough of himself to suggest to Yolande that witchcraft—membership of a coven—might give Charles confidence he wasn't acquiring from the Mass. Charles went to Mass three times a day in his old clothes. He came out just as certain as before that he'd be usurped in the end.

De Giac: The old gods are still the princes of this world— we've got Christ's word. Anyone who wants to operate in this world . . . well, the lesson's obvious.

She let him talk. He felt safe. She wasn't the sort of woman to abhor anything except financial loss. In fact she secretly abhorred witchcraft, having attended a coven as a young girl and had been shocked by the manners of the horned god.

Yolande: Who would introduce him into a coven?

De Giac: I'm sure people of standing could be found.

Yolande: One has to vow part of one's body away to Pan.

De Giac: Yes.

Yolande: You've vowed part of your body?

De Giac: You get nothing from Christ or Pan without vowing. And Yolande, the boy is not virile. He needs to run wild. With gods to smile on his wildness. Now, at the end of the Esbat, Pan favours everyone . . .

Yolande: I know, I had an aunt who couldn't stand for months.

De Giac: Well?

Yolande: It would send him mad. He's set on Christ. Don't mention horned gods to him. He'll give you to the Inquisitors.

But de Giac gave hints that Satan might be some help to the Armagnacs and to Charles. When the Comte d'Aumale

32

caught the English disorganized on the river bank at Gravelle, there was a celebration banquet at Poitiers. De Giac arranged for a massive pie to be brought into the dining-hall, and from its crust bounded a ram dyed red for England and gold for the Golden Fleece of Burgundy. An instant later a tall man dressed in animal furs and with ram's horns on his forehead exploded through the crust and slaughtered the ram neatly, decapitating it one handed with an axe, ceremonially, in front of Charles and Marie. De Giac could tell the boy didn't like it, preferred the bloodless Mass, in fact, to direct blood-red sacrifice. He decided that the therapy of the old religion was not for his prince.

To my honoured principal etc.   Dated 2 November 1422
    I am sure you have forgiven the fever that prevented me from writing directly to tell you of the death of tough and brilliant King Hal Monmouth some weeks back. No doubt you received a great number of reports of the circumstances of the tragedy, and therefore I summarize my intelligence of the matter on the off-chance it contains some item of which you have not been informed. The death took place at Vincennes. He had been working eighteen hours a day on the reorganization of the English administration in the north. According to report he succumbed on the last day of August from gangrenous piles aggravated by eight straight days in the saddle. The Armagnacs are delighted, since the new English king is, at this moment, no more than eight or nine months old.
    But the main purpose of this letter is to inform you of a more recent and equally startling death. The mad King of France has at last died in Paris, less than two months after his English son-in-law. Death came of a fit after thirty years of madness. He died with no one but a few servants around him, and only servants and the Duke of Bedford, who is the new English regent in France, followed the coffin. Bedford's motive for being there was clear. Over the grave he told the priest and the servants that the new King of France is the unweaned baby of Windsor.
    Charles Dauphin heard the news in Loches. He went into the chapel at the château and stayed alone there for

hours. It was expected that when he came out it would be to tell his servants to pack his trunks for an escape to Spain or Scotland. To everyone's happiness he emerged to tell them that although he had demanded aloud in front of the altar that God should show him once and for all whether he was legitimate heir of France or not, God had not given a sign either way and that therefore, until it was shown to the contrary, he must consider himself King Charles VII. His demeanour was one of extreme depression . . .

Bernardo Massimo

Charles confessed every day to Gerard Machet. Straight after the absolution, Machet always reassured the boy.

Machet: Be happy, my son, because you *are* God's King of France.

Charles: I suffer from an urge to pronounce the name of our Lord Jesus backwards.

Machet knew not to waste such ripe obsessions.

Machet: It's an enchantment. Perhaps your closest friends have put it on you.

Charles told Machet that he believed a martyr must die for him, a sacrifice must be made to seal and augment his kingship.

Machet: Christ's sacrifice is the one.

Charles: No, it must be a sacrifice like Christ's. But a different one.

Machet: A sacrifice will be given.

Charles: You guarantee me?

Machet: A sacrifice will be given.

The royal confessor meant de Giac would be sacrificed. He was helping Yolande arrange it.

But after a year, in spite of Machet's best efforts in the confessional, Tanguy still had treasury privileges. De Giac still slept with his king.

The council wanted Charles to demonstrate his reality by sending an army into Normandy. They suggested the money could come from mortgages. Some of them were willing to advance cash against royal property. The king's small bedrooms began filling up with mortgage papers again.

Sometimes a special clarity would enter his eye. He would send for Maman Yolande.

Charles: All my friends are working on treasury credit and using it to lend money back to me.

Yolande: I know. It's bad. It will end, I promise you. But it's time to send an army into Normandy.

On best advice, Charles bought some likely Italian companies, some Navarrese. He signed orders to put his Gascons and Scots back in commission.

Outside Verneuil, which was a quiet town in low Normandy, the English dug themselves in as they always had, behind slanting palisades of sharpened stakes.

Like Tanguy at Montereau Bridge, Charles's knights believed the only ordained way to hurt an enemy was the personal and intimate way. When the English kept winning with longbowmen, making impersonal deaths at a distance, French knights thought that was a temporary dislocation of the purer cult of war. Now Bedford, the English Regent in France, was using cannon and culverins on the battlefield, not just around towns. That too was a snide de-focusing of the fine nature of battle.

This state of mind had achieved the stature of a mental illness with the French. Man changes his nature by changing his tools and at Verneuil the tools made carcasses and captives of the ideologues, the men who followed their code, Charles's knights. All those inflexible Scottish lairds failed as well. High horses impaled on the stakes, they lay wriggling in their armour, ripe for slaughter or ransom.

Three days later the bad news got to Charles. He looked stolid and arranged a requiem Mass for the Count of Aumale, Constable of France, who had perished of the longbow the Tuesday before. At the post-communion however he fell off his priedieu. Marie was dutiful enough to do the same and both of them were carried away to their bedrooms. Maman Yolande went with Charles, not with her daughter. She ordered him undressed and had warm bricks put in his bed.

Charles: It's the indecent money. Nothing useful could come from it.

Yolande: Money is the most unmagical thing in the world. It has no supernatural qualities and it's always real inside its limits. The whole business is very sad nonetheless.

Charles: O Jesus, I have sinned.

He wanted his long fingers in her thick ones.

Yolande: Bedford never thinks like that. He never frets about the nature of his money.

Charles sensed what she was telling him: that a king could fill his kingdom to its limits with his self-disbelief. His money would then stop acting on events as money infallibly should. His armies would fail for no good reason and go on failing.

Charles: I wish we could just say yes that little English boy is the king. Then we could all rest.

Yolande: Rest?

So remotely, so alien to the word that he knew she was nowhere near the end of her political energy.

All the boy wanted was to go and lose care in Scotland or Spain. But he groaned because she wouldn't let him.

Yolande: We have to get the Bretons into alliance now.

He whimpered.

Yolande: You understand that Brittany is on our left flank and the English right.

Charles: Of course I understand it, Maman.

Yolande: Well, we need them in alliance for when the English march on the Loire. As they will.

Charles: Oh God.

Yolande began to arrange it straight away.

On a day in summer Jacques and Bertrand were sitting at the front of the house in Domremy-à-Greux. They had been drinking since mid-morning. Jacques was a born pub-keeper, Zabillet said.

Jacques's sons did the day's work, Catherine was away with the cows and her boyfriend. Jehannette was crushing coleseed in a press in the sun, and listening. A messenger with an escort of lancers cantered through the town on the highway Caesar had built. The messenger wore the Pope's tabard and seemed intense. To see and hear them as they passed made you think they were carrying some ultimate good news down to Avignon: the resurrection of the dead had been arranged for eleven o'clock tomorrow morning— some message such as that. It made Jacques angry. He stood up.

Jacques: You'd think all these bloody officials who roar up and down were doing something useful. But none of it works: they're not saving anything. Sermaize was burnt to the ground again last month. They can't do anything for us, they might as well sit by the road and pick nits out of their arses. The whole set-up is useless.

Bertrand, who liked to think he was part of the set-up, blinked a little.

Jacques: Why are you looking like that?

Bertrand flinched. He'd always feared Jacques might, in the end, resent having to fête him.

But it was the girl Jacques was yelling at.

She laid the brown eyes on Jacques. Bertrand felt an indefinite thrill to see the thirteen- or fourteen-year-old virgin's contempt in them. At least, it seemed contempt. She seemed to pass the message to Jacques that she was waiting. Waiting for the day when he would become, through old age, a child and would have to sit respectfully under the apple tree in *her* yard. And listen to her dominating the house. She was the sort of girl who would keep a husband and an old man bluffed by the time she was twenty-three.

Jacques: Does your old man make you sick?

Jehannette: No.

Grey beads of coleseed oil eked down the sides of the press into the tub.

Jacques: Why the eyes then? Why the bloody eyes?

Jehannette: Because what you say is true.

Jacques: Oh good, good.

She'd been the youngest and the pampered one. Nothing sustained in the way of work was ever required of her—the others had a sort of routine to follow, but Jehannette chose what she did each day. Sometimes her brothers could bargain her into doing what they wanted. What they wanted her to do most of the time was to take the cattle out in the mornings. It bored her. She could put on a terrible act of lethargy. She could droop at table. Looking at her, you nearly went to sleep yourself.

But, as this account will show, she could be a frantic vigorous girl with outsiders. It was only with Jacques and cattle that she slumped.

Bertrand whispered at Jacques.

Bertrand: I don't know how to put this. Jehannette . . . she's still a virgin?

Jacques thought, my girl married to the Sire de Poulengy! Madame de Poulengy! Then he remembered she had an affliction of the womb, a family secret.

Jacques: She's a virgin. Of course, Bertrand.

Bertrand: It's hard to explain. We need a virgin for our confraternity.

Jacques: Confraternity?

They did wild things in confraternities and secret coteries. It depended what the confraternity honoured: gods of black love, gods of white love, Christ God, Christ's saints.

Bertrand: Listen, Jacques, I'll tell you about ours. Myself— am I a rapist? Then Madame Hélène de Bourlémont, a nice old lady, Madame Aubrit . . .

Jacques: She's one of Jehannette's godmothers.

Bertrand: There you are. Myself and d'Ourches are the only two men. D'Ourches is a genuine . . . a *genuine* knight baronet.

Jacques: Is he good?

Bertrand: He's in the garrison. He's good. (Pause.) She'll come back a virgin. There's no need to tell you . . .

Jacques: What do you want a virgin for?

Bertrand: *Some* ceremonies only a virgin is fit to do.

Jacques: Not like the autumn riot over in Boischenu?

Every autumn there was an orgy in the forest of Boischenu. Mauvrillette in particular was favoured by the men. It was supposed to help the cattle and sheep in their breeding.

Bertrand: Can you imagine Madame de Bourlémont . . .?

Jacques: No.

Bertrand: Madame Aubrit?

Jacques had scored the young Madame Aubrit one Hallowe'en in the forest. He'd thought I'll never have anyone more beautiful than this. He'd been right.

Jacques: Madame Aubrit's all right, I suppose.

He thought, imagine Aubrit getting a redneck like me. All over the forest farmers with women, softening the year's death. And Madame Aubrit drawn from her good house into the groaning mists . . .

Bertrand: What we do, Jacques, is Christian. It helps the king.

Therefore, on a Friday Bertrand had nominated, Jehannette went at mid-afternoon to the best stone house in the town. Madame Aubrit's maid let her in and took her upstairs where Madame Aubrit herself sat in the long hall sewing by the front window. She had a straight nose and a sweet pallor: she didn't let the weather at her.

When she made stitches with her needle you didn't doubt their permanence, the permanence of her womanhood and all it touched. No free companies were going to gut this house or tear the drapes off the walls.

Aubrit: Come in, Jehannette. Did you bring your spindle?

Jehannette: I thought I'd better.

Aubrit: We'll have a nice afternoon then, working here together.

Jehannette: I'd rather do this than anything.

Aubrit: You're like me. We're not made for field work.

Jehannette: I get sick of it, Madame. It isn't the weight. It's the boredom.

Already she had the distaff under her left arm and was winding thread on to the spindle at an hypnotic rate.

Aubrit: You were no more than ten when you were here last time.

The girl frowned at her through a long silence. The red disassociated hands kept working. Madame Aubrit kept a sweet face, coughed, made a stitch.

Jehannette: It seems I've seen you a lot. It seems I've heard you talk.

Aubrit: But you haven't, have you?

Aubrit was a little off-balance from all this virgin intentness in the girl. She even blushed. She had a lover in Neufchâteau. It seemed—for a second—an outside possibility that the girl somehow knew. And Aubrit couldn't stop herself making some confession.

Aubrit: You flatter me. You shouldn't. I mightn't be a very good person.

Jehannette: I know your voice though, Madame.

Aubrit: Now . . . !

Jehannette: I love you.

Aubrit felt liberated and laughed. She thought, it's just infatuation, it isn't second sight.

Jehannette was thinking it's a lie, I loved her till last year but now . . . well, I don't love *her* anyway.

Aubrit: Do you mind fasting this evening?

Jehannette: No.

Aubrit: It's for the king's sake.

Jehannette: I'd like to be a woman in my own house. I'd like to bear children.

Jehannette asked herself why she'd said it. They were both uttering things they didn't want to.

All the time, the stealthy noises of her hands unravelling the fibre.

Aubrit: Jehannette, it will happen.

The girl shook her head.

Jehannette: There's something wrong with my womb. You can ask Catherine.

Aubrit: You can tell me.

Jehannette: I didn't want to tire you. I just wanted to say what I'd like.

At dusk Madame Aubrit had her hair done up and fitted under a net embroidered with roses. Jehannette watched in that remote avid way that distressed her father. Then the lady put on a scarlet and gold underdress. The girl blinked. It had heraldic sheep on it. Was Madame Aubrit really a noblewoman in a big way? Some great man's bastard?

Over it all she put a light cloak but fastened it up to the neck.

The girl smiled broadly. She picked up the hem of her knee-length overdress.

Jehannette: And I thought this was smart.

Aubrit: I'm not trying to outdress you. You've got what's necessary.

Her fingers softly tested the contours of the veil.

They rode the one mare south from the town, uphill away from the river. Below and behind them was a river island. It crowded the arm of river flowing past Madame Aubrit's place, making it a mere ox-bow. On the island stood the vacant castle of the Bourlémonts. All the town paid the rent, month per month, so that when raiders came everyone could go there. It had a long apron-wall with its own vegetable garden inside. The rooms were damp in the keep, but the sight of the place could sometimes give men like Jacques a luxurious sense of safety.

Far across the river, where the highway ran lined with infrequent shade trees, some businessmen were nearing town with a line of mules.

Aubrit: You don't see that often. How can they expect to get where they're going?

Jehannette's thigh was against Madame Aubrit's. The girl thought some cure might enter her womb from the direction of the lovely woman.

Around them now was forest. Chestnut, ilex, great oaks. Enchanted timber, all of it. Here you might face the aboriginal Europeans, the small people, primitive, magical, green-skinned from woad-paint, habitués of the old gut gods of the trees.

Madame Aubrit spoke loudly, as if the ceremonies—whatever they were to be—had begun already.

Aubrit: Christ save us from the entrapments of the willow. For witches bind their besoms of it. From the lecheries of the hawthorn. For it ravages your sweet brow. Give us the quick-beam rowan when demons block our path, give us a whip of rowan when our horses are unruly. Give us the oak whose fire consecrates mid-summer . . .

She went on and on. She seemed genuinely scared, you could smell a musk of fear from her.

Sitting side-on to her, Jehannette put an arm out, half-caressing the lovely woman's belly.

Jehannette: Nothing's going to happen to you, Madame.
Aubrit: How can one be certain?
Jehannette: You don't know who might be in you.
Aubrit: In me?
Jehannette: What god. What saint of God. You think you'll be let fall foul of any old witch.

The lady smiled, a thin smile. She felt it was an impoliteness on the girl's part to suspect somebody's body of containing gods or saints.

Aubrit: I hate the woods. It's even worse riding home. But there's a rule of the confraternity . . . we travel alone.

In fact she held her breath at bends.

Aubrit: I saw them once, Jehannette. I saw little green women on Thursday, over near the Ladies' Tree.

Jehannette: You should have caught them. If you were bigger than they were.

Madame Aubrit *had* seen them. She looked hard at Jehannette, and embroidered her story.

Aubrit: Two little green women. Well made. Wearing nothing. It was summer.

The girl was smiling, her own joke. Aubrit nonetheless tried to share in it.

Aubrit: Is it funny?

Jehannette: Priests say Christ God has given up the little people as lost. Perhaps the news never got through to the little people.

Aubrit: I must tell them next time I see them.

The great lady of Domremy sat stiff, saying it.

Jehannette: It'd only be fair.

Aubrit gave in and started to smile.

Aubrit: You're poking fun at me.

Jehannette: No one ought to be thrown off. Not little or big people. Just like that. Without being told.

Aubrit: What about the Goddam English?

Jehannette: They've *been* told. They've *been* told. They've heard it. From a lot of voices.

Aubrit: I suppose so.

There was a spring amongst a mesh of gooseberries. It came out of the hill over a lip of stone. When you knelt and looked deep into the place it came from you saw a clear black gloss of immeasurable water, deep and wilful and almost divine.

This Gooseberry Fountain was an ambiguous place. Every Rogation Day the priest from town read the Gospel of St John over it, as if it needed it. Arthritics washed here and, feeling better, didn't know whom to praise. Because when they thanked their Saviour for the suppler joints, they thought they could feel cynical old gods behind their backs.

A little uphill was the big beech, the Ladies' Tree, where the Oak-King had once been sacrificed at mid-summer. Its roots had taken in his blood and so its big limbs were somehow reprobate and cannibal and it too needed the

42

Gospel read to it. It was made to listen on Laetare Sunday, which was a picnic day at the big tree.

Witches came to it on Thursdays, everyone said, and everyone thought Mauvrillette was the *pucelle* of the coven who met at the Ladies' Tree. Hence (Madame Aubrit understood this) the popularity of Mauvrillette. When you slept with her you got the mad tang of hell in your nostrils, you smelt the hairy sweat of the horned god. For a second you *were* the horned hairy god. All in the price.

Madame Aubrit turned the horse from the track and crossed the Gooseberry Fountain. The ground levelled and the forest thinned. Then they came to two peasants minding horses, nearly a dozen horses altogether. The men said nothing. One of them took the reins of Madame Aubrit's mare, the other helped her dismount and then turned to help Jehannette. Jehannette hadn't expected courtesies and was already down on her feet.

When the lady walked off without a word, Jehannette knew to follow in silence.

The light went quickly and fire flared amongst the trees. There were people kneeling about the fire and a spectacular man still stood by the heaped timber. He wore a scarlet cope and black monsters writhed on it. His hat was velvet and his gown gold and complicated with heraldic designs. They were nearly all dressed that way, the man, the many women who knelt about. But a boy of perhaps eighteen years wore a thin black cloak pulled tight. He seemed to have a bare chest and to be wearing drawers. Getting up he fetched yet another superb cope from somewhere beyond the firelight and came up to Madame Aubrit and put it around her.

The spectacular man told Jehannette to kneel by him.

Jehannette: Bertrand! I didn't know you had clothes like this.

Bertrand: In the confraternity, I'm Messire. That's Messire St Michael who speaks for Christ and guards France.

Jehannette: Ah-h-h.

Bertrand: That's right.

Jehannette: You wouldn't change your mind?

Bertrand: Change my mind?

Jehannette: About being Messire St Michael.

43

Bertrand and Aubrit frowned at each other. Bertrand was nervous. He thought he was having some onus pushed on him that only Jehanne knew about.

Jehannette: What are we here for?

Bertrand: For the king's sake. A little sacrifice . . . we crown the king. In a sort of way.

Jehannette: Bertrand, have you ever told me before to crown the king?

Bertrand: I don't think . . .

The girl seemed to be petulant suddenly.

Jehannette: Do you ever stand behind things and call out to me about crowning the king?

Bertrand: Jehanne, what a question . . .

Jehannette: Do you?

Bertrand: Jehannette! What do you think I am?

Jehannette: I think you're Messire and Messire is you.

The girl dropped on the ground and took a fistful of the hem of his cope.

For some reason Bertrand flinched. All the ladies around him had a look of minor distaste to them. As if they saw some childish eroticism in Jehanne's behaviour.

When Jehannette got to her feet again, Madame Aubrit stood close on one side and, on the other, Madame Hélène de Bourlémont, the spinster, the last de Bourlémont left in the area.

Bertrand/Messire: This is Madame Ste Margaret in our confraternity and this is Madame Ste Catherine whose church is in Maxey over the river. You're to do what they tell you.

Jehannette turned to the old soft-skinned Hélène.

Jehannette: What do you want me to do, Madame?

Catherine/de Bourlémont: We'll tell you later.

Jehannette: It's just that I know your voice, Madame. I know your voice.

Bertrand/Messire frowned. Again he thought Jehannette was finding perilous meanings all around her, that she was the one holding back news of some even more exotic protocol than he and d'Ourches and their ladies were pursuing for the Friday night devotions.

He pointed to d'Ourches.

Bertrand/Messire: This is Monsieur St Denis who turned

tail on France and gave up the battle banner at St-Denis to the English. This is Madame Ste Clotilde . . .

Jehannette: It's all right. I can't take in any more.

Madame Ste Margaret who, incarnated as Madame Aubrit, knew a little about Jacques, whispered to her sister saint.

Aubrit / Ste Margaret: Her father has trouble controlling her.

They sang. The singing went on for an hour. The last song was an ecstatic acclamation for a king. Since none of them was a cleric they did not know that some of the Latin was corrupt and wizardly, a debased incantatory jumble. It elated and exalted them however. Jehannette looked from Messire to Madame Margaret to Madame Catherine and sometimes she shook her head as if a simple conclusion had come to her after a lot of grinding confusion.

St Denis, who had deserted France, was shivering with the night chill, although it was mid-summer.

But the others seemed so enriched through their long song that the woods were dwarfed by the dimensions of their happiness.

Sumptuous Messire came up to her.

Bertrand / Messire: You know about the king, Jehannette?

Jehannette: Of course.

The saints in the circle took up the questioning.

Saints: That he's called a bastard? And is disinherited by his scabrous mother? And foreigners hold the holy oils of kingship in Rheims?

Jehannette: I've heard that.

Saints: That they intend to uproot him? That if he is uprooted his scream will split open the heads of all us his children.

The girl thought that last idea too fanciful. For privileged people like these saints it was an easy thing to escape the authentic harshness of the war. As for example the day last November when Jacques and the family had been travelling to Sermaize to see Zabillet's three brothers. It was a quiet time and, so it was said, a safe area. There was a burned homestead on their right all at once. In the yard were three pregnant wives piked open at the womb, and their disembowelled husbands in a heap. There was a smell of flesh in the smoking farmhouse but Jacques forbade her to look there. She was happy to be dissuaded. But *that* was the war in France. *That* was what privileged people should talk about.

Bertrand / Messire: Do you love the king, Jehannette?

Jehannette: Kings are there.

There wasn't any argument about loving them.

Bertrand / Messire: Through your blood you are the king's sister.

He touched her face. She could smell spice on his gold clothes.

Jehannette: Blood? Bertrand, you're not going to cut me or anything?

Aubrit / Ste Margaret: No one wants to hurt you.

Mesdames Ste Margaret and Ste Catherine told her to turn her back on Messire Michael and the improper Denis. They turned away themselves, and so did the rest of the saints.

Behind them a flogging began. Jehannette understood: it was Messire Michael beating up Monsieur Denis for his unwise loyalties. The ugly pliant noise of willow on flesh went on for fifteen minutes. Madame Aubrit could see the girl did not like it yet understood she would break some wholeness of the event if she interrupted.

At last Bertrand /Messire began reading the prophecies of Merlin. On the earth sat Monsieur Denis, shivering with his cloak over him.

Bertrand: Descendit Virgo dorsum sagitarii . . . a virgin shall fall to the rear of the bowman—the *bowman* is quite clearly the Goddam English—*et flores virgineos obscurabit* . . . and her shadow will protect the fleur-de-lys. *Virgo prudens florebit et Gallia a meretrice destructa* . . . France, destroyed by a whore, shall be restored by a wise virgin from the marshes of Lorraine. From the oaky wood, the Boischenu itself, shall come a virgin for the healing of nations . . . Then she'll be slain by the stag with ten antlers . . . and on six of the antlers there will stand gold crowns.

Jehannette thought, he thinks it's me.

Incantations broke out again all around her. She was pushed forward by Mesdames Aubrit and de Bourlémont. At one end of the open place was a small shrub with

46

a peasant brown cloak around it. The girl was told to remove the cloak. The plant underneath was a mandrake, a knock-kneed and tortured little growth, cleft-rooted, threatening and precative at once, poisonous to a peasant's touch.

As the saints had said earlier, its yell—if it were uprooted out of season—could make whole populations berserk. The promise of its screams hung in the summer night.

D'Ourches took from beneath his cloak a slender purring cat. He held it above the mandrake, first gently, then by the hind legs. All the demons in it squealed like women. As it hung trying to claw him he decapitated it with a sword. Blood jumped in one viscid splash on to the mandrake.

Bertrand/Messire took her hand and she saw he had a thin little knife.

Bertrand/Messire: Put your blood with the black creature's, Jehannette.

Jehannette: Why? Why do I have to?

Bertrand: So that the cat's black world and the virgin's white one will all enhance the king.

Jehannette: I'd rather not . . .

But she let Bertrand lift her sleeve and slit her on the underarm. Madame Aubrit/Ste Margaret waved the cut arm about like an aspergillum.

Then Jehannette got down on her haunches and, without instruction, removed the sodden puppet's peasant cloak and put on top of the bush the gold coronet Bertrand/Messire gave her, and poured oil over its waxy, pink, narcotic blossoms, and dressed it in a blue cope with gold fleur-de-lys.

The evening rite was over. The pattern they had imposed on the night would convey itself in the thin air, would be transmitted by wind to large events farther west.

Aubrit/Ste Margaret and de Bourlémont/Ste Catherine were radiant.

Events farther west . . .

Yolande was having private and public meetings with the Bretons.

Yolande: Do you know de Richemont, Charles?

Charles: De Richemont?

Yolande: Arthur de Richemont, the Breton. A month ago, Bedford jostled Arthur out of an office in Rouen. They had an argument over some fiscal matters. Arthur's a very good soldier.

Charles: What do you want done?

He shivered in his bed, amongst the warm bricks. Though he wanted new friends he didn't want ferrety little ones like Monsieur de Richemont, who stank of crises.

Yolande: We could assure an alliance if you made Richemont Constable of France.

Charles: Don't ask me.

Yolande: The position is sadly vacant. Since Aumale passed on at Verneuil.

Charles: Would he have to go to war? This Richemont?

Yolande: For you. Yes. Don't flinch.

For he was certainly flinching. He could see himself taking out a clutch of new mortgages. He could see the cool venal bankers, Massimo, the Perruzzis, and the rest. He couldn't complain in front of selfless Maman. She had hocked a third of her great holdings in Provence. Yet he was king and his earth inferior to him. He couldn't sign it away without a twinge in his guts.

Yolande knew that Arthur was frantic against witchcraft. He could be a help in ridding Charles of all those bad friends who had killed cousin Jean and given the earth its excuse to subside under the boy.

So, after Richemont came, the old favourites were encouraged to go. Tanguy was talked into taking up farming Provence. Brabazon went free-lancing in Touraine again. De Giac was nervous. But even in his intimacies with Charles he saw it wasn't any use asking the boy for protection. For the brain was numb behind conjunctival eyes.

Richemont acted in the most obvious way. He had de Giac arrested one morning in Poitiers and taken to Issoudun to be tried for wife murder. He found a cook and a number of grooms who would swear to the murder and the witchery. Machet, the boy's confessor, rode over to the Auron and told de Giac he should offer his life up as sacrifice for the boy, should actually write to Charles in those terms.

My sweetest dauphin,

I know you expect that apart from the sacrifice of our Lord Jesus a further sacrifice is needed to feed and augment your kingship. I have slept by your side while you tossed and muttered. Christ dies for mankind, you said, Who dies for the king? You frequently said that: Who dies for the king? Now I offer my death. I am the scapegoat. My blood can be the nutriment at the roots of the failing oak of kingship.

I have always loved you, and did my best for you that unhappy day at Montereau Bridge.

With my deepest devotion to France's true king . . .

De Giac had only one favour to ask: he wanted his arm cut off and burned. Immediately after the amputation, grey and scarcely aware, he was sewn up in a sack like a cat. He was drowned from a bridge in the middle of the Auron.

And Charles got the letter.

Charles: It isn't any good. Poor Pierre.

It seemed Charles had an infallible nose for the one his scapegoat would be. Even more he felt remote from himself, so that he wondered was this flesh really favoured and caressed by that man, or was it just a dream of warmth? A man doesn't stamp up and down for his fantasies and—in doubt—Charles did not stamp up and down for de Giac.

He nonetheless began another fantasy with a guardsman called Camus. Camus was jumped and hacked about in the river-meadows outside Poitiers. De Richemont was again behind it. Charles saw it happen from the window of a small room in the castle. When Charles's guard brought Camus's mule to the courtyard and said Charles might like to keep it as a memory of his friend, Charles grunted and walked away. He did not believe that he was real enough to be bereaved, and therefore felt no bereavement. The emotionally subtle ownership that applies to souvenirs was something he could not indulge.

He was a mortgagor and that was it. He was paying off the Montereau Bridge debts. Paying off and paying off.

★

So there were varieties of deaths for Charles. By them he discovered how lost and null he was.

For Jehannette death had always had strange meanings too.

One day women had come wailing down the road from the direction of Greux. Someone was wheeling a hand-barrow and it gathered into it women who yelled and began to weep.

Jehannette went out to see. A sensuous spasm of grief was in her belly. She felt light yet urgent. She had been twelve or thirteen years old then—long before the Boischenu cere-monies. Does every girl have this? she wondered. The lightness, the frenzy, the feel of the frayed edges of all the world's foolishness coalescing in her guts.

It was autumn weather, very misty, and the handcart and the women came groaning at her out of a grey fug. Her cousin Mengette wheeled the cart, refusing to yield it up. In the cart, sewn in a blanket, a blood-caked bag over its head, a corpse lay. Jehannette knew it was Collot, nineteen years old, Mengette's husband, who had joined a free company contracted to la Hire, over in the Barrois. She battled with the other women to touch Mengette, to try to let Mengette know by touch how precisely she understood. For Collot had seen it was mad to be a peasant in this war, that only troopers were safe and made wages. But the god who looks after and prides himself on the zaniness of this very war had found out about him, that he was just a redneck from the Meuse, not a fine gentleman-devotee. That god had done something terrible to his face.

Jehannette thought: Christ Jesus is God. He'll make men one in battle. In a decent age the knight and the peasant will take equal risk. Amen.

She couldn't explain why she believed this. It was almost as if Collot were one of the last of the unlucky casualties, as if a new kind of equitable war were about to begin in which he would have been safer.

'Mengette, Mengette,' everyone was screaming at the widow. Jehannette gave up struggling to get close. She thought, they've *all* got fever in their bellies, *all* their wombs must feel like hives, where all the corpses and tears come home. Soon I'll bleed and be more like them. I'll give babies

50

my breast as if no one is ever going to die again, yet when they die I'll wail, I'll wail because of the weight in my womb.

Jehannette: Mengette. Oh holy Jesus!

She felt unspeakable passions for the young corpse, for the caressings its burst head couldn't take from Mengette. Poor, poor Mengette.

Later the same year a General Robert de Saarbruck came to town with five companies of soldiers and put a protection fee of two pounds tournois on every house. Still Jehannette had not menstruated.

In the new year, towns up and down the road could sometimes be seen burning at night. Then everyone dragged livestock and children over to the island, to the de Bourlémont ruins. Mad with fright, people trampled on the vegetable gardens inside the apron-wall.

Jehannette's breasts grew but there was no bleeding still. She was getting to be a private scandal to Zabillet and Catherine. While Jacques—who'd been told—thought she did it to make him look a fool.

In yet another perilous summer, the town was caught at noon by Lord Henri d'Orly, in business for his own sake. His interests were furniture, livestock, bacon, grain, and he left with so much that he had to rent a second castle to warehouse the furniture in and extra pasture for the stolen cattle. A de Bourlémont who had married out of the district lobbied all the local gentry. They frightened d'Orly into returning the cattle.

Jacques: That's the sort of service you pay for.

He had lost belief that the system would ever do any good for the people who paid up the money. But this one time it had. As if the world were considering returning to its old form.

Still that damned girl hadn't joined the race of women.

Jacques felt that if she didn't get over this seizure—he saw it as a seizure—she would never be any good. He sent Zabillet to consult Mauvrillette. The whore prescribed a perilous mixture made from crushed hawthorn. Already doubtful, Zabillet nevertheless made it up.

Zabillet: Take this.

Jehannette: What is it?

51

Zabillet: It's a mixture. For your trouble.

Jehannette: Whose mixture is it?

Zabillet: A wise woman's.

Jehannette: A *wise* woman's?

Zabillet: An expert's.

Expertise ran on a basic level in that part of the country.

Jehannette: Mauvrillette?

Zabillet: Perhaps. We have to try everything, Jehannette.

For the circuits of nature were broken in her, she was an offence to Zabillet and Jacques, and Zabillet's pity trembled in the eyes so much that Jehannette decided to drink the stuff.

First her ears began to roar; there was pain in the glands of her throat. After ten minutes her cheeks puffed, and the flesh around her eyes ballooned.

Jehannette: I can't die.

Zabillet put her to bed. She was finding it hard to breathe now.

Jacques stood back from the bed.

Jacques: Is it the change coming on?

Zabillet: It's poison, you bloody fool. Make some hot compresses.

She herself made up an emetic of aloes. The girl felt their bitterness pouring in on top of her loss of breath. A jet of bile rose up her body and Mauvrillette's poison ran from her mouth. They made her warm and soon she was mending.

Zabillet did not let Jacques forget. She shamed him by confessing in the open to the priest, stopping him in the street, insisting on instant absolution. Every day she had new stories disqualifying the whore.

Zabillet: I heard this afternoon that Mauvrillette is *pucelle* to the witches over in Boischenu.

Jacques: You ought to report it then. Straight to the Bishop of Toul. I've suffered enough for the bloody woman.

With her daughter, Zabillet took a new attitude. Since the cycles of womanhood didn't occur in Jehannette's body, the girl must be specially chosen.

Zabillet: If you wanted to join the Augustinian nuns in Neufchâteau . . .

Jehannette: No, I don't . . .

Zabillet: It's a rung up in the world.

Jehannette: They'd think I was possessed by devils.

Zabillet could make up fables of her own to soothe the girl.

Zabillet: Some women use their organs so badly. God has to ask others to do without their womanhood.

Jehannette: Some women . . .

She was thinking in fact of sensuous Madame Aubrit.

Zabillet: Queen Isabeau. She lets herself be fucked by wildcats and big German dogs.

Jehannette: My womb's dead because of what the whore does?

The concept half amused Jehannette.

Zabillet: What else can we believe?

Jehannette: I don't believe it.

Zabillet: Why not?

Jehannette was angry now.

Jehannette: Does God have to balance wombs out? Like a money-lender? I don't believe it.

Zabillet (hurt): You'd talk more politely with Madame Aubrit.

For Zabillet still thought Jehannette had a passion for Madame Aubrit.

When she was expecting her first bleed and it was late she thought, it's because I don't love anyone here enough. The house-loves and town-loves aren't sharp enough in me. She thought that she would not begin to bleed till some larger demands were made on her organs than Zabillet, Jacques and the others could make. Other girls, finding the kitchen and the town a total world, broke open like pods, bled into their surroundings, found some ripe boy by their seventeenth year, became the kitchen, became the town and a fount of harvests and children.

Jehannette knew it wasn't going to happen to her. The more she learnt about Zabillet and Jacques, the further she felt from them: it wasn't meant to be that way.

Now Zabillet had three moles on her soft upper-belly under the left breast. It was a good skin, not a peasant's. She was having a lot of pain in her belly about

53

1422 and when she bled it was a massive, disordered business. Jacques's body was gingery and where the freckles left off in the direction of the fish-white hips a sort of sweat rash began down his thighs. He had a funny navel, scarcely indented, and eye-shaped. All these and other items Jehannette had picked up seemed to distance her further from that mesh of intimate and cherished specialities her family was.

One night she woke from a dream of copulation with a goat-skinned god wearing horns and the face of her god-mother's husband (that Monsieur de Vittel who was taken at the little battle of Maxey, and was sold back to his wife at a ruinous price). Jehannette woke to find herself cleaving to Catherine. In the long bed that had once carried the whole family there was just herself and Catherine and small Pierrolot. Catherine pushed her away. No rancour in the pushing. Catherine knew what it was all about, she was engaged to be married.

Catherine: I can't help you, ask a friend. But just be a little careful you don't break the maidenhead.

Jehannette was even grateful that Catherine knew there was some lust in her: it balanced somehow her parents' fear of her freakishness. But she knew straightaway in the dark, with Pierrolot abandoned in seven-year-old sleep at her back, that if she took part in the body games Catherine and Mengette played and which were played with boys under the bored eyes of cattle out on the slopes of Bermont then she would vanish into some pattern of family and kinship. As would Catherine, very very soon.

In her scared night flesh she whispered.

Jehannette: I want to get married.

It was almost true.

But she didn't ask any of the boys and girls up in Bermont pastures for physical aid. She saw all that by-play as a sort of suicide—dragging her down into a foreign population.

However, some mania might come and then I'll bleed. She wondered if it could even be some cowboy seen in a new way, with an eye that hadn't yet grown in her head. The songs had it that way. Yet she didn't believe the songs.

Zabillet, Jacques, Catherine all went on talking about

convents. Convents—it seemed they believed—were bivouacs for dead wombs.

The idea of a convent appalled her: she didn't want the sort of obedience they had to have. She didn't want a pyramid of nuns above her all empowered to tell her to be silent and how to pray. Nor did she want the anonymous chastity of the good convents. The promiscuity of the bad ones bored her more than the flesh-play of the Bermont slopes. And nun-raping was one of the war's best sports: that had to be remembered. A disappointing way to lose your carefully kept chastity. Last, she couldn't read, had never learned her hornbook. The nearest school was in Maxey where they were Burgundian. Without learning, she'd be worked in a convent no differently from the way Jacques worked her.

At court on the Loire, Richemont, invited in by Yolande to clean out Tanguy and de Giac, was himself beyond control. In the end he took his army away and occupied Bourges, just to show Charles.

Charles, in his sleep, sang cantatas of longing for his secret and blood brother. When will you come, my special one. His kingship had near-vanished. The new chamberlain was a man called Georges de la Tremoille—Fat Georges, they dubbed him. He had a high voice which he knew sounded ridiculous. So he used it as little as possible.

Fat Georges (to Charles): I am totally devoted to your majestic kingship.

He nonetheless had grain, wine and timber concessions with the Burgundians.

A man must live, after all.

When he wrote to the Duke of Burgundy, Philip, strong son of the murdered strong man, he always began the letter:

My dearest and exalted Philip . . .

He even hoped Philip forgave him for working inside the assassin's camp.

Domremy-à-Greux was a strange town, legally considered. If you sketched it it would look like this:

55

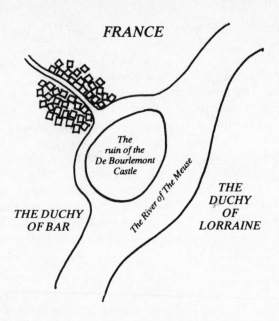

FRANCE

The
ruin of the
De Bourlemont
Castle

THE DUCHY
OF BAR

The River of The Meuse

THE
DUCHY
OF
LORRAINE

The top half of the town stood in country belonging more immediately to Charles the boy than did the southern thirty homesteads and the island. The Duke of Bar was, like his father-in-law the Duke of Lorraine, in a loose alliance with the English and Burgundians. The equivocal nature of the town sang to and echoed the two-headed nature of the war. But in the end peasants only had one nationality: they were victims. Their mothers and fathers had been victims too so that the strain was—by the year of the blind knights of Verneuil—getting strong. Knowing this, all the town paid the rent for the de Bourlémont ruin. All the town paid the same protection money with the same high sense of the insanity of the word *protection.*

Jacques lived just inside France. At the back of the house, there was a manure heap, then his half-dozen apple trees. Then a little strip of common pasture, and the churchyard and church. By the churchyard was a slab of stone that took you over a little gush of water into Bar where the other victims lived. No one could take seriously the business of the border. There was a border like that at Goussaincourt where companies of English, Welsh and Irish had already done an unsubtle massacre, not giving a damn for the feudal borders.

56

On a Saturday at the end of autumn a little after her insight in bed with Catherine, in the year in which her womanhood should have begun, she felt a warmth on her right side. It came from the direction of the belfry which at the second was ringing noon and angelus. With the warmth in her jaw and down her right shoulder and side she heard a man's voice speaking in a very loud, very jagged diction, putting weight on the words, filling them to the peals of the bell.

The Voice: Jehanne, Jehannette, a virgin, a virgin Jehanne, the king's sister, sister in the blood.

The radiance had a sort of face to it, like a lean sun with a beard of gold. You had no doubt that it was prince, god. Your guts leaped to it, your guts said yes, yes, tell me more.

The radiance went out of her eye, the delicious warmth out of her right side. She shivered amongst bare apple boughs. In her hands were Pierrolot's torn breeks. She would sometimes do domestic things for Pierrolot, her little brother.

She thought, that's the last word then: virgin, virgin, sister in the blood. Because I'd do anything for that voice, that radiance in the side.

Till Tuesday Jacques kept complaining.

Jacques: What's wrong with that bloody girl?

On Tuesday it came again, warmth, the sculptured sun for its face.

The Voice: Jehannette, Jehannette. King. Poor brother king. King without a crown. Poor brother king, Jehanne.

Then the bells stopped ringing but it stayed, the god, and wanted an answer.

Jehannette: I love you.

The Voice: It can't be helped.

Jehannette: I love you. I love you.

The Voice: Yes.

It spoke quite everyday talk when the bells weren't there for it to fit its conversation to.

Jehannette: How do I know you aren't a devil?

The Voice: If the devil were as lovely as this it wouldn't be a sin to love him. By the way, we love you. You're our darling, our sweet little one.

Jehannette: You've got to tell me . . . please.

57

The Voice: I'm Messire, you know me, the Messire of France. Monsieur St Michael, Brother Jesus's right hand. Or left. You'll listen to me, my love. And two other suns and luminaries. Brother Jesus looked at them, two sun-women, and was smitten. His god-heart broken open.

Jehannette: How do I know you're telling the truth?

The Voice: Don't be a mean little witch making bargains. You hear my voice, that's enough. Brother Jesus's heart broke open like a pod for Madame Ste Margaret and Madame Ste Catherine. Listen to them. Brother Jesus's sweet heart will break open for you. You're his little sister. You're his duckling. I carry his message. That sums it up. You're Jesus's brother-sister and the king's. You are the one who bleeds for the king like Jesus bleeding for you.

Jehannette: Bleeding?

The Voice: Do you know what I'm going to ask you to do?

Jehannette: No.

The Voice: I'm going to ask you to take the king to the holy city of France and have him anointed there.

Jehannette: But I can't . . .

The Voice: You'll get your instruction and bedazzlement from me. For comfort you'll have Mesdames Margaret and Catherine.

Jehannette: How do I know you're not one of the old gods, the bad beautiful ones?

The Voice: My love, my love . . .

But he wouldn't reassure her. You've got to take that risk, he seemed to say. Take it? She took it.

But still she worried about the old gods.

The old gods, who were many and called devil, poisoned politics, stole babies and bodies, punctured the virginity of nuns in the small hours. At night they came into the yards, up to the edge of the road, breathed on the crops. For jealousy of lovely prince Jesus had turned them malignant.

The old gods took a thousand incarnations. Lovely voices were some. The shape of farmers was another. One day only two months before, when Jehannette had gone moping up to Bermont by herself, Mauvrillette had come out from behind gorse and said did she want to see the devil?

Mauvrillette's smell and plentiful body enchanted the girl. She felt the way the men felt: I can spend a little time with her on the rim of a mad seamy hinterworld and still get home in time for dinner. They hid behind the gorse together. Mauvrillette had her arm around Jehannette: they were sisters for the moment. Within ten minutes a farmer from Greux called Guillaume Mosquillat came by with a bull he had got cheap in Gondricourt. Mauvrillette sighed and her free hand caressed the tips of the gorse fronds. But even she couldn't go out to him. The witches could greet their devil only at the Esbat.

Mauvrillette: I know his great cold prick.

The whore was proud of her knowledge and wanted to share it some active way.

Jehannette would not be recruited and dragged herself away.

Jehannette: I wouldn't have guessed the devil had gone into the shape of Mosquillat.

But the world was full of the incarnations of gods. Everyone knew it.

Two women luminaries came to her with heat in her side any old time of the day. Madame Margaret. Madame Catherine. Strong presences in France, known friends of the king's earth. She believed them outright—there was feminine softness in them. Their faces ran golden.

Jehannette: He means it, Messire does? Anointing the king?

She was in the orchard when she asked that. Mesdames Ste Catherine and Ste Margaret blossomed and blazed at her side.

Ste Catherine: He means it.

Jehannette: What do I do to make it happen?

Ste Margaret: The event presents itself. You don't make it. It presents itself.

Jehannette: I love you.

Ste Catherine: If we could we'd fuse you into our fire. Right now. Without you losing blood.

Jehannette: Blood?

Ste Margaret: Everyone loses blood. Be consoled, darling.

Jehannette coughed.

Jehannette: Me too?

Ste Margaret: Your blood is signed over to the king.

The girl screamed.

Jehannette: Jesus!

Catherine, her sister not the apparition, came out to see what she was yelling for in the slumbering orchard.

The Mass was a test. Because if Messire and his two beauties were old gods the Mass would rout them. The old gods were blood gods and sperm gods and the chaste white-bread God of Mass threw them into fits and tortured the bodies of their familiars.

She went to Mass every day and there were no convulsions.

Then she wondered if she was some god herself, some incarnation.

The voices filled in her godhood word by word: virgin, whore, king, crown, France, Rheims.

Virgin was the other test. The blood and phallus gods could not talk in a virgin. That was a principle of lore and politics and theology. She knew that there was no court and no political lobby where a virgin could be impeached on old-god grounds.

One day—

Ste Margaret: Did you notice your womb is dead?

Jehannette: I'd noticed it a lot, Madame.

Ste Margaret: It's sacred to the king.

Jehannette: Holy God!

Ste Margaret: Holy prince!

But Margaret was tough too—she couldn't help it; there were tough demands she was required to make. Of Jehannette.

Naturally, Jehannette suffered stages of wild fear. Because ecstasy is so temporary. She tried to talk to Catherine her sister whose husband had taken out a lease to farm with big brother Jacquemin on the island of the Bourlémonts.

Jehannette: Do you think it's all right to love a king you never saw more than you love poor old Jacques?

Catherine: It's easier. I got so tired of the smell of old Jacques. Young men don't smell nearly so much. Colin doesn't anyhow.

Jehannette: Kings must smell too.

But the argument was already dead. To Catherine love involved smells and skin-textures, ten thousand intimate sensations binding father-daughter, husband-wife. To

Jehannette it was a god-pressure out of some deep Hades in her womb.

Jehannette: My womb.

Catherine: What?

Catherine didn't think there was anything special to wombs. But often Jehannette had this instinct that her own womb was a more universal warehouse than other women's. All that was permanent of the war found room there. All the fragments of Collot's scream remaining after his de-faced head congealed around his dead brain. All the lasting fragments of Mengette's wail. All the belly roars of gutted farmers, and of farmers' wives who found some Welshman cutting whimsically with sharp edges at their accessible bellies.

It wasn't as warm, her womb, as other women's. It wasn't a place for babies. But it carried its weight.

She went up to Bermont on her own, where a glade of blood and phallus gods had been reconsecrated to the virgin. There was a stark shrine to Jesus's mother there made out of large grey stones. She had no fits in that place.

Jacques: She goes up there on her own. Cocky bitch!

She went up there through the birches often. An instinct seemed to prevent Jacques from complaining too much. And coming to danger in the forest was the least of her worries.

The heat, the weight in the side, the sun-voice on her right.

Jehannette: Am I a god?

Messire: The great God? What do you want?

Jehannette: I mean, Messire, a little god?

The sun presence said nothing. She could tell it was amused, as if it found her endearing.

Messire: I suppose a little god.

Jehannette: Ah.

Messire: My duckling, you'll die in your season.

Jehannette: My season?

Messire: You're the one that mentioned gods. Well, gods die in their season. After they do the great acts they have to do.

Jehannette: Great acts . . . ?

Messire: Getting the king your darling brother to his holy city Rheims.

All at once the lady presences were there.

Ste Catherine: Virgin Jehanne.

Ste Margaret: Whore Isabeau.

Ste Catherine: Crown.

Ste Margaret: Crown.

Ste Catherine: France.

Ste Margaret: Blood.

Jehannette: Whose?

Ste Catherine: Don't have any doubts. We love you.

Every week or so, maybe at the end of a meal, when terror would—without warning—take over Jacques as well as his daughter, they would start hugging each other.

Jacques: You're my favourite little cow. You little cow.

She kissed him about the face madly, as if he was already dead. And sometimes it was worst of all to think she were going to die at some high crazy feast instead of by accident, by eating the wrong thing or meeting Irish cavalry around a bend.

Jacques himself was always dreaming about her. Because she was his favourite little cow and she wouldn't have a period or attend to any of the other decencies. He complained at breakfast about his dreams. The one he had most was that she was off on the road with soldiers.

Zabillet: What nationality?

Zabillet would have been grateful for any saving symbol, and believed in Jacques's talent for dreams. He had dreamed her sister–in–law's death under a falling balcony in Sermaize in 1416. In his 1416 dream a black bird had beaten the sister–in–law to the ground with its wings.

When Jacquemin, the big brother, came with his wife on Sunday Jacques spoke to him.

Jacques: If she goes off with soldiers, I'd drown her. If I couldn't catch her and tie her in a sack, I'd expect you to.

Jacquemin: Do you think it's really going to come to that? (Dropping his voice.) Soldiers like them pretty.

Jacques: Look, whores get started with troubles they had when they were girls. Ask any of them.

Jacquemin: I will. Next time.

Jacquemin's wife hit him on the head with a wooden platter.

So in the summer when the mandrake was crowned in Boischenu, Jehannette thought, there's a way in which Bertrand's voice is Messire's, Aubrit's is Madame Margaret's, Madame de Bourlémont's is Madame Catherine's. Diminished, thinner, but somehow the same voices.

She didn't like the way Madame Margaret kept saying *blood*. She wondered too, how well Madame Aubrit knew Madame Margaret, if Madame Margaret was somehow in Aubrit's guts. And how well Bertrand knew Messire was in his. And therefore, if she said to them, do you want my blood, all of it? would they say *yes*?

For four summer Fridays the mandrake was crowned king by virgin Jehannette.

Late on the last Friday Jehannette rode home with Madame Aubrit. Jehannette was on her own father's mare. The horses trod gently over the Gooseberry Fountain among the bewitched trees. At one time Madame Aubrit heard nothing behind the thud of her mount's hoofs and turned in fright. She found that Jehannette's horse was standing still and Jehannette was sitting there dazed, straddling the saddle. Her skirt was tucked up into her girdle. Her thick ankles were white under the high moon.

Years later Aubrit would say Jehannette looked immobilized by outside forces in that second, stunned silly by decision. Perhaps that was hindsight.

Jehannette: I'm the virgin.

It sounded oracular and scared the delicate Aubrit.

Aubrit: Of course you're a virgin.

Jehannette: I'm *that* virgin. The one in Merlin.

Aubrit: In Merlin?

Jehannette: The one who makes up for what the whore's done.

Aubrit: The whore Isabeau?

A shiver of revulsion ran over the thick girl.

Jehannette: She lets her tigers shit in palaces. I'll clean the palace out.

Madame Aubrit shook her head wildly. She pointed at the obscure forests in which the rites had been performed.

Aubrit: Jehannette, it's only a little ceremony. It helps the king.

Jehannette: More than that, Madame Aubrit.

The girl actually rode up to Aubrit and put her hand, frankly, with a sort of acceptance, on the woman's face.

Jehannette: I've heard your voice since I grew up. More or less your voice.

Aubrit: My voice. We hear each other now and then . . .

Jehannette wouldn't relent.

Jehannette: Madame Margaret's voice, *Madame Margaret's.*

Aubrit: My God no.

Madame Aubrit shivered in the knowing forest.

Aubrit: That's Friday nights, Jehannette. That's the confraternity.

The girl did a brusque little chuckle. There was a tough hysteria in her, a madness with sinew.

Jehannette: You can't decide on Friday nights to talk up for Madame Margaret. Then call it off for the rest of the week.

Aubrit: What we do—it's only a formality.

Jehannette: You and Bertrand and the other lady think so?

Aubrit: It ends, it's just a little ceremony.

She remembered how all along the girl had tried to drag it beyond its modest local meaning.

Jehannette: Since I grew up I've heard voices. They come out of heat and light. They blind a person. But they were sort of familiar too. Now I understand that Messire Michael used Bertrand's voice, Madame Catherine used Madame de Bourlémont's, Madame Margaret uses yours. So you see?

Aubrit: But I'm not a good woman.

She knew it was the truth. She felt sacrilegious. And all around her the woods milled with the presences and symbols of the old religion. Poisons and narcotics ran in trunk and bough.

Aubrit: I haven't always been pure.

Jehannette: It doesn't matter. I'm the one who has to be pure.

Madame Aubrit thought, you need a damn farmer, right now, someone thick—like your old man.

Aubrit: For God's sake, Jehannette, how could you be *that* damned virgin?

Jehannette: Someone has to be. If someone wasn't chosen, someone would have to choose herself.

Aubrit: Oh my God. I'm not Madame Margaret, Bertrand's not Messire Michael. *Bertrand?* My God. Look, take me home!

Jehannette: I know you think I need a boyfriend.

Aubrit: All right. I do. And it'll happen, Jehanne. A lot of plain girls get very good husbands . . .

Jehannette: Do you think I want to be *that* virgin? Do you think there are rewards for it?

Aubrit: Perhaps you think there are. When you're young you can be attracted by all sorts of . . .

The girl was trembling. Madame Aubrit thought, she's going to jump at me from the saddle. And she's tough enough to beat me to death.

Jehannette: Do you know that I haven't yet bled? That I'm not a true woman?

Madame Aubrit coughed.

Aubrit: What can I say?

Jehannette: I don't want to be this.

The girl began sobbing. She thought, maybe I can beg off through Aubrit. Maybe I'll never hear them again. At that moment she didn't care if she never did.

Aubrit: What can I say?

Seeing the girl weep Aubrit felt stronger and thought, what a funny little piece, thinking she's chosen like that.

For in Madame Aubrit's nearly aristocratic world you were more or less what *you* chose. Madame Catherine at the Confraternity. Madame Maire on the Meuse, Jeanne to a twenty-four-year-old wine merchant in Neufchâteau. Only momentarily—as at the Hallowe'en riots—did the unchosen fall on you.

Aubrit: What *can* I say?

Soon the girl was fit to travel again.

There was an eleven-year-old she liked called Hauviette who didn't yet know, as others were finding out, that Jehannette was somehow outcast. Once when Jehannette was fifteen she went out with Hauviette and the cattle and lay on the hills while the cows grazed and Hauviette combed

her hair soothingly, all day. Even then they ran into Nicolas
Barrey peeing amongst his father's sheep on the road outside
Greux. He wagged his fluent penis in the sun.

Barrey: Hey Jehannette, come and take the cure.

She tried to be pert as any girl.

Jehannette: If a person could see it.

But there *was* the assumption in town that she needed a
cure of some kind to make her decent. Some—Aubrit,
Nicolas Barrey—thought the cure could come simply.

Autumn. Incandescent Messire began getting even more
specific with his suggestions.

Messire: Duckling! You ought to go to the commandant
in Vaucouleurs.

She asked why.

Messire: You'll need escorts into France.

Jehannette: How do I go about asking him?

Messire: Tell him I told you to ask, that voices asked. My
darling, it works. Voices scare people. You can refuse anything a farmer's daughter asks. But you take a risk if you
refuse voices.

Jehannette: Do I have to do it straight away?

Messire: Why not, love?

Jehannette: Getting away from my old man. It's not easy,
Messire.

Messire: A time will come up.

Jehannette: Yes.

Messire: Remember, always mention my name.

Jehannette: With Jacques?

Messire: Not with Jacques, duckling. But with the commandant.

Jehannette: Oh yes.

Messire: Remember how it worked with Aubrit. You had
Aubrit awed. Then you spoiled it by getting weepy about
periods. Darling. Goose.

In the spring when Jehannette was seventeen Jacques had
to go to Vaucouleurs for a damages case about protection
money he and the other victims resident in Greux-Domremy
were paying. The 1426 dues had not been collected by
February the next winter and the guarantor, a man called
Guyot Poignant of Montigny-le-Roi, had therefore had

£120 worth of horses, hay and wood taken by the Armagnac authorities.

Zabillet: What sort of person is General de Baudricourt?

Jacques: He's a wild man. But he's got the common touch. And he's human.

Zabillet: Human?

Jacques: He adjourned the case. He said, I know you people don't have the money and Vergy's getting an army to come up the river. So we'll see what happens. It's not worrying him. It's poor bloody Poignant who's paying the bill.

Jehannette: How does he speak?

Jacques: Not much better than me.

One morning on the south edge of town the girl was with little Hauviette when Madame Aubrit rode down the road. She was on her way to Neufchâteau. Two maids and eight armed employees were with her. You could tell she was afraid of the journey, of all the talk about Monsieur Antoine Vergy having got authorization from the English to supply an army and send it into the Vaucouleurs area. She was at the stage of fright when she could look at her white wrist and foresee her whole white body crumpled by the side of the road.

She rode aside to speak to Jehannette.

Aubrit: Do you still hear those things?

Jehannette: Yes.

Aubrit: My . . . my voice?

Jehannette: Yes, I hear that voice.

At the start of the journey Madame Aubrit wanted a sibyl as much as she had feared one in Boischenu. She wanted to have it said, oracularly, that she'd make it the five miles to her wine merchant . . . Jehannette saw that clearly.

Aubrit: Will I be safe on the journey?

Jehannette: It's only five miles, Madame.

Aubrit: But bad ones.

Jehannette: You'll be safe.

It was a fair bet.

Madame Aubrit smiled.

Aubrit: I'll be back by Advent.

Jehannette: You have to help me go to Vaucouleurs, Madame. If I help you . . .

Aubrit: Vaucouleurs?

Jehannette: To see the general.

Madame Aubrit coughed.

Aubrit: I know the general. The general is a friend.

The girl was ruthless.

Jehannette: They say there are Irish in Monsieur Vergy's army.

A mist of atrocities rose in lovely Aubrit's brain. She began to bargain.

Aubrit: I could give you a letter. To the general.

Jehannette: You'll do that, Madame?

Aubrit: Yes.

Jehannette: You wouldn't forget, after a safe journey?

Aubrit: No, Jehannette. I'm reliable. I'm your godmother.

Jehannette: You wouldn't tell my father?

Aubrit: Your father and I don't speak very often.

Jehannette: God give you a good trip, Madame.

Madame Aubrit came back for Christmas. The next Easter she wrote a letter that said: 'This girl is my godchild and seems to have some sibylline powers. I would be grateful, dear Robert, if you did what you could for her within reason. Her demands are likely to be high and I'm sorry to inflict them on you, but she did foretell that I'd get to Neufchâteau safely one day when I was absolutely certain I would be killed on the road or sold back to Aubrit in a heavily raped state. You understand that one has to keep one's bargains by such people. Are you worried by all this talk about the English sending armies up the river? Aubrit tells me the Lord Bishop Cauchon is handling the quarter-master work for the Duke of Bedford over in Nylons and Chalon. He says Cauchon's letting some beautiful contracts go. Are we on the wrong side? I hope your dear Alarde is well. It gives me a strange feeling still, to be able to write like this to a great man . . . Jeanne Aubrit.'

Messire, Mesdames Margaret and Catherine still recurred at intervals to Jehannette. But though there were endearments, sweetness, Messire didn't make it clear how the letter of introduction could be used.

Then she was let go to her aunt's confinement up in Burey. For one thing Zabillet seemed to consider now that

Jehannette might become a midwife, even though that was a portentous trade.

Burey was a tiny place, seven households. They called it Burey-le-Petit. A bad place to be in a war—a small un-negotiable community. But that was a quiet spring. And the homesteads at Little Burey were only two miles from the Vaucouleurs fortress.

Aunt Aveline already had a grown daughter. The daughter had a husband, a quiet man called Lassois. He told Jehannette one night he thought her Aunt Aveline was a bit old for having kids.

Aveline herself was a little timid and had forgotten a lot about childbirth. About some pains that came she was too vocal and not vocal enough about others. The laying-in ached on. Mother and attendants were mystified.

Meanwhile, in Greux during the small hours of the Sunday after Easter Catherine herself, Jehannette's sister, woke up beside her husband Colin Greux and began retching. A fever mounted at a mad rate. She had severe belly pains. After sunrise she never said another rational thing. She lost consciousness at mid-morning and died in convulsions at mid-afternoon.

Jacques, Zabillet, Jacquemont, Jehan, Pierrolot had come rushing up the road to Greux very early in the day, and Jehannette was fetched from Little Burey. From long birth to quick death.

Catherine was so nice that everyone had the sense of her death being gratuitous, more unfair than the reported deaths in the north, south and west. She was so perfectly the little wife, so full of the hint of children. Now Zabillet had only Jehannette to project her womanhood.

They all keened so much. Colin Greux's mother took time from keening to say that she was a champion at corpse-laying, but Jehannette insisted on washing the body and putting it in its shroud.

Jehannette was becoming the sort of person you looked at and thought, No, she's not worth fighting, she can make better fusses than I can.

So she was let wash the body and dress it for the resurrection.

The Jacques family were square-built. Catherine's square

belly was clammy from recent delirium. The jaw fell in a way that made her look disappointed. In the open eyes was the slightest protest. But it was a wanton death not an ordained one. You could therefore be sure she had been happy till last night. Blithe.

Outside the men dosed themselves with sour wine, the women at the fireplace wailed the old wails. It was a service to Catherine: they judged you in the new world by the noise of your arrival.

Jehannette, not wailing, not drinking, felt cut off from the warm country rites and etiquette of grief. She thought they all think I'm a cold girl. They have no idea how tender I'm being with the flannel. How delicately I rinse the sweat slick off her shoulders. How royally I do the feet and the light-brown pubis. The womb of woman corrupts first, said Père Morel of St Rémy, quoting from someone called Odo of Cluny. A wise man saw lessons in that fact. Had that Odo ever handled a dead girl, all the useless freshness of the dead flesh? So submissive that with one hand Jehannette rolls her on her side for her last wash.

Private amongst the wails, Jehanne could feel the toughness of being alone flex itself in her belly.

After the funeral she went back to Aunt Aveline's in Burey. From Aunt Aveline at last a baby boy was drawn safely by the ankles.

Then Aunt Aveline regained strength. So, after a few days, Jehannette got Lassois alone in the garden and told him she wanted to go to Vaucouleurs and give a letter to General Baudricourt. She would need someone to escort her.

Lassois's strength was not in bullying but, instead, subtly, in looking easily scared.

Lassois: Me? In the general's house?

The local landlord was a young knight called de Foug. One morning he came riding through Burey with a secretary, a chaplain, a squire, two troopers. Jehannette ran into the street and blocked their way with her head properly bowed.

She said to excuse her but she had news for Monsieur de Baudricourt at Vaucouleurs. De Foug asked her what news.

Jehannette: I've got a letter for a start.

De Foug: Who's the letter from?

Jehannette looked confidential.

Jehannette: Madame Aubrit.

De Foug made an appreciative mouth, as if he knew Aubrit well.

De Foug: Show it to me.

She showed it to him, seal-first. De Foug inspected the seal and then the writing on the front. Whenever he told the story, years after, he said the writing was jagged, done privately, not by a secretary. It was the hand of a woman who had learned to write, but arduously. The sort of hand in which love-letters often come. He coughed.

De Foug: This *is* the Madame Aubrit of Neufchâteau?

Jehannette: Nothing's happened to her, sir.

De Foug called in at Lassois's house and told him to escort Jehannette on to Vaucouleurs.

By early May the baby was starting to build fat and Aunt Aveline's milk was in full flow. Lassois left his own wife and led the girl over the riverflats to Vaucouleurs. Jonquils were in the borders of fields and all over the pastures. Cows ate them thoughtfully for their freshness and nectar. Vaucouleurs ran down a slope above the river. In their highest corner its walls became a fortress. All about it was a siege of apple orchards, a froth of pink and white. As if war had become the playful feminine thing the popular writers made it. A contest between the knights of Vaucouleurs and the apple blossoms.

From half a mile off it looked a very unurgent town. Jehannette felt helpless before such a dormant city.

There were two soldiers on the top of the south gate. The May had got to them. Looking down, they seemed drugged.

The girl didn't like cities in any case. The way the opposing balconies nearly met above your head, making a tunnel. Her aunt had died under a falling balcony in Sermaize. She smelt her aunt's terror, there in the dusk. It was such a big thing to have a balcony to sit your wife and kids on! In the market stood a dying May-tree, lopped and brought into town for the May-day rites.

Lassois: They've had a party.

There were four stalls operating in the far corner of the market, selling chickens and vegetables and tench from the river to a few pensive housewives.

Lassois: Things are slack.

Messire had instructed her.

Messire: Be rude the way Brother Jesus is with Pharisees. They remember you, you see. They won't forget *you*, my love.

A large sewer ran along the front of de Baudricourt's fortress. She asked the man at the door where the provost's office was and was sent to it. It lay in the main walk behind the outer yard. Inside, five young men were sitting talking quietly. Their off-duty, untrussed hose hung down their thighs. One spoke wild French with a Scots accent. They became silent and all together looked round at Lassois and the girl. Their eyes were very cold: they had, or pretended to have consumed dozens of thick-set girls in red dresses in their trade. They had no professional doubts about the management of farmers and farmers' daughters.

Jehannette: I want to know where Sire de Poulengy is.

The girl's bluntness frightened Lassois but the officers didn't seem to feel any insult.

Where's Bertrand? they asked each other in bored voices.

Someone: He's up with the old man, they're doing the fodder accounts.

Another: He's not here.

Jehannette: As soon as you see him, tell him I'm in the city.

Lassois flinched. The insane way that girl talked to them!

Someone: He'll be excited.

Jehannette: Tell him his *pucelle* is in the city.

They thought a second. *Pucelle* meant virgin-whore, it meant witch-madonna. It was a hazy word, a bit exciting. It had come into her mouth in a rush.

A young one looked at her and said she'd better go. She turned to Lassois and talked with him quite loudly.

Jehannette: Do you think the le Royers would put us up?

The le Royers were cousins of the family.

Lassois's voice (saying *yes yes*) was diminished and his eyes on the ground.

She walked up to one that wasn't even looking at her. He was in his middle twenties and his eyes seemed close together. His hands were big. You could see the tops of his legs between the drawers and the untied hose that fell away from his hips. The skin was dark, obviously peasant, beneath its pretensions.

72

Jehannette: What's *your* name?

She was choosing one of them for the responsibility of telling de Poulengy that his *pucelle* had come to town! Lassois's turbid unhysteric anger was rising. He was sure he'd strangle the bitch if they got home.

Jehannette: What's *your* name?

The knight-or-peasant answered. He told her to go to hell.

Jehannette: What's your name?

Someone: Tell her.

Knight or peasant: De Metz. Monsieur Jean de Metz.

Everyone whistled when he said *Monsieur*—it must have been as suspect a *Monsieur* as Bertrand's.

Jehannette: Monsieur de Metz, I want you to tell Sir Bertrand his virgin is staying at the le Royers. Henri le Royer makes wheels. (She talked over her shoulder to Lassois.) Who's the man he works for?

Lassois shook his head. He was too panicked to remember names. He kept thinking, that bloody letter, why doesn't she just give them that bloody letter?

Jehannette: Anyhow, he can find the place. It's somewhere down by the wall.

Someone: Jesus!

She walked away. Lassois walked quickly at her side. She could nearly *see* the back of his neck prickling. He expected some reprisal to catch them up.

At last they were back in the sane open squares.

Jehannette: Don't be angry with me, Durand. You're nearly choking with anger.

Lassois: You didn't tell me anything about this! This Sir Bertrand stuff! This *pucelle* horseshit! This staying with the le Royers!

Jehannette: We've got to stay somewhere till Bertrand turns up.

Lassois: Bertrand! Wait till your old man hears . . .

Jehannette: Go home if you want.

But he understood all at once that he didn't want to: he felt stimulated.

The le Royers lived in the basement of a fuller's shop. Buying their three sons apprenticeships had broken them. Mother le Royer therefore coughed proudly in her four

73

walls that ran with damp, amongst clotted deposits of fuller's earth washed down from upstairs.

She ran about in a frenzy of hospitality.

Mother le Royer: Durand can sleep with Henri, and you with me, Jehannette. I hope my croup won't keep you awake.

The le Royers, Durand Lassois, Jehannette all ate out of the one pot, like country people. They were at the long table, in a heavy mist of damp and wet fuller's powder when Sir Bertrand de Poulengy knocked on the door.

The le Royers went out walking to give Jehannette and de Poulengy a chance to talk. Lassois stayed in the corner.

Bertrand: Jehannette, don't ever say you're my *pucelle*.

Jehannette: I had to make them listen. That Jean de Metz.

Bertrand: Look, I have good friends who are canons in the collegiate church here. They don't understand words like *pucelle*, so don't use them. Why are you here?

Jehannette: It's no use pretending. I hear Voices telling me to get an escort into France.

Naturally, he said *Voices?* and *Why into France?* She told him. And further.

Jehannette: The Voice called Messire talks with your voice.

Bertrand: Mine?

Jehannette: He's got to use someone's.

He didn't argue very much. He looked pale. He was the sort of person who knows in his blood that voices and bodies can be stolen away by gods or demons, that every beggar who knocks might be Christ and every pretty boy Satan. He was frightened.

Jehannette: Also I'm the girl out of Merlin's visions. Someone's got to be that too. Someone has to get this king to Rheims where the only royal chrism is. Once that's on his head and hands no one can say he's a bastard.

Across the table Bertrand got a cloth from inside his jacket and wiped his face all over with it.

Bertrand: I don't know how to ask . . . Is it that you want to sleep with me, Jehannette?

Jehannette: Holy Christ, how *could* that be the idea!

He seemed soothed, as if he wouldn't have liked that very much himself. Jehannette was surprised by a tiny pulse of hurt.

Bertrand: Do you know where Rheims is? Do you know where the king is? How far it is to the Loire?

Jehannette: That's not my business. That's my escort's business.

There was gravy on the table. Bertrand made four dots in it, labelled them, and drew a rough line for the Loire. In this way:

Bertrand: This is Vaucouleurs. Away over here is Chinon, where the king is staying, if he hasn't already moved on. Now between Vaucouleurs and the Loire every town has a Burgundian or English garrison. It's not till you get to Gien here that you see a French garrison. The countryside is full of free-lances. Welsh, English, Burgundian, Irish. When you get to the Loire it's teeming with French and Scottish irregulars. None of them would care much if you were Merlin's virgin. So it's hard enough to get to Chinon.

Jehannette: But it can be done. With friends. With the friends I have.

Bertrand frowned up at her from his gravy-mapping. There was sensitivity of spirit about him: she had noticed that when she said someone has to be the virgin. It *had* come to him in a sharp way that yes someone had to be. But, in the same voice Messire used, he gave her human discouragement.

Bertrand: Say this virgin of Merlin's got to Chinon. All those English and Burgundian troops between Chinon and

Rheims. There'd have to be set battles. Bedford would see to it.

Jehannette: Set battles aren't bad. Not for soldiers. They sell each other back and forth.

Bertrand: They can be bad now, Jehannette. At Agincourt Henry Monmouth—the king who died of piles, you know—refused to sell thousands of knights back. He sent his men around to cut their *throats*. They'd given in because they trusted him, they thought they could depend on him. But it was just as if he hadn't learned about the codes of war. I'm sure he had, even growing up in a way–off place like Wales.

Jehannette felt a glow of that dead king who had, at least, cancelled a world of silliness by making battle real.

Jehannette: He did what he should have.

Bertrand: You ought to think what you're saying. It's a matter of law. Law shouldn't vanish like that.

Jehannette: For ordinary people it wasn't ever there. It's time it let you others down. But tell me about Rheims.

Bertrand: It would take years to get there. It'd take bankers, mortgages, treaties, contracts . . .

Jehannette: Say Messire decided to move. With gods it's different.

Bertrand: Don't say gods, for God's sake. Say God. It's safer. And I doubt God could manage it all at once.

A giddy love of Messire and rude Brother Jesus and the king came up her body. It pained, emitting itself through her throat as a bubble.

Jehannette: I know it can all get done if I just talk to him.

Bertrand: The commandant?

Jehannette: The king.

Bertrand: You *are* mad.

He had got up from the table and its slimy map and made a number of dazed circuits of the table.

Bertrand: You heard these voices only after the confraternity met in Boischenu.

It was an accusation.

Jehannette: Nonsense.

Looking beset, the almost-knight of Poulengy sat again. One elbow landed in the table-mess and he withdrew and rubbed it.

Bertrand: You can't see Baudricourt.

She told him however that she had a letter from Madame Aubrit. Aghast, he wanted to see it. He felt it all over.

Bertrand: I could get you in on this excuse. But don't expect me to back you up.

Jehannette: I won't make you blush.

Bertrand: You probably will. No wonder poor Jacques used to beat you . . .

Jehannette: Poor Jacques . . .

Bertrand: Go to Mass. Be seen there. Take the eucharist.

Jehannette: Of course.

Bertrand: And you *are . . . definitely . . .* a virgin?

Jehannette: They can send women to see.

Bertrand: I don't know why I'm doing this.

His long mouth showed fear easily.

Jehannette: Because you know the way Messire and the others work.

Bertrand: Be good till I come back.

She went to Mass in the collegiate church. Jesus was sacrificed under the forms of bread and wine. Jesus her brother, the great god with whom the Father was well pleased. Who had had voices and been unfashionably virgin and whose family had disapproved. *And* who knew that he would be sacrificed on the sacrifice day, not go by random fevers as Catherine had in Greux.

Jesus and the old oak king and she, Jehannette, knew the day of mid-summer when they would have to go painfully. Their blood was needed for kingship, people, beasts, earth, the cycles of things, the redemption of lost worlds.

People in the collegiate church were engrossed by the way she was engrossed in the bread-wine sacrifice. Some of them were there to see her, since the le Royers and Lassois and the officers of the provost's department had talked. In a dull city she was worth watching.

On Thursday Bertrand came back and told her to be at the fortress at five in the afternoon. He said she ought to bring Lassois with her. Because the general would behave better if she had a relative there to watch.

She had never been inside a castle before, or understood how furniture could impose on strangers' minds in the interests of its master. There were wonderful Flemish tapestries all the way upstairs and great oak cupboards, sideboards, chests, all garrisoned with secrets; and the secrets were wealth and power. Upstairs in a waiting-room there were pikers whose tunics echoed Baudricourt's gold lion shield painted up and down the rafters. You could have ridden a horse into the fireplace. Monsieur d'Ourches, the young St Denis, passed through the room, looked twice quickly at Jehannette. His shoulders moved slightly under his doublet, remembering the punishments in Boischenu.

A Benedictine priest, probably the general's secretary, kept coming to the door and calling out names . . . Mâitre Devise, Mâitre Fremond . . . and this or that contractor got up and went in to be interviewed. Grocers, produce-merchants, ironmongers.

They had lit the lights by the time Lassois and Jehannette were called in.

There was a great desk, racks of ornamental arms, more high tapestries and more gold lions. De Baudricourt had big hips and small unmanly shoulders. His face was tolerant in a commercial way. It stated *I understand men*. He wasn't anything like de Poulengy, had no insight into the way divinities worked on people.

De Baudricourt: How's Madame Aubrit?

Jehannette: She's well, your honour.

He put his hand out for the letter she was holding. Tearing it open he muttered.

De Baudricourt: She's a lovely lady.

Jehannette: Everyone says that.

He read the letter. Then he called out to de Poulengy. There was an edge of complaint to his voice.

De Baudricourt: This is a letter of introduction, not a straight letter. She says this little thing's a sybil.

Though de Poulengy opened his mouth the general didn't wait for words to come out. He turned to the Benedictine and told him to make a note: they were to write to an agent in Chalon, there were contracts to be tendered for.

The Benedictine agreed to remind him.

De Baudricourt: What do you want to predict then?

Jehannette: I want an escort to go to Chinon.

De Baudricourt: Oh Jesus.

Jehannette: I have Voices that talk to me with a great light. They say I have to go to Charles and take him to Rheims for anointing.

She kept his eye, she wouldn't explain any more. She thought, don't beg pardon. Make them remember you by the size of what you say.

Jehannette: I'm a virgin.

De Baudricourt: That's novel.

He had a big venal grin.

Jehannette: Messire—the Voice—tells me to ask for an escort.

De Baudricourt: Who's this Messire?

Jehannette: Messire Michael of France, King Jesus's right hand.

She thought *Try that on! Fit that in with the fodder accounts.*

De Baudricourt: You're a mad woman.

The door opened and Jean de Metz came in. The general stopped caring about the girl's sanity.

De Metz: I'm sorry, you said I was to come straight in.

De Baudricourt: Yes, how did it go in Commercy?

De Metz: I bought them twelve sols a head. Thirty prime beef. Eleven vealers.

De Baudricourt: That's wonderful.

De Metz: We'll have to send an escort for them.

De Baudricourt: You can arrange that, can't you?

De Metz: Yes sir.

De Baudricourt: All right. Would they like this girl down in the provost's office?

Jean de Metz came closer to survey her, but when he got near, she saw that although his eyes performed the livestock-judging movements they had been doing all day, they didn't touch her face or body; as if he was saving someone's feelings, hers or even his own.

De Metz: Not while they've still got their horses.

Everybody had forgotten Lassois, who now lost his temper.

Lassois: You fucking redneck.

He was screaming at de Metz.

Lassois: You fucking redneck. You're the worst kind.

De Metz beseeched the lord general.

De Metz: Let me have *him* in the provost's office.

De Baudricourt: No, listen, you've done a good day's marketing. Clear out now.

After he'd gone, de Baudricourt stood catering, quarter-mastering in his head. The demonic girl wouldn't let him alone.

Jehannette: You can afford an escort to go to the butchers in Commercy . . .

De Baudricourt: For Christ's sake, I get meat from the butcher. What do I get from you?

Jehannette: Mid-Lent I want to be with the king. I must have an escort for that.

She didn't know where that gratuitous date came from.

De Baudricourt (to de Poulengy): Has she got a boyfriend?

Bertrand played Judas.

Bertrand: I don't know, Monsieur. Perhaps you could ask the farmer?

Jehannette: I shall take the dauphin to be anointed in Rheims. I've got to have an escort in the new year at the latest.

De Baudricourt (to Lassois): Has she got a boyfriend? Is she engaged?

Lassois: She hasn't. It worries her father.

But Bertrand balanced this with an ounce of loyalty.

Bertrand: She seems devoted to the idea of being a virgin.

De Baudricourt: Why doesn't she go into the convent?

She could feel the interview beginning to close in if not close. Needle him, a voice said. Challenge him. Proclaim and be memorable!

De Baudricourt: Her father still alive?

Bertrand: They're good people. Domremy-à-Greux.

De Baudricourt: Jesus, shit-heaps outside the back-doors and they want to visit the king.

Jehannette: Merlin says Isabeau the whore would ruin France and a virgin would save it.

De Baudricourt: Ah, but your village isn't in the Lorraine, it's in this castellany.

Jehannette: It's close enough. Lorraine's just over the river.

What did he want from Merlin Magus—the family name, the year of baptism?

The commandant shouted over her head to Lassois.

De Baudricourt: Cousin! Take her back to her old man. Tell him his lord demands he punches her blue and has her named in church on Sunday.

Jehannette: I'll come back in the new year.

De Baudricourt: Jesus.

Jehannette: Don't forget me.

The commandant laughed in Bertrand's direction.

De Baudricourt: Don't forget her!

They went back to their last night at the le Royers. Lassois was in a furious daze again.

Lassois: You didn't tell me you were going to say any of those crazy things.

Jehannette: There has to be a virgin. Is that crazy?

Lassois: And that mid-Lent horseshit!

Jehannette: I made it mid-Lent because I can get back to Vaucouleurs in the new year.

Lassois: Not with me.

Jehannette: Well, it's the least you can do, I'll be helping with the confinement.

Lassois: Confinement?

Jehannette: Your wife's.

Lassois: She's not pregnant. Or are there prophecies in Merlin about that too?

Jehannette: She's missed a period. She told me last week. The child will be January.

It would be his first child. He didn't know whether to sulk or give a shout.

Lassois: She could have told me.

Jehannette: They always tell a friend first, they don't tell husbands till they're certain.

Lassois: It's not certain.

Jehannette: Oh yes, it's certain. How else can I get away from Jacques in the new year?

Lassois: If I was going to have a daughter like you . . .

Jehannette: Don't worry. It only happens to a few people.

Poulengy came to take her home the next day. At six o'clock he arrived outside the le Royers' basement with his two archers and his piker. They wore oddments of armour and looked a little ragged. Lassois rode pillion with the piker in the rear of the party as far as Little Burey. His wife was

81

waiting for him. It was early June and she had more signs still that she was carrying a child.

If he took it a little dully it was because he had never had so many people mislead and misdirect him in such a short time. His wife, the mad girl Jehannette, de Poulengy. Poulengy had told him *not* to make any ardent reports to Jacques. *Not* to set up the punishment the general had ordered, to climb down at Burey-le-Petit many miles short of Jacques.

There was a pack-saddle well forward on the shoulders of de Poulengy's mare for Jehannette to sit on. Though their bodies did not touch he seemed to be weighing her; as if he really wanted to pick her up and test how she hung in his arms. As if *that* would give him clues.

He said the English were letting out contracts in Champagne. It meant there should be an assault on Vaucouleurs before autumn. Therefore the confraternity had put off the mid-summer rites for that year. She could feel in him the attraction for, a terror of vision, prophecy.

They rode into Greux. Women looked up from the presses and boughs in all the gardens of Greux on a fine June day. Even the two archers and the piker grinned behind their sire's back as if Bertrand were a comic knight grotesquely in love with the square girl.

The highway went straight here. At the last homestead of Greux you could see the first homestead of Domremy-à-Greux.

Bertrand: The general can be frightened all right. He likes to have all possibilities covered. He can be frightened by the sort of things you say.

Jehannette: I know that.

She thought, I'm understanding people as I've never understood them before. She was full of the wonder of that. In her cool dead womb was manipulatory knowledge.

The first brats of the town, Thiesselin's boys and Guillemette's, were already running beside them.

Bertrand: But you have to know the sort of people you're dealing with. For example, the general has written off to an agent of his in Chalon to offer a tender on wine and timber to the English forces Bishop Cauchon is supplying. If he gets the contracts the English could be outside Vaucouleurs in

82

September drinking wine he sold them. Shoring up their excavations with his timber. They're very strange, these big nobles. None of them is as straight-out as you. Or even as me.

The Domremy bells roared, dull village bells, no refinement in their throats today. Was it a death or marriage or famine or hour of the office?

Both he and the girl, together, in the same instant, felt a crippling sadness and crouched on the big horse.

But three days later the sun-face of Messire took her again from the right.

Messire: Great Christ and brother Jesus knows you are a true sister, duckling. Seed and fire in his heart for you!

Jehannette: Is the new year all right then?

Messire: You can't do wrong. Little red apple.

A boy called Nicolas Barrey, who had once waved his man-root at Jehannette, got interested in her because she had ridden home with an escort. Jacques encouraged him, let him sit in the garden in the long evenings and feel the enchantment of the girl's rugged disinterest.

Barrey: Come out with the cows and and me? We could have a nice day, Jehannette.

Jehannette: I couldn't take the excitement.

The Barrey boy was nineteen, you couldn't wish for anyone more pleasant, and his father was one of the girl's godfathers. And Jacques couldn't help feeling that the joy of a young husband might loosen up the frozen machinery of her womb.

The boy pretended light irony but was actually hurt and jealous.

Barrey: It isn't any use trying to interest a knight's lady.

Jacques: There won't be any more of that knight's lady horseshit.

Selectively misinformed by Bertrand, Jacques had beaten the girl up nonetheless as any good father would. After, Zabillet told him there was no question she was still a virgin. Sometimes he wished something unequivocal *would* happen to her body so that he could take up a permanent attitude to her.

Jacques: According to the Sire de Poulengy, she was carrying a letter from Madame Aubrit to the general.

Barrey: Oh-h-h-h!

Jehannette: If you think she wrote it for her own sake . . .

Jacques: For whose bloody sake could she have written it? *Dear General, this is my little friend Jehannette and I'd like you as a personal favour to marry her off amongst the gentry or make her an abbess.* (He turned to the girl.) What was in this bloody letter?

Jehannette: I don't know. I never had it read to me.

Her remote eyes flickered over Jacques, keeping him mercilessly confused.

Jacques: I'll have a word with Madame bloody Aubrit.

But he knew he couldn't: he was disqualified somehow because he had had her by accident at Hallowe'en and here she was writing off to a general. The arrangement gave him a form of vertigo.

Barrey: We could have a great time up on Bermont. (He knew he had Jacques's permission to roll his eyes when he said *great time up on Bermont.*) Don't tell me you're not interested.

Jehannette: I won't tell you then. You can guess.

She sat actually lusting for the blazing return of Messire.

Jacques went to old Jean Barrey and agreed on a dowry. Then a dowry agreement was drawn up by the notary in Greux. Two good milkers, a family of pigs and two pounds tournois would go with Jehannette if she could be got into church for the betrothal ceremony.

Jean Barrey found out from the parish priest in Greux that you could bring breach-of-promise pleas to court even if the betrothal hadn't taken place in church. A dowry agreement between the two families was good for evidence. He told Nicolas and they both told Jacques.

Jacques: Get a subpoena from the court in Toul and I'll pay the fee.

When de Poulengy went to see Madame Aubrit that summer they talked about Jehannette for the whole visit. Aubrit's eyes twinkled with some intoxication of fear for the girl. In fact she had been very sad to miss out on the repetition of the rites.

In the end she invited Jehanne to visit. Jehannette brought her spinning gear to keep herself amused.

Aubrit questioned her about General de Baudricourt.

The girl told her what was said by the general, de Poulengy, herself.

Aubrit: And you're still a virgin? (Aubrit was trying to make the business chatty, whimsical.) After meeting all those handsome soldiers.

Jehannette: A virgin has to be a virgin. Inspect me if you like.

Aubrit: No. No.

All at once she began shivering.

Aubrit: I'm not a good woman for a god to use my voice . . .

But the girl could somehow see an erotic content to the lady's terror, a history of sexual spasm there. A weird anger buzzed in Jehannette. She could have hit Madame Aubrit very easily, many times. For not being pure. For the coyness of the confession. *I'm not a good woman for a god to use my voice . . .*

Bertrand visited her in July. Jacques wouldn't invite him in or pour him a drink. So Bertrand and the girl went out and sat on stools in the orchard.

Bertrand: The general's mentioned you in a report to Chinon. The king believes in visionaries, he has an astrologer, Germain de Thibonville, with him everywhere he goes. He sends off for horoscopes to Pierre St-Vallerien and others. They charge him the earth but he's happy.

Jehannette: I wouldn't charge a cent.

Bertrand: I know. Look, nothing's possible for the moment. If Antoine Vergy's army arrives at Vaucouleurs by the end of summer, the general hopes to come to an arrangement with him, a conditional surrender.

An arrangement. It sounded characteristic; farmers' families would be eaten whole. All over the castellany would be unburied corpses, on doorsteps, in the yards. But when the forces faced each other, there'd be an arrangement then.

Bertrand: Like this: the general will say let's stop fighting and if I'm not reinforced by Easter I'll march out and you can march in. I can see you don't like the idea of this sort of thing.

Jehannette: I don't understand why it can't be done for peasants.

Bertrand: Anyhow, if there *is* a conditional surrender all

85

the general's professionals will have to look around for new work by next Easter. So some of them might be willing to travel and join the army on the Loire. You see, we might get an escort that way.

Jehannette: You'll come too?

He closed his eyes tight and swallowed. Just like a man nagged. He had never been in a skirmish and true fighting men were as remote from his understanding as titans would be. The idea of Vaucouleurs besieged by English and Burgundians made his hands sweat. Even though everyone in the provost's office seemed to yawn and say it would just be a tableau, a set play.

Jehannette: You'll come too?

Bertrand: On conditions. The general should have settled things well before Christmas, but I don't want you hanging about till then. I want you to be good for Jacques. If people in this area get convinced a person is mad, you know what they do?

Jehannette: Sometimes they chain them up in the woods near Bermont.

Bertrand: Yes, and they also put them in ducking-chairs and half-drown them. So behave.

The girl yawned.

Jehannette: Is that all the conditions?

Bertrand: No. The last one is: never take for granted I believe what you say. You might be straight up and down crazy. But the king seems to listen to strange people. All the despatches—and all the rumours—say that.

Jehannette: So there's nothing to be lost.

Bertrand: Holy God!

Vergy came early. His Swiss burned Commercy in mid-July and the accustomed horrors were performed in the little towns. Lassois and his wife and parents-in-law went and crammed into the le Royer cellar in Vaucouleurs. Lassois was sure from what he had seen of the general that nothing too uncomfortable would be allowed to happen in the general's city. A lot of people came down the road from Greux making for Neufchâteau which was wholly inside Lorraine and therefore safe. The nine-year-lease the town had on the de Bourlémont castle had expired. If they locked themselves in there and the place was taken, they would all be killed on the grounds that it wasn't decent for peasants to hold a castle against professionals. Even the Swiss, who were a peasant army which had sliced up knightly armies, would have felt that the properties had been violated.

The town doyen, sheriff, mayor, and elders voted for a quick remove to Neufchâteau. The cows and wives of Domremy-à-Greux joined strangers' cows and wives on Caesar's road.

Neufchâteau stood on a hill of vines. It had a public house called the *Ancient Cock* where Jacques himself had stayed a time or two. The landlady was a brash woman with wiry ginger hair. She rarely covered it with a hood. All the men liked her and called her *la Rousse*. The pub was full, but she let out the stables cheaply to refugees. Because she and Jacques winked at each other and pretended to have had robust times together in the past, she gave him two stalls for a few sols and let him keep his horse illegally in the yard.

The provost of Neufchâteau had made a regulation that refugees were to pasture their livestock day and night on the hills outside town, and boys like Nicolas Barrey stayed out there with them all the time. One day Jehannette took Jacques's plough horse out of town for exercise and the boy saw her.

Barrey: Why don't you stay? It's nice out here in the evening.

She wouldn't answer.

Barrey: My old man has a paper for you. It came from Toul, just before we left home.

Jehannette: What sort of paper?

Barrey: It's from the bishop's court in Toul. The bishop doesn't like bitches like you.

You could smell the town of Neufchâteau half-a-mile down the road: all the sewers had overflowed. The locals were saying that's what the provost gets for being merciful. Did he think none of these people were going to shit?

The stableyard at the back of the *Ancient Cock* was paved with raw sewage which had overflowed at night and was baked dry by the sun. You held your breath when entering the yard, it was like coming into a new element. Then, after half an hour you began to take the stench for granted.

87

At one of Jacques's two stall doors, old Jean Barrey presented a subpoena from the bishop's court in Toul. It called on Jehannette daughter of Jacques formerly of Sermaize to explain in early August why she would not make a betrothal in church to back up the dowry agreement Jacques and the Barreys had made.

Toul was twenty-five miles north, beyond the cinders of the abandoned harvests Vergy had set light to. Jacques looked around the fouled yard. He hadn't suspected that canon lawyers would go on issuing cool Latin subpoenas in the hot stink of this summer crisis.

The girl was so furious she said she'd go.

Jacques: They can't expect you to do that.

Jehannette: I'll go. Who are you sending to lie for your side of the case, Farmer Barrey?

Jacques: You little sow! You can't say that sort of thing to Farmer Barrey!

Barrey Senior: No one can go. Vergy's men are all round Vaucouleurs. They've started mining the walls. (He stood regretting the legal advice he'd taken in Greux.) When things settle down, we might be able to arrange another hearing.

Jehannette: I'm going *now*. (She made movements of her hands as if she were actually putting spare petticoats into a sack.) Because you're not going to marry me off, that has to be settled.

Barrey Senior: Jehannette, we'd be very proud if you'd consider . . .

Jehannette: Would you be proud to have *no* grandchildren? Because I don't have periods, I never have had.

Barrey Senior: I don't understand you.

Jehannette: Oh, my old man didn't tell you that. He would have had to promise you an extra porker for it. Given that I'm not very bloody pretty in the first place.

Jacques was set to punch her but she took hold of a rake.

Jehannette: No more of that knuckle stuff.

She held the rake by the neck and there wasn't any doubt the intent to punish him was there.

Barrey Senior: Look, what if we forget it for now?

Jehannette: No, get a notary to say in a letter to the bishop's court that you made a mistake. You made the settlement without knowing enough about Nicolas and me and you don't want to go on with it. You don't have to go as far as saying I've got a dead womb.

Barrey turned to Jacques who still stood under threat of the rake handle.

Barrey Senior: I think we'd better do that, Jacques. Nothing seems right at the moment . . . I'll pay the fee.

When Barrey began to leave he saw that there were dozens of people watching the quarrel from the back windows of the *Ancient Cock* and over the stable partitions.

He told them, with a tired movement of the hand, to go inside and called to Jacques.

Barrey Senior: I don't believe everything she says. I know she's upset.

Jehannette: You're a decent man.

She put the rake down. Instantly Jacques punched her full-force on the bridge of the nose. She fell hard, no bending at the hips. No one came to help her as she woke. She understood after some minutes that her capuchon had been knocked off her head and her hair hung loose in the sewage.

For the rest of her time in Neufchâteau she waited on tables for la Rousse and slept with the servants. At Vaucouleurs, early enough to save Neufchâteau from an epidemic, General de Baudricourt made exactly the contract with Vergy that Messire/Bertrand had predicted that July. Vergy would go back to the Marne. At Easter next year de Baudricourt would give him the whole castellany if he still wanted it.

While the people from Domremy-à-Greux were marshalling the cattle and pigs at the north end of Neufchâteau to drove them back home, Jehannette saw old Jean Barrey. He called to her in his gentle way.

Barrey Senior: Nicolas went off, did you hear? He went missing just after your father and I had our talk.

She felt a coldness in her belly. As if he were the first casualty of her mission.

Barrey Senior: Oh, he wouldn't sulk, I don't mean that. I wonder why he went, that's all. He took a horse.

The unmarried girls helped drove the cattle home. The dead dust of the burnt crops filled the wind that blew down the valley; the waste of the year fell in black smuts on their heads.

At the first houses of the town women began to leave the column to mourn the damage. Broken oak furniture filled the yards, fires had been lit anywhere and many roofs had been burned. The houses were full of excrement. Apple trees had been cut down. Women kept screaming *Oh look, oh look!* as they verified that the beds consecrated by loves, deaths, fevers and dreams had been chopped up and some Swiss piker had crapped in the stew-pot.

Madame Aubrit's house had had its top floor burnt down. The roof had fallen in. Fragments of Flemish needlework blew around the threshold. The church was burnt too, the roof of Jacques's place gone. People wandered the streets looking vacant. Vergy's men had done this quickly, it was clear. They may have stayed only one night, lit their celebration fires, put a torch to the crops, broken up the furniture and then gone on. That's the measure of our permanence, you could see people thinking; one night's work and all our meaning's burnt or has shit on it.

Jehannette saw by the church the bloating body of a horse. It was almost a release to see this death of animal flesh amidst all the inhuman wreckage. Jacques and other men were standing beyond the body of the horse, their backs to it. They had discovered the heart mystery of the town's ruination: that was the impression Jehannette got. So she crept up on them.

Nicolas Barrey was lying stark-eyed and grey, some days dead. There was a cross-bow bolt in his throat and his belly was a city of maggots.

She fought them to get near, but old Jean Barrey held her off firmly, seeming to exclude her from some last intimacy he wanted to share with the boy. Jacques beset her, hissing in her ear as she groaned and felt authentically widowed.

Jacques: Why weren't you kinder to him then?

After that, a sort of genial and final despair of her appeared in Jacques. He began hugging her again. He said, in a valedictory way, *You little piglet, you fat little goose, you mad little bitch.* He had somehow understood he couldn't love her through the flat of his fist any more.

There were too many indications that that phase was over. She had lost a lover, was a sort of widow. She had carried Madame Aubrit's love-letters to a general. Using on him (so said the non-committal Lassois) the same catty disdain she used on her old man. She'd come home with a knight's escort and her very individual virginity untouched. And she had been Poulengy's white *pucelle* in Boischenu.

Zabillet: I've told him not to beat you up any more.

Jehannette: Thank you. It was my hair full of muck I couldn't stand.

Zabillet: He's just a little scared.

Jehannette: So am I. I don't know what will happen.

Although two parts of her knew differing certainties. In her chest and shoulders she was certain she would always be here, Jacques's funny unmarried daughter. In her gut, however, she was certain of what happened to you when you were incarnate god the way she was: first the giant act, then the flesh-blood sacrifice. Jesus who was God of gods, also knew. In the Gospel of St John the knowledge was in his gut like a growth, like a baby in his mind's womb. Now in hers like a baby. So the certainty in the gut was the worst: the chest and shoulders just had trouble imagining what would happen, that was all. First, the entry into Jerusalem or Château-Chinon. Then, the iron through the wrists.

She was scared and *did* know what would happen.

Jehannette: I just don't know what will happen.

De Poulengy rode down from Vaucouleurs with Julien his servant in mid-November. He wanted to tell her Jean de Metz would certainly travel now. Because Orleans had been attacked by an English army early in the month and had invited knights to join the garrison.

Bertrand was of course appalled by the English assault. It was against all law. They had the Duke of Orleans a prisoner in England.

Bertrand: You can't attack the city of a prince you've got prisoner. That's all.

Jehannette felt relief. All the crazy old protocol of battle was under cancellation now. The demonic English had woken up to it. Hal Monmouth wouldn't take prisoners at Agincourt. Then the English Royal Council refused to sell the Duke of Orleans back. Now Bedford had sent troops against the Duke's city. She thought, things are simpler

91

now, things were naturally vicious, unfantastical. She felt that if she wanted to intrude she wouldn't need to know all the weird etiquettes that once ruled wars.

Bertrand (over and over): You just can't do it, it isn't allowed.

Jehannette: They're doing it.

Bertrand: Maybe. But they've already suffered for it.

It seemed that on the first Sunday of the siege the Earl of Salisbury had been looking at the city fortifications from a tower outside the walls. They heard nothing, Salisbury and the English generals, but one of the sides of the window recess blew away and bore half Salisbury's face with it. He'd taken four days to die. The story was it was a child who had gone up on the walls of Orleans to play and accidentally set off a mortar. The one stone ball found the one window where the violator of world law stood! God had done it, Poulengy said.

Jehannette: I suppose God gave Henry Monmouth piles too.

What she saw was that this Earl of Salisbury had died the same way Mengette's peasant husband Collot had, by someone's remote action, indecently. That too somehow made the new world seem simpler, more malleable, than the old.

Bertrand: A child! An innocent child set the mortar off!

Jehannette: That's a good story. I wouldn't change it if I was them.

Bertrand: What's wrong with you?

Jehannette: So this Jean de Metz wants to leave Vaucouleurs?

Bertrand: I've only discussed it in basic terms. But he seems willing. D'Ourches can't leave the district. His father's sick and he wants to oversee next year's harvest.

Jehannette: But this Jean de Metz hasn't anything to oversee.

Bertrand: That's right.

Jehannette: He'd think it was a great joke to rape me.

Bertrand: I'm sure he can be talked out of it. He isn't so bad.

Jehannette: All right. I'll travel with him.

Bertrand: You don't sound grateful.

Jehannette: What's gratitude got to do with it? You'll have an exciting journey.

Bertrand: Hm.

She thought, he'll cancel if he's given the chance, he'll back out.

In the new year Jehanne Lassois was due to have her baby. At Epiphany Lassois called for Jehannette, as Poulengy had told him to. The girl didn't pack any petticoats, trying to imply she'd be away just a few days.

Jacques: Are you going up to Vaucouleurs?

He asked dismally. Since last August it had become *her* business if she went to Vaucouleurs or not. But he let her know that her tripping round would distress her old man very much.

Jehannette: I don't have the clothes for it.

She showed him her empty hands. Lassois didn't say anything.

It wasn't till they were going through Greux and were safely away from home that she began to give people full-value farewells. Little widow Mengette was in the sun amidst the glaring snow in her mother-in-law's garden. The girl came up and started weeping over Mengette's knees.

Mengette: What's the matter? You're only going to a confinement.

Jehannette: I'm going away. But don't tell Jacques. Perhaps in a month or so . . .

She made a ceremonious goodbye to the Guillemettes who were out in the snow in their yard and to Jean Waltrin of Greux. Lassois understood she was making up for the off-hand way she'd left Jacques and Zabillet.

General de Baudricourt had been asked by de Poulengy to include a memorandum in his January despatches. It said:

May I remind Your Benign Majesty that last May a virgin said to have Sibylline powers came here to ask for an escort to you. She claimed to be the Oak-wood Virgin of Merlin's prophecy. She's a very rugged sort of person, goes to Mass and doesn't have fits. She says she's heard voices ordering her to take you to Rheims. If Your Majesty should happen to wish to examine her, I could provide an escort of officers of this garrison who want to join the army on the Loire. I would of course examine her as thoroughly as I could here to test her political and moral nature. They call her a *pucelle* but a white *pucelle* . . .

Mid-January a Lassois baby-boy had been born and poor Durand kissed his head and straightway took Jehannette to Vaucouleurs. Mother le Royer was waiting for them in the street. She was shivering and slipped on the iced stones in her sabots.

Mother le Royer: That gentleman Monsieur Bertrand is here, he's been here every afternoon for a week. (Having that gentleman in the house all the time embittered her a little.) It's no use having important people in here to talk to you. There's nowhere for the rest of us to go to let you be private. Except out in the cold. It's different in summer.

Bertrand: Hello Jehannette.

Jehannette: I'm no one's Jehannette any more, no one's little girl. You'd better call me Jehanne. No one would call a spinster Jehannette.

Bertrand: Thanks for bringing her, Durand. You're doing better things than you understand.

Bertrand seemed full of spry faith today.

Lassois fended off the knight's gratitude, protected his brain from it by putting both hands palms-out on his forehead.

Bertrand: I've been talking to d'Ourches and the general about Orleans. It's the centre of the set-up now. Like this.

Fuller's dust, drifted down from the floor above, lay over the table. Bertrand made marks on it.

Bertrand: That's the river and here's Orleans on the north bank. Down here is Chinon and here is Blois where the relief forces are supposed to marshal and here's Gien where the king has a garrison. That's the place we'd go for first if we were making for the Loire. Now Rheims is right up here, as I told you.

He pointed to the top right-hand corner of the table, spearing the dust half-a-dozen times with his index finger, emphasizing that the holy town was an island of impossibility.

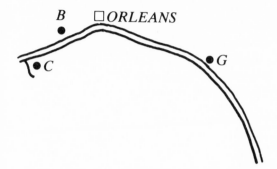

Mother le Royer didn't like the way he was treating her table. The names were unknown to her, the pattern may have been unclean for all she knew.

Bertrand: If they take Orleans, Blois and Gien will go, then Bourges. They'll be deep in the king's country then. It's unthinkable. Even as it is now they're right across the line of travel from Chinon to Rheims. You have to understand these things if you want to talk to the general.

The hard geography he had drawn depressed her. She began to yawn.

Jehanne: You mean they've got to be driven away from Orleans?

Bertrand: Yes. And don't think there isn't a road from Paris to Orleans. In every town there's an English depot and garrison. And between the line of the road and Rheims there are towns called Montargis, Melun, Auxerre, Troyes, Sens—Holy Mother, endless towns that all have a garrison of Goddam-English or Burgundians!

The girl waved her hand, dismissed the eastern half of the table.

Jehanne: You told me about them last May. It's Orleans that's the trouble.

Bertrand: Yes, yes. It's the trouble.

He sounded exhausted by his knowledge of the map.

Jehanne: De Metz still wants to come?

Bertrand: Yes. There are lots of English nobles down there. He wants to get himself one and put him up for sale.

Jehanne: When are we going?

Bertrand: The general wants to see you first.

Jehanne: No.

Bertrand: How does he know you're not a witch? You come here using words like *pucelle*. It gets around.

Jehanne: I was told by the *pucelle* of the witches of Boischenu, a whore called Mauvrillette . . . *you* might know her . . . I was told the devil services the witches with an ice-cold member. How can I be a witch if I'm still a virgin?

Bertrand: He doesn't know you're a virgin.

Jehanne: I've got a body like a child. Because I haven't bled.

Bertrand: He doesn't know that.

Jehanne: I won't tell him. I don't want *him* to know.

He hushed her down, pointing to the roof.

Bertrand: You've already told the fuller, Jehanne.

The girl sat and began to huddle. Motherly Mother le Royer recognized a frightened child there and came out of the corner, taking her by the shoulders.

Bertrand: We're going to Chinon all right. (Bertrand was brotherly as Mother le Royer was maternal.) But he's waiting on an answer from the king for a start.

Mother le Royer: The king knows about her?

And at once there was a fever of strength in the girl's belly, an intoxication. Of course, I'm in the king's knowledge now, she articulated to herself. My pattern is in the king's knowledge. The excruciating map de Poulengy had drawn in dust was blown out of her memory, remaining valid only at the back of the brain, not in the guts where godhead pawed like a baby.

Messire: Orleans is an eye in the king's head, a tooth in his mouth, love. Its walls touch Jesus's brow.

Jehanne: Orleans?

Messire: Orleans.

Jehanne: Yes.

So Jehanne went back amongst the sable lions of de Baudricourt and the cavernous fireplaces. Raging now with de Baudricourt timber, she saw. Timber contracted to Monsieur Antoine Vergy last August, when Domremy-à-Greux, Greux, Burey-le-Petit, Burey-la-Côte and two dozen towns had been ruined.

De Baudricourt: Well, you said you'd be back. And you're back. (The little shoulders shook genially, and the unheroic gut.) Just in time. We'll be moving out at Easter.

She didn't want his unmixed goodwill. It would yield more to keep him bewildered.

Jehanne: You lost the city but won some contracts.

For a second he was offended. He'd only been trying to be nice.

De Baudricourt: That's the way of the world. Someone has to get Cauchon's contracts . . . But I'm not going to explain myself to you.

Jehanne: I wouldn't be very interested.

De Baudricourt: Jesus, you're the same rude little cow.

Jehanne: Yes. When can I have the escort? There's Orleans to look to now.

De Baudricourt: Messire's added Orleans to the list?

Jehanne: I can't help Messire, general. Amongst what he says is Orleans. When can I have the escort?

De Baudricourt: I want to talk with you first, I want you to call me Monsieur because that's what I bloody well am to you. I want you to confess every few days to the priests at the collegiate church. I want to talk to Mother le Royer . . .

Jehanne: She knows I'm a virgin. We went to the baths together today . . .

The general raised his eyebrows—almost like the father of a wise child—towards the Benedictine and Poulengy and some middle-aged official in a long woollen overall. The official refused to share the general's pride.

De Baudricourt: Go back to your cellar now. (The general told her softly, again like a father. She wondered was she visibly orphaned; the speed at which le Royer and the general offered themselves as new parents astounded her.) And don't give Mother le Royer any cause to change her mind about you.

Jehanne: If you have to make these jokes, I suppose I have to tolerate it.

De Baudricourt: That's right. Get out now, get out.

97

Outside she asked de Poulengy who the middle-aged man in the long tunic was. He told her it was the Chamberlain to the Duke of Lorraine. The general thought the Duke might be talked into giving them safe conduct papers.

Jehanne: Would that do any good?

Bertrand: Perhaps a little.

Jehanne: The general wants to share the joke. The joke I am.

Bertrand: Perhaps.

Jehanne: Bertrand?

Bertrand: Yes?

Jehanne: I *do* often mean to thank you. For what you do.

Bertrand shook his head.

Bertrand: No, I'm honoured. It's my . . . my only chance.

She looked at him, knowing he meant my only chance of knighthood, honour. At first she wanted to laugh at such an imperfect knight's intimate ambitions but after a second was ashamed of herself.

Jehanne: You have to fix it so that we start soon, Bertrand.

She was begging. She could feel a sort of hilarious disbelief rising in her, in the static air of Vaucouleurs. Waiting for the commandant to try out his squalid tests.

At the collegiate church she confessed to Père Jean Fournier and not without some cunning. For example:

Jehanne: I was arrogant towards a lord higher in the order of things than me. But he wouldn't do what's needed.

Fournier: Needed? Who by?

Jehanne: By Messire St Michael.

Fournier: You don't mean to tell me . . . ?

Jehanne: Yes, by Messire St Michael. I wouldn't say it if it wasn't true.

Père Jean Fournier knew who he had there, behind the black screen.

Fournier: What else?

Jehanne: I despair.

Fournier: You despair?

Jehanne: Because things take so long to arrange, great men move so slowly.

Fournier: Nothing happens in a hurry in this world. Especially for the arrogant. Especially for those who despair.

Ho-hum Père Fournier, she thought.

He asked her did the voices tell her to be arrogant. She said the arrogance was all her own.

And why was she a virgin?

Because Christ was. But she didn't tell him she was victim: clerics like Fournier didn't like girls to make claims.

Some days she went back to Burey-le-Petit to see the baby. One afternoon she spent three hours with de Baudricourt and even asked him how to deploy a company of troops. He enjoyed himself, calling the businessmen in from the waiting-room to use as moving pieces. The businessmen formed the men-at-arms in the centre. Mounted or dismounted according to the nature of the action, the ground where you stood, whether it had rained or not—a dozen other considerations. The Benedictine monk and a few officers were arranged around them as wedges of pikers and archers. So the general had turned the social order upside down, making the local tradesmen the knights for the purposes of demonstration, and making the knights and the clergy the common off-siders and flankers.

De Baudricourt: Don't worry about the chinless wonders in the middle. The longbow counts for a lot. Not so much the crossbow. It takes too long to crank it up and fit a new bolt. But when you're defending a town the crossbow's fine. Like at Orleans. You can have men on the walls all day cranking their bows. Bertrand will tell you we had ordinary citizens up on the walls sending bolts off all day at Vergy's Burgundians and Swiss. The Swiss are scared shitless of them, to coin a phrase. You see, a bolt can do awful things.

Nicolas Barrey's image, desecrated by bolts, burnt her eyes.

De Baudricourt: It's the English who are really good at all this.

When the businessmen and officers had been sent out, the general and the girl suddenly began laughing, laughing.

Jehanne: Please send me.

De Baudricourt: I can't yet. You know all the reasons why. And you can't be a general. You've got to start learning *that* at five.

Jehanne: Listen. Listen, my lord. I don't want to be a general. I just want to tell the generals what to do.

Again they laughed.

Jehanne: But seriously . . .

De Baudricourt: Aren't you ever going to marry anyone?

Jehanne: Of course. And have three sons. One Pope, one Emperor, and the other one King.

The general murmured in a thin voice made for conspiracy and womanising.

De Baudricourt: Let me start your little Pope off.

Jehanne blinked but his desire stayed in his face, was no mis-sighting. After the afternoon's clowning with tradesmen he wanted her. He thought she was a nice little piece. Her back-chat had an erotic sting. Seeing him thinking it, she felt a little aggrandized.

Jehanne: Someone will let us know, if it's ever time for the little pontiff.

Her lids prickled with tears and she couldn't stop herself smiling.

De Baudricourt: Do you mind going to see the Duke of Lorraine?

Jehanne: I'm not a circus bear, Monsieur.

De Baudricourt: I know that, my love.

Jehanne: I am not your love.

De Baudricourt: He can give you a safe conduct. That will help you a little, as far as the Loire. No one's really safe out there.

Jehanne: He's on the English side.

De Baudricourt: The alliance isn't active.

Jehanne: The alliance?

De Baudricourt: He doesn't help them much. You might have gathered by now: the lines of alliance aren't kept very strictly.

She remembered his wood and wine contracts with Cauchon. She wondered why she was gentle with this mean-shouldered fat-gutted traducer? Because he had once—for ten minutes—desired her?

One day de Metz spoke to her as she dismounted in the inner yard of the fortress. He watched her closely, for she'd been riding country-style, her dress tucked up in the middle into her girdle. All rednecks gaped when girls got down from horses—it was just a country custom.

De Metz: You won't travel like that, will you?

Jehanne: Why?

De Metz: You'd be much safer dressed like a boy. I don't have to explain, do I?

Jehanne: No.

De Metz: I mean, I *know*.

Jehanne: I suppose you do.

De Metz: I've been in this business since I was twelve. I was a big child.

Jehanne: When will the general let us go?

De Metz: When do you want to go?

Jehanne: Better today than tomorrow. Better tomorrow than the next day.

De Metz: Jesus, you're impatient.

Jehanne: No one else can save him.

De Metz: The king?

Jehanne: Yes, *no one* else. Even if he marries his baby boy to the Scottish princess . . .

De Metz: Who told you he would?

Jehanne: Monsieur the General.

De Metz: The general doesn't tell me things.

Jehanne: You're just a country boy. You have to be something special to be told things by a general.

De Metz: You little tart.

Jehanne: You think I ought to wear boy's clothes?

De Metz: Doesn't the idea interest you?

She thought, it ought to. It ought to be significant. But I don't give a damn.

Jehanne: Either way it makes no difference.

De Metz: That might be truer than you think.

Jehanne: I suppose that's a joke.

De Metz: Well, you're not the prettiest little piece . . .

She shook her head.

Jehanne: No, I know I'm not the prettiest little piece!

His grin made him seem seventeen yet his eyes were blunt and antique, two old stones, a statue's weathered eyeballs. All the fires he had set, and the rapes and cuttings and impalings, had convinced him this was the only way things had ever been done in the world. It was the way the world rolled on.

Hence a dozen de Metzes with their attendant archers

101

would make a short hell of any town, just because *that* was their picture of the world.

In the end Baudricourt got a letter by king's messenger. It said that with the emergency in Orleans there was no chance of reinforcing Vaucouleurs. And yes, His Majesty would consider seeing the sibyl, the *pucelle*, the virgin. She could come to Chinon if she wanted and make application to the Master of Requests. Neither message surprised the general very much.

First Jehanne had to go to Nancy, to see the old duke. She didn't think she could tolerate the trip, the fifty dead miles she'd have to travel. In the old red dress she'd brought from Domremy. She remembered that de Metz had said she'd be safer as a boy. Now, apart from safety, she thought suddenly she would reveal and assert herself in menswear. She started to tremble.

Lassois's second doublet lay in a corner.

Jehanne: Hey, Durand, have you got any long hose?

She began to dress behind a screen in the corner and felt light, recreated by Durand's black doublet which was tight on her breasts and over the shoulders.

She called out to Mother le Royer.

Jehanne: Catherine, see if Alain's got a doublet. Durand, what about those long hose or haven't you got any spares?

Lassois: What about a cloak?

Jehanne: I'll slit mine up the back.

Mother le Royer came in with a woolcap of Alain's, and long liripipe she could use as a scarf. And a riding cloak, red wool. The girl groaned, choosing whether to wear it: she liked its cut and colour.

Jehanne: I was going to alter mine.

Mother le Royer: No, use this one. Look, it's got warmth, you'll be glad once you're on the road.

There was difficulty getting the light brown hair up under Alain's cap.

Jehanne: I ought to get it cut but there isn't time.

Lassois: Wear my hood if you like. I'll wear the cap.

Jehanne: I don't want to hurt you, Durand. But the cap's much nicer. This nice blue . . .

Looking down at her body rendered strange in Alain's

and Lassois's oddments, she felt reinforced. She liked the tightness at the crutch and in the legs, the altered limbs. It occurred to her that the dead womb didn't weigh on her now. Perhaps it's just the newness of the clothes. But now I'm someone else. I'm not Jacques's disappointing child.

De Metz was to escort them into Lorraine, but de Poulengy rode out along the Toul Road with them for a mile or two.

De Metz: How do you like the style?

He asked Bertrand so that Jehanne could hear. But Bertrand wouldn't joke about it. For a few hundred yards he rode at Jehanne's side.

Bertrand: I'm sure it was the only thing to do. But you must realize that once you've dressed liked that nothing will ever be the same.

Jehanne: But I didn't want it to be. I can't sit back and enjoy sameness.

De Metz took them as far as Toul. Whose bishop Nicolas Barrey had appealed to against her breach of promise. Then they were in Lorraine with the duke's pass. No one would have touched them.

Three days later, at cold dusk, they came back to le Royers. The girl was silent, unwinding the liripipe from round her neck, but Lassois was riotous, pacing the cellar, giving the le Royers the story as if the girl wasn't there. In ways, she wasn't. As de Poulengy had said, nothing was the same. The way the duke had treated her told her this; that she was on the line of godhood now, she was launched. No one again might ever think, there's a girl, let me father, mother, or love it.

Lassois: She was so bloody rude at times. But the old duke ended up giving her five francs and a black mare. (Lassois had never known before that arrogance paid.) That house of his—the fireplaces are bigger than Burey! And the furniture . . . Jesus! But she walked about as if she'd always lived that way.

Jehanne spoke in a daze.

Jehanne: It's the only way to behave.

If you were bemused at this or that item, they remembered you were from the country.

Lassois: All the old duke was worried about, all he thought

103

of, was his bowels and kidneys. He asked her did she know any incantations for those organs. She said she was sorry to say she wasn't any good at that sort of thing. He asked her what she was specially good at and she said saving the kingdom was her only speciality. He asked her was she worried to tell him that because he's an ally of the Goddam-English? She said she wasn't worried because he didn't believe in her anyhow. If he believed in her he'd send his son-in-law to help Orleans. He laughed, he laughed . . . if I'd said it . . . but he laughed with *her*. And gave her presents.

The girl snorted. *Five francs!* A present of contempt. She went and lay on a bed, still wearing Alain's good red thigh-cloak.

Lassois went on informing them, more secretively, of her ways with great men.

Lassois: Then she told him that his kidneys might improve if he went back to his wife. She said those six bastards worry you and they worry ordinary people. Jesus, I didn't want to be there then. But that old duke's a gentleman. He didn't tell her to go to hell like the general always does. He was just a bit thoughtful and coughed a lot. Then he gave her a horse, a bloody horse!

She could see the le Royers watching her. Thinking what is it? Has the world turned over? In the morning will the dukes and generals come along to get their orders from us?

Not that Mother le Royer was perfectly happy about the clothes. She still had a parental conscience for the eccentric creature on the bed.

Mother le Royer: Were the clothes comfortable?

Jehanne: Oh yes, comfortable. The hose were baggy.

Mother le Royer: Do you think you'll wear them a lot?

Jehanne: Yes, Kate. It's only sensible.

Mother le Royer: Goodness, we didn't know what was starting, did we? That day you came here first.

The girl slept dressed like that, in some sort of dedication to her new lineaments.

Later on people would say she dreamt Messire. But she lay stark awake when Messire showed up on her right, obliterating with his dazzle the sleeping hump that was Kate le Royer.

Messire: My little he–nun, my little she–soldier. You're ready now for arms and armour.

Jehanne: Armour, darling Messire.

Messire: Your brother–king has armour to offer you.

Jehanne: Amen.

My little he–nun . . . she could feel the rightness of the male clothes in which she immediately turned on the side warmed by Messire and slept deeply.

In the morning Catherine and she went to the collegiate church to Père Fournier's Mass. She was such a different being now, in garments of male musk and shape, she wanted to be reassured all over again: by the test of the bloodless blood sacrifice of Christ which made the wrong gods writhe, spit, convulse. Nothing happened, though people looked. They knew, however, that she was travelling to the king and there was reason for disguises.

Straight after breakfast, at a barber's at the Avignon Gate, she had her hair cut *à soldade,* a basin-crop, the hair shaved to above the level of the ears.

Mother le Royer: Oh, that's ugly.

Jehanne: Yes, but Jean de Metz and Bertrand tell me it's the only way to get a helmet on.

Mother le Royer: My God!

The story was that postulants in convents always wept when their hair was cropped. Hair was supposed to be a crucial sacrifice for a girl to make. In fact Jehanne felt no emotion at the barber's for the brown hair she lost. It had been foregone since she dressed up to go to Nancy.

The evening of that same day the general arrived outside the le Royers'. He had an escort of four men–at–arms and a priest and a young Benedictine attendant. The priest and the monk dismounted with de Baudricourt and followed him into the cellar. Getting up from the le Royers' table, Jehanne saw the priest, Père Fournier, saw the demon–hunting firmness of the face. She was frightened, she could sense the line of terrible authority rising from Père Fournier through bishops to the Pope. This was the price of speaking: that they'd never stop testing the question: *was she virgin, whore, demon, possessed by demons?*

Out, out, out de Baudricourt called to the le Royers and Lassois.

Lassois had learned something about talking up from his cousin-in-law.

Lassois: It's cold out there.

De Baudricourt: Sad. Get out!

Jehanne was in her dress. Her cropped hair beneath a capuchon.

De Baudricourt: You know Père Fournier? And this is Brother . . . Brother Etienne. All right?

Meanwhile Père Fournier had kissed a purple stole and put it carefully around his neck for protection.

Jehanne: What are you going to do?

Brother Etienne took from under his scapular a gilt pot of holy water.

Jehanne: No! This is nonsense.

De Baudricourt: Is it? Better you have a holy-water fit here, in front of a friend, than way over there. They're subtle, witch-hunting bastards over there in Viennois.

Fournier: Adjuro te, Satane . . .

The priest began, feeling for the holy-water pot.

Jehanne: But I confess to this priest! I confess to him two and three times a week . . .

The general assured her above the burr of Fournier's Latin exorcisms.

De Baudricourt: He doesn't know if you're lying or not. I'd kneel down if I were you. They're convinced . . . all these people . . . that witches will *not* kneel to them.

Jehanne: Damn!

But she knelt. Fournier noticed it but kept on with the exorcism formula.

De Baudricourt: You can say the *Paternoster* in Latin?

Jehanne: I don't think so.

De Baudricourt: Sad. They're convinced witches can't say the *Paternoster* in Latin. I don't think it's much of a proof.

Jehanne: Monsieur general, you make jokes all you want. I'll always remember this as an insult.

Jesus, she screamed, sister to brother. *Jesus,* she began weeping softly.

At once Fournier stopped enunciating.

De Baudricourt: I think you can take it she isn't a witch.

The girl faced Fournier. Her face was bunched, intimate, hurt.

Jehanne: I confessed to you. You *knew*.

Fournier: It's no ultimate test.

Jehanne: I went to your Masses.

Fournier: Yes. I hope you come to a good end.

He nodded to Etienne to take the water bucket back to the collegiate church. There was every chance, such a cold night was it for Lassois and the le Royers waiting outside, that it would freeze over before he got it there.

Jean de Metz had a squat, solid body-servant called Jean de Honnecourt. Since Durand's long hose were chafing her in the breach Jehanne rode across Vaucouleurs to ask de Metz for his servant's old clothes. De Metz lived in two upstairs rooms at the *Green Man,* and she went there after he could not be found at the provost's office. In the yard she saw Jean de Honnecourt emptying the slops bucket, as if his master had just got up after a lie-in. But the servant did not see her as she turned up the outside stairs and walked into the room the stable-hands had pointed to.

De Metz was lying across a girl. One eye focused with a luxurious slowness on Jehanne, then he got up in a hurry and rushed into his drawers. In a way Jehanne was surprised he was so easily shamed.

The girl on the bed turned on her side and went on sleeping. Jehanne's belly was a pocket of fury. She wanted to beat the profligate white arse that faced her. As once she had wanted to beat Madame Aubrit.

De Metz: It's my sister come over the Novillompont.

Jehanne: She's had a hard trip.

The unanswerabe fury ate her: she had to get out of the room. De Metz had a shirt on now.

Jehanne: I want your man's clothes. He's about my build.

De Metz: All right. Come through here.

He blew his nose: his discomfort was over and he was actually whispering for the whore's sake.

He took her through into de Honnecourt's thin little closet and forced the shutters open. The room was neatly kept, a little dusty, and in the corner was a chest de Metz opened. Standing back from it, he looked a very big man with his thick tall legs bare under the shirt. His grey eyes said *don't expect me to change my habits, I'm your travelling companion, that's all.*

De Metz: Take anything you like. A gift from me.

Jehanne: Shouldn't we ask your man?

De Metz: I bought everything he has.

Jehanne: You ennobled him too, did you? You called him *de* Honnecourt.

De Metz: You can get away with these things in a war. Just look what you're getting away with. No, don't take the mended ones, take the best pair.

When she got back to the black mare in the yard she put her forehead against its rump and began weeping privately. She kept telling herself: but you don't *want* to be that girl, you don't like him, there's no desire there. Why won't you be consoled, you silly bitch?

Because now she was dressed for the journey: that was why. There were no chances for her outside the journey. She couldn't be someone's sister from Novillompont. She couldn't even die by accident: the day for her blood had been arranged.

Later in the day Bertrand came to tell her they were to leave secretly in the early morning of Wednesday. The party would gather before six in the inner ward of the palace. There would be Bertrand and his man Julien, Jean de Metz and de Honnecourt. Then the king's messenger Colet de Vienne, who had brought the despatches earlier in the week, and de Vienne's archer Richard.

Jehanne: Six men! He kept me waiting all this time for six men!

But six men were safer because less noticeable, he said. They would dress like businessmen.

At the same time, a committee led by Monsieur Alain thought de Honnecourt's clothes weren't good enough for her and raised money to buy her a shirt, cloth doublet, long hose, short hose, a red thigh–cloak, ankle boots, a wool cap with flaps.

To my honoured principal etc   Dated 12 February 1429

Though I have now served the Bank of the Family Gondisi for ten years in its dealings with the Armagnac enclave and have often found their behaviour strange and erratic, I have never seen them in such a state of impotence as seems to have afflicted them this winter. The fact of the Orleans siege has dazed them to the extent that they can manage only pitiably small forces of men, pitiably small supply convoys for that city.

Meanwhile their minds seem to be moving in fatuous directions. When Queen Yolande visited me today she spoke mainly of a report from some small garrison town on the Meuse. The report puts forward the merits of a country girl who makes predictions and has offered to take the king to Rheims, not before liberating Orleans. A military sibyl, Yolande called her. The Queen went on to say that although such people always abound in times of emergency it could be useful to have a prophetess on the staff, so to speak, to encourage Charles perhaps. If only this girl were the right sort of person, said the Queen. I asked what the right sort of person was.

She replied, the girl has to be a virgin, it is necessary for a prophetess to be a virgin. Otherwise there was no sure way of telling where her prophecies came from, heaven or hell. She admitted that this girl was probably un-suitable. The courier who brought the despatch says there is a rumour that the girl is the area commander's mistress. As Queen Yolande confessed this her disap-pointment was genuine and so, sad to behold.

Charles stays close to his bed all day, except for hearing three consecutive Masses at mid-morning. If anyone mentions Orleans he closes the bed-curtains and sleeps for the rest of the day . . .

To my honoured etc, by the same despatch bag.

Dated 13 February 1429

Lent has begun with what seems at first sight an Armagnac disaster. Yesterday, the first Sunday of Lent, a French army was routed in the open field. The details, as far as I know them, follow.

On Saturday night the Bastard-Royal, Jean Dunois, heard in Blois, the mustering area of the French army on the Loire, that an English convoy under Sir John Fastolf was on the Paris road, coming to feed and strengthen the English in the mud outside Orleans.

Dunois rode out with the Count of Clermont and the Constable of Scotland to link up with a French and Scottish force from Orleans itself led by Lord Willie Stuart and the famed la Hire. Though this latter group was small and had to dash out of Orleans through the English lines, it was the first to sight the three hundred English wagons. La Hire sent back to Clermont for permission to attack them while they were still in single line along the road. Clermont refused permission, saying la Hire must wait for the army from Blois to come up.

This was a fatal decision. Fastolf, it seems, used the time to line his wagons across the valley and dig in pointed stakes facing towards la Hire. But somehow, about the time Clermont and the Bastard reached Rouvray town, just south of la Hire's Gascons and Lord Willie Stuart's Scots, a mad charge towards the English wagons began amongst the Armagnac cavalry, whose discipline is deplorable.

The results are said to have resembled Verneuil. If Lord Willie Stuart was, as many say, responsible for the onslaught, he paid for it. His horse ripped its belly open on a stake, he fell out of his saddle and squirmed on the ground until some Welsh or English peasant emerged from the stakes and wagons, unbuckled him and disembowelled him where he lay.

As this was happening, Clermont couldn't manage to make his soldiers advance from Rouvray, which is a wine town. They started breaking into cellars and tasting the vintage. Dunois the Bastard-Royal was disgusted and went on up the road with a few friends. He was able to liberate some French and Scottish knights by charging the English escorts from the flank. All over the field were parties of English longbowmen cutting throats and looting the dead. One of them paused to fire a shot at him. The arrow punctured his steel shoe and entered his foot.

With the arrow sticking in his foot he rode on to a hill where la Hire had eighty knights marshalled. The English were avoiding this group and la Hire was considering attacking the wagons, since so many of the English and Welsh had left them to plunder the corpses lying about. The Bastard however told la Hire that it was no good, that there was no one to support him, because all Clermont's men were drinking wine in Rouvray.

La Hire and the Bastard and even Clermont got safely into Orleans after dark last night. The English rout stopped at Rouvray where so many of Clermont's Auvergnois drunks lay about for the English to deal with.

By dusk yesterday the English outside Orleans knew about their success. The French courier who brought the bad news this evening (Monday) says they were shooting arrows wrapped round with bulletins into the outworks of Orleans. The bulletins told the French that Fastolf's column was bringing pickled fish for Lent. Therefore the English are choosing to call this confrontation at Rouvray the Battle of the Herrings.

The courier who carried the news from Orleans to Chinon rode all last night and most of today. His message seems to have done some good here at Chinon, where the Royal Court is now situated. Since it seems that Orleans is still intact, everyone is talking about the urgency of doing something about it. Yolande is speaking practically again, and even the King is said to be in better heart now that disaster has taken the more definite shape it did at Rouvray . . .

Bernardo Massimo

News of Rouvray got to Vaucouleurs ten days after the rout. Bertrand brought it to her from de Baudricourt who had got it by way of Monsieur de Saarbruck, Commandant of Commercy.

All the nap and freshness went out of the clothes Alain's committee had given her. She felt time, present time, smothering her. As if she were packed in it and it were wadding. She tried walking up and down, to break out of the prickly seconds. They quietened her with a pint and a half of red wine, which made her sleep for half an hour.

Catherine had her up in the small hours. She fed Durand, Henri and Jehanne on fresh bread and mulled wine. She was a little tipsy with the concept of journeys. Just as the concept of arrivals had excited her the first day Lassois and the girl had come. After the breakfast le Royer and Lassois fetched

111

the two horses, the grey and black mares, from the *Brazen Magpie*. The girl would take both with her, ride one and lead one, because she had no money to buy remounts. The le Royers rode the grey and Lassois and the girl were on the Duke of Lorraine's black horse. All but Jehanne got down at the collegiate church where Jean Fournier, exorcist, was robing to say Mass. Standing, Lassois could reach his arms round Jehanne's waist while she stayed on top of the mare. The le Royers were both weeping: they could smell finality. They thought the bluff that had worked at Vaucouleurs could kill her in another and more canny city.

Lassois's embrace crushed her belly.

Lassois: You've bit off a mouthful, you poor little cow.

Jehanne: Not by accident. Kiss the baby for me.

Lassois: It's been such pure bloody fun. It'll be hard to settle down again.

Mother le Royer: We'll wait at the Porte de France, Jehanne. And wave you by.

Only de Vienne and his archer were in the inner court when Jehanne rode in. They stood talking together by their horses and wouldn't look at her.

She called to them.

Jehanne: I'm the girl. I'm the virgin.

Archer: Good morning.

De Vienne turned to her. He was a small joyless man full of a funny professional pride.

De Vienne: We usually travel alone. Forty trips a year. We know how it's done.

Jehanne: We're all very lucky then. To have you with us.

From the archer's saddle hung both crossbow and long-bow; he had a quiver of arrows on his back and a bag of bolts at his pommel. The crossbow shone with lubrication. A real specialist. Yet he was friendlier, had less of de Vienne's gross professional pride.

Archer: I'm a virgin myself. It's best not to tell anyone. We're a scarce class of people. Why have you got two horses?

Jehanne: They're all I've got in the world. And my clothes.

De Metz, de Honnecourt, Julien led horses in from the outer yard and Bertrand, the Benedictine secretary and de Baudricourt came down the front steps of the palace. The

112

general had dressed for the event: he had a tunic of de Baudricourt lions over his clothes and an orle of twisted silk green and white, around his head. He carried a small sword by its sheath. His mood was the same as that of Lassois and the le Royers: he could have been a member of the family, and kept snorting and aggressively sighing in the manner of Jacques.

De Baudricourt: Christ knows what's going to happen to this girl. (He called out for them all to hear. He even turned to Jehanne.) Christ knows what's going to happen to you.

For a long time he thought about this. Colet de Vienne sneezed to bring him back.

De Baudricourt: But if she doesn't get there, I won't forgive any of you and I'll complain to the Chancellor of France and the King. So get her there. Do you swear you will?

He offered them all the quillon of the small sword. They touched it one after another and spat. *Bless them*, he told the Benedictine. While the monk was still speaking, the general came to Jehanne and put the sword on to her belt with two latches.

De Baudricourt: You poor little cow. Burgundians, Lorrainers, Swiss, Welsh, English, all over Champagne and Tonnerre. Will your Messire look after you?

Jehanne: Of course.

He took her by the elbow.

De Baudricourt: Why don't you stay and we'll have that little pope.

Jehanne: I wasn't born for that sort of trouble.

Monsieur the commandant hugged her briefly round the waist—he could not reach her shoulders, since she was on the horse. As she touched the back of the general's hat she saw the archer grin and shake his head.

Bertrand gave his instructions. De Vienne and the archer would go first, then de Metz and his man, then Julien, Jehanne and Bertrand himself.

While they were riding out of the yard the general was able to walk beside her for a few seconds.

De Baudricourt: Haven't you got a saddle?

Jehanne: I'm used to riding just with the cloth. Don't let my grey mare tread on you.

It happened to be the last and politest thing she ever said to him.

There was mist all that day across the middle of the country and only beyond the walls, after not looking at Durand and the le Royers, that Jehanne saw the density of it.

And then she thought with some regret that when she got into trouble, de Baudricourt would blame himself. Oh, Brother Jesus, why did she always forget to reassure people?

BOOK TWO

King meets Sibyl

It would one day become fashionable to call the journey prodigious. De Vienne himself gave it for most of its course an air of major dangers reduced to minor ones because of his expertise.

In dripping Sept-Fonds forest, for example, they stopped to bind their horses' hoofs with rags. Jehanne went up to young de Honnecourt. She had a bundle in her hands.

Jehanne: These are your clothes back. I hope you didn't mind . . .

De Honnecourt: I've nothing of my own. I go out to empty their shit and when I come back all my clothes are gone.

Jehanne: Don't sulk, I haven't got anything either.

Vienne told Bertrand the way they'd go: off the main road immediately. Lanes and goat-tracks as far as Montiers. Back to the highway for a mile or two, but ten miles from Joinville they had to take to forest tracks again. That was the worst part. At St Urbain Abbey they would be under sanctuary. If they arrived late at night and left early no one could have a chance to report them to the commandant in Joinville. And so on.

The country was hilly the first day and the mist stayed down. It was very cold. Bertrand kept groaning and his nose ran. Unexpectedly at noon, light savaged her right eye. Mesdames Margaret and Catherine came:

Margaret: Don't fret.

Catherine: For Jesus's little cherry there's no ambush . . .

Margaret: No rape . . .

Catherine: No sharp edges.

Margaret: Love the king . . .

Catherine: Jesus's weak brother.

Then wet Bertrand replaced them.

Bertrand: What?

Jehanne: What?

Bertrand: You said *hold me up*. You were slipping sideways.

Yes, she could remember the heat forcing her off her horse.

Jehanne: I don't know why I said that.

Sour Colet led them to river fords and along chalk tracks over the hills, amongst the bare presence of dim vineyards. At mid-afternoon they were single-file on a bridle-path when Colet and the archer stopped. The archer turned and pointed urgently to a thin ditch beside the path. Bare shrubs filled it. They led their horses down there. Colet came on foot down the ditch to see Bertrand and Jean de Metz.

De Vienne: We heard them.

De Metz: What?

De Vienne: Didn't you hear them?

Bertrand: No.

De Vienne: They were talking English.

Jehanne: Jesus. Where?

De Vienne: Up there. On the track.

Bertrand: Listen.

All the girl's limbs tingled. The outrage of foreign sounds threatened to jump on her out of miasma. The core outrage, the deepest enemy. The Goddam voice.

De Metz: I can't hear anything.

De Vienne: Shhh!

He had prestige to say it, he had been closer than anyone to English tongues. He slipped between their sentences with the king's letters.

It began to rain. De Metz dismounted and grabbed his man's elbow, pointing to the top of the ditch. The girl could see it dimly: de Honnecourt white in the face, de Metz punching him in the back to make him more obedient. Together they vaulted out of the ditch and drew out their swords. De Honnecourt tried to look everywhere simultaneously.

De Metz called out a challenge at the top of his voice. It frightened Bertrand, for he stood with his mouth at full stretch and his breath cowering down in his throat.

De Metz: Kneel down you Goddam bastards. You're my

prisoners. (He repeated the word emphatically since they were aliens.) *Pris-on-ers!*

De Vienne and the archer, still shoulder–deep in the ditch, began hooting, and the rain came down harder on de Metz and his man.

De Metz: There wasn't anything?

The couriers doubled over their pommels. It was the first time all day de Vienne had laughed.

De Metz gestured into the ditch with his sword but its tip couldn't quite reach de Vienne. De Vienne laughed so thoroughly that he threatened to fall off his horse.

Archer: You were going to take all their gear? And sell them back their lives?

De Vienne: You're such a brave bastard. Such a business-man.

Jehanne: I don't think it's funny.

Her nose had begun running: that much was permitted to happen to Jesus's cherry.

Bertrand told de Vienne there wasn't to be any more of it. But for an hour afterwards he would now and then laugh privately.

When they rested at dusk, de Vienne said they were only half-way to the abbey.

An hour after dark they were deep and blind in a dripping forest. The girl's thighs were aglow with saddle pain, and Bertrand, rash and exhausted, yelled from the back of the line.

Bertrand: Is this another joke?

De Vienne: No, this is la Saulxnoire. A dreadful bloody place. Witches everywhere.

Beyond the forest they would often look up to find themselves in a blind little village, where all the lights were doused. In such a place de Honnecourt dropped back two paces to ride beside the girl.

De Honnecourt: Can I sleep with you when we get to St Urbain?

Jehanne: Damn it all! (She was so tired.) You weren't thinking of that this afternoon. When Jean made you climb out of the ditch.

De Honnecourt: He's mad, he'd do anything for money. Will you sleep with me?

Jehanne: If I wanted to sleep with any old redneck I would have stayed at home.

De Honnecourt: That's a bitch of a thing to say.

Jehanne: Would you sleep with a nun?

De Honnecourt considered and made a face that meant it might depend on the state of his temperament, but altogether he'd rather not.

De Honnecourt: It's sacrilege.

Jehanne: All right. Messire calls me his duckling. God help any man who has me.

Messire didn't frighten de Honnecourt enough.

De Honnecourt: You only want to sleep with knights.

Jehanne: That's right. Of course.

De Honnecourt: Bloody Sir Bertrand.

Jehanne: If you like.

De Honnecourt: Hopeless idiot he is! Dresses up like women.

Jehanne: What?

De Honnecourt: Every chance he gets. Every time there's a party. Dresses up like a bloody woman. Gets all the other officers to court him.

Bertrand had said, *Once you dress like that nothing will ever be the same.*

Jehanne: What's wrong with that?

De Honnecourt: It isn't very natural. Is it?

In the middle of the night she heard a river on her right. De Vienne sent the word back. It was the Marne in full flow. They were amongst the houses of the abbey suburbs then. The mist had thinned from the frantic rain and she rode with the others under an arched gate into the abbey's outer yard. She saw carts, stables, straw and cow dung: it was a homely place.

De Vienne knew the place in the wall to knock at, for the king's messengers always used the abbey. It had been the place of sanctuary from the Counts of Joinville for three hundred years. One of the whimsicalities of law gave Jehanne a bed tonight, just a few miles south of a Burgundian fortress.

A middle-aged brother let them in the gate. Holding up his pitch-pine torch, he knew de Vienne.

Brother: You've got a lot of friends tonight, Colet.

120

De Vienne: They're de Baudricourt's friends.

Brother: Well, we'd better find them room in the men's house.

Jehanne: Can I stay in the women's house?

The monk squinted at her and looked shocked.

De Metz: Jacques always wants to get in with the women.

So they were all taken through into the men's dormitory where two big beds stood in a clean cold room. The brother porter lit the fire and put his torch in a wall-bracket.

Brother: You can show your friends the latrines, Colet. *Benedicamus Domino.*

All: Deo gratias.

Brother: You're very welcome.

The second he went de Metz bent and kissed Jehanne on the side of the neck.

De Metz: This is going to be a nice night, duckling.

Bertrand: Jean, myself and Jehanne in this bed, the four of you in the other.

Archer: That isn't very brotherly of you, Monsieur.

Bertrand: Jean and I will sleep with all our points done up.

There were rude noises of disbelief from de Vienne's end of the room.

De Metz began to unlatch his hose, shivering. His boots were still on as if he intended to wear them in bed.

Bertrand: I mean it, Jean. We'll all keep fully dressed.

De Metz: Oh God Bertrand, it's cold.

Bertrand: She's never bled.

De Metz: What?

Bertrand: Madame le Royer says she's like a child. She belongs to gods. Do you want someone who's got diseases and belongs to Messire?

De Metz groaned. He didn't want to interfere with anything as strange as that. As portentous. He believed Bertrand. Bertrand was reliable in that area.

The girl had got into bed wearing even her cloak.

De Metz: Don't you want to go out the back?

Jehanne: I wouldn't dare.

Fatigue seemed to have brought out freckles on her face. He grimaced with a sort of pity.

De Metz: I'll take you.

Jehanne: No thanks.

De Metz: It's all right. I know what sort of virgin you are.

Jehanne: You know I might as well be dead as raped.

De Metz: I know.

Jehanne: Nothing will stop me. Something will happen to you if you try to spoil me.

The electricity of the gods ran down his neck.

De Metz: Trust me.

Jehanne: I'm really very uncomfortable.

She got up.

The latrines were in a narrow earth-floored corridor. He stood back, holding the torch. He wasn't at all curious, when there is a world of women it was lunacy to touch a freak, a girl with omens.

When the girl was finished she laced up her hose to her doublet tightly and let herself be taken back to bed where she fell asleep straight away. It wasn't so easy for Jean de Metz. He went and roused de Honnecourt.

De Honnecourt: What's the matter? You've got the girl.

De Metz: She's some sort of magic virgin. Didn't you know? Come on. It won't take you long.

De Honnecourt: Oh hell.

De Metz: Come on.

Colet and the archer knew their business. They knew where to cross the Aube after rain, every wrecked homestead, and the whole mad filigree of secondary tracks. Colet was all sour dedication. He watched the girl lie down fully dressed in some barn, between Bertrand and de Metz. For some reason the sight made him seem to hate the three of them. Bertrand was a little frightened he might have Burgundian contacts and arrange through the pub in some village or other to sell the three of them.

The Seine above Bar was beginning to flood but Colet knew a place where the horses could be swum over. By travelling at night they got to the hills above Auxerre on Sunday morning. It had been raining all night, and their skin was puckered and half-rotten with water. Colet said there was nowhere they could cross the Yonne in flood tide except the bridge on the near side of the city.

Jehanne: Let's all go down there then. We could see the cathedral. And have a meal.

122

Archer: They serve Chablis.

In the crypt of St Etienne's Cathedral that noon the girl saw a wallpainting of Christ in doublet, cloak, boots, riding out with four friends. On the road to be God, King, and Sacrifice. She shivered but felt glorified—validated.

At the end of a long meal at a good hotel, de Metz and Honnecourt and Julien all said there was no reason why everyone shouldn't spend the night there.

De Metz: You could even take your hose off for the first time. In a nice house like this.

But Colet said some of the Burgundian knights in the Auxerre garrison had a business going: they went around the pubs in the evening, found out who was staying there and—if the trouble was worth it—met them on the Gien Road next morning and made them pay extortion.

So they dragged off through the suburbs. The hills ahead looked mute in the rain. You couldn't believe there were fires or warm cordials in all that countryside. According to Colet the King's Loire was over there.

The girl was singing.

Jehanne: King Noah he had a golden Ark.
            There's one more river to cross.

Now there was no trouble using the towns. But Colet said the free-booters here were as bad as in Burgundy. They would take you and keep you in a pit until someone paid for you. Still he kept on the minor tracks, and Bertrand and Jean wondered was he paying them back for something by making the journey long and uncomfortable like this.

On a muddy Thursday they rode into the mean little town of Fierbois. The pub was called the *Blind Godefroi*.

De Vienne: It's time to write your letter.

Chinon was fifteen miles west and she was meant to pause here, to write a letter to the king.

De Metz sent Honnecourt to fetch a secretary to the *Blind Godefroi*. But when the man arrived it seemed preposterous, just to come into a miserable little place like that and begin a letter to a king.

Even if he was drunk, the arriving notary could see her doubt.

Notary: Monsieur, Fierbois is the threshold of the court.

I myself have composed dozens of petitions for visitors to our sovereign. You begin *Most Benign Majesty, a humble servant begs* . . .

He seemed to know what he was talking about. She wanted him to cast a letter that said these thing: She was a virgin from Lorraine (close enough) who was meant to send the English from Orleans and lead him to his anointing. She had been ordered to do these things by Messire who was king amongst gods . . . no, make that King Jesus's right hand . . .

Notary: As you say, monsieur. A more seemly phrase. More calculated to reassure.

Jehanne: And beg him can I see him.

Notary: All right.

Bertrand: Can you embellish the thing?

Notary: Yes, Monsieur.

Bertrand: Do it as well as you can. We'll pay for good work.

While they were all waiting at the *Blind Godefroi* for the letter to be embellished, Colet came and sat by the girl.

De Vienne: You are a virgin, Mademoiselle.

Jehanne: Yes, you were told . . .

De Vienne: A man of my experience doesn't necessarily believe just anyone. But you put it in you letter . . .

Jehanne: Yes.

De Vienne: You know, they'll check.

Jehanne: Of course.

He sighed and gave her the name of a respectable pub in Chinon.

Three hours later the notary came back. The hands that offered the letter were trembling. De Metz poured the man a glass while Bertrand inspected what had been written. He grimaced at a few of the extravagances.

Bertrand: It's all right. It's fairly strong. But there's nothing anyone could complain about.

Jehanne was the only one who saw Colet and the archer away. The others still resented their professional arrogance and that joke of theirs in the mist.

Jehanne: You'll see the king before I do.

De Vienne: I never see him, Mademoiselle. I just deliver the letters. Some go to the Chancellor's office, others to the Grand Master of the Household, others to the Master of Requests. I saw him once in Poitiers. He was walking by the river. He's an awkward young man. But he likes walking.

Jehanne: Thank you for bringing us.

But he wouldn't be complimented.

De Vienne: I'll let them know at the Requests offices where you're staying.

She went walking in the freezing mud of Fierbois. A girl of fifteen was milking a steaming cow in a yard. *There's a shrine?* Jehanne asked her. Gravid with the Loire winter, mute in a sad nation, the girl pointed to a broad track up into the alder forest behind her. She was not a happy girl. Jehanne however felt suddenly all the lightness of the tourist who is not bound to the meanness of a particular landscape.

The forest was a miserable place in its final and totally silent death before a spring now one month away. Two hundred yards in stood a little church, no bigger than the wrecked church of Domremy-à-Greux. When she was near to it two frightful people jumped out of a birch-bark hovel at the side of the track. They seemed ravenous for her. They had a sort of scabies all over their faces and their throats were bloated with goitres. In intimate birch-bark squalor they had given each other terrible things. The man saw it was one visitor and ducked back into his house.

Woman: Do you want to see Madame Ste Catherine's chapel and hear some of the amazing stories . . . ?

Jehanne: Yes.

Woman: It'll cost you a sol.

Jehanne: With all my heart.

For the woman was so commandingly ill. She wasn't as old as Zabillet, probably not thirty-five or thirty.

Inside, the place looked a little like an ironmonger's. Chains hung from the beams, old armour, swords, lances, pennons.

The terrible scarlet and lumpen face, its eyes shining, spoke to her.

Woman: All the gifts of grateful and gallant knights, Monsieur.

125

Jehanne: Oh?

Woman: Escapers, tournament-winners, sires held for ransom. Maybe you've had trouble yourself in that way?

Jehanne: No, not yet.

Woman: Once, only about fifty years back, this place wasn't anything but ruins. But a local sire called Godefroi used to come here. He'd got an arrowhead in his spine at Crecy. He had paralysis and he was blind and a bit ashamed, because you can't get an arrowhead in your spine from the front.

Jehanne: Maybe he got it while he was retreating the legal fifty yards.

There *was* a knightly maximum retreat. Ordinary people were permitted to run like hell. Successful soldiers like la Hire were wise enough to adopt the same vulgar practice.

Woman: You're too kind, Monsieur.

Jehanne: Where is blind Godefroi now?

Woman: Dead.

Jehanne: Rest in peace.

Woman: Blind Godefroi knew that Charles Martel himself had buried his sword behind the altar here, so he used to have himself carried here by his servants. The place was a ruin. They had to cut their way through the briars to get blind Godefroi close to it. They put him down here. He told them to leave him for two hours, to wait in the town. And while he was alone Madame Ste Catherine told him he was to build the place up again. It isn't the first time a god has spoken straight to a person.

Jehanne: No, it isn't the first time. You tell the story very well.

Nonetheless she found an eeriness in eloquence from a face like that. You could see, the more you were with her, that she was younger and younger. Twenty-five?

And she could read Jehanne. She spoke softly.

Woman: I wasn't *born* with ulcers. I wasn't *born* with tumours . . .

Jehanne nodded. She began to finger the locks and chains, the entire suits of armour, hanging stained in the damp air. They felt remote from radiant Madame Catherine.

The terrible woman followed Jehanne about amongst the iron thickets and undergrowth.

126

Woman: Godefroi had the place rebuilt. He could immediately see again. He could immediately walk.

Jehanne: Immediately?

Woman: I saw him when I was a child. Riding into Fierbois, talking to people, cuffing apprentices' ears. He got his pride back by doing what Madame Ste Catherine told him. Look. (She pointed to a reliquary with a lump of rusting metal in it.) That's the arrowhead. A surgeon cut it out of his spine after he died. These manacles here belonged to Cazin du Boys who was taken prisoner by the Burgundians ten years ago and kept in a cage in Sens . . . He woke up one night to find the cage unlocked and all the guards asleep. Now these are more remarkable still. They were on the hands and feet of Monsieur Perrot of Luzarches. The English caught him at Verneuil. While he was asleep one night in prison he had a dream about Madame, he talked to her. When he woke up he was back in his house in Luzarches. He yelled and his sons came and cut the chains. You can still see the hacksaw marks, here. These belonged to Jean Ducordray who escaped from Belleme castle this year. He strangled two Burgundians, dropped twenty feet without hurting himself, and stole a horse.

Jehanne: Madame Ste Catherine is pretty broad-minded about strangling people.

Woman: Nine months back, everyone was here, the Great Bastard, General la Hire. One of the Duchâtel boys had brought along the armour of an English knight he had fought and killed in single combat after asking Madame for help.

Jehanne watched the vacant armour move itself slightly in the draught from the porch. Was Madame honoured by all this crass hardware?

Jehanne: Thank you for showing me all this.

Woman: Monsieur. You can have me in the porch. The porch isn't sacrilege, as it would be in here, in the body of the church.

Jehanne stared at her.

Woman: You wouldn't catch these things from me . . .

Jehanne thought, this being doesn't consider herself beyond the sisterhood. This thing is more woman than I am, this thing has bled. In her own belly she felt such loss. Oh Brother Jesus, what have you made of me?

Woman: I'm twenty-three years old. Not so old.

Jehanne's left hand touched the trim sword de Baudricourt had lashed to her waist. She felt grateful for it now, for having a strong recourse.

Jehanne: Get out!

The woman put her body against Jehanne's right shoulder, the belly against Jehanne's right hip. As she said, it was palpably a young body. It seemed to radiate some sort of useless fertility. Jehanne felt murderous. Her thin sword was unsheathed in her right hand before she'd thought and the woman had begun dodging for the porch amongst the hanging irons. Jehanne landed a blow with the flat of the thing on the woman's hip

The woman yelled from the porch.

Woman: When Madame takes these curses from me, I'll still be young. You'll beg me and I'll spit at you.

Jehanne: Go to hell!

Woman: Sow's arse! If you're a prisoner ever, I'll beg Madame to keep you in place. I'll *beg* her.

Jehanne came stamping to the porch but the woman had gone. Outside, she could see both her and her ulcerating mate vanishing into the bare but thickly-sown alders. It seemed they expected the offended young Monsieur to split their hovel with a few sword-blows. Jehanne ran to it as if she would. A sodden blanket lay half out the door and water from the wattle roof dripped on it.

She felt shame. She very nearly vomited for grief. Secretively, as if watched, she put the sword back. Amongst the black stalks of timber she began running for Fierbois. At one time she heard a low slow voice from the forest.

Voice: Hey, pretty-boy!

The board of the *Blind Godefroi* showed a knight with his head blindfolded. Beneath it Jean de Metz waiting in the mud.

De Metz: Where've you been? Thank Christ you're back. Bertrand's buying wine for a heavyweight from Chinon and it's costing him a packet.

He dragged her by the wrist into the main hall. The radiance of a fire gave her flesh some enthusiasm back. She began rubbing her hands, then shook the water out of her cloak. All the time she watched Bertrand. He sat at table with a priest dressed in the red cassock of a doctor of theology. Jehanne could always spy by instinct the warm and shaky self-regard of a former peasant or farm-boy. It was something apart from the cold invincible conceit of hereditary rank. She thought the doctor of theology was a peasant. But, across the table from him, Bertrand looked red and honoured.

Bertrand: This is Maître David Gaucherie, a Canon of Loches . . .

Gaucherie: Astrologer-visitant to the court of Charles VII and Fellow of the Faculty at Poitiers. This is the girl?

De Metz: She had to dress like that for the road.

Jean had become even a little protective since he'd heard of her affliction.

Gaucherie: How do I know she isn't a boy?

Jehanne: If I'm a boy, Maître, I'll be found out, won't I? You'll hear my screams in Loches.

Bertrand could tell the dislike between them and tended to babble.

Bertrand: Maître Gaucherie has just visited the king.

Jehanne: You saw him?

Bertrand: Oh yes, Maître Gaucherie is brought in to do astrologies for the king.

Jehanne: Soon the king won't need astrologies. He'll move the stars himself.

Gaucherie: I hope not altogether. It's useful to be called in. It helps pay the wine bills.

Bertrand: We'll pay, Maître.

Gaucherie: I didn't mean today's wine bill in particular.

Bertrand: Tell her about the astrology you cast.

Gaucherie: It's rather confidential.

Bertrand: But you said the king told people at dinner.

Gaucherie: Some people.

Jehanne: You enjoy your secrets, don't you Maître?

When Gaucherie looked at her he seemed very intent, very official all at once, as if he had been waiting for her to arrive and was carrying a message for her.

Gaucherie: One secret I can let you have, girl. When he was a child the king got this idea from somebody that there always had to be a special sacrifice to keep a king robust. That some special person had to die to nourish the king, to . . . to irrigate his aura, you could say. I don't know who it was told him that. But he always believed it. Like Jean Baptiste dying to nourish the aura of Herod. Of course, Charles always intended to be a better king than Herod. But that gives you an idea. A person never knows, going into his presence, whether he—or she—is that sacrifice . . .

The girl frowned for him, looking the way country people ought to when faced with scarlet cassocks, closed capes, doctorates in divinity, inside knowledge.

Gaucherie went on to tell the story of how de Giac had once tried to become the sacrifice for Charles. When he looked at Bertrand, Jehanne would think he was just gossiping, when he looked at her she again got the idea that it was all a planned message from him, a planned inspection of her.

Bertrand: I thought you ought to hear all this, Jehanne. (His funny tenderness was on him: he was even a little fearful that hearing these things might be too much for her fabric.) It sheds some little light on the king.

The girl was thinking, he's been waiting all this time for my blood. The king's instincts on the Loire knitting in with hers on the Meuse. A high terror brought out sweat on her. Bertrand saw her skin turn bilious. She could feel the smothering limits of her godhood, like de Giac who'd once tried to be sacrificed for the king, feeling his sack with hand, forehead, excruciating stump, before they drowned him in the Auron.

Gaucherie: Some theologians would consider the king's attitude unorthodox. Christ's blood sacrifice is supposed to be the ultimate and adequate one. On the other hand, it's possible to argue that other offerings have their power through association with Christ's . . .

Jehanne: What is the astrology you cast the king?

Gaucherie: I can't tell you that. You could be anyone.

De Metz: He stills thinks you're a cow-boy, Jehanne. Show him your tits.

Jehanne: I'm bound to the king. The king and I are the one breath . . .

Jean de Metz said to tell her and shrugged his hips as if to balance himself for the taking out of weapons.

Bertrand: Jean, you can't talk that way to a royal dignitary.

De Metz nonetheless had Gaucherie by the eyes—or the other way round.

Gaucherie: The details are quite secret. But one thing I can tell you. Anyone can see it, just by looking. Virgo is in the ascendant, Venus, Mercury and the sun are half-way up the sky. Every village astrologer knows it. It's the interpretation that counts. And the interpretation you *cannot* have. The king is my client in that matter.

Bertrand: I'm very sorry. My friend doesn't realize . . .

De Metz: Listen, your friend's all bloody right.

Gaucherie: Excuse me, I'd hoped to visit the shrine of Ste Catherine before it's too dark.

Jehanne got in front of him.

Jehanne: Thank you Maître. I've learned so much.

Gaucherie: Virgo . . .

He was looking at her closely to find likenesses between her and the trim constellations he'd seen deploying above Chinon. Then he went out to meet the tumour-lady and see Ste Catherine's hardware.

Although the question of blood sacrifice raised by Gaucherie had resonated in Bertrand, he tried to soothe Jehanne.

Bertrand: Don't take that sacrifice seriously. But the stars! Very meaningful, very meaningful.

Jehanne thought the king had sent that Maître Gaucherie to look at her and if Gaucherie's report was good she'd get straight to the throne-room.

Jehanne: Bertrand, Jean, can we go straight on in the morning?

Bertrand: Yes. Fifteen miles. We might be there by noon.

Jehanne: I'm going for a walk.

What she wanted on her walk was to see a Mass or at least a crucifix. The Mass and crucifix were cool. They told you the blood, the impaling, the smotheration did not go on and on and on. The blood of a sacrificial god didn't hurt forever.

In the empty village church Christ was resting on his gibbet as never he did in the hot agonies of Golgotha.

On a dripping Sunday afternoon they took rooms at a pub Colet had recommended just inside the Lorraine Gate of Chinon. It was the Sunday they called *Laetare* and at home, in Domremy-à-Greux, the priest would have read the Gospel of the Beloved Disciple to the incorrigible king-oak of Boischenu. Afterwards all the unmarried sat down and ate rolls under the tree, and hard-boiled eggs.

From the Lorraine Gate of Chinon you could see the river, brash ice floating in it, and the thin jumbled town. Above it all, on a ridge following the river's line, the knotted skein of great towers. In one of those, the king, his under-nourished presence!

Jehanne felt very tired. The complicated walls and forest of turrets on the mountain ran across her vision like some code she could not deal with. She thought, perhaps he's *not* reading the general's letters about me. Perhaps he won't. Perhaps he'll say go home. You can't disobey a king.

The landlady forced supper on her, a herring stew. It steamed in her face. She ate it quickly, with lumps of bread.

Later, while Bertrand and de Metz were out, Colet the messenger called in and told her about the tangle of royal masonry above the town. It was three castles in fact. In the northern one, called Coudray, a lot of officials lived. In the centre, St Louis, where the towers were highest, lived the king. In the southernmost, St George, was the military governor and the garrison.

Jehanne: I suppose it could be days and days . . .

She meant *before the king sees me*.

De Vienne: Maybe. But people know about you up there. The whole family's very hot on prophets. Charles's crazy old man always gave them a hearing. He used to give audiences to a sibyl called la Gasque. She told him which of the Popes was the true one. She turned out to be wrong . . . But he'll see you.

It was five days before anything happened. Even then the happening was oblique: two horsemen wearing royal blue tabards with gold lilies came for de Poulengy and de Metz. Jehanne argued but wasn't taken: she wasn't in their instructions.

Only a few hours before, Bertrand and Jean had bathed and bought new doublets and were now grateful for it. Jehanne had also bathed—not at the public baths but in a back room of the house. But it counted for nothing.

She lent Bertrand her good cloak because his was a mess from the journey. She gave Jean de Metz instructions.

Jehanne: Tell him I'm the one he has to see. It's urgent.

De Metz made a face. He'd never met a king before and intended to feel his way.

In the church of St Maurice, where she wandered that afternoon, there was a weird fresco. Christ faced a crowd of well-dressed people. Their faces glowed with a gentle enough interest. But he was looking over his shoulder, frowning, as if he didn't want to get any closer. The crowd had begun to make a path for him in their midst. Whoever painted it . . . some Italian probably . . . knew how it was with gods.

They weren't back till dark. They couldn't sit. Memories kept stinging them, memories of poor phrasing, of ineptitudes, timidity before interrogators.

The afternoon's history came out in jagged pieces. How small the little room where the king worked. Monsieur de Gaucourt bullied them. De Gaucourt? The Master of Household. There were three bishops with the king, four other theologians, suspecting them of espionage or witchcraft. The Queen of Sicily, Yolande, large, square, dark, silent.

Hearing it, the girl hissed and hit the wall.

Jehanne: I should be seeing her for myself.

Bertrand: And there was Maître Machet, the king's confessor.

Jehanne: I should be seeing him.

Bertrand: We did our best.

She asked had the king asked anything.

De Metz: Just twice.

He'd asked his confessor, Maître Machet, if *that part of the country* (round the Meuse) wasn't famous for witches. He'd asked if she was still a virgin.

Bertrand actually winked at Jehanne. He was highly stimulated by his afternoon with royalty.

When Jehanne asked them what he looked like they argued. Bertrand idealized him and de Metz reacted with worse and worse and even obscene depictions of his bad features—the heavy eyes, the long nose.

They agreed he didn't dress well.

133

Jehanne: Did you tell him the only one to talk to was me?

Of course they hadn't, they felt they'd been lucky enough to be able to breathe in that exalted environment. Now they went downstairs and started drinking. A little celebration. They were thinking, this is the one time we're ever going to get close to the king in our lives. Have we made enough of it?

They weren't sure.

That night three priests came to question Jehanne. One was Maître Machet, the king's confessor, and another Pierre l'Hermite to whom the king also confessed. They introduced themselves and were not hostile. She told them the same things she had told the general and Fournier in Vaucouleurs. It already depressed her a little, all the reiterating she must go on doing. In the intimacy of a hotel parlour they didn't seem very special men, however prodigious they might have looked against a court background. Had she belonged to a coven? Did she often confess? (The king confesses daily, said Machet. *You have a powerful ear, Maître,* she very nearly told him.) Why did she want to stay a virgin? Did she want to be a nun?

She said there were some things she couldn't tell them, she could only tell the king.

They got ready to go: their notaries were shuffling together the record of their dialogue.

Jehanne: When?

Machet: This is a question for the Council. There's a Council meeting in the morning. Perhaps after that, perhaps never. I can't say.

Jehanne: You can tell him things in the confessional . . .

Machet: I don't use the confessional in that way . . .

Jehanne had already heard rumours however that he did.

Jehanne: It'll all happen in the end, anyhow, Monsieur. We might as well get things going.

Machet: God in heaven!

But he did not hide that he was some way pleased by her quality. The rumour she had heard was that he was devoted to Maman Yolande.

Saturday.

The two messengers from the castle came in the early afternoon. It was to be seven o'clock at night, in the Grand

Logis. She was dressed at four in the clothes given by Alain's committee and wouldn't eat supper. De Metz and de Poulengy sat with her giving her confidence. They knew that, after all, entering a fixed path amidst well-dressed people was what frightened her.

All the bells of Chinon rang Vespers—from the castle, from the city churches. Immediately Bertrand was found to be weeping.

Jehanne: Bertrand?

Bertrand: You won't be coming back. You're out of our area now.

She found that Jacques had been right: she had no graciousness for saying soft things at such times.

Jehanne: You'll be riding up the mountain with me, won't you?

Bertrand nodded and brushed his tears one at a time off his lashes.

De Metz: You won't be coming back though. Whatever happens. And anything could happen. That worries Bertrand too.

Jehanne: Only one thing can happen.

She ached to say softer things. She saw de Metz's strange discoloured eyes on her. Soon they might return to their old enthusiasms. Their old certainties: fire, rape, the trading of persons, the loot business. For the moment they said *in mercy talk to Bertrand!* She could say nothing to either man, she went and sat in a corner. While she was there she heard de Metz talking to Bertrand.

De Metz: Tonight, when we get back, we'll get in Honnecourt and Julien and have a proper booze-up. And you can get dressed up and fool around . . .

Outside the pub a crowd grew. It pressed the door and trampled the garbage. From the upstairs windows you could see its breath going up like incense. They began to chant *Noël.*

Jehanne: Why are they doing that?

Bertrand looked radiant.

Bertrand: For you, Jehanne.

He opened a window and began to shout down at them. *Noël, Noël.* There was that about Bertrand: he liked to savour *occasions.*

135

He and de Metz had to force her through the crowd, swords drawn, when it was time to leave.

Jehanne kept asking the people why they were there, who had given them the enthusiasm. She got no answers.

Bertrand and de Metz had to leave her at the Barbican Gate. There were six young knights there in buffed white armour and rich tunics. On the tunics were heraldic falcons, beeches, barrels, stag horns, all the mysterious symbols of high birth. Bertrand seemed discomfited, shame-faced, not having any fine symbols for his own blood.

Thanks, Jehanne said a few times, *thanks.* Her attention was on the six pretty knights and the breakneck track up through the main gate into the outer yard. It would take ten minutes on foot.

She asked one of the knights.

Jehanne: Can't we ride, Monsieur?

He rattled his cuirass.

Knight: It's too hard on horses and we don't want to have a fall in this stuff. Monsieur de Gaucourt sends his respects and says he's waiting for you in the main yard.

Jehanne: The main yard?

Knight: Up there.

The terrible mountain overbore her, the king on its top. She'd be panting when she saw him.

She walked in the middle, three of de Gaucourt's handsome boys on either side. On their foreheads silk twisted white and blue, indisputable knights' banneret. She could smell their indifference under the cold moon.

They carried their helmets at their waists, ornate salades that terminated in steel eagles' and griffins' heads. She was amongst the aristocracy. Brother Jesus, teach me to be rude.

At the inner gate the guards asked them to wait and someone went to find de Gaucourt. He had obviously been talking or drinking or both at once in one of the military apartments in the main wall.

When he came he was smaller than his knights. He wasn't cold anyhow. He was unambiguously hostile.

De Gaucourt: They're all waiting.

Some way inside the inner yard, past a white chapel, she could suddenly hear a crowd of talkers. She could hear people laughing, men and women. She kept looking straight ahead towards the old keep, its windows all shuttered, but knew it could not be the source of the noise.

De Gaucourt: Over there.

There was a vast hall, two floors high. Some of its upstairs windows were glassed and lights shone under the glass.

De Gaucourt: Have you ever been to a castle before?

Jehanne: Vaucouleurs.

De Gaucourt: Vaucouleurs? Oh yes. You'll find this bigger.

She wanted to tell him *you won't get me to play the hick*.

The six knights went ahead, up the steps into the hall and then up the inner stairs.

De Gaucourt: Do you know what's in there?

Jehanne: The king, Monsieur.

De Gaucourt: Not only the king. Three hundred knights dressed like me. Officials. Their wives. Superbly dressed. Bishops and theologians. You see, you're famous. But imagine how angry they're going to be if you waste their time.

Jehanne: There is no need to talk to me like that.

De Gaucourt: Everyone says Virgo's in the ascendant. Just the same, if things weren't so desperate, you wouldn't get a look-in.

Jehanne: If things weren't desperate I wouldn't want to try, Monsieur.

She put her gloves back on her sweating hands. The count went ahead of her upstairs. At the top his knights were waiting for him behind screens that cut that end of the hall off from the rest. Over this part was a low wooden roof through which footsteps could be heard and the twanging of stringed instruments. That was the musicians' gallery and the players were tuning up. The noise from the body of the hall was high, sounding fatuous and hostile. Even in this cold porch the heat of all those voices was unwelcome.

De Gaucourt: Go ahead.

It was so bright in there, it was all terrible splendour. She was grateful that for many seconds no one noticed she was there. Down the centre was an aisle. On one side were three hundred knights . . . Gaucourt said there were three hundred, there looked to be three hundred. There were capes, cloaks, tunics over their steel. On the other side scarlet-gold-blue lords and their ladies. Some of them caressing against the walls. Royal stewards, blue and gold, knowing the audience had started, moved amongst the nobility, whacking them over the shoulders with short staffs.

Now people were beginning to see her. She could not believe she'd ever get through all the symbols that challenged her from clothing. Fishes and apples, dogs and tusked boars, black elephants, formal roses, towers, falcons, fishes, checks and crescents, hearts and oak fronds. Shells, crows, keys, roosters, bridges, onions, sheafs, hammers, ships and fettered swans. A hot interest in the eyes above the symbols. A hot fusty interest. She preferred the coldness of the six young men.

A lot of them, on both sides of the hall, were clearly drunk. They all wore their hats.

At the end of the room was a dais. A confusion of men sat there on chairs all of equal height, and two women. Both wore small circlet crowns. They were dark, the young one much slighter than the older. It was the queen of France and her mother Yolande.

Machet came down from the dais and took Jehanne from de Gaucourt. She scarcely recognized him. He was in armour with a tunic of pomegranates.

Jehanne: I didn't know you were a knight, Maître.

Her voice pulsed.

Machet: My family are lords of Blois. Come and meet the king.

He looked a prisoner between two heavy men sitting on his left and Madame Yolande two places off on his right. Even by the standards of March he was a pale man. His eyes were heavy as everyone said, his nose like someone's chilblained finger. The fat unhappy lips seemed to quiver with questions.

Behind the lips, the mystery of kingship her blood was written off against!

Her head rang. It was like waking up to find yourself married to a stranger.

He would not take his strange drugged eyes off her. He was dressed in an unevenly quilted gown. That was a visible sign of their connection: they were the two worst dressed people in the Grand Logis.

She went on to the dais, got on her knees, kissed the hem of the quilted gown. It smelt of mould.

Jehanne: My name is Jehanne. I'm a virgin. Since I was thirteen I've had Voices telling me I'm to lead you to Rheims to be anointed. Lately they talked about Orleans too.

He said nothing, didn't look any more or less pained.

Jehanne: Messire told me to tell you these things.

The King: Messire?

It was a thin voice, the bones showed through it.

Jehanne: Christ our brother wants it all to happen.

The King: Is Christ our brother? *Our* brother?

The close relationship seemed to appeal to him. Though he had suffered greatly from close relations.

Later, people would wonder why he took to Jehanne so quickly.

It happened that from that second he could smell a sort of deliverance in her. Her brown protuberant eyes had a non-political guile in them. All she wanted to do was achieve her own victimhood. He could tell that and was excited.

Jehanne: There are other things I could tell. Only you.

The King: All right. Over in the bay. (He called over his shoulder.) Put two chairs there.

The dais grew to be an alcove at one end. Two seats were put there, only two.

He did not get up yet. He said, *You go ahead.* Everyone watched her go and she turned her head and tried to outstare them. Even far and away above France's finest people, the musicians sat silent and agog, their instruments lying in their laps.

Machet and a bearded official in red and purple were arguing with the king. He was tamping down their arguments with a lazy left hand. At last he got up and came and joined her.

The King: What are the other things?

Jehanne: I know this from the Voices. I've known it since I was fifteen, at least fifteen.

The King: Yes?

Jehanne: I'm the blood sacrifice set aside for you.

The funny eyes looked inadvertent.

The King: What?

Jehanne: I'm your victim.

There was some temptation, for the first time, to apologize for the grandeur of the claim.

Jehanne: Christ our brother was the big blood sacrifice. But a king needs another blood offering all over again for his kingship.

The King: You've been coached by some theologian.

Jehanne: It's the last thing I want to sound like: one of them.

His big mouth hung. He trembled.

The King: You wouldn't lie?

Jehanne: I wouldn't lie to you. The Voices have been getting me ready for you.

He giggled lightly. His upturned face quivered slightly.

The King: We're not a very pretty brother and sister.

Jehanne: It doesn't matter. We have our uses.

The King: Holy Christ, Jehanne . . . If you're a liar or a witch . . .

Jehanne: No, you can tell.

The King: Or a spy . . .

Jehanne: Give in. Give in to what you know about me.

Under closed eyes, he swallowed.

The King: I don't want anyone to die for me. I don't want any more murders. I carry the blame for the murder of cousin Jean when I was sixteen . . .

Jehanne: It isn't our choice, sweet king. It's all been arranged. Others will see to it.

The King: This is hard to believe. That I'm talking to you like this.

Jehanne: Imagine how it is for me.

The King: You're some sort of incarnation. The theologians won't like that.

Jehanne: This is news for you alone. You have a right to news of your own. After all, you're going to be anointed.

The King: This is ridiculous. You say you're going to be sacrificed and we're both delighted about it.

Even his laughter and excitement was creaky, angular.

The King: Your friends say you go to Mass.

Jehanne: Yes.

The King: You confess?

Jehanne: Yes.

The King: You're a virgin?

140

Jehanne: More than a virgin. I've never bled, sweet king. But don't tell all these people.

The King: Never bled.

Jehanne: It's full of meaning, of course.

The King: God in heaven.

Jehanne: Give me a relief force and I'll go to Orleans.

His gaiety vanished then.

The King: I can't. Not just like that.

She said nothing.

The King: You'll have to be examined.

Jehanne: After we've been so close? You still don't know?

The King: It isn't so much for my sake. It's more for theirs.

Jehanne: After you're anointed, you'll be able to make up your mind like *that*!

She slapped her hip.

The King: No, no. All these people would have to invest in a relief force. They deserve to *know* . . .

Jehanne: All these people?

The King: Maman Yolande—I mean, my mother-in-law, Her Highness the Queen of Sicily. My chamberlain la Tremoille. The portly one there. And even the archbishop. They all have to raise money. So do I. They deserve to know . . .

Jehanne: Isn't your word good enough?

The King: I want to be sure too.

She couldn't help her lips tightening, or stupid tears coming out of her lids.

The King: Look, don't be hurt, Jehanne. You're lucky enough to be here.

Jehanne: Dauphin, that won't ever be my attitude. You're the one who'll have to be grateful.

The King: My God! To you!

Jehanne: To Messire.

The King: There's a prophecy about a virgin of Lorraine . . .

Jehanne: I'm nearly from Lorraine. Lorraine starts at the river. The Duke of Lorraine sends his respects by the way.

The King: The sacrifice . . . !

They already seemed so familiar to each other, so knit to each other's horizons. It was like falling in love: you looked

141

at a person and understood she'd always been there, a germ in the brain, a hint in the blood.

The King: Please, Jehanne, come and meet the queen and my council. It's astonishing the way poets and martyrs and prophets keep coming on. Endlessly. And now you.

Jehanne: Yes, yes.

She agreed from politeness. She was enthralled by the straining necks and tip-toe postures of the nobles of France in the body of the hall.

The King: Maman Yolande's been saying for ages that something has to be done about Orleans.

He led her by the hand out along the dais. All the Council stood except the two queens. He took her first to Yolande, the mother-in-law.

The King: Her Highness Queen Yolande of Sicily and Provence, Duchess of Anjou.

Queen Yolande had a square murky face, not at all handsome, not even for a fifty-year-old. Her hair was hidden under veils, nets, templers which all looked like a joke on top of that rugged militant forehead.

Yolande: Maître Machet told me about you. That you're a likely girl.

Jehanne: I hope more than likely, Queen.

Yolande: I'm sure something can be done for you.

Beside Yolande, slight Queen Marie complained to the king.

Marie: Listen, aren't you supposed to introduce guests first to me?

She was tiny, peevish, skin as murky as Maman's.

The King: Is it so important?

Marie: I think so. It's always happening. Either the Queen of France has precedence over the Queen of Sicily or . . .

The King: The Queen of France *does* have precedence. But your own mother . . . !

Marie: All right. If you're so keen on informality, try it out on the Council and see if they tolerate it. Introduce Machet before Clermont and Clermont before Chartres and Chartres before Georges.

The King: Jehanne, this is my queen.

Beside the queen Maman Yolande was once more casting up her eyes and smiling.

Jehanne knelt down and picked up the queen's hem. It was a brilliant gown—black velvet vines on cloth of gold. A fur collar. It smelt of newness and spice when Jehanne kissed it. The queen seemed unaware of this gesture of submission, so Jehanne got up again.

The large man at the queen's side was Monsieur de la Tremoille, Fat Georges, the Lord Chamberlain of the Kingdom. His eyes were sharp, blue, young, knightly in a face of sweat. They did not move, the face wasn't interested.

Chancellor Regnault de Chartres, the Archbishop of Rheims, had blue age-marks on his pallid skin. His forehead was peeling, flakes of dying skin being on his clothing. At least he nodded.

Jehanne: Is the holy ampoule safe in Rheims, Monsieur?

Regnault: How quaint of you to ask. I suppose it is. I haven't yet had the happiness to visit my city.

Jehanne: This year then. I promise.

But he wouldn't give her the benefit of his eyes.

The King: Be a little grateful, Monsieur Chancellor. Jehanne's not only going to pack the Goddams out of Orleans. She's going to take us to Rheims as well.

The girl felt for a second let down, as any girl would whose lover used their intimacies just to get laughs from his friends. She could tell that, with this lover, it might happen a lot.

When they came to Monsieur de Gaucourt, the king asked him to find her apartments in Coudray.

The King: We can't have her mobbed—I believe she was mobbed down in the town. That can't go on. Also you must arrange a servant for her.

De Gaucourt kept a sort of affirmative silence, bowing slightly.

Later they all sat, the dais people. The splendid beings in the hall, the knights as well, kept standing while music was played.

The King: What does your father do?

Jehanne: He's a farmer. He's doyen of Domremy-à-Greux.

The King: I can't say I know it.

It was like being told God didn't have Domremy-à-Greux on his books.

Jehanne: The north half of it is in France, Dauphin.

The King: The other half?

Jehanne: The other half belongs to the Duke of Bar.

The King: Ah, my brother-in-law. Whom were you born under. Him or me?

Jehanne: Under you, Dauphin.

The King: Good.

Jehanne, as a girl of simple targets, most of which she hit squarely, could barely suspect, let alone define, the complexities she now moved amongst.

For example, during the music de la Tremoille rose and went and stood behind Maman Yolande's chair.

La Tremoille: You got that mob together tonight, Madame. The mob outside her pub.

Yolande knew the fat man's quick eyes were off down the Grand Logis. He liked small pale women who were imperceptible under him, whom he could lie on and almost forget they were there.

All his weight was on the back of Yolande's chair at that moment.

La Tremoille: The crowd at the pub . . .

Yolande: How could I get a crowd together at the pub?

La Tremoille: You got half a dozen of your Franciscans to preach about Lorraine virgins in the market today. *After* the Council meeting. If we'd known you'd take advantage of us like this . . .

Yolande: We need a new impetus. It's time.

La Tremoille: It doesn't matter to you that you might upset our diplomatic connection with Burgundy.

Yolande: You mean the contracts you have with the Burgundian army.

La Tremoille: You know what I mean. I mean with the duke. Who can't be beaten front-on.

Yolande reminded him that if Orleans went Charles wouldn't be in the market for money-loans any more.

La Tremoille admitted that, in the long term, Orleans had to be relieved. Yolande said she had some first-rate plate Fat Georges might care to advance money on.

They discussed whether the girl might be a witch, and how it was Machet's first impression that she wasn't

La Tremoille: They tell me you've sent Gaucherie to Orleans.

144

Yolande: Yes.

La Tremoille: To tell them Merlin's virgin is coming to help them.

Yolande: It won't hurt to tell them that.

La Tremoille: Reprehensible. Playing on people's hopes.

Yolande: It's time they were turned back, those Goddam English.

La Tremoille: Only because you don't want them all over your real estate in Anjou.

Yolande: It's time. For lots of reasons.

La Tremoille: Reprehensible. Playing on people's hopes.

His high-pitched squeak of appal died. He went and sat down.

He would never be told that Gaucherie had travelled by way of Fierbois. Where he looked at the girl and perhaps gave her news of a private hope the king had.

For Yolande knew that true visionaries take up that sort of hint with zeal. She had known the mystic, Marie de Maillé, a frightening woman, whom poor old crazy Charles had consulted often around the century's turn. And every time she told him she could see weapons hanging from the clouds and a mad king sitting in his own filth. But he had never been able to stop himself calling her in periodically to tell him of the awful times coming. *She* would have died for the young Charles if it had been suggested to her.

Yolande liked the way Charles was talking to Jehanne. The way he sat up when he spoke. Soon he would find out that in Orleans they were calling aloud for the girl.

Later in the night Jehanne was taken out of the Grand Logis, drunk with terror, crazed with impressions, pretending to talk and walk straight. Through a tangle of walls, over bridges, they got into the inner yards of Coudray. She walked behind Monsieur and Madame du Bellier. Servants carried lights. She already had a high-summer headache from all the lights in the Grand Logis. And she was supposed to sleep now, in the utterly foreign apartment of the du Belliers. This was in one of the antique towers—a lot of screens and opulent drapes hid the windows, but the shutters could be heard shuddering in the wind.

Jehanne and Madame du Bellier sat in high-backed chairs

waiting for Jehanne's bed to be got ready. Hot bricks wrapped in flannel were put deep down amongst the sheets.

Du Bellier: Maman Yolande is a fine character. She saves the king from his friends.

Jehanne: I'm his friend.

Du Bellier: I didn't for a moment mean *you*, Mademoiselle, I think Maman Yolande is very pleased with you.

Two maids carried in a massive chamber-pot, but Jehanne asked to be taken to the latrines. It was simple curiosity. How did people in high towers rid themselves of their wastes?

A maid showed her into the hall, then down a little passageway with two right-angles in it to baffle fetor. Behind drapes were twin holes in the masonry. She could hear a river deep, deep below them.

Maid: It's an underground stream, Mademoiselle. It washes the whole mess down into the Vienne.

Jehanne: Above or below the town?

Maid: I'm not sure, Mademoiselle.

Jehanne: It's an important question. For the town.

Maid: Shall I wait for Mademoiselle in the corridor?

When they got back to the place where she was to sleep, Queen Yolande sat there. So too Madame du Bellier, her head turned chastely to one side.

When Yolande spoke the words sounded habitual—like yet another midnight conference out of many.

Yolande: Jehanne, have you ever heard of Maître Gelu or Maître Gerson?

Jehanne said she hadn't.

Yolande: They are great scholars. Expelled from the University of Paris by the Duke of Burgundy for being Armagnac in sentiment, you understand—for loving the king. Like Père Machet himself.

Jehanne: I see.

Yolande: The Council has written to Maîtres Gelu and Gerson asking their opinion of you. Now one thing is likely to be troublesome. I believe it's forbidden in the Old Testament for women to wear men's clothing.

Jehanne: I didn't know that, Queen Yolande.

Yolande: It isn't the sort of thing a parish priest has to tell most girls.

146

She put her big chin up and scratched underneath it, like a man whose stubble is itching him.

Yolande: Why *do* you dress like that?

Jehanne: Jean de Metz advised it. Then the voice of Messire . . .

Yolande: Do you think it was good advice?

Jehanne: It was the best way to travel across France . . .

Yolande: But the journey's over now.

Jehanne: No, I haven't gone to Orleans.

Queen Yolande gave a whimsical grunt. Jehanne tried again.

Jehanne: I should be at home. I should be having children. Except that wasn't allowed and I had to take on new clothes.

Yolande: Like a nun?

Jehanne: Messire called me his little he-nun.

Yolande was well satisfied.

Yolande: Ah, like a nun throwing off her old clothes. I'll most certainly tell Maîtres Gerson and Gelu you said that.

Jehanne: I don't need anyone to plead for me, Madame.

Yolande: It *might* be your business to believe things are fated to happen. It's my business to arrange them. Let's respect each other's business. Now, you're supposed to be a virgin as well.

Jehanne: Yes.

Yolande: You can't object if Madame du Bellier and I verify it.

Jehanne stood silent, minding. The queen shrugged and looked suddenly tender.

Yolande: You'll have to put up with a lot of this. I've sent off to Orleans telling them to expect a great virgin. I'll look silly if the virgin's fallen from her state. Undress now and lie on the bed.

Jehanne went to the screen that was meant to shield the bed from draughts. She took off her clothes and hung them on the screen.

Yolande: Now lie on the bed. Ah, at least you've got breasts.

Jehanne: Of course, Madame.

Du Bellier: Her Majesty is thinking of a clique who consider you a boy disguised. Some royal bastard . . .

Yolande: Now, lie as if you were being looked at by a physician.

Jehanne: I've never been looked at by a physician.

Yolande: Of course not. Well, like this.

The Queen of Sicily actually rolled on the bed and disposed her large legs. Then she rose and indicated Jehanne should do likewise. Jehanne did. She could see squinting Madame du Bellier and the Queen of Sicily framed by her knees. Her head side-on on the pillow, she flinched as if they would attack her.

Yolande: Madame du Bellier, Madame . . . quite remarkable. Quite . . .

Jehanne looked at Madame du Bellier, who was frowning and peering devotedly.

Jehanne: I've never bled. Please don't tell anyone.

Yolande: You're a good girl, Jehanne.

But Jehanne hated that timid adjective.

Jehanne: I'm more than that, I'm a freak. But Brother Jesus planned me.

Yolande: You're a most necessary freak.

Jehanne: My blood belongs to Jesus and his weak brother . . .

It was immensely more than she'd intended to say.

Yolande: Ah. Thank Christ you came.

Still lying on the bed with her knees up, Jehanne began weeping, weakly. It was a little hard to breathe, she felt so far above the earth in the arc of her godhood, so uselessly furious at the Voices. Disconnectedly, she thought how nice it would be to sleep in a haystack again, all her points done up, between de Metz and Bertrand.

The queen came up the side of the bed and patted her short hair.

Yolande: You'll learn to trust only me. And to look out for spies.

She didn't say whose.

The king's first Mass was not till mid-morning so Jehanne had to fast till then. Early however the maid came and told her the du Belliers and Monsieur de Gaucourt wanted to see her in the hall.

There was a great fire out there but Jehanne shivered both

for subtle reasons and for the cold. The tower was three hundred years old, Madame du Bellier would tell her later. It hadn't been put together for comfort.

De Gaucourt had a boy-child with him, an ill-fed pretty face. The boy wore a dusty blue jacket with black crows on it: he was someone's page or squire.

De Gaucourt: This is Louis. Or something.

Boy: Minguet's my common name.

De Gaucourt: But what were you christened, for Christ's sake?

Minguet: Louis, but everyone calls me Minguet.

De Gaucourt: All right, Mademoiselle Jehanne, you're welcome to him, he's your page.

The child smiled, bowed to her. Beside him, de Gaucourt shrugged. In his way he was as appalled by her success as Durand and the le Royers had been.

De Gaucourt: Just remember. He's a noble. His father lost everything to the Goddam English. You're not to beat him up. You can thank the du Belliers for him. He's from their staff.

The du Belliers bowed. So did Jehanne.

De Gaucourt's eyes didn't see her—all that high-born impercipience, just like last night's.

De Gaucourt: Do you have any other money to employ servants?

Jehanne: No.

De Gaucourt: The king's first Mass is at ten. You're to come. This . . . Minguet will show you the way. And the money . . . I'll see the Queen of Sicily about that. She seems to be the one interested in you.

After de Gaucourt left the boy stood there smiling in a way that made you doubt whether he was very clever.

Madame du Bellier came up and said she knew she should have asked Jehanne to sleep with her the night before but had got some stupid fright about it. Would Jehanne share her bed that night?

She waited for an answer. A grey woman, square, fifty years, restful.

Jehanne felt a rash of gratitude all over her cheeks.

Mass in the chapel of St Lawrence. Christ's victimhood bloodlessly restated while rain throbbed on the roof. At the chancel, on opulent prie–dieus, the king and queen of France, bloodless themselves, carved from soapstone rather than from marble. Behind them the Queen of Sicily, the Chamberlain and his family and secretaries, then the sloughing Chancellor and his staff. Machet. De Gaucourt. Two dozen others. Jehanne knelt at the back.

As the king and queen left the chapel, his heavy eyes rested without affection on her face for some seconds. She thought, sweet Jesus he *will* let me be butchered, the same limp way he let de Giac go to be sacrificed.

The lights were going out, the air was full of the smell of stanched candles. Members of the Council stood whispering in the half–light, making the day's, the month's, the era's cliques.

Little Minguet, noble numbskull, came up beside her, saying the King wanted her.

Charles was waiting in the passageway outside, in a draught. There was a remote savoury warmth from the kitchens. Only Machet stood close to him and a few court officials were off out of hearing, within call.

The King: They're using you to pester me. Did you want that? Is that what your Voices prescribed. My mother–in–law and my Chancellor. They've already conferred with bankers. This morning. Before I was even up.

Jehanne: Orleans, Dauphin?

The King: Where you come from, do they think I've got a lot of armies in a bag and I pull them out one at a time? Is that what your old man thinks?

Jehanne: I know he loves you, that's all.

The King: What a sentimental answer that is! I might go to Spain or Scotland and live in peace.

Jehanne: It wouldn't be allowed.

The king roared and his roar cracked into hoarse fragments around her.

The King: I know that! Oh sweet God, I've got no peace from letting you into Chinon.

He went and only Machet stayed to tell her about putting in an account to Queen Yolande's treasurer. As he was going, he smiled at her.

Machet: That's the way to do it. Speak up, full force. That's how Queen Yolande does it.

But she had no need of Machet's encouragement. She had noticed something crucial about the king: that he'd been beyond himself but still hadn't let out the secret about blood, about victim. When he yelled at her it hadn't been like an assault from some stranger, it had been a quarrel between members of a family. In which certain ultimate secrets are never mentioned.

Minguet was there, shivering a little.

Jehanne: Have you ever been to Orleans?

Minguet: I was born there. My father worked for the duke, the great duke the Goddam English won't give back.

Jehanne: You'll see Orleans again soon.

She almost promised him the duke as well, she felt so full of potency from the way King Charles had fought her.

Jehanne: And don't stand smiling like that. It makes people think you're stupid.

To my honoured principal, etc   Dated February 1429

I was not invited to witness the arrival of the girl-wonder. Only knights and ladies of the court were admitted to that particular levée. Queen Yolande nonetheless had me invited to a dinner at the château de la Milieu at Chinon last night. Since the girl was present I shall describe her before I go on to detail the pretext for the dinner.

She is about average height for a girl but very broad-shouldered. Her eyes are very large and a little protuberant. I think they too are brown, like her hair. She wears male clothes without embarrassment, as if she was raised wearing them. Apart from the clothes and the very large and penetrating eyes, I think you would see thousands of girls just like her on any journey in France or the north of Italy.

Yolande seems very pleased with her and likes to thrust her forward, and did so at last night's dinner. The occasion for the dinner was a remarkable diplomatic stroke brought off by Monsieur Georges de la Tremoille (Fat Georges). A month ago, Monsieur de la Tremoille suggested in council that the magistrates of Orleans should send envoys to Duke Philip of Burgundy and beg him to accept the onus of protecting the city. Since Duke Philip's troops were in entrenchments outside Orleans, working with the English, he could accept the city only if he talked the English into withdrawing. Bedford and the English Royal Council wanted Orleans for the very obvious reason that it gives them the heartland, the very core of France. Philip wants it so that he could use its weight to score off both sides at once.

On secret orders from the Royal Council and the King, two Orleans ambassadors were sent to Dijon to offer their city to Philip for protecting. Philip took them to Paris to confer with Bedford and get English approval for the idea. But in fact the English duke was angry at Philip for being so willing to accept the city. He is reported to have said, I'd have every right to be upset if someone else takes the birds after I've beaten the bushes so hard. In the end the Duke of Burgundy walked out of the meeting and took the Orleans ambassadors with him. He sent an envoy into the lines outside Orleans with a trumpeter and called all the Picards and Burgundians to leave the siege. They marched away from Orleans, the English whistling them.

Queen Yolande, who has her own spies in Orleans, has spent the day speaking to members of the council to add more colour still to the hopes raised by Monsieur de la Tremoille's diplomatic success. She points out that the English are living in wattle huts. They have already stripped the vineyards on the north of the city for firewood and have actually been reduced to burning horse-dung for some warmth. Their floors are crawling with mud. Such, says Yolande, are the conditions for knights and men-at-arms. God knows what amenities common archers and pikers find. Yolande is especially delighted by a report that Talbot makes his soldiers carry the night's dead far up the Châteaudun Road for burial, so that the people inside the city won't see the death rites and find hope in them.

Her Majesty admits that the Orleanais inside the walls aren't much better off. There is a sort of madness in a city under siege—panic, hatred, unneighbourliness. The population of Orleans is so crowded that last month the one cannonball killed twelve people.

I was present in Queen Yolande's apartments when she

told a gathering of her friends that the English Council has garnisheed a quarter of all English officers' pay to help little King Henry win the war. There were times, she said, when the French might have considered the same course if they had ever managed to pay their officers in the first place. There was much healthy laughter at this . . .

Bernardo Massimo

Jehanne heard the news of de la Tremoille's diplomatic coup from Yolande herself. In the afternoon, some hours before the celebration dinner of which Massimo told his principal, Machet came and fetched her from her room in Coudray. She was taken to Yolande's apartments which were somewhere near the chapel. There Yolande maintained a staff of her own: her own chamberlain, treasurer, master-of-house, Augustinian secretary. Three ladies-in-waiting sat with her when Jehanne went in. Her secretary was transcribing on to vellum with a frown on his face.

Yolande turned to Jehanne and told how Philip had been weaned away from Bedford, and about the misery of the Goddam English.

Jehanne began to press her. When would an army go? Before the mud dried out? Before the vines put out new shoots?

Yolande laughed but it was a warning laugh. It said *Don't presume!*

Yolande: It's slow work seeing to the interests of a king. I've looked after him since he was ten. Since ten years of age, since he was betrothed to Marie in the Louvre. What a ceremony that was. The mad king was called in to watch. He'd been wearing the same clothes for eight months. Isabeau the queen smelt of wild animals and lovers—the sort of lovers she takes you can't always tell the difference. Bears and monkeys used to defecate in the corners of her conference room at the Barbette. She had a leopard on a chain. My ladies-in-waiting were terrified of it. I knew he wouldn't survive, growing up in that family. So I took him to Angers with Marie. She was nine, he was ten. It was just supposed to be a break for him, a trip to the provinces. But I never sent him back, though he visited her when he was fifteen and begged her to get rid of the beasts and stop rutting all day. Begged her weeping. To stop rutting.

There was still a new toughness in Yolande when she looked at Jehanne. It was like the banked venom of a mother whose boy takes up with some unlikely girl. The unlikely girl, Jehanne was permitted to observe, was herself.

Yolande: Of course, he still wants her. There's nothing sadder or longer-lasting than the love of a child for a totally unsuitable parent. Perhaps he wants to be loved by her more than he wants to be called king in Paris.

Jehanne: When does the army go to Orleans? The French army?

Yolande: If I've waited since he was ten, you can wait a few more weeks. That's my point. Look, this front of fetching country arrogance you put on works in public but don't try it when *we're* talking together.

Jehanne: Before the mud dries, though?

Yolande: The mud won't dry till April. It's going to get worse. You're going to Poitiers in the meantime.

Jehanne: Poitiers is away. Away from Orleans.

Yolande: You have to be examined if you're going to be of use.

Jehanne: I'm supposed to be more than *of use*.

Yolande: God!

She looked around at her ladies and her secretary. Jehanne saw they were all working. Two of the ladies were predictably embroidering but the other one was reading, had the power of the word in her head. *That* was like having Voices. Jehanne fought an urge to be apologetic.

Jehanne: Queen, you examined me.

Yolande: Yes, but that wasn't recorded. You're not to mention it. This examination is by the Faculty of Poitiers.

Jehanne: The Faculty.

Yolande: They're all scholars expelled from Paris by the Burgundians. Unless they have posts down in this part of the country they're very poor. I tell you that for this reason: they'll *want* to decide that *God* is in you, and not demons. Because they *want* the English turned back. And that is true of all of us, even of Fat Georges now. I don't say Fat Georges exactly *welcomes* you. But he understands Charles needs something like you and so do Charles's people in Orleans.

Something like you? The Voices in their heat, the pressure in the guts, they didn't say *something like you*. They tolled, they roared, *You! You! You!*

Yet Jehanne knew she could never improve Queen Yolande's attitude. Yolande went on.

Yolande: The Council can easily prove you untouchable if they want to. It would be unjust. But that's court politics. So be grateful and come to Vespers with me.

Yolande and Jehanne and the ladies-in-waiting met the king's massed entourage at the chapel door. De la Tremoille was on one side, the incisive eyes which amidst all that lard had seen how to pry England and Burgundy apart. On the other Regnault the Archbishop of Rheims, looking sick. Today his cheeks were sloughing.

There was that second's intimate bemusement of the eyes between Charles and Jehanne.

Charles: Good news, Jehanne. Good news.

As everyone had said that day.

Jehanne: I've heard, Dauphin.

He waved his entourage to go ahead into the chapel. Only old de Gaucourt and two knights stayed back as some sort of bodyguard. Charles took her by the elbow secretively. Exactly like a lover who wants to re-tell and have re-told his first meeting with his girl.

Charles: A victim? A victim for my kingship? Do you mind it, Jehanne?

Jehanne: I was born for it, Dauphin.

And at the moment he himself had no lack of enthusiasm for the idea.

Charles: And the Voices said it.

Jehanne: The Voices said it. And I can tell it in my blood.

He coughed.

Charles: So can I. In my blood. And I recognized you the second you said it, as if you were my sister or something.

She nodded and nodded. It was all true.

Charles: Not a word though. Not a word about *that*.

Jehanne: No. Not a word.

Charles: Don't think it doesn't make me sad.

When he went back to where de Gaucourt was standing however he called out to her and there was joy in his throat, a joy in suspecting you were valid king.

Charles: We're having a big entertainment tonight. Acrobats, two performing bears and a play called *Judith and Holofernes*. Appropriate. Perhaps one day you'll bring me Talbot's head.

That night she went into the Grand Logis in the king's party, and all the court called out *Noël, Noël* to congratulate the Council and de la Tremoille. On red carpet beneath the dais two blindfold bears stood, paws out interrogatively, massive but trembling. They reminded Jehanne of prisoners captured from the crazy court of Isabeau, and their handlers talked to them very threateningly to soothe them down.

Soon Charles wanted to see her again. He lived in a small room formed by screens on the ground floor of the Grand Logis. Next to it, even smaller and just as temporary, was his bedroom. Unless the whole mountain shifted, he was safe. It was no use people crowding in. In any case he didn't like a grand entourage except on the days he was feeling temporarily kingly. So he kept a monk in the room to say the office and called in one person at a time to share the small space.

In his little box his mood swung about crazily but the Augustinian went on intoning under his breath. Sometimes you felt it was that hissing priestly monotone that held Charles together.

Early in their third and cramped meeting he warned the girl.

The King: I don't want you to nag me, Jehanne.

Jehanne: Yes, Dauphin.

The King: Why do you call me dauphin all the time?

Jehanne: I'll call you king again once you've been to Rheims.

The King: I told you not to nag me.

Jehanne: I was just telling you, gentle king.

The King: There, you forgot. You *said* gentle king.

The Augustinian kept on and on saying his breviary in a murmur, part of a divine self–conversation.

The King: Let me just look at you?

He studied her again like a lover. Verifying her. She studied him. He still wore the faded blue gown. At his chest the cloth was violet from age. The five gold lilies sewn there

156

were all shredding, as if he half-agreed with his mother and had no rights to them.

Occasionally, he asked her questions about Coudray, whether she liked it there. He did not understand she had no earlier accommodation—apart from a few pubs, the farm-houses of Domremy-à-Greux, the stable of la Rousse in Neufchâteau, the le Royers basement—to draw on for comparisons.

About three the king fell asleep. His bony ankles were visible. The rain on the window was a sort of rival prayer to the Augustinian's. At three o'clock, a servant brought Archbishop Regnault de Chartres in. The king stirred and sat up.

Regnault: It's all done. I've sent letters of appointment to members of the Faculty and to Machet. I shall of course preside myself as the Council recommended.

Jehanne watched his face flaking as he spoke. She thought if I can stand to look at you, you rotting old man, you can stand to look at me. But the Chancellor refused to see her.

Regnault: The girl will stay at the Judge-Advocate's place, where the court will hold its minor sessions. For full sessions it will meet at the cathedral.

Charles: How long do you think?

Regnault: They're first-rate brains. They won't rush. But then the army won't be ready till spring in any case.

Jehanne: Is it *my* examination? Is that *girl* me?

Charles: What date?

Regnault: Myself, Machet, the girl will leave on Saturday. Queen Yolande is coming too.

Jehanne: Archbishop, am I the girl?

The Archbishop glanced at her, went on talking to the king.

Regnault: Maître Machet will give the girl her instructions. Your mother-in-law, by the way, has the friars preaching about her. It's too much. The Queen of Sicily seems to have the Dominicans, the Franciscans, the Augustinians, all in the palm of her hand.

He looked sideways at the chanting Augustinian, kissed the king's passive hand, left.

Without warning the king behaved with exhilaration.

Charles: One day I'll take you to see my baby boy, Louis.

Regnault went to Scotland to arrange the betrothal. Did you know my Louis is engaged to the Scots princess?

Jehanne: Monsieur de Baudricourt told me once.

Charles: Of course, she's an older woman. He's three, she's four.

His laughter was like choking. The bones of the joke stuck out crookedly as his ankles.

Charles: The Chancellor didn't like Scotland. So don't take it personally that he doesn't love you.

He began to tell the story of the de Chartres family. The more he talked, however, the more she understood that it was a story he told himself, to prove to himself he had friends.

De Chartres, said the king, had three brothers killed at Agincourt. He and his father had been prisoners of Jean sans Peur in Paris ten years ago. One day Jean sans Peur turned the contents of the Cabochien prison over to the Paris crowd. Now Regnault was in a basement cell, his father on the ground floor. He always believed he heard his father call out *Regnault, no tears at all.* The crowd took an hour to get to the basement, for the slaughtering was done by professional butchers and watched by the others: tailors, bakers, carpenters. Regnault vowed, while waiting for the craftsmen to get to him, that if he escaped he'd fast every Wednesday of his life and have no breakfast on Fridays and Saturdays. A monk, let in to absolve and anoint the steaming quarters of old de Chartres and others, somehow got Regnault out disguised as a corpse. Regnault had now kept his vow ten years, but last December had asked the Pope to dispense him from it on the grounds of ill health and because he had so much travelling to do as a diplomat.

The king's face glowed with the story. He was saying *look, no one would desert me for enemies such as those Burgundians.* Jehanne felt she ought to destroy that sort of illusion.

Jehanne: I've heard both Regnault and that fat man have contracts with the Burgundians.

For a second he hated her, raising such questions.

Charles: How else can they find the money to underwrite my armies?

It seemed he felt lucky to have any sort of loyalty from anyone. He didn't want to question the terms.

He yawned.

Charles: I don't think I'll go to Vespers today.

Back in Coudray the orders were Jehanne was to eat no supper and stay in her rooms. It was as if a meeting had been arranged and she stayed sitting quietly with Madame du Bellier. Madame du Bellier embroidered, had a name as an artist. Jehanne idled with a spindle, waiting for the event.

At eight o'clock the Queen of Sicily came in with a man about Gaucherie's age, dressed more or less the same—perhaps a lawyer, perhaps a theologian from Italy.

Then Jehanne saw the man's servant carrying a drug case. A physician.

A physician who had produced a cup from his cloak and was thumb-clicking for his servant to open the chest of drugs and pass the right mixture.

Jehanne: What's this?

Yolande: A test. Just a test that has to be attended to.

Jehanne: But what is it?

Physician: It isn't harmful.

He offered her a grey mixture to drink.

Jehanne: No.

Yolande: Jehanne, I want you to go to Orleans with an army. I want the army to look at you and say there is our entry into Orleans, our outbreak, our victory. But first, you must pass tests.

Jehanne: What test is this?

The physician was immobile with the proffered cup—a highly professional posture. Yolande slumped a little but chose to be patient.

Yolande: Bishop Gelu, the great scholar, advising the Council by letter says it is appropriate that God should send someone humble to ruin the Goddams. He refers to you as *a flea on a dung-heap*. He says fleas from dung-heaps have often inconvenienced the progress of evil. He says women have too—he nominates Judith who sawed Holofernes's head off, and Esther and all those other ladies. He does however warn us that it's possible that a person could be fed to the ears with venom by other persons, human and demonic, and then be sent off to poison the king with a kiss.

Jehanne: The test is for poison?

Yolande: Yes. I don't think what Gelu describes is possible. I think our friend the doctor here thinks it's insane. But Gelu has suggested it and so it must be attended to. Drink up.

Jehanne: It's going to make me feel strange.

Physician: For a moment, Mademoiselle. No more.

Jehanne drank. Her head tolled and her ears blocked. She repressed vomit when it was already at the back of her throat. Receding bile burnt her palate.

Jehanne: Dear God. I very nearly sicked up.

Yolande: You were supposed to.

Jehanne's eyes were closed. She did not see the physician's servant move behind her. He was young and large. One of his arms wrapped her at the middle, the other hand smothered her face. When her mouth opened to attempt biting, the doctor's hand, suddenly ungloved, rushed down her throat. When she was sick the brisk servant had suddenly moved from behind her and caught the mess in a bowl.

She was trembling from the terrible possession they had taken of her. The doctor stirred the bowl with a long-stemmed spoon, lifted gobbets of the matter, sniffed with distaste. Other liquids and powders were dropped into the bowl and changes—if there were changes—were noted.

Physician: Maître Gelu was one of the greatest of French brains. Perhaps he's too old now.

Yolande: So?

Physician: It's just vomit. What Gelu suggests might be possible with a toad, but a young woman is not a toad. And the king wouldn't want to kiss a toad.

Yolande put a hand on the girl's shoulder, gingerly, aware of the girl's outrage.

Yolande: It all goes to show . . .

The girl thought, men are so damned harsh. What if they ever beat me up, raped me, used weapons on me?

Jehanne: Well what?

She was weeping gratefully for the big brows of fire dazzling her in her apartments in Coudray.

Messire: Be wise as the rose bush . . .

Madame Catherine: Jesus's sweet rose . . .

Messire: Rest in your place. Obey the wisdom of the soil . . .

Madame Catherine: Respect the gardener . . .

Madame Margaret: Sting and puncture all uprooting hands . . .

Messire: Be wise as the rose bush, sweet rose . . .

Madame Margaret: But impatient for the spring!

King Charles called for her again the following afternoon. When she reached the cramped royal closet she found a narrow-chested boy sitting with the king. At the first sight and in some lights he looked younger than Minguet. At a second look you saw twenty or so, a grown man who wouldn't get bigger.

As Jehanne was brought in the runt jumped up and made the sign of the cross. Then he danced up to her.

Man: This is the dear girl?

Charles nodded. He wasn't enthusiastic.

Man: Alençon. Jean.

Jehanne: You're related, Monsieur?

The family likeness was there: the boniness, the lost mouth and suspect eyes.

Alençon: The king's cousin.

Jehanne: The more princes turn up the better.

Charles told her—in a bored voice, as if Alençon had reminded him of the story too often—that Alençon had been captured by the English at Verneuil when he was just a boy, fifteen years.

Alençon: I've barely paid off the ransom. All my estates are in Normandy. The English have them. So it's hard to raise money on them. I've been five years in prison . . .

Charles yawned.

Charles: I suppose you'll want some military award? Marshal of France maybe?

Alençon turned gracefully to his sacred cousin, arms outstretched as if hard put to it to contain the fullness of the honour.

Alençon: If my royal cousin could find a place . . .

Charles: Your royal damned cousin has more places than he has men to fill them.

The young duke kissed the king's forehead and rushed back to Jehanne.

Alençon: I believe you hear Voices? I was out early this

161

morning shooting quail when a Dominican arrived at Saumur—full of you, so to speak. I called my beaters off.

Jehanne: You didn't mind if others took the birds?

Alençon: What?

Charles: I think, that Jehanne is echoing what Bedford said to Philip of Burgundy over Orleans.

The king was, in fact, almost asleep.

Alençon: Oh yes. Do your Voices mention Normandy?

Jehanne: They have enough trouble arranging for Orleans. All people do is set me tests. They even hunt through my puke. But they won't send me to Orleans. Let alone Normandy.

Alençon: I have to put up at an abbey. My wife and mother-in-law and myself. A cousin of the king! Having to find *board* at a *monastery*.

Charles: Things will improve. Things will improve. Don't talk any more . . .

In the silence you could hear the monk murmuring some rollicking Latin hymn from the minor hours. The king went to sleep.

Now the duke and Jehanne had to whisper.

Alençon: Have you ever soldiered?

Jehanne: No.

Alençon: Have you ever carried a lance on horse-back?

Jehanne: No.

Alençon: My dear girl! *Have* you a *horse*?

She had and had forgotten. She'd handed it over to a groom before climbing the mountain three nights before.

Alençon: We'll send your page for it. They have a pretty fair tilting yard over in St Georges's.

Jehanne: St Georges's?

Alençon: The garrison fortress, next door. I know the armourer. Come on.

She frowned at slumped Charles.

Alençon: Come on. Don't be polite.

The armoury of St Georges's was a stone barn. The armour of lords and knights in garrison or court at Chinon stood on racks marked with the heraldry of each owner. But there was spare equipment for visitors. The relicts of dead or forgetful soldiers.

Jehanne could tell that the armourers were laughing as

162

they strapped her into a cuirass and plates. Thin-legged Alençon looked ridiculously over-balanced in upper armour without leggings. Perhaps she did too, but that wasn't the only reason they were laughing. It was the quaintness of being ordered to mix elements considered unmixable: steel and woman, thorn and rose.

They gave her a cloth cap to put on and over it went a helmet. They latched it to her cuirass. There she was in a private hard-sided world where the light was different. She felt distinct guilt. *I oughtn't to be here,* she felt. *Not on anyone's orders. Even Messire's.*

She wondered if she could still breathe in there.

Alençon gave a muffled and metallic order to the armourers.

Alençon: Put the visor up!

She could feel fingers and thumbs working on the sides of her helmet. The visor lifted. It was still a different way of living, inside that steel. When you got used to the weight on your shoulders you began to feel a little drunk, vain, gifted, potent.

Alençon: Tilting lances! Light ones!

They waded into the yard where Minguet held the horses. He had already put tilting saddles, high at front and back, on both the mounts.

Jehanne: How do I get up?

Minguet: I'll get you up there. That's what pages are for.

When he'd managed it, he led her off to the tilting ground. It was levelled ground on the north end of the summit. A white fence ran down its middle, and towards the end of the course and on the far side of the fence a target shaped like the upper quarters of a knight on a saddle hung from an arm that could be spun.

Alençon showed her how to rest the lance on the bracket on the right breast of the cuirass and sight it across her body for the target. His small hand had trouble keeping his lance up, but Jehanne felt comfortable with hers. He had been in prison since he was fifteen. Was he a good tutor?

Alençon's face inside the helmet was shedding sweat.

Alençon: It's harder than it looks. But you seem to have the gift.

He explained how the target should look as if it were

163

facing the middle of your lance as you began your run. You had to hit the target from the front, never to turn your lance across your body to strike the target from the side. Otherwise you could be torn off your horse or break your ribs.

So he kept on giving hints as his hand strained and his face sweated.

Alençon: I'll show you.

He galloped his horse, but put the lance into the target too glancing and sidewise, and was pulled forward sharply across the high pommel and the horse's withers. When he rode back his slight face glowered with a sort of disapproval of himself. There was heat rash down the side of his chin. Behind a hand, Minguet was laughing at him, like an equal.

Alençon: You see what can happen? Be careful.

But she knew she didn't have to be. What a strong family the family of Jacques from Sermaize are. Because she had no strain carrying the lance. She knew what angle to carry it at. She was under a sort of inspiration, some expert spirit wouldn't let her miss. She hit and spun the target three times out of three.

Alençon: You've done it before.

Jehanne denied it. She liked the way he accepted her talent, his mouth slightly agape.

He whispered.

Alençon: Then there *is* virtue in you. You're not yourself. You're being *moved*.

Jehanne: Perhaps.

Alençon sat still on his horse and watched her do it some more times. Then he noticed she was weeping.

Alençon: What's the matter? Why the tears?

Jehanne: I don't want to be good at this.

Alençon: I'd love to be able to do it.

Jehanne: I know.

She could have told him it's the simple things the saint-and-demon-struck can't do. Like menstruate, treat their people normally.

Alençon: You have a genius, a *genius* for it. Let me give you a horse. That horse of yours . . .

Jehanne: You're broke, my lord. I heard you say.

Alençon: Not that broke.

He had dropped nearly all the courtly mannerisms he had

164

shown when they'd met. A child of twenty, he whispered again. He liked whispering.

Alençon: I want you to talk to my wife and mother-in-law. Would you? Because they won't let me campaign. You know what they're like. They say *you'll ruin us if you get taken prisoner again.* If I give you a horse . . .

Jehanne: A little horse? . . . something comfortable?

Alençon: Yes. Will you come up to Saumur and talk with them?

So she rode up to Saumur one rare sunny Wednesday. She could tell the Duchess of Alençon was grateful to see she was so lumpy, unwomanly: she trusted her husband's new enthusiasm more for that reason. She was twenty, but she was older in the head than him, was sharp and pretty. It was she who had raised all the mortgages to buy her husband back after he had gone for that short bloody gallop at Verneuil. It was she who knew the exact dimensions of their poverty, which wasn't—Jehanne noticed—like the poverty of ordinary people at all.

For their apartments were crammed with wine, tapestries, chaplains, heraldic servants. Billeted at St Florent, in the suburbs of the abbey, were two hundred men-at-arms with their squires and archers, all getting pay from the duke. It seemed that if princes went broke, it meant they had to start spending bankers' money rather than their own. But nothing else changed.

Duchess: Jean isn't very mature.

Alençon: Yes I am.

Duchess: No you aren't, my darling. He was captured at the age of fifteen and the English warden in le Crotoy treated him like a son.

Alençon: It wasn't all a picnic. The English were getting ready to pike me that day I was on the ground. I didn't have any breath and I had too much armour on—we'd sat in it all morning, on horseback. Imagine, dear girl. Then an officer noticed the huke I was wearing. He said *don't touch him, he's royal family, you stupid bastards.* He would have saved my duchess a lot of trouble by not coming along . . .

The duchess smiled at both the duke and Jehanne with the sort of unmasked indulgence people use only on very small and easily out-foxed children.

Duchess: Nonsense, Jean. It's a fact though that we'll never be out of debt until the splendid city of Alençon is taken back off the Goddams.

Jehanne: I can't promise anything about Normandy.

Duchess: I see.

Jehanne: Let him come with his soldiers though. Let him. I promise he'll be safe.

Duchess: I've had him back only a year.

Suddenly, Jehanne could see how deep in physical love the duchess was with her boyish duke. Jehanne felt loss, a movement in her womb, a shiver of love and longing for this sharp maternal girl who fell open like a rose when the duke went to bed with her.

Jehanne stood up, sweating from love and conviction.

Jehanne: I'll be with him. Nothing will go wrong.

Alençon: Can't you tell, my duchess? There's *virtue* in her.

The duchess shook her head a little. Finding *virtue* in people, she half-implied, was another of his child's games. However, she was impressed.

Alençon had given her a light Barbary mare. It wasn't as easy to ride as farm-horses, or the horse Lassois and Alain gave her, or the big black Belgian she got from the Duke of Lorraine. It moved with delicacy, a feminine sort of spirit was in it. Coming out of the barbican above the town she felt that she was sitting lightly on top of the morning, on the back of God's hand. And the hand was definitely moving, even if the movement was temporarily southward. She wanted to make someone pay for it being southward. She decided to pretend she didn't know about Poitiers, that she thought she was on her way direct to the army at Blois.

There were five knights banneret with her, their squires, archers, pikers. They loudly crossed the Vienne by a bridge at the quays and went south.

Jehanne: Where will we meet the Queen of Sicily?

Knight: At Loudun, Mademoiselle.

Jehanne: Loudun?

Knight: Yes.

Jehanne: Loudun's away from Blois.

Knight: You have to leave all this to me, Mademoiselle.

Jehanne: Damn you, Loudun's south, away from the army.

Knight: You have to ask the Queen of Sicily about that.

Jehanne: I'm asking you. Are you too scared to tell a girl the truth?

Knight: Mademoiselle, they told me you're difficult.

Jehanne: Who? Who told you?

He wouldn't say.

Knight: I'm allowed to truss you up and hang you from my saddle if it's necessary.

She roared at him, her little Barbary propping beneath her in fright.

Jehanne: Damn you, where am I going?

Some of the common archers and squires were laughing at the knight.

Knight: It happens you're going to Poitiers. To be asked questions by scholars.

She pretended that was news.

Knight: Mademoiselle, the Faculty of Poitiers is going to decide whether you're a witch or not.

He wasn't wearing a helmet and his eyes suggested he knew the answer already.

Jehanne: What's your name?

Knight: Monsieur Lucien d'Estivet, Count of St Luce.

Jehanne: When the Goddam English leave this country, I'll see you're given the last square inch. You can be lord of that.

Knight: We'll both be old before anything like that happens.

Jehanne: That's the trouble with you lot. You can't believe anything's going to change.

He was just young and vain enough to be hurt. He should have laughed with his archers but it was beyond him.

The squire of the Count of St Luce sang deliciously, a soft tenor.

Squire: She stood in her scarlet gown,
     If anyone touched her, the gown rustled down,
     And she called out *Eia*.
     But a better girl by far
     Was a girl in a saffron gown,
     And when I alone touched her
     The gown rustled down.
     And she called out *Eia*.

She thought of Jean Duke of Alençon and his Duchess waking warm as bread in each other's arms this morning. What with sun and journey and the Count of St Luce edgy about his dignity, it was nearly possible to think about it without pain.

Ahead, outside a pub four miles from Loudun, flags were flying—the flag of Anjou, Sicily, Jerusalem. Horses grazed the common and soldiers lolled on benches. But someone saw Jehanne's party coming and the flags were uprooted and Yolande—in white satin and side-saddle—rode out along the muddy highway to meet her.

Yolande: Do you want to stay the night here or go on?

Jehanne: I'd rather go on.

Yolande: Then it can all start earlier.

Jehanne: Yes.

They rode off to one side. The Count of St Luce went a little pale in case he was bad-mouthed to the Queen of Sicily.

Yolande: Two things you'll have to remember about Poitiers. Nearly all the men who'll examine you are hard-up. There are no endowed seats at Poitiers, no official university. They were all Paris professors once, as I said, but the Burgundians expelled them. There's a Parliament in Poitiers, but it scarcely sits, it never has cases brought to it. Cases can't *get* to it. Because of the state of the country. Doctorates of law, civil and canon, doctorates of theology . . . they're spilling down the stairs in Poitiers.

Yolande sat on a war horse. Her mouth seemed to Jehanne to be four feet above Jehanne's head, and the big square face filled a quarter of the sky.

Yolande: Now the Advocate-General . . . you'll be staying at his place . . . he's quite broke, all his property is in the north. He's living on banker's money. Most of us belong to certain north Italian banking families. Except men like Fat Georges—he's in business for himself. *And* owns himself. By the way, the Advocate-General has the best house in Poitiers, so you'll be very comfortable. But that's the first thing, everyone is broke and wants the King to send an army to Orleans and knows he'll do it for *you*.

Jehanne: How do they know it?

168

Yolande: The preaching orders keep saying it. The Franciscans and Dominicans. Charles hears them. He believes them.

Jehanne: I'd hoped he believed me as well.

Yolande: He does too—don't be touchy.

It's my business, Yolande had said, *to believe everything is arranged.* She would have tried to arrange the birth, death and resurrection of King Jesus.

Yolande: The second thing to remember is that they have some sort of pride that won't let them rush things. Don't make enemies of them by being too impatient. You'll be there, in Poitiers, some time.

Jehanne: How much time?

Yolande: A month. You can count on a month.

Jehanne: Dear God.

The city sat proud on a fat knoll in the flat plain of Poitou and by the gentle river Clain.

Regnault de Chartres, Chancellor of France, set up an office for the Royal Commission in a house in the north of the city. From this office small committees of theologians would go to the Hôtel de la Rose, where the girl was lodged, to interrogate her. After each session of questioning the interrogators would report back to the Commission as a whole and the theological arguments would begin to fly. Sometimes the entire Commission would question the girl, either at its office or in the cathedral of Poitiers.

The Inquisitor Turelure and Père Sequin filled the house with the collected works of Jerome, Origen, Tertullian, St Ambrose, St Augustine, Odo of Cluny, Albertus Magnus, Aquinas. Their mentality was: it is impossible that in these books somewhere there is not a key to that girl at the Hôtel de la Rose.

Archbishop Regnault himself had that hatred of sudden reversals and lightning rearrangements that most statesmen have. He wanted to send an army to Orleans, he even wanted to go to Rheims. He didn't want Charles, the Armagnac party, to be made ridiculous through the lunacies of a little Mademoiselle Christ.

Queen Yolande's part in making the girl's reputation through sundry preachers appalled him. He would tell the

Commission that its first work was to find out whether the girl was actually sane.

Two Armagnac bishops, apart from Monsieur Regnault himself, sat on the commission. Machet also, and Pierre de Versailles, Abbot of Talmont and a royal ambassador.

Yolande somehow took apartments in the same house as the Commission used. After three or four weeks it was clear she was trying to influence it from the outside. The Franciscans in Poitiers preached about the girl—not as if she was a person but a divine event. Everyone knew the Franciscans were Yolande's people.

The Commission was begun with a solemn high Mass in St Pierre's on Monday morning.

Jehanne attended it with Madame Rabateau, her hostess, then walked back to the Hôtel de la Rose and heard nothing from the commissioners for two days. By Wednesday breakfast time she was frightened. What were they talking about? All Monday, all Tuesday? She began to wonder if they were finding ways of challenging her that de Baudricourt and the King had not used.

There had been no light or Voices since she left Chinon.

On Wednesday morning the waiting ended. Four commissioners visited her. The inquisitor Turelure, Pierre de Versailles, Maîtres Jean Erault and Jean Lombard, professors from Paris.

From the moment Turelure spoke she felt a rush of confidence, her blood crackling in her ears in a sort of celebration because they were men without benefit of Voices and their information all oblique, through books and precedent of law.

And she could be impatient with them, she saw, and must be impatient. Because they were the canny sort of men who might say *if her Voices say things are so bad, why isn't she more impatient?*

Turelure began by checking her for insanity, heresy. Being an inquisitor, the two were one and the same to him.

His questions were:

Do you believe Our Lord Jesus Christ is God?

Is the Second Person of the Holy Trinity?

Is One Divine Person subsisting in two natures, Divine and Human?

He watched her, for the formulas of belief themselves had power to make witches fall frothing on the floor.

His further questions:

Do you believe the world we see about us was created by God or Satan?

Do you believe that coupling within marriage is approved of by God?

That the Eucharist should be given to people in the form of wine as well as in the form of bread?

Jehanne: No. None of that sort of thing is ever thought of in the countryside.

Turelure: No? Suppose I told you that two years ago, outside Toulouse, a knight fell in love with a freehold farmer's daughter. When he told her he was going to make a marriage contract through her father she said she loved him but if she lost her virginity she'd go to hell. The young knight went to a canon of Toulouse for advice. He said, *I'm afraid your girl sounds like a Catharist heretic.* Catharists think Satan created the visible world, that all copulation is evil. They are a threat to society and they are widespread. For example, the farmer's daughter had picked up the heresy from some local noblewoman. Both women were jailed and the noblewoman repented but the girl wouldn't and was burned alive in the end. Do you think she was right?

Jehanne: No. She was brave.

Turelure: Wouldn't you say the bravest thing of all is to say *no, my conscience can't be right in this matter, the Church must be right.*

Jehanne: I can't say, Maître. I can't imagine myself turning a knight down for such bad reasons.

That first day they asked about the origins of the Voices. It had not occurred to her to tell General de Baudricourt about the mandrake-crowning rite in Boischenu: the incarnations that Bertrand, Mesdames Aubrit and de Bourlément were. Now she knew not to tell Turelure and those others: that they would misunderstand. The Boischenu events were for her, to inform her and help her see the mystery. The experts had no rights to them.

171

She felt roseate, having managed the Commissioners well that day.

And on Wednesday night the rain began again. The Queen of Sicily was dining with the Rabateaus and Jehanne.

Yolande: Let's hope it's making mud on the Loire.

Yolande had this hopeful image of the Goddams hardly anyone else in Chinon or Poitiers seemed to share. They lay in mud. The mud crawled beneath them and edged them towards the anonymous silts of the Loire.

Yolande: Are you being polite to the gentlemen of the Commission, Jehanne?

She gave a pert answer.

But the gentlemen of the Commission knew how to work on a person. Sometimes half-a-dozen commissioners sat with her all day asking and repeating questions. Sometimes one or two would come with one or two questions. The answers would be portentously written down and read back to her as if she were being given a last chance to recant some dangerous opinion.

Her victories were scarce.

For example, with Maître Aimerie, who sat testing her for some brand of heresy whose name she didn't know.

Aimerie: Your Voice told you God would save the people of France in their agonies. But if he intends to do that, why do we need an army?

Jehanne: Maître, the normal arrangement is the armies do the fighting and God decides who wins.

He nodded at that—he approved. For some reason his approval made her very angry.

Jehanne: It seems to me you could have answered that question for yourself.

Aimerie: The question was: could *you* answer it?

Jehanne: I'd have to be an idiot not to be able to answer *that*.

Maître Sequin de Sequin from Limoges questioned her in his broad-vowelled southern accent.

Sequin: What sort of French do your Voices speak?

Jehanne: Better than yours.

That got round. It became one of the commissioners' favourite stories.

But Jehanne was breathless with inertia. She would have

welcomed seeing boyish if not childish Alençon. She wanted to see Charles. Her brain yawned but she slept badly. And was once woken to find the heat in her right side had become a pain and there were the golden brows of Madame Ste Margaret.

Madame Ste Margaret: Tell them, rosebud, they must hurry, hurry. They must hurry, hurry, rosebud.

At one time they didn't come near her for four straight days. They seemed to be trying to prove some thesis to her about God moving slowly. Regnault de Chartres never came at all.

In Holy Week Sequin challenged her.

Sequin: We've concluded that you're not to be believed, you're all talk, you haven't given a sign.

Jehanne: Dear God, send me with the army! I'm not here to give signs. What do you want? Orleans is the only sign I can give you, you'll get more signs than you can handle at Orleans. For God's sake, signs!

She was allowed to walk about during interviews and she always found herself on her feet when the questioning was finished. That day she was at the first floor windows, looking down rue St Etienne.

In the wet square the children of Poitiers were catching cats, pagan animals, familiars of demons. By the cathedral stood wickerwork cages built like men with horns, built like Satan, the horned god. Here the cats would be locked up and tomorrow night, after Christ's death, the cages would be ignited and the burning animals would scream weirdly enough to convince all the city that a sort of justice against the black world had been achieved.

Jehanne: If you want signs we might as well give up and join the cat-chase.

Sequin was a farmer's son and had a southerner's lack of malice. He even enjoyed the status he had: the commissioner Jehanne slapped down most.

They asked her if she had to send a manifesto to the English generals, what she would say. Maître Jean Erault took it down to be examined by the Commission. It didn't give them much: it told Talbot, Suffolk, Glasdale, la Poule to go home, and if they wouldn't to expect the worst.

★

173

That Holy Thursday four women of good reputation were sworn in as witnesses to the girl's virginity.

The four women were Yolande (included in the sub-committee only because she was known to be able to handle Jehanne), Madame de Gaucourt who was older than the queen, Madame Rabateau who was older than Madame de Gaucourt, and an eighteen-year-old, the Countess de Trèves.

On Holy Thursday night, after the Eucharist had been moved to a side chapel and the tabernacle on the high altar of St Pierre lay open and empty, Yolande told Jehanne she would be examined by the four noble ladies in the morning. Virginity was a state that could easily be altered, Yolande said. Not mine, Jehanne said. Mine's beyond cure. The other examination had been private, for Yolande's own sake, said Yolande. It couldn't count with *this* court.

Jehanne: Have you told the other ladies to expect a shock?

Yolande: I don't know what you mean.

Jehanne: That I'm a full-grown child. That I've never been troubled with troubles.

Yolande: Just let them see for themselves. They're all kindly creatures. Even me.

In the morning of Good Friday an iron framework such as was used by wealthy women in childbirth and gynaeco-logical disorders was set up above Madame Rabateau's bed. Jehanne took off her clothes and lay with her feet in stirrups.

She arched her neck and squinted at the wall behind the bed. When it became too painful she looked down the length of her body at the pursed faces of the sub-committee. A fury came over her. None of the women moved, all frowning self-seriously at her genitals, each of them a self-serious tool of the commission. Through Queen Yolande, Madame de Gaucourt, Madame Rabateau, the Countess de Trèves, the commissioners paid you back for the un-accountable and obscene gifts you carried. Obscene because they weren't earned in any Faculty. Through these four dupe women the men repaid you for laughing at their accents.

She shut her eyes. Immediately she felt a soft hand on her pubis. She sat up.

Jehanne: Don't touch me!

The vacated stirrups swung before the sub-committee's

174

faces. The little Countess began crying. Madame Rabateau edged up the bed to comfort her. But Madame de Gaucourt and the Queen stood impassively where they were. Two calm violators.

Yolande: Last time I didn't touch you. One can see certain obvious features just by looking. And it was unofficial. But you can't really tell without using your hand. We've sworn to God to be decent but thorough. You'll have to bear it, Jehanne. Without nonsense.

Jehanne opened her mouth and screamed at them.

To my honoured etc.   Dated 1 April 1429

On Easter Sunday in the cathedral of Poitiers, His Grace Regnault de Chartres was forced to sit on a throne on the high altar and listen to one of Yolande's Franciscans preach a sermon that went close to comparing the girl to Charles Martel. The preacher pawed the pulpit and roared on about France and Christ who bled for it (it alone, it seemed!) and the girl, in male clothing, sat and listened beyond the chancel.

It appears that the Commission has argued in plenary session the verse in Deuteronomy which says, 'The woman shouldn't wear men's clothes or a man dress as a woman: such behaviour is odious to God.' Queen Yolande tells me that Maître Machet suggested that since the prohibition was not mentioned in the Gospels it could be considered to have lapsed, to be merely an injunction for the ancient Jews. Maître Erault reminded the commission that in Compiègne the relics were preserved of Ste Euphrosyne, who had lived thirty years in male clothing to underline her virginity.

It seems therefore that she will get clean away with her strange habits of dress.

Meanwhile the Franciscan order is preaching wonders about the girl all over Poitou as far away as Bourges. Franciscans are sneaking into Orleans to preach the new hope she implies . . .

Bernardo Massimo

In Easter week, the small party of Franciscans who had been sent to the Vaucouleurs area to look into Jehanne's origins came back to Poitiers. Regnault had hoped the Burgundians might have caught them, but a king's messenger had got them there and back using back roads, fog and night. They were Yolande's people, with Yolande's vision of the girl. They weren't of much objective use to the Commission. Yolande very kindly sent one of them to tell the girl how things were in the Vaucouleurs castellany.

He found people mustered in front of the Rabateau house, not rowdy people. They looked as if they were waiting for a birth or death to be announced. Later he discovered they were a changing crowd—everyone passing stood there for perhaps ten minutes, or longer if the Queen of Sicily or Monsieur de Gaucourt were arriving or leaving.

Inside, the Franciscan found the girl sitting with Madame Rabateau. She had spindle and distaff and was working very fast with them. At first she wasn't very warm. She'd seen too many theologians lately.

Franciscan: Queen Yolande sent me, Mademoiselle. I'm just back from Vaucouleurs.

Jehanne: What did you do in Vaucouleurs, Brother?

Franciscan: I talked to General de Baudricourt. I talked to your people.

He saw the spasm of pain in her face. The spasm of guilt.

Jehanne: Is the general giving up the town this Easter?

Franciscan: After the Duke of Burgundy had his argument with Bedford, he let Monsieur de Baudricourt keep Vaucouleurs. To spite the Goddams. And for a cash consideration.

Jehanne: Whose cash?

Franciscan: The general's. He paid it himself. He took out a mortgage with Italian bankers. On property he owns at Bugeaumex.

Jehanne: But he began some special tax to cover himself?

Franciscan: No.

Jehanne: No.

Franciscan: He said tell her . . . meaning you . . . tell her I bought Vaucouleurs back out of my own pocket.

Her body glowed for his sentimental gesture.

Jehanne: Did you go to . . . to Domremy-à-Greux?

Franciscan: I met your father.

Jehanne: How is he?

Franciscan: He finds it hard to talk about you. Your mother talks more freely. Your father said you were always a good girl.

Jehanne: He never told me that.

Franciscan: He said he heard you were staying with relatives and were under the guidance of a good knight, a man called . . .

Jehanne: Bertrand.

Franciscan: That's the name. Then he heard you'd started dressing as a man. He went to Vaucouleurs to talk to you but you'd left two days before.

Jehanne: He used to call me his favourite little cow.

Franciscan: He put me on to a lady of the locality. Madame Aubrit.

Jehanne: Dear God.

Franciscan: She asked me if you'd told us about Voices. If you'd told the king. I said yes. She said *Dear God.* Just like you.

Jehanne: Thank you for telling me all this, Brother. I like your style better than some of the others . . .

Franciscan: Some of them are questioning whether there can be virtue in someone who won't do what their old man tells them. But there are precedents. Jesus stayed behind in Jerusalem when he was twelve. That was some sort of disobedience . . .

Jehanne: Thank you for the kind words.

Yolande had Italian banking officials in her apartments all day, the eternal Monsieur Bernardo Massimo, the Poitou representatives of the Perruzzis of Florence. All the paperwork kept her rosy.

In Orleans, she told Jehanne, the English had occupied the slopes of St Loup, a suburb on the east of the city. Throughout March they built a bastion there of mounded mud and timber palisades. From it they could watch and command the road to Gien and the river upstream from Orleans. In Holy Week they finished a massive redoubt on the le Mans road to the west of the city. They named it London—nostalgically. They would be building others, Yolande told the girl. The reason for the bastions was that they didn't really have enough men to surround Orleans and needed somewhere to run to if the Orleanais shook off their phobias and decided to assert themselves. So, anyhow, ran Yolande's reading of events.

In April it became known that the Commissioners were writing their report for the king.

Yolande: Charles wanted to be here before this. But he's had a stomach infection. Besides, he gets sudden enthusiasms and then gets all floppy for weeks. You mustn't mind him, Jehanne.

Jehanne: Will they tell him to give me troops?

Yolande: Their style isn't to give instructions. It's more to say there's no reason why he shouldn't.

In the second week of April the Master of Requests came to Poitiers. He called Jehanne to an interview with Yolande at the queen's apartment, and when Jehanne got there she found Regnault the Chancellor in the room.

Master of Requests: Mademoiselle Jehanne, you didn't meet me. I was in Italy on business when you arrived at Chinon. The king wants me to tell you the findings of the Commission he appointed to investigate your nature and the validity of your requests. The Commissioners find that you should not be sent away since your promise is so great, even if the promises are unfounded. The king should not be too hasty to accept you either. But he should continue to test you by two means—first by praying for a sign, secondly by continual enquiry into your life, morals, motives. Now since you've come to Chinon he's applied both methods. The king has kept you close to his royal person for six weeks, for although he has not been all that time with you himself he has appointed the best brains to be with you and the Commission is a limb of his sacred person. In the time you've been observed you've shown no evil, you are direct, honest, simple, good, and a virgin. When asked for a sign you said the sign would be Orleans and that was that. Now since the king's commissioners haven't found any evil in you and since we can only test your claims about Orleans by sending you there . . . Is anything the matter, Mademoiselle Jehanne?

There had been a massive and omniscient wink from large Queen Yolande. Like a trunk closing.

Master of Requests: Please listen . . . and since your answers have been consistent, the Commissioners say the king might be rejecting help in rejecting you, rejecting the best of help, rejecting the Spirit of God. That is the essence of what they find. Now Monsieur Regnault wants to warn you.

Monsieur Regnault looked better, the face pallid but firmer in texture. Perhaps the papal dispensation allowing him to eat breakfast had been granted.

Still he didn't look at her. He could have been talking to Yolande.

Regnault: You have to be given a chance to beg off. You've said that there's a divine guarantee working in you. First Orleans, then Rheims. If nothing happens we'll know you've been lying on heaven's behalf. The penalties are high . . .

She thought: I'm not going to put up with all this princely ignoring of me.

Jehanne: If I'm lying there'll be none of the king's men left to punish me. But I'm not lying.

For the first time his eyes came to hers. She could see that he understood perfectly what her track was: that she'd be sacrificed, hanged, piked by soldiers, burnt perhaps. Burnt dear God! He knew it was all going to happen: he made her certain about it, was even pained by its prospect. The muscles of her legs began jumping.

Regnault: You'll have to wait and see if we're doing you a service.

Yolande: Don't discourage the girl.

But the chancellor's eyes had withdrawn, he wouldn't be giving her anything more.

Master of Requests: Mademoiselle Jehanne, the king requires you to travel with a supply column to Orleans. Entering the city won't be easy because the English have earthworks and forts on all the approaches to the city from Blois and on both sides of the river . . .

She felt terrible power in her guts, her dead, her un-assailable womb.

Master of Requests: You will of course be travelling with royal officers who know how this sort of operation is carried out.

She whispered.

Jehanne: Oh brother Jesus.

Master of Requests: You will travel to Blois by way of Tours. There the Treasury has ordered armour for you and there you will speak with the king . . .

Jehanne: Armour?

She remembered the sense of entrapment it gave.

Yolande: You can't campaign in shirt and stockings.

All at once there was a long silence. No one had, for the moment, the talent to break it. It seemed that everyone there, even the queen, Machet, the Chancellor, the Master of Requests, knew everything that was going to happen, had the scent of all her possibilities in their nostrils. The scent in particular of her royalty and death.

Riding to Mass next morning she saw a long column of horsemen moving down the rue St Etienne. Madame Rabateau plucked her sleeve as if to say they ought to move aside and let the group pass.

Jehanne: But why?

Nonetheless doing what Madame Rabateau said.

She saw Monsieur de Gaucourt leading the column. Machet sat beside him in a brilliant coat, ermine and cloth of gold. And then Alençon rode past her, looking sober as a lost brother returning in a dream. Behind him, wearing a cap of fur, and miserable with the morning cold, the king. Then lords and knights, archers, pikers, monks, stewards, a hundred people.

Jehanne: The King. The King's been *here*?

Madame Rabateau: You have to understand, he isn't a strong man . . . Queen Yolande tells me he's simply afraid.

Jehanne: Afraid?

Madame Rabateau: Of what's been started here. The mortgages. Committing the army.

Jehanne: He doesn't have to be afraid. I'm the one . . .

Madame Rabateau: I know. I know.

There was a little room to ride after him on Alençon's little gift-horse between the walls and the flanks of the column and under the unsafe balconies. *Dauphin!* she screamed over the chatter of knights, the noise of hooves. *Dauphin!* She galloped after him. He deserved to be flogged.

180

In her short gallop up the side of the convoy she under-stood she was immune from punishment. Anyone could have pulled her up with an arrow or a drawn sword. But she had the same amazing amnesty from all discipline as those mock kings had in old stories. Who were appointed by true kings to have one hectic season of royal authority before they were killed for the king's health.

Jehanne: DAU-PHIN!

De Gaucourt had wheeled back from the head of the column.

Her horse ran in under the muzzle of his and rebounded off its shoulder. It was going to fall but there wasn't room. Her own leg was crushed sideways against the wall of a shop-front and the horse got back its balance by dancing furiously on its hooves.

De Gaucourt: Jehanne, the king will see you when he wants to. In Tours.

She could see that Alençon too had turned back and was frowning over de Gaucourt's shoulder. De Gaucourt seemed petulant that the king's escape from Poitiers hadn't evaded her. There was a childish exchange of insults between the girl and him.

De Gaucourt: He doesn't talk to pig-girls who call him dauphin.

The king was already looking over *his* shoulder saying softly, wearily *Let her through, let her through.*

Jehanne: You came close to breaking off my leg at the knee. I hope you can manage the same trick with the Goddams.

De Gaucourt: Sow!

Jehanne: Cretin!

De Gaucourt: Bitch!

Jehanne: Bloody peasant!

Charles: Let her through, let her through.

The king's nose glowed weirdly in the morning cold. Some cold blue royal stones sat on his fingers, outside his gloves.

Gaucourt let her by. Riding towards Charles she could feel the bruising of her leg. She looked up at the king on his big Belgian horse.

Jehanne: I'm your truest mother—not that whore who

181

keeps pet monkeys and not even Yolande. I'm your mother in Brother Jesus and you need my blood. Why won't you damn well talk to me?

Charles: Do I have to talk to you all the time?

Jehanne: Do you believe me, Dauphin?

Charles: I don't have to talk to you all day. Or is that the contract?

Poor Charles was trying to do the remote act with the eyes that Regnault and Fat Georges were so good at.

Jehanne was speaking quietly now, was a woman offended to her roots.

Jehanne: You saw me every day at Chinon.

Charles: I don't have to be the same all the time. Then I was excited. I didn't know how much trouble was involved.

Jehanne: I want to be with you. You're my only love.

Charles: And I respect you, I respect you. Fair enough?

Jehanne: Then you should have told me you were here.

He actually showed his teeth.

Charles: Because you're my mother? Motherhood's a very sore subject with me.

Jehanne: You should have let me know!

Charles: You would have bullied your way in.

Jehanne: I'm not a bully.

Charles: My God!

Jehanne: All my blood is for you.

Charles: Don't talk about it all the time!

Jehanne: I beg your pardon, Dauphin!

Charles: What do you want? I'm buying you armour. I'll give you horses and a flag with *my* lilies on it. I'll make you my limb. All these soldiers understand it. Otherwise you could be dead already for your continued lack of politeness.

Jehanne: Except Monsieur de Gaucourt. He doesn't know I'm your limb.

Charles: It's nothing to crow about. Scapegoats get away with murder. Till their throats are cut.

Her eyes stung and she started crying at his crass manners. Pain blazed in her damaged knee-cap.

He closed his eyes.

Charles: Will you let me go now?

Jehanne: You're the king, Dauphin. You go where you wish. And talk to who you want to.

She backed her palfrey to the wall where Alençon the giver waited. The royal column began moving again, watching the girl as they went by. They seemed so many eyes ratifying the existing arrangement.

Alençon: If you see the furniture wagons outside the bishop's place, ask them to hurry.

Jehanne: Yes.

He put his hand on her wrist.

Alençon: My little soldier.

Jehanne: Don't talk down to me, Monsieur.

He shrugged, he was a little hurt. But she couldn't have him taking over the dominance in their relationship. *My little soldier!*

Alençon: How's the horse?

Jehanne: First-rate. Otherwise Monsieur de Gaucourt would have really skittled us.

Alençon: Not a word to anyone. But they're talking of naming me commander-in-chief.

Jehanne: I hope it's true.

Even she knew it was an honorary title. The authority would be with strange men—la Hire, the Bastard—of whom she'd only heard fables and legends.

In Tours there was an armourer by appointment who took her measurements for a steel suit. To be made quickly. While she stood in his front room and he ran around her chattering, Jean de Metz knocked on the door and wanted two mail suits for himself and his man de Honnecourt.

His eyes narrowed. He said *Jehanne* as if he was looking at her across a river. His eyes said *no high-class armourer's going to be very sedulous about me and poor bloody Honnecourt.*

She heard him talking to one of the armourer's journeymen about mail.

Jehanne: Listen, they tell me that mail won't keep arrows out.

She spoke too loudly and eagerly because of the illusion of distance between Jean and herself.

De Metz: Neither will this stuff.

Jehanne: They tell me it depends on how the arrow strikes.

Armourer: You have to be a little unlucky for an arrow to pierce steel. A bolt will, of course, there's no protection against bolts. But mail . . .

Jehanne suddenly thought, it's all useless, this stuff. It's only old–fashioned politeness that forces a person to get fitted out with it.

De Metz: It's a matter of finance. I don't suppose you offer credit . . . ?

Armourer: I'm sorry, sir. I'm holding so many credit notes from the Treasury. I have to raise credit myself. On the credit. The banks are the only ones who win.

Jehanne: I'll talk to Queen Yolande. You ought to have a steel suit.

De Metz: I wouldn't want that.

The ancient brutal eyes of Jean de Metz, who had started in the business at the age of twelve, warned her off arranging favours.

She would have liked to give him the rights to her suit—she didn't want her armour. It would be like living in a perpetual dusk.

The king was feeling well in Tours and being a canon (honorary) of the cathedral agreed on a Thursday to touch people for king's evil on the steps of St Gatien. Yolande, Chancellor Regnault and the girl went there and stood behind him. But the clergy had made it their own spectacle: canons of the cathedral flanked the king and the dean read a vast speech in Latin to the scrofulous people in the square. At its close the sufferers made a long and patient line up the stairs. They were interested, you could see, in how bad the person in front was: had the glands ulcerated yet, had they split open into a permanent sinus? This column of people with awesome throats wavered forward like phantoms in distorting mirrors. There were babies too, carried by mothers. Elected early in life to the king's evil.

Each victim the king touched on the head with a gloved hand. The glove would be burned later. The glove took the disease from the sufferer, the fire took it from the glove, the upper air took it from the fire.

At each touching a priest intoned a formula that said, *The King touches you, the Lord God restores you.*

And across the square a thin deacon in a green dalmatic was taking three sols from everyone who had been touched.

The canons started processing back into the cathedral with the glove that had soaked up so much swelling and putrefaction. The deacon strolled across the square squinting into the open velvet mouth of the collecting bag.

Jehanne took the king's elbow.

Jehanne: Should they sell your touch?

She pointed to the thin deacon. He had reached the cathedral stairs and had put on a face less fiscal to pass his lord king and dignitaries.

Jehanne: They shouldn't sell your touch.

Yolande: Come now . . .

De Gaucourt: For God's sake!

Jehanne: They can't sell the king's touch!

Charles: It's all right. They're building an ambulatory at the north end.

The deacon bowed and went through into the nave.

Jehanne: You know how much it's worth to them? Three sols a time! They value the king's touch at three sols.

De Gaucourt: People can't pay more. For God's sake!

Jehanne: Sir Deacon!

She had yelled. She heard the Chancellor sigh behind her. She rushed into the cavernous dusk of the church. Under the great vaulting the little deacon looked as if he might bolt with the bag of sols, down the nave past the sepulchres of dead bishops of Tours to sanctuary beyond the chancel.

Jehanne: You must give me that bag, please.

The king and Yolande had come in behind her.

Charles: Jehanne, Jehanne, let it go.

Jehanne traced the outline of the impossibility with her hands, a little tentatively, since the man *was* clergy.

Jehanne: You just can't sell the king's touch.

Deacon: Mademoiselle, I . . . Your Majesty . . . I must obey the Dean.

Yolande suddenly broke the impasse.

Yolande: Give it up, Brother Deacon. I'll speak to the Dean.

The deacon came up and surrendered it to Jehanne.

Yolande: Tell the Dean the money will be returned to all with king's evil.

185

Charles: Tell him I'm sorry.

He had said in Poitiers she was his limb. Now he was begging pardon for some unmanageable part of his anatomy.

The deacon turned away. Jehanne imagined the Dean in the sacristy, his cope off, his account books open, waiting to make the tally.

Jehanne: You ought to have more pride, Dauphin.

Charles wiped his nose.

Charles: No doubt, no doubt.

Yolande left them—out of some sort of sensitivity.

Charles: Those people—they get their scrofula cured. Who cures me of my king's evil? Who cures me?

Jehanne's ears prickled.

Jehanne: You know who.

Charles: And you're like the glove that gets burnt.

She bit on her fear, but found with pain that it was her chapped lower lip her teeth were savaging.

Jehanne: It ends, my pain will end. And Brother Jesus . . .

Charles: Yes?

Jehanne: His heart will open to me. I'll walk about . . . in there. In his garden.

Charles: I don't want you to suffer.

But she could tell his mind had already drifted from her. She could suspect that he might not feel any deep fever of bereavement on her day.

Except that when he was an old king, refined by her sacrifice, he might wake with an inconsolable pity in his thin heart.

She was sent to tailors in Tours! They ran up a houppelande, blue with lilies, for wearing over her armour. She had forgotten what a lust for good male clothes, for cloth-textures, she had.

Then a terrifying fitting at the armourer's, in the stink of metallic dust and metal polish. Putting on the tomb of metal.

The armourer told over the names of the pieces as apprentices strapped them on.

Armourer: Well, first we have the breast plate, then the backplate. Then further down the pansière to protect your belly and the garde-reins to look after your kidneys. And just to prevent a lance getting under your breast plate, these metal strips from the waist down called tassettes. Then six pieces for the arms: the cannon, the épaulière . . . you'll get to know them . . . and four pieces for the legs. The shoes are called solerets.

They were strapping her legs in greaved steel. All the time she sweated and felt she might scream in panic.

Jehanne: It seems very heavy.

Armourer: It's the lightest we make—you'll get used to it. About sixty-five English pounds.

On her walks around Tours she kept meeting knights whose property was now in English hands. Each of them wanted her to say, once Orleans was relieved, her insight would tell her to lead the army in exactly the direction of his lost real estate.

So when someone called Sir Jean d'Aulon stopped her in the street she thought, it's just another hard-up gentleman with a mortgage and lost property north of the Loire. He was a quiet man, but direct.

D'Aulon: They call me honest Jean. By that they mean I'm the poorest knight banneret in the army. I'm not married because no girl's old man is very interested in estates that have been in the keeping of the Goddams for the last eleven years. I have to state I live off the credit of Monsieur Georges de la Tremoille, the Chamberlain. But I'm not his spy, he keeps me out of kinship. I've fought with la Hire and Poton, who are the only two decent generals in the French army, apart from the Bastard himself.

She nodded—she'd been listening to the same speech all week. The next sentence would be *I think that after Orleans the offensive has got to be in the direction of le Le Mans / Château-dun / Etampes / Montereau / Montargis.* They could prove it always by making little invisible maps on the palm of their left hand with the index finger of the right.

D'Aulon: I'll be very happy to give you every service.

Jehanne: You don't understand, Sir d'Aulon. The king's paying my bills and they're big bills. But I've got twelve sols in my purse, that's all. My page is supported by the du Belliers, my clothes are paid for with treasury notes.

The Duke of Alençon gave me my best horse. I can't pay wages . . .

He was thin, she noticed, but all that was there had the appearance of muscle. His face: tanned. Features: leathered by pilgrimages or campaigns.

D'Aulon: They didn't tell you: the king appointed me your equerry. Yolande arranged it. She trusts me. And I take an oath to you so you can trust me.

Jehanne: What does an equerry do?

D'Aulon: He . . . *I* manage your staff, your pages and heralds, their upkeep, our upkeep. I act as your treasurer too. I will have ample finances to pay for escorts for you, or outfit a limited number of troops in your name if you order me to. I arrange your accommodation, pay your bills and eat with you and your chaplain if you don't dine out.

Jehanne: All with twelve sols?

D'Aulon: I believe you also got a bagful from the canons of St Gatien.

Jehanne: If I'd known I was going to have an equerry I'd have kept it.

He was about thirty-four or five. If Jehanne had always been by instinct angel of contempt for the ageing codes of knighthood, he would be stubbornly perfect knight. Contradicting each other they would get on together very successfully, and he would wonder and she would respect.

What else can be said about him? If he ever stepped down from his simple dimensions and went out looking for whores or singing risqué songs, no one ever reported it. Or reported if he ever wept.

Jehanne: Sir Jean, this is my page Minguet.

D'Aulon: Hello Sunshine!

In Tours she stayed with the du Puys, friends of Queen Yolande. One afternoon she found visitors waiting for her in the du Puys' upstairs hall. A young Augustinian monk sat by the wall. He kept his eyes to himself. You could tell he was from a good convent; was freshly ordained priest and awed by it; wasn't a career cleric.

A soldier waited there also, in a mail coat, facing and

admiring the big fireplace. For it was built like a small cathedral, spired and buttressed. When the knight turned it was Bertrand. He had a smile as broad, as remember-the-good-times, as you could ever expect him to wear.

He held out a ring.

Bertrand: Your mother sent this.

It was a gold-coloured ring with writing on it.

She held it, believing him, and a terrible lust rose in her for the sweet, tight, unreasonable griefs, loves and pities that filled kitchens in Greux and Domremy-à-Greux.

Jehanne: My mother.

Bertrand: We met at le Puy on Great Friday. I know that's a long way from the Meuse, but the country's all pretty safe.

Le Puy was a pilgrimage place: they had a black Virgin there, brought from Egypt by Saint-King Louis. They said that before the Virgin was born the prophet Jeremiah had sculpted this statue in sycamore wood.

Jehanne: Did Jacques go?

Bertrand: Just Zabillet. And Madame Aubrit. And Madame Hélène de Bourlémont. They've heard all about you. What they hadn't heard I told them. It frightens them a little.

Jehanne: Imagine how I feel.

But she nodded in the direction of the priest, who didn't seem to be, but must be, listening.

Bertrand came up and whispered to her. His breath was thin, very sour.

Bertrand: They're frightened if you don't drive the Goddams out they'll be burned for impersonating saints.

The Augustinian went on keeping custody of his eyes and ears in his chair by the wall. He seemed guileless and didn't want to overhear any secrets: not being a political monk, one would hope.

Jehanne: What are they, children?

Bertrand: They feel they started all this off. With the confraternity.

Jehanne: They think Madame Aubrit in her own flesh and Madame de Bourlémont in hers are *that* important?

Bertrand: I worry about it a little myself.

Jehanne: No one will ever hear about it. It's my business.

It's no theologian's business. Madame Aubrit in her own flesh hasn't a thing to worry about. What are the words on this ring?

Bertrand: It says Jesus–Maria.

She found herself not only kissing the ring but sucking at it as if it were nourishing.

Jehanne: Who's the monk?

Bertrand: Père Pasquerel. Your mother and Aubrit met him at le Puy.

He called out to the boy. He *was* just a boy and looked utterly virgin with a flat dark face.

Bertrand: This is Mademoiselle Jehanne.

Pasquerel: I met your mother in le Puy.

Jehanne: Sir Bertrand said.

Pasquerel: She asked me to . . . to look after you.

It was in his favour that he could tell on sight that *looking after her* was a little beyond his limits, as creditable as these were.

Pasquerel: I'm lector at the Augustinian monastery here, I went to le Puy to get the plenary indulgence that operates in the years when Good Friday coincides with the Feast of the Annunciation. It did this year. The crowds!

Bertrand: The crowds!

Pasquerel got to the point.

Pasquerel: Mademoiselle, do you want me to be your chaplain? Your mother asked me, my prior says he will arrange it with the Queen of Sicily if you want it. I say Mass very delicately, I don't rattle through it. If you confess to me I'd rather die than give anyone any intelligence about what you confessed . . .

Jehanne: I would like it. Could you say a Mass in St Gatien for my equerry, my page, Bertrand, and myself?

As d'Aulon had predicted, she suddenly had a chaplain.

And although Yolande objected to the man she chose, it wasn't so important for Yolande to know what a sibyl confessed, to place a corruptible confessor on the girl's staff when, in any case, the girl talked freely enough at table and wherever else they met.

On the first floor of a nearby town house Jean, Duke of Alençon, was committing grotesque adultery. Madame

Christine du Rhin stood above him grinning into an Italian drug-pot.

Alençon: What is it? Henbane? Hemlock? Belladonna?

Madame du Rhin: You'll fly, darling. You'll see wolves and bears and take on animal shapes and copulate like a donkey or a bull. You'll think me the sweetest lady bear you've ever seen.

She went on rubbing the grease into his genitals, up the walls of his thighs, over his chest. The influence of the drugs entered his body through lice bites collected in an old inn on the way from Poitiers to Tours.

He was losing power in his legs, but once the witchcraft took over and he became the menagerie of rutting beasts she promised, then there'd be no chance to talk business. He would wake in the end, but Christine would have gone home.

Alençon: Did you talk to your husband about Mastracoute?

He had had the idea of offering a six-year lease on three of his châteaux in Normandy from the date of the expulsion of the English in return for a short-term lease on one of her husband's châteaux now.

He wanted her to understand that the offer was serious, not just a pretext for getting her to bed.

But his animality ballooned at speed and he sank in its amplitude, bounced and somersaulted on its vast elastic surface. In the Flemish tapestries on the walls the animals pawed, barked, roared and moved forward to lick him. A unicorn on his left rose on its hind legs and winked at a vast bear. In the roots of the grass minuscule people roared sexual joy. He felt his feet leave the ground. Soon he would fly like a witch against the rosy firmament of her vulva, leap like a salmon up the falls of his seed. So he had to remind her about Mastracoute now.

Madame du Rhin: He's never home, my love. Yolande's pawning real plate, real plate. (His land, she suggested, was—being in occupied territories—almost notional.) He's spending all his time with the usual people: bankers, financiers . . .

Alençon: I might become the only commander-in-chief who's ever had to live in a bloody abbey.

A unicorn nuzzled his left ear as if to console.

191

Madame du Rhin: Don't think of it now, little ram.

Yet his last sane thought was of resentment. Her father had been a silk manufacturer ennobled by the mad Charles. A royal cousin now had to make financial arrangements with people like that and mess around in bedrooms with their daughters! Though, as he was torn into a pink upper air, she was a good craft to ride in, for her belly was firm and her breasts enabled a flying man good hold and emotions of heady safety.

The peopled earth lay far beneath them now. Imagine, he thought, all those tiny things bothering to raise grotesque structures of finance; imagine them lobbying, imagine them fucking in politic ways, always the right woman. He felt the same contempt God felt. In fact there was every chance—he must think about this when his brain got used to the altitude—there was every chance he was *himself* that ancient and potent gentleman. Steering her peasant tits he bounced off stars.

She said his body was sensitive and took in all the witching lotions very eagerly. When they began falling they fell together. In their falling there was no threat of splitting open on hard surfaces. There were no hard surfaces in the unlikely country Madame Christine knew so well.

When he woke he had not yet returned to Tours. He could smell butterflies and stallions about him, he was a wolf in the thick randy air and the wolf-goddess of the oak snarled far-off at him down avenues of gaping bears.

He got up to join her, moved the taffeta bed curtains aside and made for the vixen. He hurt his groin on a long table by the fireplace. He didn't stop. Christine's voice came from behind him, from the bed, not from the vixen down the corridor of great bears.

Madame du Rhin: Jean darling, what's the matter?

She came after him and caught him, for he found it hard to make headway against the size of his lust.

If he got to that vixen, he thought, what a grasp of the nature of things I'll be granted. How much more amenable will death, hell, goddesses, beasts, timbers, metals and earth be to me.

The vixen was displaced by an opening door. There stood

192

a monster, badly focused in a red cloak and black hose. It said nothing.

Lady du Rhin ran back to bed yelling out where were the damned servants?

The terrible thing in the red cloak, instead of becoming a member of the docile erotic landscape, punched him on the side of the head.

Giant: You. With the wife you have!

It punched him again on the ear.

It pulled out a thin-bladed sword and went to stand near Christine whose head alone could be seen, framed by the blue bed curtains.

Madame du Rhin: Mademoiselle, have some pity for those who are weaker than you are . . .

The deformity swiped at the curtains with its sword. Christine withdrew her head. You could hear her begin to sob, besieged in the draped bed.

Meanwhile Alençon was sweating with nausea and was grateful to recognize the floor as a floor and sit on it. When he looked up again he was no longer a wolf-head and Jehanne stood over him shrunk to her normal squatness.

He felt furious at her for finding him in this state.

Jehanne: Your squire and her maid tried to stop me on the way in. I told them I had a warrant from the king. I've just heard from Yolande that you *are* going to be named commander-in-chief. That it's settled.

Alençon: I knew it was more or less settled.

Jehanne: The smells in here!

Alençon lost his temper with her, with himself for letting himself be found like this, greasy with lust and herbal lotions.

Alençon: You've got no right to treat people the way you do. Just because you heard voices out in the pigshit somewhere. (He whispered.) This is only business.

Jehanne: In your bare balls, commander-in-chief, you don't look much different from the run of mankind.

Alençon: Nice talk for virgins!

Jehanne: I had brothers. All better built than you.

But she saw that she must stop the argument, that she kept it going because she wanted him to beg *her* pardon, not

Jesus's or the Duchess of Alençon's. If she had had something soft to weep on at eye height she would have wept with loss as on the morning she found Jean de Metz with a whore and put tears all over her horse. As well, she wanted to be provoked into beating up that soft white tart amongst the taffeta bed curtains.

This is worse than honest lust, she saw. Be sad for that poor dark businesslike duchess at Saumur.

He had found a wrap and was putting it around himself.

Jehanne: I won't have whores with the army. I won't have our army pouring its virtue away in whores' bellies.

He answered her quietly.

Alençon: A chaste army's hard come by.

Christine had her head, only her head, out of the curtains again.

Madame du Rhin: Mademoiselle, if you forgive me and agree not to report this to my husband or the Inquisitor, I'll make a general confession and go on pilgrimage.

How she wanted to hit the pale sensual face.

Jehanne: Why does she talk about Inquisitors?

The commander-in-chief was taking his clothes from the places they'd been dropped. His hose were strung light-heartedly over a lectern near the fireplace.

The sweet, tainted face appeared again amongst the curtains.

Madame du Rhin: A total general confession, Mademoiselle, and a Rome pilgrimage.

She was afraid of what curses Jehanne would leave behind in the air. The suspicion infuriated Jehanne, who turned to the commander-in-chief. Alençon had one leg in his hose and had a shirt on.

Jehanne: About the army: soldiers won't blaspheme. No swearing on the netherparts of saints of King Jesus.

Alençon: You're very simple-minded about soldiers.

Jehanne: Am I? I don't think I am. I know what soldiers are. They start fires in the middle of the floor and shit on the hearth. They cut pregnant women open just out of lack of *virtue*. Well, ours are going to have *virtue* . . .

She was using his own word against him.

Jehanne: Now will you come with me?

194

Alençon: Why?

Jehanne: Surely there's enough for you to do. Arrangements . . . orders . . .

He nodded and got his doublet on and latched up his points. On the way to the door he hesitated and called over his shoulder towards Madame du Rhin besieged in bed.

Alençon: Goodbye . . . Goodbye Madame . . .

There went Château Matracoute!

The armourer had asked does the young lady want a proper sword.

Jehanne thought of the swords at Fierbois. Hanging from the rafters because they had virtue, had figured in victories often prodigious.

Père Pasquerel, her chaplain, wrote to the priest-curators of Fierbois asking for a sword.

The next night Yolande mentioned it at table.

Yolande: Charles Martel's sword is said to be buried at Fierbois . . .

Later the same night Mesdames Margaret and Catherine visited her.

Madame Ste Catherine: Rose takes sword . . .

Madame Ste Margaret: As wife takes husband.

Their voices went on like a pulse in her blood. Their persistence was only partly a comfort.

By noon the following day there was a story in the town that she had sent for the sword of Charles Martel in Fierbois, giving exact instructions about the place where it could be found by digging.

She complained to Yolande. Yolande said it was necessary to conjure up names. Even names from seven hundred years back.

Jehanne remarked satirically that after being in the earth seven hundred years, the weapon wouldn't have much of a cutting edge.

She began to feel all the tracery work Yolande and the Franciscans did on her was a kind of assault.

Jehanne: I'll tell people it isn't the truth.

Yolande: Deny a little and you deny the lot.

She smiled, that Queen of Sicily. That cool, percipient,

195

unafraid smile that had harried Charles from boyhood on.

Very early the next day, Pasquerel heard her morning confession in a corner of the first floor apartment where Jehanne slept with Madame du Puy. She thought Pasquerel an innocent. She decided to ask him about Yolande's hectic legend-making.

But however personally lilywhite Pasquerel might be, he had caught some sort of subtlety from his professors of theology.

Pasquerel: Even Jesus had to tolerate it. The story for example that he and the good thief shared the same bath when they were babies. Maître Gelu says it's a fantasy. Yet it's got this much truth in it: it's a story about how they were fated to each other from babyhood. Now the story of the sword of Martel has this much truth to it: that you're expected to do to the Goddams what Martel did to the Arabs. You see. Maître Gelu would say there's no sense in denying that sort of story.

But she was afraid of operating on such a ground where truth had varieties and there were varied species of it. It was the ground where Yolande and Regnault were masters. Even Pasquerel seemed to see this fear.

Pasquerel: Look at it this way. You won't stop people spreading stories.

Altogether it had been a preposterous week for Père Pasquerel. He had been made a chaplain on royal pay, heard the confession of a royal duke—how Alençon had gone flying adulterously about the earth with some affluent witch. And day by day, he (Pasquerel) learnt in confessional secrecy the girl's conscience.

When the sword came it was very large and in good condition, newly greased, five little crosses on the hilt. Yolande had sent a page to tell Jehanne to come to the hôtel de ville and accept it in front of various councillors, with ceremony.

Jehanne got Pasquerel to write a letter.

It said Jehanne preferred to accept this weapon in private. All the executive of the Armourers' Guild brought it to the du Puys', but only the man who had run up Jehanne's armour was let upstairs. Jehanne and Pasquerel were by the fire. Pasquerel was reciting Matins. The armourer stood drawing the blade in and out of its red velvet scabbard on which stood blue lilies.

Armourer: It's lovely work.

Jehanne: But so large. How can I carry it?

Nonetheless she had stood and was accepting it little by little into her hands.

Up the river from Tours, the city of Blois sat pleasantly on the north bank. The French army, the volunteers and the bought, sat there in the first haze of spring in drying tents on the slopes around the town. The slopes were drained well, the French army had not suffered that winter as Yolande said the Goddams had. All that month of April corn and cattle had come in from Gien, Bourges, Châteaudun. Corn depots and pastures were found across the river in the suburb called Vienne.

On an April day when broom was beginning to bud on the sides of the Tours-Onzain-Blois road, Jehanne found a timbered place five miles from Blois. There she went amongst the trees, taking Minguet with her. She stripped to her undershirt and drawers and Minguet began to arm her. D'Aulon was also put into armour by his young squire. In the sunlight at the side of the road Pasquerel waited, also her second page called Raymond, and the two heralds, Guyenne and Ambleville, appointed to her from the king's staff. Guyenne sang a song about love-making in Poitou and Limousin so lightly that one would think that to love was as easy as to breathe.

Jehanne called through the elms to d'Aulon.

Jehanne: All this must be awfully hot in summer.

She had been riding the palfrey the Duke of Alençon had given her. Now Raymond brought her charger, which he'd been leading all the way from Tours. It was black, a dozen years old. The boys, Raymond and Minguet, got her up there by way of a set of folding wooden steps. Minguet carried them about at his saddle as part of his professional field equipment.

Up there, folded in steel, she felt so clumsily arrogant that she couldn't help expecting some large hand to swipe at her out of the broad day.

Come on! she called out. D'Aulon was on his charger. One of the heralds had her white banner. Minguet carried her white standard. On the standard, Brother Jesus held the world in his hand. The words from the ring her mother had sent from le Puy were painted there—not in some sentimental recompense to Zabillet, but because they were appropriate to her own case. She thought nevertheless it would be good if Zabillet could one day know—it made her feel a slightly better daughter.

When she rode in sight of the first tents and hovels on the slopes north of the road into Blois she called for her standard. There was a notch in the chamfron for her to put the butt of it, but her hand shuddered and it took two tries to place it there. The standard itself was made of buckram and did not flap in the wind off the river. This made it harder still to hold up.

Oh Brother Jesus, and Maria carrying the unasked-for god-baby!

The two heralds rode to the front of the line, little Raymond who had pimples and was short-sighted blew a horn.

Men came loping out of the shacks and the marquees. They very quickly knew what dignitary it was, they started calling their friends out from indoors. Some of them wore rough shirts and clout-cloths only, bare-legged. They seemed men of large frame and reddish complexion and she could not understand what they spoke.

D'Aulon: They're Scotsmen, Mademoiselle. A strange people. Very wild. A backward race.

They kept very quiet, just watching. South of the road, in the river meadows, were Piedmontese. You could smell the metallic mud in which they were camped. They were watching too. They whistled and yelled out small barrages of greeting, but without much zeal either way. They had a corpse amongst them, some soldier dead of spring fever, wrapped tight in a shroud, and Jehanne had the impression that he was levering himself on his shoulder-blades to watch. The French camp, high up by the château walls, was noisier. They whistled too and called *Noël,* but perfunctorily. They called, *Going to slice up Talbot, sweetie?*

She told them, *If Talbot isn't wise enough to go home.*

It would have taken a campaigner's ear to judge how much of all the noise was mocking and how much applause, or what proportions of each were in a given soldier's throat. You could guess there were reptilian obscenities inhabiting that tangle of noise. All you could do was hold on to the standard and look them in the eye. Your army.

A French knight rode out of the château and met them. He said d'Alençon had sent him to invite her in.

D'Aulon: They're in a strange mood.

Knight: They haven't been paid. The duke has to go to Tours to see about it. There are so many slip-ups.

D'Aulon: They won't just wander off, will they?

Jehanne thought, this is immovable, this army and me. Neither of us are going home for any reason.

Knight: The duke's given them his word. You know what the hold-up is. Fat Georges.

D'Aulon said nothing, since he lived on credit extended by de la Tremoille.

When she went into the great hall striped with daylight d'Alençon came to her and kissed her hand. His eyes clearly said *Am I forgiven, cleared to take part?* She thought, if they were all like this . . . !

Alençon: Come and meet two officers from Orleans.

He led her to a trestle table at one end of the room. A weathered little man with a delicate, bunched mouth watched her come. He had one hip hitched on the table-top. Beyond the table was a taller less fragile Monsieur. They both wore long loose luxuriant gowns of satin and braid.

The Duke of Alençon caressed the elbows of the smaller man.

Alençon: This is Monsieur Etienne Vignolles.

There was a sort of blue torment in his eyes such as you see in very good monks who are straining for *the vision.* Had he stood he wouldn't have been an inch taller than her.

Alençon: You might have heard of him under his pet-name.

Jehanne: Oh?

Alençon: La Hire.

La Hire: Mademoiselle.

Jehanne: Monsieur la Hire, in the Barrois they use your name to frighten children.

La Hire whispered *Mademoiselle* again, in apparent gratitude. He couldn't even stand straight, this newly introduced nightmare, his shoulders stooped forward as if he'd damaged his back while terrifying some population.

The upright man was Monsieur Florent d'Illiers. He lacked savage by-names.

D'Illiers: How's my little brother-in-law Minguet? He's a bit of a dreamer. Kick his arse if he gives you trouble.

Jehanne: When Monsieur de Gaucourt gave Minguet to me he reminded me the boy was of better blood than I am. He told me not to kick him anywhere.

D'Illiers: Nonsense. Kick him wherever presents.

General d'Illiers, said Alençon, was taking the first contingent into Orleans in a few days. General la Hire had been there most of the winter. He had a sketch-map of the state of the city, which he showed. As he spoke there was no echo of screams from the Barrois in his almost scholarly blue eyes.

La Hire: There are two ways of getting to Orleans. Either along the north bank or the south. The English have made large earthworks and forts to cover all the main roads both north and south of the river. The one here called St Lorent is the biggest but maybe not the most important. You can sneak into the city by crossing the Paris road here, just south of the forest. And you can even get through in small numbers between any two of these forts on the west, even though the English have a ditch running all the way between them. On the other hand you can come down from south of the river, cross a few miles upstream and come down to the Burgundy Gate here. The English fort there is undermanned, and that makes approach from that end a very wise business.

Although there was that story about him flinging his helmet in the mud at Rouvray, at the battle in February when Fastolf rolled up the French and the Auvergnois troops got drunk, he didn't seem to have any passions. He spoke exactly and always said *the English,* never the mocking names: Goddams, coués. He was an engrossing monster.

With the logic of her gut, with the logic of her stature as sister-king, Jehanne knew certainly which way to go. By tapping the map with her right hand she suppressed la Hire's appraisal. Forgetting how he was in her screaming dreams at nine years of age.

Jehanne: The way I choose to go is this way, fair up against the forts . . . this one here, what's its name? . . . St Lorent. And this one . . .

La Hire: Croix-Boisée.

Jehanne: Indeed. Then straight in the main gate.

D'Illiers: The English wouldn't let it happen. They'd deploy most of their men against us before we got to the line of their fortresses.

He was surprisingly willing to discuss her idea as with an equal. He turned and asked la Hire. *Etienne?* he said.

La Hire: They'd have to. They've got the city people feeling helpless, they couldn't afford to let us in, to let *you* in, Mademoiselle. The Bastard's mentioned *you* in speeches.

Why is he admitting this to me? she asked herself. *Is he an ally of mine, this tiny killer?*

Jehanne: Very well. That's the way we get them then.

D'Illiers: It's not all as rosy as that. The way they can't afford to let supplies in, we can't afford to lose them, and there's risk of losing the battle and the supplies if we force a *tête-à-tête* between the river and the Paris road. (He added something, with a rough, not-very-loving indulgence.) We could even lose you, Mademoiselle.

Jehanne: It won't happen.

La Hire: You can't be sure, Mademoiselle.

Jehanne: It isn't the season for that sort of thing to happen to me. It just isn't time. You can be assured of that.

She was pleased with the way she'd regained her brusqueness—treating them the way she'd treated de Baudricourt.

D'Illiers: Mademoiselle, I don't think your seasons are the sole consideration.

Jehanne: I thought it had all been settled by the Royal Commission. You've been told about the Royal Commission.

D'Illiers: Which one, Mademoiselle?

Jehanne: The one into the question of whether I was a witch and heretic.

D'Illiers: That one.

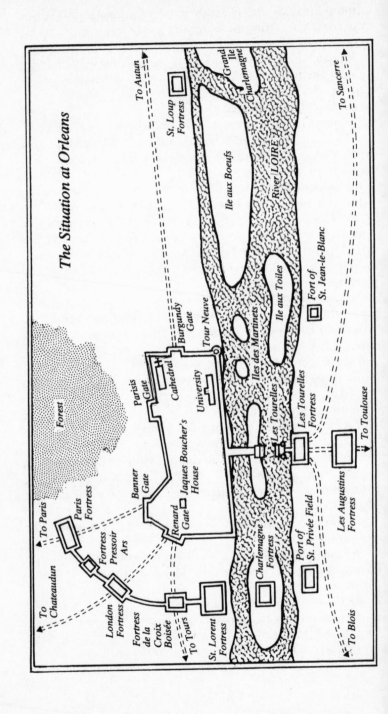

The Situation at Orleans

D'Illiers winked at la Hire. It wasn't a nice, uncle-style wink. What if there were generals with whom the Royal Commission didn't count for much?

Jehanne: Why in the name of God would the king send me? Fit me out with weapons and equerries? All that? If I'm not to give orders?

One of la Hire's shoulders dipped, as if in respect for the Royal Commission. She was glad d'Illiers would be leaving for Orleans soon and la Hire staying on.

La Hire: You have your certainties, Mademoiselle. I don't think the Royal Commission said they were absolute certainties. Monsieur the Duke and all of us . . . we have to acquire our certainties with a bit more difficulty.

Jehanne: There is a royal warrant. It says I have to be consulted.

Alençon was a little panic-stricken between his generals and his prophetess.

Alençon: And you shall be, Jehanne.

La Hire: But there are more generals to arrive yet.

D'Illiers: And all of us are subject to the Royal Council.

He could have been saying, *that six-week circus in Poitiers. What does it mean to us?* Jehanne remembered a story she had heard of la Hire: how at the siege of Le Mans he dismounted to ask a priest for a quick absolution. The priest asked him to confess; he said there's no time to confess, just time for absolution. The priest refused. Back in his saddle, la Hire said, *God, I want you to treat General la Hire the way General la Hire would treat you if he was God and God was a general.* From a man like d'Illiers or even de Gaucourt it would be a good joke. From la Hire it came with a cold workmanlike madness.

That night Maître Machet came to tell her the Council wanted her to send a letter of summons to the English outside Orleans.

She wondered how you got a letter to the English. Well, her heralds would take it, Monsieur Ambleville, Monsieur Guyenne. She remembered Guyenne's sweet lyric voice.

Machet: It's all right. They've got immunity.

But only under the weird laws that had given Orleans its immunity. The Goddam English had annulled those laws. So, in her guts, had she.

Machet: They'd have no sane reason to detain heralds. Believe me.

Jehanne: Ambleville and Guyenne . . . they can take it right into St Lorent and put it in Talbot's hand?

Machet: I'll send a secretary.

Jehanne: Père Pasquerel must read it to me in its final form.

Machet: Of course.

The letter she worked on called first on the English king (seven-years-old, what must he think of the jagged world dad Hal Monmouth left him?), on Bedford, Suffolk, John Lord Talbot, and Thomas Scales, all to give up and surrender the keys of all the king's cities they had taken in France. Divinely sent, she'd come to ask for the be-Englished Duke of Orleans and his city back. (Had the Voices spoken of that duke or was it the daily subcutaneous voice of Madame Rabateau?) All soldiers, gentlemen or otherwise, in the English army outside Orleans, go home. The king (said the letter) and I are willing to make peace if you do. The King of England must understand: I am a leader whom you can't argue with. The English king can't hold France because Brother Jesus refused to recognize him. Brother Jesus recognizes Charles, the virgin Jehanne recognizes Charles and Charles will enter Paris in the end.

Late at night the letter was impressively embellished in a small hand in Blois château. Pasquerel read it aloud to her. He liked it. Quite strong. She was tired enough to doubt if he was an authority on strength. Ambleville and Guyenne were sent for.

Meanwhile, it was found that some businessmen in Tours and Blois had agreed, after late-night consultations with members of Yolande's council, to underwrite the army's pay.

At ten o'clock that morning, under a streaky sky that promised no such surprise, a twenty-five-year-old boy called Monsieur Gilles de Rais, Marshal of France, rode into camp. With him three hundred peacock knights and their staffs. They could have arrived the night before but Gilles had made them camp down the road to polish armour and enamels and have their servants unpack the best silk tunics and dress the war-horses. Like Yolande's Councillors and the financiers they must have worked half the night.

He was Breton and his spectacular battalion were all Bretons. He was said to be the wealthiest young man in the country. First, he rode glowing through the dusty bivouacs. He wore white silk, blue pomegranate trees covered it in groves and on the blue branches, orange pomegranates. Behind him, a forward guard of twenty immaculate knights. Next, on belled pack-horses, pieces of piping.

Alençon and Jehanne watched from a window of the château.

Alençon: That's his portable organ. He takes it everywhere with him. Forty pack-horses! He's a music-lover. Not only that. Look.

Beyond, and far enough behind the pack-horses so as not to be tainted by the dust they raised, a choir of little boys and young men, all singing in Breton under the direction of a backward-walking and stumbling choirmaster.

It was a pity that raw music from the Scots camp blurred their song.

Within half an hour he walked into the great hall of the château. His legs were long, he moved beautifully, was beautiful with eccentric blue eyes and red lips moist as if always in hope of some special word or event alighting between them. Something really special. Nothing as mundane as kisses. His hair was somewhere between red and gold. Had Jehanne ever seen a more dazzling man?

He came straight to her and took her hand. He was slightly cross-eyed with fervour.

De Rais: You've got no idea, Mademoiselle, how much the things you say interest me? Do you know alchemy?

Jehanne: No, Monsieur.

De Rais: You're a disciple of the Arabs!

Jehanne: Disciple . . . ?

De Rais: Or a gifted herbalist?

With his questions he was a sort of pagan version of the Poitiers examination.

Jehanne: I'm not very strong on herbs. With herbs, you've got to know what you're doing.

205

De Rais: Indeed. You've got no idea how much you excite me. Would you like to hear my choir?

Jehanne: Yes, yes.

At length he spoke to the others. Machet didn't like him much, kept niggling at him.

Machet: You still keep a choir, my lord? Of small boys?

De Rais: You know how I prize a well-harmonized choir.

Machet: Actually, there are a lot of good tenor monks in the camp.

De Rais: Lumped together from a dozen places, untrained. The nearly good is worse than the execrable. My boys are the sweetest voices I can buy. From Normandy some of them, others from Périgord, a number from Lombardy.

Machet: Your interest then is straight musical?

The half-mad blue eyes blinked.

De Rais: You know my passion and what I will spend on it, Maître Machet. However, no one could have thought of or bought a woman like Mademoiselle Jehanne. (It was an adroit tack.) You must give us your orders, Mademoiselle.

La Hire, who was there, nodded as if he was keen for orders from her. She doubted it.

At night, during a dinner in the great hall, she overheard Monsieur de Rais roaring into Admiral Culant's ear. He had drunk a lot of straight Muscadet brought in by his own supply wagons.

De Rais: But so squat, so plain, so young. Who would have expected the forces of light to show so much imagination?

She didn't like to be talked of in the same tone as was used for wonderful storms, plagues, victories or curious animals from the East. It seemed that Yolande, two places away, noticed her pain. When the dinner ended she pulled Jehanne to one side of the hall. Beyond the window they could see thousands of camp-fires, ordered, almost votive burning in a camp becoming more and more ritually pure. Tomorrow Gilles de Rais's choir would sing at the morning Mass in the priests' camp.

Yolande: Before you start forming opinions about that boy de Rais there are things you ought to know. He's a good soldier, better than your sweet Alençon. He's massively cunning, a diplomat. Once more, your Alençon doesn't come up to him. We need his help—his Breton companies are the best fed, best clothed, best armed. Last of all, he is one of the three soldiers *you* can trust. You might wonder why?

Jehanne wondered.

Yolande: Because he's got a passion for the colourful. For prophecies, visions, flashes from the blue. That's your strength. He'll give you money, time, sweat, because the mystic and the supernal are the things he's really willing to pay for. He is, in fact, a thorough freak.

Jehanne shrugged. She would have been happier with more homely virtues, more stable talents than Monsieur de Rais.

At noon the next day she was riding back with d'Aulon and her pages from High Mass in the clergy's camp when Bertrand stepped out from a line of tents and held his hand up. Quickly, as if afraid of being accused this time of yet grander impersonations than Messire, he pointed to two men on his left.

Both soldiers were grinning in moleskin trousers and shirts. They were her brothers, Jehan, a year older than her, and Pierrolot, fifteen years old.

She shifted on her horse and smiled at them. But there wasn't room for them in her scheme of things, where they wanted to be.

Jehanne: I can't get down off this big horse. It's all this steel I'm expected to wear. Whenever I get down the saddle looks higher than a roof.

They laughed again.

Jehanne: How do you like it here?

Pierrolot: What a crowd!

Jehan: It isn't comfortable in the camp.

He'd always been a main-chancer.

Jehanne: What do you want?

Jehan: A room maybe. In the château?

Jehanne: Full up.

Jehan: A pub?

Jehanne: Perhaps that. A room in a pub.

Jehan: What is it? (His voice was raised.) Why are you this way?

Jehanne: I'll get you food, bedding, better equipment. But you aren't going to live with me.

Jehan: Jesus.

He looked at Pierrolot, invoking family memories of her bloody-mindedness. Her grandeur about taking cows to pasture. Pierrolot didn't co-operate: he thought she'd promised them the world in promising food and something better than a blanket under the moon.

Jehanne: I have a small treasury now, you see. My equerry manages it.

Jehan: Equerry, Jesus!

Pierrolot: Equerry.

Pierrolot said it slowly, feeling it over like an artifact drifted in from Bohemia.

Jehanne: I'll look after you. I won't be living with my family any more. That's the way of it.

Jehan: Well! Thanks!

Jehanne: Come to Orleans. You'll be safe.

Jehan: Like Cousin Collot? Got killed by a mortar. Mengette bringing him home in a handcart.

Jehanne: It won't happen to you. Their great Lord Salisbury got the same injuries as Collot. Rednecks have got as good a chance as anyone. War's changing.

Jehan: Is it?

Jehanne: Yes.

Jehan: Why?

Jehanne: Because I'm here.

Jehan: Jesus.

Jehanne: Where's your wife?

Jehan: With her mother. In Greux.

Jehanne: You understand: whores aren't permitted in the camp?

Jehan: The soldiers sodomise. The whores come in dressed as men.

Bertrand (pacifically): Not very many.

Jehan: Guess who they learned the dress-up trick from?

Jehanne: I'll see to them. I'll see to my sad sisters, brother. Have you got siege-hats?

Siege-hats were flat-crowned, steel, with a wide steel rim.

Pierrolot: What?

Jehanne: Siege-hats. For when the English drop things on you. They have fortresses all round Orleans from which they drop things on people. Hadn't you heard?

They were all pale and silent. Jehan, almost her twin, spawned as soon before her as Zabillet and Jacques could have managed, twinned to her by name, kicked at the track with the ball of his foot.

Jehanne: The forts are called St Lorent, St Loup, Croix-Boisée . . . you'll see them. I'll send Raymond and Minguet with three siege-hats.

Pierrolot: Raymond and Minguet?

Jehanne: My pages.

Jehan: Pages! Big horses! Equerries! Pages!

Jehanne: I've got two heralds too who are away on business at the moment. And then there's my chaplain Père Pasquerel. When you see him, feel free to confess.

Jehan: Jesus almighty Christ riding on a horse!

Jehanne clapped the neck of her mount.

Jehanne: Riding on a horse . . .

Pierrolot was simply pleased to be there, kept smiling at her privately, as if to say *I've eaten and slept with you and seen you crap and scratch yourself, and look at you!* What a roaring joke it is. Without Pierrolot, with two Jehans say, it could have been a nasty meeting.

At night the tall sun-face of Messire moved in her right eye, in the tropics of her right side.

Messire: The rose has its triumph in la Beauce. In King Jesus's garden of vengeance in la Beauce.

She went straight to Alençon's apartments and had him woken. Much influenced by the air of adventurous chastity Yolande's priests had created in the camp, he'd been sleeping. He gave you the idea that neither lust nor visitors usually woke him after eleven.

Jehanne: My dear duke, if someone said the la Beauce side, what would it mean to you?

Alençon: But you heard the other day. La Hire told you. La Beauce and Sologne.

Jehanne: I didn't hear anything about la Beauce and Sologne. Till just now.

Alençon: But they talked about nothing else. North bank. South bank. La Hire and d'Illiers said them by name.

Jehanne: I haven't heard the word la Beauce till now.

Alençon: La Beauce is the north bank, where the city is. Sologne the south, the suburbs of Orleans. La Hire and d'Illiers . . .

To his appal she took his face in both her hands. She held it very tight and he was frightened.

Jehanne: Will you believe me, lovely duke? I heard nothing of the name la Beauce till tonight.

Alençon: I believe you. It doesn't matter.

As a reward, she let his little face escape.

Jehanne: Anyhow, the army has to go by the la Beauce side. Fair up against the Goddam forts.

Alençon: Oh?

Jehanne: It will all happen in la Beauce.

Alençon: I see.

Jehanne: Will you give that order?

Alençon: I have to meet with the others first.

Jehanne: When? When?

Alençon: Tomorrow morning.

Jehanne: I'll be there?

Alençon: If you . . . all right.

As if to soothe her he told her to be ready, they'd be marching very soon. That didn't satisfy her. At last he had to be exact.

The war leaders would meet in the great hall at eight o'clock the next morning. Their decisions would go for immediate approval of the Royal Council. They could be on the road the day after tomorrow.

Jehanne: Ah!

The next morning was Tuesday. At eight, mist still filled the encampments but there was a strong sun behind it. At eight, Jehanne and d'Aulon were the only people in the great hall. Jehanne stamped from the conference table to the windows and back.

D'Aulon: You've got to remember that they're used to war, they've been warring for years and years. They don't feel as urgent about it . . .

De Gaucourt came in with a secretary twenty minutes late. Taking his seat, he said nothing to her. Then la Hire, mumuring Mademoiselle. He sat, joined his hands. Again like a good monk. He closed his eyes.

Then Marshal Gilles de Rais with a beautiful boy equerry, a skin so white-ripe your impulse was, as with fruit, to touch and test.

Gilles: You slept, Mademoiselle?

Jehanne: Thank you . . .

Gilles: Any prophetic dreams?

His lips were moist to take account of them.

At table, Monsieur de Gaucourt snorted thunderously. He must have had sinuses you could fit your fist in.

Then Culant, Alençon walked in.

Alençon: We haven't been idle, Jehanne, we've been inspecting the convoy.

All the others followed him in, found a place at table. The doors were locked. They all sat silent, waiting for Alençon's initiatives.

Alençon: The question of route. Jehanne's counsel indicates we travel by the north bank, direct for the city gates on the west.

In this way began Jehanne's first experience of those rituals called war councils. She didn't know that morning, but the rite was performed as a means of conjuring up power for the generals, that they might have some measure of rule over their army. The decisions that arose at the close of the ceremony were sometimes doomed to be overruled by the politicians. Often as unrelated to truth as the statement of the priest at Mass-end: And the light shines in the darkness and the darkness does not consume it. As if that day were to be somehow brighter than all its dead and squalid brothers. In that same spirit, the generals held formal councils.

Jehanne didn't yet understand that these were hopeful rites as well as military assemblies.

Alençon intoning therefore.

Alençon: Jehanne's counsel indicates we travel by the north bank.

De Gaucourt: Does the young lady's counsel understand that the English have two garrison towns between Orleans nd Blois? One at Beaugency, one at Meung. Both north of the river.

Jehanne: I think my counsel knows more about the Loire than you do, Monsieur.

She still heatedly remembered her injured leg in Poitiers.

De Gaucourt: This means that we have two garrisons on our flank all the way up to Orleans. They can make assaults on the convoy from the sides and have walled towns to withdraw to. Then, if anything goes wrong in front of Orleans, we have these same garrisons on our flank for the retreat.

Jehanne: My counsel guarantees things won't go wrong in front of Orleans.

De Gaucourt: Your counsel hasn't outlaid money. We all have. All of us. Except you and your counsel.

Jehanne: They're crude ways of thinking. We won't get anywhere thinking like that.

Marshal de Boussac and Poton were both laughing.

De Gaucourt: You'll go out the door. On your ear, girl.

Jehanne: Yes, on my ear. My knee-cap in Poitiers, my ear in Blois. You're really working me over, Monsieur.

Poton was hitting the table with two fingers and hissing *Lovely, lovely, lovely.* Gratification showed up too easily in the girl's face. De Gaucourt saw it.

Gilles, having heard she hadn't dreamed last night, was asleep. It was a question: whose gallantry would save the girl?

La Hire's voice had a sudden quality to it. *It* saved her.

La Hire: It isn't impossible, of course, the north bank. We all know from Rouvray that attacking a supply column has its dangers. If we keep formed up tightly, the English at Meung and Beaugency won't dare ride out. Now, when we get to the forts outside Orleans the greater part of the army can form up between the Paris road and St Lorent fort and the convoy with a strong guard could cross the same Paris road well to the north of the English line and come down to the Bannier or Parisis Gate, safe home.

He coughed resonantly—his little body sounded quite hollow.

Culant: I think we're all aware that yesterday Monsieur d'Illiers got his company of four hundred men into Orleans by the la Beauce bank.

De Gaucourt: You're not seriously backing up this idiocy.

Culant: I'm simply giving information.

Boussac: What's wrong with the Sologne bank? If we went by Sologne the best things of all would happen: the army would *get there* for a start . . . no bloody small consideration . . . the supplies can be barged down river to Orleans from a few miles upstream . . . the people inside the walls would get the girl the Bastard promised them. It has to be faced up to. The Bastard's made big of this girl. (The words had a double meaning.) Or will if given his chance.

Poton again hit the table with two fingers, saying, *Lovely, lovely, lovely.*

Jehanne: Marshal de Boussac, I understand your joke. It's a pity Marshal de Rais is asleep. I don't think it's his kind of humour.

Again Poton with his fingers . . .

La Hire began speaking. No one caught his first words. By his fourth or fifth there was entire silence. His authority was the highest at the table.

La Hire: . . . needed something to make much of. Both outside and inside Orleans, for the English and for us, conditions are bad. Outside, the English are short of men, they live badly, supplies are irregular, the English Council in Westminster have other problems—the west country, Ireland. They happen to be quite sick of demands made by the English Council in Normandy. It's a wrong-headed policy. Poor Johnnie Goddam outside Orleans feels he's the tip of a finger of a long hand and a long arm, and the head that works the arm and hand and finger-tip doesn't give a damn for him. He's ripe to be destroyed. But the people *inside* the city can't even see it. Once you go into that city it's like going into a kingdom of the mad. They can see the Goddam mud and misery from the walls and yet they can't see. The English have supernatural stature in the minds of the people inside the walls. The poor Bastard Royal has to make promises to balance that out. His large promise is the girl. I share Monsieur de Gaucourt's concern for the convoy.

213

But whatever else fails to be brought to Orleans, the girl has to be.

Alençon: Then isn't the surest way the Sologne bank?

La Hire: Even if we meet the English head–on in la Beauce, the girl can easily be slipped round the flanks. The English, you have to understand, are short of horses.

Boussac: All right, the girl aside, we can win a set battle on the north bank. But we've all seen . . . haven't we . . . the full–scale battle thing fall flat before against a hungry, muddy pack of bastard English. I won't mention names . . .

Jehanne: Agincourt.

Boussac: I won't mention names!

The talk went on for hours. Far away in the camp Jehanne heard some consecrated trumpeter calling the camp to the daily Mass. She knew that sort of thing would quickly lose its power amongst soldiers unless the army moved soon and in the right direction.

Then, all at once, there was no problem. Culant wrote on paper and showed what he had written to Boussac and then to Poton—but it could have been a joke because both men smiled. From that time de Gaucourt was abandoned by the others. Even though it was a marvellous ceasing of opposition it made Jehanne uneasy, as if she and de Gaucourt were the only two innocents in the room.

A little later still Poton suggested that the army and the convoy could travel along the south bank as far as the ford near Clery, well past Meung. Then the army—or most of it—could cross to face the English forts and the convoy could continue far inland on the south bank until Checy, some miles upstream from Orleans; there barges would meet it and take the supplies downriver to the Tour Neuve wharf in the south–east corner of the city. Would this satisfy the young lady's counsel?

She looked at la Hire for signs either way. The troubled blue eyes looked fair back at her. There was no message in them.

She stared down the table at de Rais. He slept still, his superb head nearly upright but tending to his left shoulder. He was very, very tired.

Jehanne: Will you all vote on your honour?

De Gaucourt: I'll certainly vote on mine.

So they voted to do that: to travel on the south side but cross the army in time to run up against the English positions on the west of Orleans. De Gaucourt voted against it, Boussac wouldn't make up his mind.

The plan which, it appeared, the war council had decided on can be indicated by a simple map.

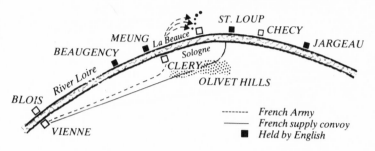

On those numbers the rite was consummated at two o'clock. Alençon said that subject to Royal Council assent, the wagons would begin to move out of the south-bank suburb of Vienne after dawn. They would all be told their positions in the column before evening. The camp would be struck at seven o'clock following a solemn blessing by the Chancellor of France, Monsieur Archbishop Regnault de Chartres. He thanked them for their time.

In a corner, Boussac, Poton and Culant soothed de Gaucourt. It seemed very curative talk. His old eyebrows unknotted. They took him out by the elbows.

Jehanne got up from the table feeling unreal.

I ought to be grateful, she thought. They're doing what I want and here I am frowning about it,.

Alençon saw her, bowed quickly with a painful grin, and began to rush out.

Jehanne: Why are you so nervous, my sweet duke?

Alençon: War. War.

Jehanne: Is that all?

Alençon: Jehanne, I don't know the river. I don't know the country north or south of the river. I was ten years old the last time I went to Orleans and I didn't look at it with a soldier's eye.

Jehanne: Why are you saying this?

215

Alençon: Don't blame me for what happens . . .

Jehanne: Happens? Nothing will happen.

Alençon: Jehanne . . . don't stop having special . . . *affection* for me.

He went out before she could give any guarantees. There was Marshal de Rais still asleep. She tiptoed to him and touched his shoulder very gently. Instantly he woke. His weird lively eyes jumped to her face.

Gilles: Tell me, Mademoiselle. Are you any good at *interpreting* dreams?

BOOK THREE

Brother Jesus's Garden of Vengeance

To my honoured etc.   Dated 29 April 1429

As I informed you in my last letter,* having discovered in the Marshal de Rais a greatly wealthy man who wishes to assist his king's cause by large monetary embursements, I now find it necessary to put on armour and follow him towards Orleans so that I might complete my business with him.

The march to Orleans began yesterday morning from Vienne, the suburb of Blois that lies on the south bank of the Loire. The army was to march with the supply column and the herds of cattle, sheep and pigs, but the Marshal himself and the girl were to lead, so that I too was in the leading party. Although General Poton had sent scouts ahead of us, my honoured principal can understand that a banker would not treasure being at the head of an army column. The supplies gathered were all larger than the largest city market, the herds and wagons had been concentrating for two months. Now wagoners' boys ran along the sides of the wagons hitting them with sticks to drive the rats out of the grain.

Beside the road were the Marshal's choristers in black cassocks and ruffs. Then his Breton knights, very handsome soldiers indeed. There were seven hundred priests round about, tucking up their cassocks for the long walk.

Jehanne, the girl, joined us before dawn, in her armour but wearing a cap on her head. She has a few knights and pages and such people to travel with her. Trumpets began talking to each other up and down the lines and north towards Blois where much of the army still waited to cross the bridge and join us.

*Not quoted in this account.

219

Our journey began stylishly. The Marshal's boys and the monks sang *Veni Creator Spiritus*, a touching anthem for that time of morning and in that light. The Marshal is passionate about choirs. He kept raising his armoured fore-arm in time to their chant, or in praise or disapprobation. All his knights were round him, unhelmeted. I heard the girl ask him ingenuously were all Bretons so handsome?

If the road was level it was very churned from the winter rains, yet the boys and the priests didn't stop singing till nearly nine o'clock. One of the songs the boys sang was a chant in praise of love between males. It struck the priests dumb. And although the girl did not under-stand the Latin wording it made her uneasy. The Marshal claimed it was arranged from an old chant his choirmaster had found in the library of St Julien de Vouvantes. Jehanne said, strange monasteries they have in your part of the country. The Marshal replied softly, strange monasteries they have everywhere, Mademoiselle.

By noon the boys were all lying exhausted on the wagons. The road was uphill. Everyone was quiet, deal-ing with horseflies. Everyone except the Marshal and the girl. The Marshal spoke endlessly about prophecy and divination, as if the girl would be amused by talk of her own trade. He told a story about King Hal Monmouth, who had learned astronomy at the English University of Oxford. Everywhere King Hal went he took two astro-labes with him. One horoscope he cast by means of them indicated that his son should not be born at Windsor, the Goddam castle of which one hears. The reading of the astrolabes suggested that what had been won in France by Monmouth would be lost by Windsor. He sent urgent messages to his queen, Catherine, ordering her to keep to other castles than Windsor, but before they reached her she went into labour at that very castle.

The girl told the Marshal that it wouldn't have mattered where the child was *dropped* (her word). It was all going to happen anyhow.

That night we camped in empty fields. It is only when you get into open country and find the earth idle every-where that you understand the monstrous nature of this war.

I had six blankets but was still uncomfortable. The girl insisted on sleeping in her armour, I cannot think why. Her short-sighted page called Raymond took off only her garde-reins and pansière which together make a bell-shape at the waist.

This morning she was therefore very stiff. When the priests said Mass thousands of soldiers and wagoners milled to see the consecrated hosts, because they thought they might have to fight the English today. The soldiers often crackle as they walk, because they have periapts wrapped around them beneath their shirts—parchments on which incantations are written to protect them against being wounded.

We all breakfasted with the Marshal. The Bretons ate smoked fish, bacon, cheeses, glacé fruits, and they drank hypocras. But still they complained about how harsh it was, soldiering.

It became a warm day. All this morning we were amongst hills, where it was time for someone to see to the vines. But there was not a soul there with fork or shears to do it.

Rain started to fall early this afternoon. The Marshal chattered away at the girl. He had two astrolabes himself and says that Sagittarius has wandered deep into the house of night. Sagittarius is apparently England's star.

About four o'clock this afternoon, a contretemps arose between the girl Jehanne and the army leaders who, apart from Gilles de Rais, were well back in the column. At that hour the sun got under a cloudbank and lit up the far-off Loire and what at first sight looked like a vast walled barge afloat on it. It was in fact the city of Orleans.

Now it seemed that the war leaders had told Jehanne that the army would leave the supply column in plenty of time to cross the Loire and take on Talbot's fortresses on the west of the city. The Marshal de Rais knew nothing about this undertaking, since he slept through the entire meeting. On seeing the city to the left and a little behind where she now rode she began to shout and heave herself upright in her stirrups. She said her counsel had told her the army had to attack the Goddams in la Beauce, that that was where the army should be now. Monsieur Gilles said her counsel was probably right but he didn't think the Royal Council would easily commit the army to a hit-or-miss onslaught against Talbot. He was highly apologetic for the fact that Royal Councils were not as well informed as she was. Or even as he with his astrolabes.

She called out, 'They put us here. Two simple-minded people to lead the army by the wrong road!'

She insisted on riding back down the column until she found the generals, who were all together at the head of a great force of cavalry. We didn't see her again at the front of the column until an hour passed. She was still raging. The Royal Council and the Bastard had both forbidden a head-on attack in la Beauce. The army was to remain at the side of the convoy. The girl had asked them what had been the use of the meeting the generals had held two days ago at which it was decided the army should cross to la Beauce and charge at Talbot. The Duke of Alençon and de Boussac had both told her the generals had decided that way out of politeness to her, knowing the Royal Council would never allow it. De Gaucourt also told her that strictly d'Alençon shouldn't be with the army, not yet having bought back the prisoners he left standing in for him at the English fortress of le Crotoy.

She came back to Marshal de Rais damning the ransom system and the small minds of the Royal Council. All the flags were sodden and the choir-boys and knights coughing, but she was a sharp, bright point to the army.

In the end we came down to a temporary encampment some distance upstream past Orleans. It is to the east of Orleans that the English fortresses are weakest and so supplies can best enter Orleans from that direction. The girl's rage is, in human terms, unreasonable.

This letter is being written under shelter of a wagon. It is a miserable evening, with a strong wind from the east . . .

Bernardo Massimo

Jehanne, daughter of Jacques of Sermaize, sat trapped at the point of an antic army that hadn't taken the right direction. As they waited there was a shift of wind, squalls first, then a gale. All the great men lifted their cloaks against the west-bound downpour.

There was a tent out there, on the river, or rather a tent on a barge. It nosed in through the haze and moored below them by a crude wharf, in what should have been deep water. Nonetheless those who came ashore waded across the silt. They wore fur-trimmed cloaks over their armour.

A very tall man with a fringe of black beard led them. He kissed de Gaucourt on both cheeks. His wet boots creaked. Yet he had the delicacy of moving that Alençon had been trained to have and could in fact do well enough but which only people like Gilles and this man were good at.

Jehanne: Are you the Bastard?

She could hear de Gaucourt grumble. She'd cut across his reunion, which should have been given more time.

She skidded down the river bank towards the newcomer. His eyes were soft, but to the point of authority. There were no possible eccentric vices there, as there might be in Gilles. You could bet, too, he didn't keep astrolabes.

Jehanne: It was your order to do it this way?

Behind the Bastard, Culant, de Loré, de Rais turned their faces into the wet gale, discussing its omens like fishermen.

Bastard: I gave the order. And others wiser gave it.

Jehanne: Does it appeal to you, the idea that it could have been all over by tonight?

Bastard: Yes.

Jehanne: You've heard of my counsel?

He spoke very softly, yawning now and then.

Bastard: Of course I have. I'm not being rude: perhaps though your counsel hadn't heard that an English column under John Fastolf has left Paris for Orleans.

Jehanne: I've been told all that, Monsieur.

Bastard: By your Voice?

Jehanne: Voices! No, by Monsieur d'Alençon.

Bastard: Please, Mademoiselle Jehanne, we must work hand in glove.

She was sure at once only the Bastard would understand her anger. She got close to his left shoulder by means of tiptoe.

Jehanne: The Voices said la Beauce. La Beauce, la Beauce!

Bastard: I'm sorry. How was I to know? If I'd known . . .

Talking to him was nearly as pleasant as flirtation. But she couldn't let him honey her down like this. If it worked, he'd try it every time.

Jehanne: Don't absolve yourself so easily, Monsieur. You managed to mislead me. But not half as much as you misled yourself.

The army leaders were all around them now.

Gilles: How can you get barges up here against this wind?

Bastard: We can't. Not even by tacking. Also the river's too low. If Talbot knew he could come up from les Augustins and bundle us all up while we're waiting.

Alençon immediately had scouts sent out to the west to see if any such illumination had struck Talbot.

The Bastard said it was a pity they weren't there half an hour earlier, when the wind had been fair. The water had fallen right away in the last half hour too. The tides were very tricky around here—it might have something to do with the islands in midstream. She could see at once the fear in him. Of the loss of the city perhaps, the city so personal to him.

Jehanne: Don't worry. We haven't come all this way to be stopped by wind and low water.

He took hold of her elbow.

Bastard: It's the little things, Mademoiselle. Always the little things that ruin one's chances.

Jehanne: That's why my counsel said *la Beauce*.

Bastard: Indeed.

But at dusk the rain stopped, the wind turned north-west and moderate and the water level rose, sucking at the piers of the dock.

The barges came up from Orleans in the twilight, their blatant square-rigs shielded from English gunners in St Loup by a vast island close to the north bank. All the knights along the levée clapped and called *Noël*. But as if they too were in the wrong-side plot, the barges moored on the north bank of the river.

Jehanne: Why *that* side? Why in holy Christ's name?

La Hire told her in his remote way. If the barges moored on this side and they spent the night loading they couldn't spare the men to watch out for the English who might move soldiers over the river in the dark or might send a raiding party from Jargeau in the east or might do both . . . or might, or might. This ogre of her girlhood stood beside her with all the cool reasons.

The Bastard whispered to her that it was time for her to cross the river.

Bastard: We have a nice place for you in Checy. A fire. And supper.

She remembered there *was* a weight of steel on her and pain in her kidneys.

Jehanne: If a farmer ran his herd the way you run this army, he'd starve and deserve to.

Bastard: Perhaps, Mademoiselle.

Raymond and Minguet blindfolded the horses, even their own. There was clapping as she limped forward with Pasquerel and d'Aulon over the silt. The barge had come close in, ignoring the wharf, so that horses could be loaded. She had taken her armour off and waded in kidskin boots.

There were shouts of goodwill along the embankment of happy voyage. La Hire had two hundred lancers who were also to cross to Checy that night. In the drizzle she saw Jean de Metz in his old-fashioned mail, his man de Honnecourt from whom she'd once stolen clothes. Bertrand was there, bare-headed for some reason, wet hair slicked around his ears. With him his three men—Julien, and Jehan and Pierrolot, her brothers-in-Jacques.

Jehanne: All right Bertrand, Sir de Metz. And bring your men.

In the morning, the barges were loaded and cattle and corn sent down river. The Orleans garrison went skirmishing around the English fort of St Loup, so that the barges would not be troubled by the firing of bombards, mortars, culverins. All the fleet found safe moorage in the moat under the east walls.

At noon that day, at the pleasant château of Checy, a meeting was called. When Jehanne came in they were all around a long table. Alençon, the Bastard, de Gaucourt, the Marshals de Boussac and de Rais, la Hire—all of them. She caught the sense of established lunacy in all the minds around her. Because they were all talking about an improbable proposition that had been given standing amongst them: that the army would go back to Blois. It was as if they had spent all morning convincing themselves this should happen.

Jehanne: Why?

Bastard: I don't have the boats to bring them over to Orleans. If I tried to bring those barges up-river again, the English wouldn't let it happen, not a second time.

Jehanne: Do you mean that you told the army to come this side, knowing they couldn't cross?

Bastard: That's so. I had the convoy in mind. The convoy was more important.

Jehanne: So you've got food now. To feed your fright on. And that satisfies you.

Bastard: One can't play around with the English. Did you know they've kept your herald Guyenne?

Jehanne: Guyenne . . .

The singer!

Bastard: Ambleville they sent back to Orleans. They're threatening to burn Guyenne.

Jehanne: Why?

Bastard: For carrying messages for a witch and heretic. I think it's only a bluff.

Jehanne: Witch and heretic . . .

La Hire: I don't think we should leave. I think we ought to cross no matter how long it takes. The soldiers all *feel* right, they've been to confession, they want to be with girls. They want to die in the next day or so if they have to.

Bastard: I'm sorry. I'd take you down to Orleans if I could.

De Boussac: They'd rather have the girl and the supplies than just another army.

Bastard: That's the flat truth.

La Hire: Would they want an army that beat its way into the city from les Tourelles, repairing the bridge as it went?

De Gaucourt: The sort of suggestion you'd expect from someone not putting up the money.

Stooping, la Hire lit up with hilarity. In his eyes, seeking those of others, was a conviction of his own decency of soul.

De Gaucourt: I've seen all the royal armies go out. This is likely to be the last. It isn't for gambling with.

La Hire: I won't go back. With your permission, Monsieur Bastard, I want to go into the city.

Gilles: You always knew you'd do that. Hence your transfer of two hundred lancers to the girl.

La Hire: An improvement on choirboys, Monsieur Marshal.

There was no hiss or fury between them, they were masters of dispassion.

Gilles: We're permitted a few comforts.

Jehanne was distracted by the Marshal's sublime ripe throat stretching in discussion.

Alençon: Jehanne, if you go into the city with the Bastard and la Hire, I swear to you that I'll bring the army back. Along la Beauce.

Her hand lamely beat the table top, its knuckles still smarting.

Jehanne: . . . the way I wanted to come anyhow.

She thought, how right I am never to apologise to *this* crowd for my strange view of matters.

Alençon: Monsieur de Rais has kindly written off my ransom.

That roused them.

Culant: On the basis of your Normandy properties?

Alençon hung his head. There was a poor boy's shame there.

Gilles: We're going to get Normandy back. It's in the stars.

Alençon: So I'll take the army back to Blois and return with it. Will you go into Orleans, Jehanne?

La Hire: Jesus Almighty.

Jehanne: If you guarantee this: Père Pasquerel, with my standard, will lead the army. All soldiers will continue to confess. No whores will be admitted to the camps, even dressed as men. No soldier will lose his fighting edge on a whore or swear on the genitals of King Jesus or the saints— the French will die by that sort of talk. Do you promise?

Gilles: A new idea. The virgin's virgin army. Beautiful.

Downstairs delegations of businessmen, magistrates, ridden out through the supposed English cordon, to invite her into their city, into the unreality inside the stones and towers. They all knew so much about her. Cowled

Franciscans with no more than a cheese knife for defence, had crept through the night or fog-bound English siege with a freight of legends.

At eight that evening she rode out of the Checy walls on to the Orleans road. There were hundreds of men with her: knights from the Bastard's garrison, the Bastard, la Hire with his or her two hundred knights-mercenary, de Gaucourt with a similar company of horsemen, the Marshal de Boussac with more still.

She could see fires burning in the dusk on the left of the road. She knew whose they were. The coués, lighting their night-fires in la Beauce, in Brother Jesus's vengeance garden. The kindling was damp, long grey streaks of smoke blew towards the city, melancholy smoke such as from the burning of garbage or old clothes.

Bastard: That's their St Loup bastion.

He didn't disapprove of their St Loup bastion—he didn't sound angry—brotherliness instead, as if he knew things were hard for them in there. He said the town militia and some of the garrison had attacked the bastion that afternoon, had broken down the palisades and climbed up the earthworks inside. An English knight had been killed and his pennon taken. Five other Englishmen had died. The English in St Loup had few horses, so weren't likely to pursue.

Then there was enough light to see the city walls.

Bastard: This will be tiresome for you.

There was a low barbican at the city entrance, and beyond it the walls with nine towers on that side alone. Braziers and pitch torches burned all along the walls and sometimes men moved there and threw shadows over the lights. She saw lights too on top of the square cathedral spires; and bouncing from a tangle of roofs. A tangle. She felt terror of the smothering city encircled with armies.

Bastard: The house you're to put up at belongs to my father's treasurer, Monsieur Boucher. He lives right across the city, on the central street called rue des Talmeliers. The main gate on that side is called the Renard Gate. From it you can get at St Lorent, la Croix-Boisée, the Rouen, Paris, London forts. At Talbot.

Jehanne: They're holding Guyenne over there?
Bastard: Yes.

She called to Minguet, Raymond. She'd been going to ask them to hold off the crowds, but she could see they were children in a column of full-grown men. Poor little Minguet had to ride first with her buckram flag into the teeth of the welcome.

Jehanne: It's all right. Don't get lost in the crowd.

Minguet and Raymond went in the Burgundy gate and then she rode in on the Bastard's right. There was a sharp roar, not like ordinary barracking, more like some near-limit of pain or ecstasy. Riding into their tight city she punctured the circle of their fever, all the ill breath of their mania came out of their mouths. She could see light on the under-chins of people yelling this way on balconies. On the ground the canons of St Croix cathedral bayed by the walls; on the left the captains of citizens' militia holding helmets, and themselves roaring.

She looked at the Bastard. His lips bunched over the line of neat beard. But she couldn't have heard him even if he did speak. His eyes said *You see, you've been made necessary to them*. He had speciously soft brown eyes which he used for melting women.

The great moan and bark of the release of the garrisons and people of Orleans! They would hear it in the fort of St Loup, amongst their sad fires. They may hear it in St Lorent, Guyenne too, or in that muddy fort on the cold island of Charlemagne in mid-Loire. They would cross themselves, call for priests, draw magic circles, wrap themselves in parchments, pluck hairs from white horses, dismember rabbits for lucky organs.

Meanwhile, the pitch-pine torches were putting mystery on the grey the king had given her from his stables in Tours. It was as white as a symbol; if Christ God had ridden a horse amongst the people of Israel in the night of some Italian painter's fresco, the horse would have been as white and moved like this old horse.

At her entry to Orleans, she felt for the first time in many weeks the intoxication of her godhood. She felt the excitement of exorcising madness, raising it in a cloud above the city, drifting outwards into the eyes of the English. She reeled with the joy of the light on her simple steel suit. *Oh my people*, she said. No one could hear her. She stood in the stirrups, in the high-brimmed saddle, and raised her right hand. Women with goitres touched her horse. A large pitch-spark fell from a balcony and the the white pennant in Raymond's hand began to burn. He stared bemusedly at it, trying to focus. She spurred her grey and somehow—the management she had over the horse astounded her—turned him around at Raymond's side. She could see Raymond's green eyes, drugged with light, quietly considering the flame. She took the burning tassels in her gloves and crumpled the fire. She felt delighted by this little feat. Likewise the crowd. She rode back to the Bastard, one singed glove raised to him. He laughed. As if he were saying *you're just a peasant after all.*

Boucher's house was four storeys high. It had strange tall false windows with stone tracery and true windows inside them, an expensive way to save on glass. Stone figures leaned realistically over false stone balconies outside the false stone windows. It was all curious and delightful.

The Bastard shouted for her to dismount, and took her up the steps. A man of perhaps forty-five years, clean-shaven, waited smiling there in a gown of blue and gold lilies. He bowed and his little speech of welcome could not be heard. He pointed to the crowd. She could see her brothers there, red-faced, beyond themselves.

All at once she was in the quiet of the front lobby. A thin woman stood by the stairwell, four servants around her. The thin woman had on velvet, green and gold. It smelt of spices. There was a beautiful girl-child at her side, plump. The child's eyes blazed with disbelief in siege, the true presence of Goddams beyond her back garden, child-rape, transfixion. If stone projectiles flew over the rue des Talmeliers and broke into someone's kitchen and shattered to deal a few deaths, then it was an event as disembodied and ordained as lightning or heavy hail.

The Bastard pointed out Boucher as his father's treasurer. Madame Boucher. Little Charlotte. Named for the duke who now lived in the Goddams' misty nation.

Jehanne: Do you get letters from the duke?
Boucher: Yes, Mademoiselle. The English go to a lot of

trouble to see his letters reach me. It's one of their gallantries. You must want to disarm before dinner.

Jehanne: What will happen to my brothers?

Boucher: They can stay here. There's a meal in the kitchen for them and beds on the top floor. You must understand it's hard to accommodate all your attendants on the level they deserve.

Jehanne: They'll be quite happy. Could I have my page to help me get out of this stuff?

Madame Boucher: Let me, Mademoiselle.

Boucher: She's good at taking armour off. I never use a page.

Madame herself talked all the way upstairs.

Madame Boucher: He's always up on the walls, poor man. He has to look after repairs to the west wall. Those wretched Goddams are beating away at the stonework half the day . . .

Jehanne got the taste of their connubiality, of Madame Boucher doing lover's and page's duty after dangerous hours above the Renard Gate. Even on this night she felt a second's loss.

In an upstairs bedroom Madame Boucher unlatched her quickly. Jehanne felt shrunken and sore in her shirt and hose. Minguet had brought her other clothes up, sulking a little at not being allowed, this night of all, to do his trade: the unbuckling and soothing of knights.

When he'd gone, Madame Boucher kissed her shoulder between the shirt-collar and chafed neck. It almost seemed she'd forgotten whom she was undressing.

Madame Boucher: Will my child grow up?

Jehanne: Yes. Of course.

Madame Boucher: They have been living in mud, those coués. Boucher knows. They're thick with lice, the wine they have is very bad. They think you're a witch.

Jehanne: My God.

Madame Boucher: If ever they get inside the walls, they won't leave anyone standing.

Charlotte stood with full lips, her eyes blazing with the almost insane security of the sort of childhood she had been given to enjoy. She didn't seem to hear her mother.

★

In the middle of the council at Boucher's place, in the middle of the Saturday morning, Jehanne could tell that her prophetic tone had lost her the general called Gamaches.

He called in his ensign and folded up his flag and said he resigned. *Bloody little sauce-box,* he kept shouting.

The Bastard spoke to her in the corner. La Hire spoke in his dull authoritative way to Gamaches, who was at last bullied into handing back his flag to his ensign and offering to kiss Jehanne.

She and Gamaches kissed each other in a cursory way. She could tell he was about to say something sexually demeaning. So could la Hire, whose hand was suddenly on his arm as a warning.

Jehanne: I'm sick of councils. So sick of delay.

At Mass at Boucher's that morning, Messire and Mesdames Catherine and Margaret burnt on her right.

Messire: The rose climbs towers in Jesus's vengeance garden in la Beauce.

Catherine: The rose climbs towers.

Messire: Blood-red sister-rose, blood-red King Jesus's sister-rose.

Margaret: Thorns for their flesh. Quick.

Messire: Quick, love.

Catherine: Soon.

Margaret: Have pity for all poor soldiers. Sister-rose.

Catherine: Soon.

Outside in the streets around rue des Talmeliers the militia had been lined up in oddments of armour since dawn. When she walked out on Boucher's steps she saw their exquisite but fragile conviction of the rightness of the day. She knew it shouldn't be wasted. But at noon the Bastard, de Gaucourt, all of them, were indoors wasting it.

Jehanne: Will there be anything to stop me calling out to the Goddams from the bridge?

De Gaucourt: No. Take your steward and tell him to shout if there's any sign of arrows.

La Hire: Especially if they appear suddenly in his body.

So in the afternoon she went out with d'Aulon and some French knights from the south gate on to the Loire bridge. It was a dry grey afternoon. There were gunners in a wooden palisade by one of the piers of the bridge. They called out

Noël, mademoiselle! The commandant of the gunners whistled out of a mouth of rotten teeth. The French knights waved back.

Jehanne trembled under her armour, the big horse moving lumpily and to her pain between her thighs.

Knight: That's Maître Jean the master-gunner. The coués in les Tourelles are so frightened of him that sometimes he throws himself over the stonework as if he's been wounded, and has himself carried away on a litter into town. The Goddams yell and cheer. Half an hour later back comes Mâitre Jean large as life. Dealing them death.

I've never spoken to any Englishman before, she was thinking. The English knights spoke Norman French. The archers would call out to her in jagged Goddam ways she couldn't predict.

Jehanne: I've never spoken to an Englishman before.

D'Aulon: They're like us. They don't want to die or go to hell.

Jehanne: Aren't you afraid?

D'Aulon: I was their prisoner for two years. I taught them to play chess. They use a lot of profanity. But then . . .

Far out across the pathway of the bridge was a wooden tower with a few French watchers on top.

Jehanne and d'Aulon went inside: it was cold and dark in there. Around the walls were palliasses, a French guard lay on one of them. There was an incisive smell of sap and sour-wine piss. The staircase had no banister. When she got on to the platform upstairs one of the watchers raised the parley flag. Waiting for an acknowledgment, the French knight pointed out the features of the place. They were only six metres up there and the structure trembled every time someone put down his foot. In front of it, tumbling against it, was a mound of earth and faggots, then a gap in the bridge, perhaps twenty-five metres across. The water looked deep, strong, abiding, muddy, flowing in that gap.

Where the gap ended and the bridge began again was another mound of dirt and faggots and a wooden tower just like this one. There were two flags flying there: red lion on gold, black boar on blue. Alarm ran up and down her arms. Men stood on their platform over there, holding up a parley flag. She could see an English knight standing still, waiting

233

to hear with green and white silk around his head. Behind him stood the towers of les Tourelles, a fine stone castle, and beyond it the complicated earthworks of les Augustins.

D'Aulon: My mistress wants to talk to Monsieur Glasdale.

Knight: Is your mistress the cowgirl?

D'Aulon looked apologetically at Jehanne.

Knight: Come on, is it the bloody cowgirl you people are using?

D'Aulon: It's the girl, the *pucelle*, the virgin. Monsieur Talbot has her letter. And her herald.

Knight: There's a bonfire at St Lorent for her too. Why doesn't she visit over there?

D'Aulon: Monsieur Bastard won't let her. Will you or won't you get Glasdale?

The knight went. The men he left behind could speak the language brokenly. They called out cowgirl, whore, harlot, cock-sucker. They invited her behind the earthworks to milk them. She was bare-handed, one glove in either hand. She ground the gloves into her ears. They cackled and whistled and pissed over the ramparts.

Jehanne thought, I ought to be taking this better. I ought to be laughing them off. Why aren't I?

D'Aulon: Would you like to wait downstairs?

Jehanne: They're just village wits.

Ribaude! they kept calling in their weird voices. *Vachère!*

Glasdale did not come for half an hour. He was large and moved easily in armour, though not with the hereditary ease of the Bastard and Gilles.

No one said anything.

In the end Glasdale asked was there to be talking or not.

She began calling to him before she understood what she was saying. She'd been entranced by his movements, by the movements of the other English. All dead and they don't know it.

In that state of mind she began the talks.

Jehanne: Monsieur Classidas (it was his French pet-name) you're all going to die. Give up that place and go home with your lives. For Sweet Jesus's sake.

Everyone on the English platform answered, knowing they were permitted to. It was consecrated hatred over there, Glasdale had somehow let them know it was a holy

234

and right hatred. He didn't bother to restrain them for some minutes. In the end Glasdale spoke in a jagged passionate voice, a little short of breath.

Glasdale: My good friend Talbot has a bonfire for your herald. I've got one for you. You're a peasant and a whore and a fucking disgrace and when I get you I'll let my men at you, then I'll burn you without consulting the University of Paris or any of that cowshit. They can convene on the question of your blistered arse, sweetie. Can you hear me?

One of the French knights was sitting in the shadow of the parapet cranking up a bolt in a crossbow. He called out to the man holding the parley flag.

Knight: Haul that thing down and I'll put a bolt into the bastard.

D'Aulon kicked the bolt out from between the man's greaved legs. He was angry with everyone and didn't want to be tempted in this way.

D'Aulon: What if she got captured? What would they do to her after a thing like that?

The English redoubt thudded with weird sounds, hurrays and hip-hips, whistles, rooster-calls, pig-grunts. Jehanne went downstairs, crying in the dark fort. *You silly bitch, it's just words.* But it was like Jacques's hatred in the days when she first failed to become a woman, a hatred of her organs and of *her* mystery. Out of all the mysteries they could have chosen to hate—wounds, rape, homesickness—they chose only *her* mystery. Gratuitously.

To my honoured principal etc.   Dated 1 May 1429
    Last night Monsieur the Bastard tried to persuade me to underwrite the garrison's pay immediately, which including back-wages came to a total of more than seven thousand pounds tournois. I might have considered doing so on security from Monsieur Gilles de Rais, but that gentleman could not be found. The Bastard out of hand presumed him to be holed up in one of the city's pleasure houses, perhaps one that deals in children. I replied that the Marshal's vices, whatever they were, had no bearing on his credit, so that I was prepared to wait for him to re-emerge. The Bastard nonetheless saddled up this morning and, with a body of forty knights, slipped round

the northern flanks of the system of English fortresses outside the Bannier Gate. Before he left I reproached him for not waiting the little time it would take to find Monsieur Gilles. He replied very reasonably that his purpose in going was not only to obtain the pay cover-notes from the Council itself, but to lead the army back now that the girl is installed and the Orleanais are ready to act.

Before going he asked the girl to swear in front of Monsieur de Gaucourt (who is afraid of her rashness) that she would attempt nothing military before he got back to Orleans. She swore.

She is said in any case to have pleurisy. Madame Boucher pointed out at table that a man's spleen and kidneys are further from his backside than are a woman's from hers. (This on a night I had been invited to Boucher's.) The girl said she hadn't come all this way to be held up by the closeness of her spleen to her behind. She is argumentative but succinct. To prove her equality with men she rode out in front of the Paris fortress with la Hire and six hundred knights to cover the escape of the Bastard. The English in the fortress simply watched them and yelled abuse . . .

Bernardo Massimo

Tuesday. La Hire had her woken at five. The first outriders of the army had just cantered down through the rubble of the suburbs to the Bannier Gate. La Hire took her up into the Michaud tower and she could see a haze of movement far out beyond the farthest olive bay of forest in the north-west. An hour later riders, a few dozen, raced their horses down past the Paris fort towards the city. By then, she could see her own banner, and hear *Magnificat* being chanted. Pasquerel was even bringing the priests back.

La Hire: I suppose we have to feed all those bloody clergy.

Jehanne: They won't have an easy life. The army will stay confessed. There'll be no whores. Anyone who gets hurt will have to have last rites.

La Hire's cavalry rode out to face the Paris fort again and screen the army's entry to Orleans. The bombards of Orleans were let off for celebratory reasons and all its bells tolled. And you could hear the solid line of hate and curses the English threw up, for it was the best they could do by way of solid lines. For the first time it came to Jehanne that yes, they were very frightened, those poor coués.

Jehanne, Raymond, Minguet, Bertrand sat their horses by a heap of old bricks outside the Renard Gate. The first General Jehanne saw was Marshal de Rais. He was grey-faced from his all-night ride, wheezing from some—as yet—mild fever. His remarkable lips were parted and dry.

Jehanne: Where's your choir, Monsieur Gilles?

Gilles: The Bastard says he can't afford to feed them, dearest Jehanne. But they sing better than the priests.

Jehanne: They can't absolve people.

Gilles: There's that.

Jehanne: What do your astrolabes say about today?

His improperly beautiful eyes looked at her with the appearance of knowing her down to the wish-bone.

Gilles: They say that today you'll see your first dead coué.

One delicious tremor snaked out of her belly and swelled in her throat.

More supplies came down from the Sologne side that morning. The Bastard was up at Checy, everyone said. D'Aulon rode in, Pasquerel, ecstatic with exhaustion. Alençon (said Gilles) had been retained in Blois by Maman Yolande, for she thought he had some talent and should use it on Fat Georges to sustain the flow of money and supplies. Jehanne did not quite believe that story.

Noon rang. Jehanne lay beside Madame Boucher in the screened-off bed of the large apartment upstairs. D'Aulon, who had ridden all night, was sleeping with his boots off on a settee far down the room near the windows. The sun lay over exactly half his face, like a clown's paint, but he was too deep asleep to know it. In a courtyard at the back of the house Charlotte sang.

'Brown squirrel, brown squirrel,
Tell me where's your store,
If you've more than seven nuts you couldn't love them
more,

If you've more than six nuts you'll hold them in one paw,
If you've more than five nuts you needn't close the
door . . .'

The cry from that distant and entrenched childhood in which
Charlotte subsisted drugged Jehanne to sleep. Immediately
she was deep in a forest of veins, pale red and umber, thick
as aspens. And beyond this curtain Madame Aubrit and
Madame Hélène de Bourlémont looked around lost and
moved gingerly on their feet. She saw then that they were
stepping around something wide-eyed and sacrificed. It
was a young man's face, not Nicolas Barrey's nor the king's
nor Alençon's, but she had travelled all her life towards the
sighting of that face in her sleep. His throat was half cut
through and its face at weird right-angles to its body.

She woke on her feet by the bed.

Jehanne: Why didn't anyone tell me?

Poor D'Aulon sat up, shaking himself dutifully out of
sleep.

Jehanne: It's started. No one's informed us. But it's started.

Madame Boucher had put on a gown and came out of
bed.

Jehanne: They're killing Frenchmen, Madame Boucher.

D'Aulon: Down there!

Below his window you could see a middle-aged militia-
man with a bolt in his thigh. The bolt itself had been tied
with cloths to stop the bleeding but the cloths were slick
red. Three friends chaired him down the rue des Talmeliers.
He called *Oh, oh, oh* in a way that clearly said *Tell me it isn't
true that my whole skin hasn't been penetrated.* He was white as
junket, and his friends had been lugging him for a long time
and were cursing each other for being awkward.

D'Aulon called to them not to carry him like that for
Christ's sake. It kept the wound bleeding. Carry him on
his back! Well, get a door or something. For Christ's sake
knock one down and pay damages later.

Children came running behind this engaging tragedy.
D'Aulon asked them where it was all happening. Someone
said there was an attack on St Loup.

Jehanne: Where are those bloody boys? Get me dressed,
get me dressed!

238

Of course Madame Boucher began to strap her into the uppers of her suit.

The Sire d'Aulon excused himself and left to look for his squire. There was no fever in his movements.

Jehanne: I don't need leggings or shoes.

Madame Boucher: You'll be top heavy.

Jehanne: I want to get there.

She dodged away as soon as Madame Boucher had strapped the plates across her belly. She carried the long Fierbois sword under its cross-member and ran down the stairs. Madame Boucher came after, little arms heaped with greaves, leg-pieces, helmet.

From the steps she could see Minguet fifty yards down the street talking to Pasquerel and some monks. For standing so idle she could have beaten them all.

Jehanne: You damn child! Why wasn't I told Frenchmen were getting killed?

Minguet ran up, blinked, reached for the heap of steel Madame Boucher still carried.

Jehanne: You get my horse! Madame will finish me.

The boy ran away, shamed.

Jehanne: Père Pasquerel. (She grunted, Madame Boucher tied the knee-piece tight.) Didn't you see that old man carried past?

He could feel the edge of her voice and put one on his.

Pasquerel: My brothers and I were just saying: we thought that sort of incident happened every day in a city under siege. And the wound seemed hardly fatal.

Jehanne: My information's different—there are Frenchmen getting killed beyond the Burgundy Gate.

Their sacramental duty stirred in them quite automatically, they looked around as if they wanted someone to hand them a horse or a stole.

Jehanne: Ride over to St Croix for holy oils. You can get horses from Villedart's.

Pasquerel: I ought to stay with you, Mademoiselle.

Jehanne: It doesn't matter. I'm not dying today.

Madame Boucher was kneeling in the straw and horse-dung, buckling solerets over her riding shoes.

Jehanne: I don't need those, Madame.

Madame Boucher: I never let Boucher go up on the

239

walls, let alone outside them, unless he's completely protected.

A minute later Minguet came running down rue des
Talmeliers with her horse. She liked the way its legs bounced
on the stones. A young man was carried by on a litter. His
face was grey and his eyes gone, only white showed. Blankets covered his injuries.

Minguet and Madame Boucher pushed her up into the
saddle.

Minguet: Aren't you going to wait for me, Mademoiselle?

His concern for his page's pride when she knew there was
death down the road made her furious.

Jehanne: How in the hell can I?

Madame Boucher: D'Aulon. Wait for d'Aulon.

She put her heels into the grey's belly and he was glad
to run. The heart of the town was empty and the square
near the university. She met three or four wounded men,
militia, carried by friends glad to be out of battle and to
have other wounds than their own to gesture about. At the
Burgundian Gate she stopped. D'Aulon, Minguet, Raymond
were only a little way behind her. As d'Aulon reined up
beside her a man with a pushed-in chest was rushed into the
city. Someone must have thrown large stones at him. His
sodden shirt flapped where jets of blood rose under the
fabric.

Jehanne: Oh Brother Jesus.

D'Aulon: The priests will meet him.

It was quiet outside the walls. This had been the suburb
of St Aignan and a few stone houses still stood roofless, but
the French had burned the suburb down so that the English
wouldn't have winter shelter. It was a place of charred up-
rights. The English army, fossicking there in the mud-
bound winter, had somehow desecrated the place, so that
there was little spring growth. Jonquils bloomed in the
ditch by the road, however. A mile up this road they could
hear men calling. A little farther, a Breton knight was dying
on a palliasse at the side of the road. His pages had stuck his
standard in the soft earth. It made its futile heraldic boast
to the empty road. A crossbow bolt was under his eye and
went down into his head. The right eye was monstrously
swollen but the left seemed to watch them pass. The squire

240

bullied the pages, as if there was something that could be done.

Jehanne: A priest ought to be with him. There's a whole damned regiment of priests with this army.

D'Aulon: Perhaps they weren't told. *We* weren't told.

Ahead they could see earthworks, palisades, and inside them a belfry and cloister roofs.

Jehanne: This is the one that used to be a convent?

D'Aulon: That's right. The convent of St Loup.

Many hundred of metres off, in the ruined meadows, warhorses were tethered. Companies of militia rested by the road amongst piles of faggots, ladders, axes. Some lay on their backs in pavis, back-shields, like upturned tortoises. But she got the idea they were more awed than exhausted. They looked at her with staring eyes.

Jehanne and d'Aulon turned in amongst them.

Distantly, like a man who finds himself saying something excessive while drunk, she spoke to them.

Jehanne: There's no need to feel bad. We're all going to get inside that place.

They watched her promises pass. Who could tell if they believed her?

Further into the fields, across a few irrigation ditches, were groups of mercenaries with General Poton, who waved to her. Beyond them, standing about talking quietly, hundreds of knights and archers, men from Brittany, strung out in groups of a dozen. Fifty metres ahead of them, on his own, Gilles watched the English outworks.

She climbed down and gave her horse to Minguet. Already her thighs were aching. She felt ridiculous too, waddling over uneven ground with all that steel suiting on.

Jehanne: Why doesn't the Bastard let me know?

Gilles: Know, dear lady?

He sounded contemplative and his eyes were fixed on the English earthworks.

Jehanne: When these things are happening.

He explained the Bastard had intended only for the militia to demonstrate outside St Loup while the barges slipped down from Checy. But it became a battle and the English had done a lot of injury to the militia. De Boussac found out and had gone round waking up the army. It was as well.

241

The militia companies wanted to give up the fight at St Loup and return to the city to cut the throat of every uselessly drowsing knight they could find. At the moment, Gilles told her, the Bastard was at Checy, the Marshal de Boussac and la Hire round at Parisis Gate to deter Talbot from coming to help St Loup.

Jehanne: I mightn't know much about military things. But it doesn't look to me as if it needs relieving.

Gilles: It will, it will. Give us time.

A Sir Henri de Longnon got badly hurt in an assault on the walls, said Gilles. That had appeased the militia.

She could see there were weird and plentiful resources in Gilles's eyes.

Jehanne: How should it be done?

Gilles: Well, we ought to talk to Poton and the militia. I think we should go in the middle, dismounted of course. Our archers ought to carry lots of faggots, ladders, axes. Half Poton's company and half the militia on our right, the other half of each on our left. If we can light enough fires at the palisades we'd blind them with smoke, because the wind's westerly. Come and see Poton.

They went and talked, Jehanne thinking all the time how she hadn't known the planning of death could be a craft, could be so cleanly intoxicating in the brain. Messengers were sent to the militia companies by the road. Jehanne and serene Gilles walked back to the centre. Squires adjusted breast plates and belts for knights. Militia-men hugged faggots under their arms and found the point of balance of ladders and let their grip rest there.

Everyone began walking at once.

Jehanne: What will they shoot at us?

Gilles: Dear lady! Cannon. Arrows. Bolts. They'll throw stones too. But of course the stars say you and I shall be untouched.

Jehanne: Someone says it.

Gilles: Someone says it.

Jehanne: Your knights could wait back until the archers get the palisades alight?

Gilles: Dear lady, do you think knights—once arrived—could tolerate standing back in safety while their poor commoners take the risks?

Jehanne: All the dead are poor commoners. Your poor Sir Henri was beginning to discover it back there when we passed him.

Gilles: But you ought to consider: he's safe dead, with his honour intact.

Jehanne: My God, you should have seen his eye.

Gilles: I saw his eye, Mademoiselle. (He made a concession.) When we get to the wall, we will of course help with the equipment.

They were two hundred metres away. *Brother Jesus* she kept muttering, as a promise, as an utterance of delight. They would be inside St Loup in la Beauce in Jesus's garden of vengeance.

St Loup stood on a hill. There was a ditch, a mound, another ditch, the palisades. Gilles told her the English had manned the mound outside the palisades that afternoon, but been forced to run indoors.

Gilles: Don't tread on a caltrop, dear lady, it's very painful. Keep your face down, don't look at the top of the walls. A pair of upturned eyes attracts their archers. Once we have the walls broken, stand back and rest.

They were now within bowshot of the palisades. Everywhere men were saying incantations and blessing themselves.

Jehanne: They've got a dog.

She could hear a big dog barking twice inside St Loup. A big blackbird flew above her head.

Gilles: That's the cannon, that's not a dog. You see, the stones landed away behind us. Can you run? Soon everyone will start running.

From the parapets an Englishman was calling at them in French. *Go back. Go back.* Quite hopefully.

A small flock of arrows rose out of St Loup and landed somewhere amongst the mercenaries. There was a scream there so disembodied that it seemed to be the sound of some mechanism.

Archers with pavis on their backs began to run into the first ditch and up the mound. Jehanne, in the bottom of the ditch, put her foot down beside a rusted jumble of iron spike. She had seen it only that second. Against Gilles's warning, she looked at the parapet, since she couldn't die

243

today. She saw longbowmen letting fly, but once the arrows left their strings she couldn't see them.

Climbing the mound she called for Minguet. He had her flag and he was so close behind her that she bumped him in half turning to look. They both very nearly fell over in a steel tangle.

Gilles and Poton stood on the mound.

Poton: They're piss–weak. Maybe a hundred archers. Half as many knights.

By some expert use of tinder, someone had started a torch burning and faggots were blazing against the palisades. French archers were firing upwards, through the smoke. No one seemed to be hurt, or to put the ladders up to the parapets.

And this is battle, thought Jehanne. Simply work. Like burning off the trash at the end of harvest. She noticed too that everything was both very fast and very slow—as time is to the intoxicated. The men under the palisades moved leisurely. A ladder went up the wall. Amongst the smoke an Englishman relaxedly pushed it away with an axe, and without any appearance of malice. She watched, she couldn't believe this was the nature of war.

Then everywhere, the walls were burning. Smoke funnelled up the flutes of the wall and you could hear men coughing and shouting oddly, Englishly, to Jesus and Mary.

Knights and archers like brothers raked the blazes together and began knocking holes in the burned timbers.

Gilles: Step through, Mademoiselle. If you must.

Breton knights had rushed in ahead looking for saleable English.

Inside, the world was different. Wooden shacks burned in the grey fog. Somehow there were dead on the ground, dirty with soot and blood and open–eyed. It wasn't always clear where their wounds were, though there were cut throats and near beheadings. The sharpest points of the mess were the eyes, the terrified crystals.

How did this happen? It was honest work at the base of the palisades. It couldn't have made all these black dead English.

In King Jesus's garden of vengeance in la Beauce . . .

She and Gilles strolled across the killing-ground to a cloister whose roofs had fallen in.

Gilles: It's all terrible: it's the only way God gave men of settling his affairs.

Jehanne: I see.

Gilles: One gets used to it . . .

All at once she was very angry with the dead.

Amongst the columns of the cloister an English boy in engraved armour gave up his sword to a Breton knight. The boy was weeping. Six Englishmen passed her in the smoke. One of them looked her in the eyes. They all ran on. Where were they going?

From the end of the cloister nearest the chapel, a French mercenary stepped. He wore tapestry over his shoulders like a cape.

Jehanne: They're starting to loot. Does that mean we've won?

Gilles: It seems so.

They began walking side by side towards the looter. Gilles raised his visor.

Jehanne: And all the killing over?

Gilles: I think so.

Jehanne: It's all very quick, isn't it?

Gilles: Yes.

At the edge of the cloister, however, an Englishman lay in a long smear of gore. His guts flopped red and grey out of a long belly wound. His eyes were open. His mouth was moving very slowly. He was so intent on his words; like a rehearser.

Jehanne was overtaken by mad hope.

Jehanne: If we tucked them back. In the right way.

More offal slipped suddenly from the wound. The coué closed his lips.

Jehanne: There must be an order. For putting them back.

She was about to go on her knees and try to puzzle it out. Gilles took her by the shoulders and jolted her against a pillar of that ruined cloister. Her breath left her for some seconds. Her head rang.

Gilles: He's gone, dear lady. It can't be done, there's no right way to replace a man's viscera. He didn't suffer.

Jehanne: Savages. Bastard savages.

245

She wasn't sure whom she was talking about.

Gilles: You saw him talking quietly. He didn't suffer.

She spoke in a daze.

Jehanne: Don't let them kill anyone in the church. The army mustn't get unclean. Don't let them loot the place. There's a man there stolen a drape.

Gilles: Dear lady.

She put her helmeted head against the stonework in King Jesus's garden of vengeance in la Beauce. She could hear Gilles asking the soldier with the tapestry where it had come from. Gilles sounded very quiet, very terrifying. Two or three other soldiers too had come into the open with loot and Gilles asked them acid questions while, in their hands, rich cloth rustled and precious metal clicked.

She could hear axe-blows and raised her head. Beyond the apse of the chapel stood a bell-tower. Militia-men were cutting at its door with axes. Knights and gentlemen strolled about amongst the wreckage. A thousand knights and gentlemen in the fort, inspecting the outnumbered dead. Some chatted with their English prisoners. Only the militia-men were still war-like, hacking at the campanile door.

Gilles told her he'd put guards on the chapel. They walked through the murk to see what was happening at the tower.

Jehanne: I expected when we got inside we'd find the English laid out, washed . . . you know. Anointed . . . in clean shrouds.

Gilles said nothing.

When the campanile door broke down militia-men trampled each other to get inside. They were convinced of their immortality now, they had unbuckled their pavis which lay, great husks, all over the cloisters. Within the tower, finding the last enemy, they were laughing.

Jehanne: Tell them to bring them out.

When Gilles tried to he couldn't be heard. Then Englishmen were forced out the door. They were dressed ridiculously in badly-fitting Augustinian habits. In dalmatics you could see moleskin breeches or bare legs beneath. In chasubles over filthy drawers. The cloister was all at once thudding with rampant male laughter. The crowd unflexed itself and Gilles led Jehanne through it. Soon they were facing a tall Englishman. His monk's habit came as far as his calves. His eyes were not funny. But Jehanne began to laugh at him because she knew she could save him, that the eyes boggled like that without any necessity.

He said, *Lady, you can't risk killing us, we're clergy*.

Gilles went into the middle of the robed English and gestured that he wanted everyone to be silent. He could tell and was grateful that the sight of all those antic hairy calves had broken her despair.

Gilles: The English came last October. Since then you've had no success with them. Generals promised success but produced its opposite. That dear lady came last Friday evening, promised success and here it is on Monday afternoon. You shouldn't do anything with these English clergy unless you ask her. Why? Because you never know what divine pattern you upset by not asking her.

The militia all looked to her. For some reason she found herself laughing again and she could see the militia-men think, certainly she's going to say *slaughter*, and could feel the impulses of their blood burring at her heart unexpectedly.

I'm going to say *yes*. I want their comic blood. When she said *no* she was arguing with herself as well as them. She said no, the clergy had to be saved, not cut about or beaten. She said *King Jesus lusts for mercy the way we lust for worse things.* She said *Obey me!*

Englishmen gave way at the knees. They put their foreheads to the ground and cried.

At night in Orleans, Jehanne confessed to Pasquerel her guilt for the dead, her hour of blood-lust. Pasquerel said of course, of course. She was angry at him for being unimpressed. And as well for caring more about the doctrine of suffering than about suffering itself, the doctrine of death rather than about death, the doctrine of whole skins rather than the fact of strewn guts.

She was still in a state of unease at dinner time. She felt they're in hell now, consumed, wasted. What meat and wine can put a coating on that fact?

So she was petulant when the Bastard came to dinner with his thanks.

He said the fall of St Loup was more than he and de Gaucourt could have hoped for. They had put a garrison

247

there while workmen filled the ditches, levelled the mounds, knocked down the palisades. They were working this very night by torchlight. St Loup couldn't have fallen at a better time. The news was that Fastolf was in Janville, though no one knew how true that was. Janville was only a day's march north.

Jehanne: Fastolf, Fastolf!

She said it *Fastoff. Fastoff*. The way she—and others—called Glasdale Classidas, and Suffolk Suffort.

Bastard: You'd rather not be told about him.

Jehanne: If I'm not told I'll have your head.

Bastard: I've a tough neck. But I'll remember.

She went to bed shivering that summer's night beside warm Charlotte.

To my honoured etc.   Dated 1 May 1492

Today was Ascension Day and the girl, who seems to be given all credit for yesterday's capture of St Loup, went to Mass in Sainte-Croix without any armour. There is a rumour that the slaughter she saw has made her less militant. But all the militia were drawn up in companies in the cathedral square and cheered her for a solid half-hour.

Monsieur de Rais tells me that the generals are alarmed in case all the militia and knights cross the river tomorrow to take on St Jean-le-Blanc and leave the town denuded. Some of them tried to tell her the next attack will be a sortie against St Lorent. She refused to believe them. She said she had asked her squire, who had told her every soldier knew the next step was an assault on the St Jean-le-Blanc, on the les Augustins side.

The Marshal is dazzled by her. His taste is for her sort of exalted impudence and intuition. La Hire also appreciates her: they both have the same peasant temperament.

The English are not so easily endeared to her. In fact there are signs that she is their greatest fear. This afternoon she went out across the bridge to the south of the city until she came to the place where the French have broken two spans and built a fort facing les Tourelles. As on an earlier occasion she wanted to warn them, but this time she asked a French archer to shoot a letter she had written

248

into the English fortifications. I think she hoped by this stratagem to avoid being called names. For someone so sure of her mission, she is easily hurt by the insults of others. As the archer shot the arrow with the letter bound round it she called out 'Take this and read!' As she turned to come back into town she heard an English knight yell, 'News from the Armagnac whore!' This shout is supposed to have distressed her very much . . .

Bernardo Massimo

At five o'clock the next morning the militia companies lined up in the rue des Talmeliers. They stretched from the Renard Gate out of sight in the direction of the centre of the town. About half-past six they all started barracking. *Les Augustins! Les Augustins!*

Jehanne could hear it and was frightened—it sounded such an unmanageable roar.

D'Aulon: They ought to quieten down. Talbot could overhear them.

Jehanne: I'll tell them.

She went out on to the steps with Pasquerel and d'Aulon. Seeing her, they stopped being coherent and let out a long deep scream of acclaim.

A half-dozen city magistrates stood at the base of the steps. They advanced. In the centre a boyish man, sleek, about thirty. They all bowed.

Magistrate: Mademoiselle, we cannot accept de Gaucourt as civil governor. His interests fight the interests of the city and the Orleanais. It suits him if the situation drags on, it suits the knights and free companies, because we feed them while they take and sell prisoners. They don't really like headlong assault because the militia kill too many negotiable Englishmen, you understand. General Poton complained to the captains of militia that they killed too many English knights at St Loup.

Jehanne: You surely think we ought to let anyone surrender who wants to.

Magistrate: I express it badly. What I mean is that it's business to them, but to us it's a fight for our lives.

For our sanity, one of the others admitted.

Magistrate: De Gaucourt can gain from forcing the Council

to raise another army still. He pretends he's mortgaged himself for his king, but he's really on the money-lending side. We can't fit another army into the city. We can't feed it or support it. If we aren't allowed to start doing now what has to be done, we would consider giving the city up. I say that so you'll see how serious we are.

The militia were screaming. *St Loup, les Augustins!*

Jehanne: I want to go over the river today. Does that suit you?

Magistrate: It makes us ecstatic, Mademoiselle. De Gaucourt has boats ready to ferry knights . . .

Jehanne: The knights will come too. I'll be with la Hire and Monsieur de Rais.

She looked up and down the lines of red morning faces. It was an hour of the day, under a clear sky narrow but radiant above the balconies and gables of Orleans, when no one believes in death, in the abstract let alone in the particular.

D'Aulon and the magistrates managed to quieten the companies closest to Boucher's door.

Minguet got her horse and Raymond her armour. She told Raymond to hang the armour from his horse—she'd put it on outside the walls—and not in his short-sightedness to drop any. Her brothers were there, mounted, and Bertrand wheezing for air—so much of it was burnt up in the fervour up and down rue des Talmeliers.

All together, and with the magistrates, they rode down the lines of militia-men who took the whole far wall as far as the cross-roads at rue Ste Catherine, half-way across the city.

It took a quarter of an hour from there to the sight of the Burgundy Gate. In the square in front of the gate were one hundred and fifty armed knights and horsemen. At least as many archers stood on the parapets over the gate, facing the centre of the city.

D'Aulon knew what they were for. *They're there to stop us,* he told Jehanne.

She found the magistrates had ridden forward on her flanks for the confrontation. She looked them in the face, as if to assure them the right sort of fury was in her.

D'Aulon: That's de Gaucourt's flag.

He pointed out a knight in the centre. At that second a

knight rode forward and raised his visor. It was old de Gaucourt's face inside.

De Gaucourt: I could hear them yelling *les Augustins*.

Jehanne: You're a fool if you think I told them.

De Gaucourt: Who told them?

Jehanne: They knew. They could smell it.

De Gaucourt: All a matter of noses.

Jehanne: It's good to see you ready for war, Monsieur. Even if you're all facing the wrong way.

De Gaucourt: This crowd isn't leaving the city, Jehanne. When we go to les Augustins it's to be done properly.

Jehanne: *I'm* going where no one can stop *them* going. That's all.

There was a clean whistling sound. All the archers on the parapet had armed and drawn their bowstrings. Their leather wristlets glistened, tight-packed with sinew.

Jehanne: The people behind me will fight you and then the Goddams. That's a fact.

Magistrate: They'll fight you, Monsieur.

The militia were crowding the buttocks of the horses, the magistrates' horses were skidding forward towards de Gaucourt.

De Gaucourt: For Christ's sake, if they do it . . . the les Augustins thing . . . it'll be a shambles.

The archers on the wall were being whistled, hissed, booed. Militia-men were taking off their mail, opening their jackets, calling out, *Kill a Frenchman if you want to. Sow's arse. Bastards.*

Magistrate: They'll kill you, old man.

De Gaucourt hissed and punched the rampart of his saddle.

D'Aulon: Don't do that, Monsieur. Your archers might think it's a signal.

De Gaucourt called over his shoulder for the gate to be opened. His knights couldn't move for militia-men. Their horses hated being immobile in the crowd and began snorting out their terror.

De Gaucourt: There aren't enough boats to get this crowd over quickly.

Jehanne: A good thing we started early.

De Gaucourt: I'm not responsible for the shambles we'll see today.

251

Jehanne: They can't be controlled.

De Gaucourt: You're very pleased, Mademoiselle. That they are out of control.

Jehanne: I don't think you can say that, Monsieur.

De Gaucourt: I needn't ask: your Voices all say today's the great day.

Jehanne: Perhaps they do.

De Gaucourt: Have they read Vegetius on *de Re Militari*?

Jehanne: They don't admit it.

De Gaucourt: It'll be a great day for blood.

De Gaucourt rode out of the barbican with her. The jonquils trembled in the ditches. Even the weeds binding the misused earth of St Aignan suburb looked vibrant.

Soon they could see a fleet of a half-dozen barges moored near the little river islands called les Martinets.

De Gaucourt: See. A half-dozen to ferry all this crowd over to Ile aux Toiles.

It appeared that a bridge of two barges, moored overnight, connected Ile aux Toiles with the south bank. It was only a short throw from the isle to the south bank.

The magistrates said that the barges ought to be packed with militia-men, who could then wait on Ile aux Toiles for Jehanne, de Gaucourt and whatever other mounted troops took it into their heads to come. De Gaucourt and Jehanne agreed.

Jehanne: Raymond, get me in my hardware.

The boy came to her, peering to make sure where the limbs were on which he was to clamp the items of her suit.

With these defiances and in these casts of mind a day began so confusing that by the afternoon no one could tell who had been right—de Gaucourt for his caution, Jehanne for being blithe, the militia and magistrates for being enthusiastic.

Militia-men and some knights were already sailing for Ile aux Toiles when la Hire led his companies out of the Burgundy gate. Jehanne asked could she speak to la Hire. They rode a little aside.

Jehanne: The magistrates say all you knights and generals don't want to finish the English quickly. It's not in your interest.

La Hire: Maman Yolande has made it in my interest.

252

She realized he had achieved what was for him a summit of honesty.

Jehanne: Thank you. I want to stay with you today. Not de Gaucourt.

La Hire: My honour, Mademoiselle.

It was two hours before there was room on a barge for Jehanne and la Hire, their frightened horses, the frightened horses of their equerries and attendants. She didn't speak to that pale incarnation of Messire called Sir Bertrand de Poulengy, who had in any case to wait for the next barge.

The river ran deeply, potently, and the horses had to be soothed.

Look, la Hire told her.

The day's first and basic confusion was commencing. From mid-river they could see not only the Ile aux Toiles, but on the south bank the English mud-and-palisade fortress called St Jean-le-Blanc. To the west of St Jean, a half-mile away and hazed by the exhalations of the river, stood the complex of les Augustins—les Tourelles.

So it was like this:

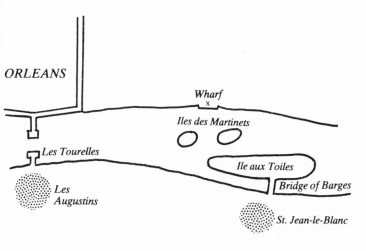

The English were leaving St Jean-le-Blanc, climbing west over its parapets. A roar of French joy from the militia on Ile aux Toiles gusted the English west to where they could join their colleagues in les Augustins.

La Hire: They'll run wild now, those militia. *Wild!*

And hundreds of militia left the island and ran over the barge-bridge to St Jean-le-Blanc and struck their company flags all over the mounds and set fire to the palisades and the hovels inside.

The flames looked nearly companionable at that distance, in the sun and under the light wind.

Jehanne: Is it such a bad thing? To get a fort so easily.

La Hire: It won't do them any good. They'll think it's a compliment to them.

Jehanne: Perhaps it is.

There was all the delirium of amateur-soldiering in her too that morning.

La Hire: Glasdale's making les Augustins stronger. That's all.

Soon Jehanne, la Hire, d'Aulon and fifty other mounted soldiers were on Ile aux Toiles, amongst the thick forests of rowan trees. Beyond a rise were the anchored barges by which they would get to the south bank. The barge trembled in this deep and narrow channel. The girl's belly knotted. It would be hard to lead the war-horses across them.

D'Aulon came to talk to Jehanne and la Hire. He came, in fact, in delegation—a red-haired Scot called Lord Hugh Kennedy, a Spaniard called Don Partrada, and d'Aulon, bankrupt Armagnac.

D'Aulon: Monsieur, Mademoiselle, it's obvious what's going to happen. The militia are going to run on to les Augustins . . .

La Hire: I know. Expecting the English to clear out of it as well.

D'Aulon: The English will in fact chase them all the way back to the bridge here. Unless there's a good rear-guard set up on the south bank . . .

La Hire: I know, I know. It's going to be an abattoir.

D'Aulon: De Gaucourt was right by accident.

La Hire: It hasn't escaped my notice.

He counted heads. There were twenty of his own hired knights, there were Partrada and a half-dozen Spaniards, there were four Scots lords, Jehanne, d'Aulon, squires, Minguet, Raymond, and, by now, her brothers and Bertrand. About eighty people, all mounted. They'd take station on the west mound of St Jean-le-Blanc if it wasn't too hot there from the burning walls. Every time the English crowded the militia back to the bridge la Hire's people would threaten and terrify them. The bridge of barges had to be kept a reasonable, a peaceful thoroughfare where men and horses could cross without panic.

Amongst the trees squires blindfolded the horses and led them over the flat-boats. Everyone picked a rowan branch, for rowans were reputed best when dealing with unruly horses. There was a beach of soft brown silt for them to step on to at the south bank.

D'Aulon: It's happening already.

The militia had gone sprinting for les Augustins. They ran through the trampled earth and few charred doorposts of what had been the south bank suburb of le Portereau. The bad winter diet they had eaten told on them. They could see too that English knights and archers were coming out of the gate of les Augustins and standing on the piled earth and logs outside. Bending English crossbowmen were coolly at work on the ratchets of their weapons.

It occurred to the Orleans militia that les Augustins was not going to be like Jericho. They pulled up and stood gasping, hands on belts. Some of them even lay down amongst the weeds where the market gardens had been in years of peace.

La Hire lined out his eighty people in the steep mound of St Jean-le-Blanc. Jehanne kept an eye on her brothers in siege-hats and mail-coats, mounted on the sort of horses you'd use as pack-animals in more peaceful times. Already a few militia-men were strolling back towards St Jean and the bridge. A middle-aged man stopped under the mound and called out to them. There's a giant up there, a Goddam giant. *There*, outside les Augustins.

All the knights began pointing out to each other an English soldier in armour, who did look big, treading up and down the outworks of les Augustins. He was a depressing symbol.

La Hire knew the militia couldn't deal with such symbols. He had dismounted but climbed into his saddle again to ride out and order them back from the wasteland in front of les Augustins. He saw though, they all saw, the militia get up in silence and more or less at once and begin to walk towards the English. What weird shift in their vision, what incantations of the coués made them do it? The English waited on their mound or behind barriers of stakes. Ready as bridegrooms.

Flocks of arrows flew out of the breastworks. Hundreds of English knights, a few of them mounted, came yelling downhill. The militia died like sleepwalkers. A half-minute later they woke and began running.

La Hire dismounted again. He told his people to shelter behind their horses. If any squires or others had bows or crossbows they should get them ready.

Not everyone obeyed. The Scots were arguing. Two Scots lords wanted to ride straight up the Sancerre Road, through the running militia. La Hire talked to them, using their own Scots obscenities. He told them how soon the militia would all be milling out of breath to cross to Ile aux Toiles and how the English would be all round them, lofting arrows into the dense and indiscreet target.

Lord Kennedy: You're entitled to tell mercenaries what to do. Younger sons and hard-up farmers. You can't tell lords a thing.

La Hire didn't argue. He just kept up the presumption of command. He watched the shafts of the English long-bowmen—whom he was known to admire—catch sunlight at their apogees above the Orleanais rabble.

La Hire: Save up your death for this afternoon, Monsieur Kennedy. I think it might be needed more then.

The militia-men were now walking back in a leisurely way, stopping to let wounded friends spit blood or get their balance back. It was soon that they'd run.

La Hire spoke quietly, professionally, to Jehanne explaining how the English worked, the archers in squads, the knights running out all at once to hack up their enemy, then returning to the screen of archers who fired all at once in squads. The crossbowmen in amongst the longbowmen, letting go with terrible bolts all together at someone's word. Then the knights emerging again.

La Hire: We never do anything as well as that. Too much false pride, I think.

Jehanne saw that the sun was high.

Jehanne: Is it noon already?

La Hire, squinting at the sun as if it too were obdurate, admitted it was already noon.

Soon all the militia were running, very slowly, and the English—who had eaten badly themselves that winter—slowly following. In la Hire's company on the slope squires and suspect knights unhitched crossbows from their saddles, fitted bolts, cranked the weapons.

La Hire asked d'Aulon to look and tell him whose flags were flying on Ile aux Toiles. D'Aulon went down to the river bank to make a survey. When he came back he told la Hire that he'd seen de Gaucourt's, de Villars's and de Rais's flags amongst the clearing high up on the spine of the island.

La Hire made a detached comment on the report.

La Hire: The old man will keep them there all day. Just to show he was right about the militia.

Jehanne: Surely Gilles . . .

La Hire: Maybe Gilles will come.

La Hire nodded at d'Aulon. You could see he liked d'Aulon's tranquil style.

So the Orleans militia came gasping back through the flattened suburb of le Portereau. They milled on the bad road. Their mouths hung, they looked identically vacant, and inept with their feet. The English pattern la Hire had indicated to Jehanne had now broken up because of the number of French prisoners taken, all from Orleans and so easily saleable. On the road below St Jean-le-Blanc a militia-man from Orleans who had no breath left stopped to lecture la Hire's force.

Militia-man: They had a giant . . . two-handed bloody sword . . . like a scythe. Why weren't you there?

One of the Scots rode at him, but he danced to the side and barked for breath and joined the queue for the bridge.

Some knight had walked up to argue with la Hire. *We should have ridden up to the militia*, he said. *We ought to do it now, while the Goddams are feeling good and have lines of prisoners to look at.* La Hire didn't answer.

Now the English archers walked away a little and sat down to rest. The militia got across the bridge and there was wide rural quietness in le Portereau and on the slopes of St Jean-le-Blanc. You had to look hard to see the corpses along the river flats.

About one o'clock Monsieur de Villars crossed with a small party and joined la Hire.

At the same time, defiant Englishmen marched out of les Augustins and pretended to picnic in the rubble of le Portereau, half-way between their fortress and the mound where la Hire's people waited. After taking a little bread, the Goddam archers began firing at la Hire. Everyone on the slope had at least a hide shield which they put up when the arrows made the black well-ordered dive for their flesh.

La Hire said the English were trying to force them back to Ile aux Toiles. Once they managed that they'd knock holes in the bottoms of the barge-bridges and the day's war would be finished.

Proud knights, poor knights, squires, adventurous peasants (Jehan and Pierrolot for example) sheltered under shields and behind horses of varying value. When arrows struck or pierced a shield it was a blow that could knock a man on his backside. So, comically bowled over and open to the sky he could be caught by the next volley. In this way a few of la Hire's men were wounded. But of a dozen volleys not one shaft struck Jehanne's shield or her old grey.

The English could see it all had scant effect and sat down again to think.

Jehanne put her shield on her shoulder and went to see her brothers. Downhill a Frenchman's horse was bucking and galloping with a shaft in its withers. Another was on its front knees with an arrow deep in its eye. A boy, struck in the belly, was praying aloud in a level voice, very business-like. He seemed to be acknowledging that praying aloud was the professional thing to do when an arrow found your belly. She stopped and kissed his face but he didn't know. He wasn't as alive as he looked.

Jehan was peasant-bitter. When were those lords and cowards on Ile aux Toiles coming? *Why are you crying? Am I crying?* she asked him.

Pierrolot: I wish I had a crossbow. Couldn't you afford me a crossbow?

She remembered what de Baudricourt had told her about crossbows, one zany afternoon in Vaucouleurs.

Jehanne: They're very slow to load. You have to be taught.

Pierrolot: I'll learn.

He was willing to undertake any course of learning if he got off that hill.

Jehanne: Don't be frightened. Your big sister tells you. Don't be frightened.

Pierrolot: I wish more people would come.

Bertrand was there in his mail and siege-hat, stooped more than the other stoopers, behind his horse. In his white face the veins at the sides of his nose were an expanse of purple. It seemed they might have burst from terror. He appeared old and unhealthy and looked up at her as if he was saying *yes I know what I am, a vain threadbare knight, I confess it.*

She stood by his horse and laughed at him lovingly and he half-laughed, half-sobbed back at her. They both knew too that the other was thinking: yes, *that* was the best time, when the pattern was simple, with de Baudricourt or on the flooded roads with the king's messenger.

Jehanne: Nothing's going to happen to you, Bertrand.

Bertrand: There are a thousand Englishmen there, Jehanne. How many of us? Are there a hundred, are there as many as that?

She told him that nothing would happen to him because he was Messire's voice, there were incarnations, and he was an incarnation.

Bertrand: I'm not aware of being Messire's voice. When the arrows start falling I'm not aware of it. Why don't they run up on us?

Jehanne: I don't know.

Bertrand: You have to go back to la Hire?

Jehanne: Yes. Do you know, none of those generals are like humans at all.

He laughed. Because he thought she was apologizing for leaving.

Jehanne: It's the truth.

Her visit had however done him good.

Bertrand: Put your shield on the other shoulder going back. It's not much use to you facing Germany.

When she had walked a little way away she turned again and they laughed with each other under the terrible sound, again beginning, the glissade and hiss of arrows in the air.

He called, *Put your visor down.* But she felt happier with it up, as if she might ultimately escape entirely, even from Messire, through that little hole.

She saw the praying boy had died and was being carried down behind the mound into the charred ditch of St Jean-le-Blanc.

The air cleared again. It seemed the English had put up a flight of arrows just out of bemusement. Now they sat down again.

A half-hour passed. Everyone except la Hire was angry. Jehanne was angry. Knights were calling overland to Ile aux Toiles. *Gaucourt, Gaucourt, Gilles for Christ's sake!*

In the wasteland the English stood up all together, then divided into two unequal parts.

There were hundreds of Englishmen running at them, hundreds for the flat-boats. Only two dozen English knights were mounted.

La Hire told his people to stand on the mound. He signalled around him and acquired some Gascons, the Scots, the Spaniard Partrada, and d'Aulon. You could hear the English shouting. There was a crunch of lance-butts as la Hire and the others couched their lances in the sockets on the right chests of their armour. Jehanne remembered to call for her own lance from myopic Raymond.

Her belly jumped when she homed its butt in the socket near her right armpit.

La Hire said undramatically *Montjoie St Denis,* the old French battle-cry. He admitted later he thought it would be his last utterance of that nearly meaningless but cherished French slogan.

Jehanne, uninvited, jolted downhill with the clutch of horsemen la Hire had signalled for. Her visor was down. Her impetus, the impact she would make on something down on the riverbank, alarmed her. But she was grunting in a sort of exaltation. Through the grate of her salade, she could see English knights and soldiers turning, trying to form up for the shock of la Hire, d'Aulon, don Partrada, some Gascons, some Scots, her potent virgin self.

She could tell they wouldn't be able to stand it. Even if they were hundreds, with axes for knocking holes in the flat-boats. They all caught terror from each other in one holy instant. She saw a Gascon catch an Englishman on lance-point, lift him broken in the air, discard him on the road.

Time, like a hand, took her as it takes the drunken and flung her, with d'Aulon and la Hire and Partrada side-on to the Englishmen running at the mound where Bertrand and young Pierrolot, with his ambitions regarding crossbows, waited on their poor horses.

Again you knew the English would run away at an angle.

The Orleanais militia watched this success from Ile aux Toiles. With them as with the Englishmen hope and despair came in epidemic spasms. In epidemic hope they came jogging over the bridge back into Sologne.

Most of the knights had taken English prisoners and Jehanne watched them pass her. They were a lean race. They were sent into the ditch of St Jean-le-Blanc where the praying boy's fresh corpse lay. The earth there was black and still hot.

La Hire: Oh holy Christ.

Again the militia were chasing the English all the way back to the outworks of les Augustins. No one could stop them. Watching them freshly and fatuously inspired she had the same sense la Hire suffered: that although it was mid-afternoon the morning's idiocies were repeating themselves. And she was tired now.

La Hire thought it safe for them now to go forward into the wasteland of le Portereau. Militia companies passed them and called back commendations.

La Hire: We'll have to do all over what we've done all day. Just the same, it *can* be done.

But her horse that had seemed so hectic and fluid on the slope moved heavily now.

Behind them the Marshals de Boussac and de Rais and old de Gaucourt at last crossed. Jehanne, turning painfully, saw de Gaucourt's great flag coming forward, green leeks on a red ground. God damn him.

Breton knights suddenly rode all about them shouting *Noël.* Celebrating them. She asked la Hire if what they did all day was the right thing then?

La Hire: It was the only right thing that's been done all day.

Gilles: Noël, dear lady.

The Marshal de Rais, bright-eyed this afternoon, had

ridden to her front, making his big horse step crabwise in salute.

La Hire: It would have been pleasant to see you earlier, Monsieur.

Gilles: I was ill the whole morning in Orleans.

La Hire: Your flag was on the island.

Gilles: I had my man put it there. As an inspiration.

He smiled, a loving broadness of smile along the delicate lips.

La Hire: Jesus Lord Almighty!

Jehanne: You might have sent us your knights, Gilles.

Gilles: I had to be *bled*, Jehanne. The omen! I couldn't send my men out under such an omen.

La Hire: Mother of God!

Gilles: Remember I had that fever yesterday? A recurrence. I was too sick to instruct my servant on the correct herbal mixture. I'm an excellent herbalist, Jehanne. Any village from Lorraine to the sea would be quite proud of me.

La Hire: And de Gaucourt's story?

He was so quietly angry, his blue eyes drugged with it.

Jehanne watched them. Gilles still rode sideways up the plain. She was fascinated, as if she might find out now which one was the more dangerous, the least human.

Gilles: I simply warn you. When I tell you I had a fever you are not to talk as if it's fiction.

La Hire spoke through Jehanne.

La Hire: Monsieur wants me to fight him so he can establish the good name of his puke, of his fever sweat. There's no question of its good name. I wish he'd been here, that's all. Even the lower gentry are permitted wishes.

Gilles: Spare us the story of your farm boyhood, Monsieur.

La Hire inhaled and rode away to the right flank.

Gilles: He puts on this calm act. But he's really very touchy.

Away to the right de Gaucourt rode in a broad convoy of knights.

Jehanne: That old man. He should lose his head.

Now Gilles was riding more normally, at her side.

Gilles: You mustn't make rash judgments, Jehanne. I had a fever. De Gaucourt spent the morning finding barges. The

Bastard is menacing Talbot in front of St Lorent to stop him crossing over here. All reasonable activities. Just look at that fellow!

They were nearing the corner of les Augustins. As at St Loup you could see monastic masonry beyond the palisade, a campanile like the one where the frightened English at St Loup had dressed as priests. On the walls, above the main gate, facing south towards the hub of the king's France, the English had their giant standing. He must have been seven feet tall inside his armour, but his helmet was fantastical and high, the kind they made in Germany, swept up above the crown in the form of an eagle's head. He stood there as some sort of argument—symbolic, mythical, biblical, magical—that to try to burn down les Augustins was against nature, decency, reason.

The militia piling faggots under the palisades were suffering and being killed. They would run in a company at a time to start a fire under the parapets. But there were so many English on the walls that the arrows fell like a shudder of wind running through silk.

There was no one up there to say do it all together. The other companies sat spectating or fussing over wounds or regretting the dead.

Gilles found la Hire and spoke to him as if they'd never argued.

Gilles: Etienne, would you look after the rear as before? I'll take the Bretons and do the thing properly.

Jehanne: I can come too, Gilles.

Gilles: I don't think so.

Jehanne: Don't your discs say I'll be safe?

La Hire: You *can* get hurt under the walls.

Jehanne: Monsieur, don't you know I'm Jesus's sister?

She was half-joking at him. If not to herself.

La Hire: I wish the English knew it.

In the end she was permitted or, at least, couldn't be stopped.

Gilles, his Bretons, Jehanne, d'Aulon, Raymond, Minguet, all dismounted. Bertrand, Jehan, Pierrolot seemed not to notice that they also had an option to go. The light was late afternoon. Two thousand, three thousand militiamen were facing the south wall of les Augustins. They looked at the giant above the gate. They watched other companies run up the mound into the ditch, up to the palisades, heap faggots, moving gently as beetles under their back-shields. The black downspout of rocks and arrows fell on their backs. This or that back or back-rib snapped or a bolt punched through into a spine. But the faggots were alight in a few places. The wounded were carried back through the ditch, over the mound to the watchers. The English poured water on the fires, leaned over the parapet with pails. The giant remained, over the gate, quietly hexing all the waiting army.

Perhaps two hundred knights and squires and boys. They edged through the middle of the militia. The militia numbly watched them through. Gilles walked along the front of the line, telling them they had to light too many fires for the English to put out. The girl was with him, he said, pointing to her white banner. (It was in myopic Raymond's hands.) The girl said there wasn't any special virtue in that giant. It wasn't clever to be bigger than *someone* else and it wasn't clever to be bigger than *anyone* else, it was an accident of birth. His knights would break down the gate under the place where the giant stood. Would they come, would they do it, many many fires to show the dear lady . . . ?

Those militia-men who were to live on in Orleans, working out their trade, remembered Gilles's speech for decades. For they could tell there was some kinship between Gilles and the girl. And over many years it was confirmed: both would be killed for witchery. The girl because her witchery was white and won earth for the undernourished king. Gilles because his witchery would turn black and he would grow, in the end, a beard and dye it blue, and cut living children apart in Brittany in his fortieth year, and make love to their bloody fragments and whisper endearments to their excised hearts and spleens.

The militia listened as if they dimly guessed the outline of the potent futures of Jehanne and Gilles. What you might call a magic moment held them then.

The English too could tell that down there, in a weedy flood plain, Gilles was breaking the spell they'd tried to make with their crass giant. They took to artillery. Culverins and mortars began to spray the militia with lumps of stone, some of it heavy river stuff to crush men, other coarse-textured and explosive to slice or penetrate. Once there was a short formal scream from somewhere in the Orleanais ranks. As if from a sportsman acknowledging a touch or a well-placed football.

Gilles: Mademoiselle, would you consent to carry your own flag?

He gave her what he'd given the militia: the idea that he had special knowledge about what would work.

Jehanne: You're a funny one.

His eyes on her, he drew out his massive sword. Jehanne went to Raymond and took her flag—his hands didn't easily give it up, he was in a dream.

Jehanne: You get an axe, Raymond.

She stood near d'Aulon. All the gentlemen pulled down their visors. She did. She was very used to the smotheration now, terror kicked only feebly in her belly. A bagpipe rant from somewhere in the lines entered the grille in front of her face and became quite refined, sweeter, inside her little steel cell.

As at St Loup, everyone had to walk. No one could actually run. They were so burdened one way or another. The mound was very steep and slippery, although the militia had come up it so often today.

She climbed it on her knees and one-handed. The flag in the other hand bucked and tripped on her knees and dirt got on it.

At the crest everyone stopped a second, throwing their weight back on their heels. Jehanne looked into the pit. It was full of shadow. There were three dead men lying in the shadow. Because they lay steeply downhill or uphill they looked to be floating.

Then she ran down into the ditch on her heels. She felt some sort of trip-wire grab her foot and she sat backwards in the soft dirt. Minguet and Raymond, not saying a word, lifted her up by the elbows. It took long, slow effort.

The slope out of the ditch, out of the dark, up to the palisades. She could see splashes of blood on the black earth. And there was so little room to stand at the top, so little room to pile wood or wield an axe. She was very nauseated but knew it would be a bad omen if she puked.

265

Heads down, heads down, everyone kept yelling. But it was senseless not to look up to the top of the walls. Because she wanted to see how the English looked. She could however see no shapes or faces, but far above her, hung in the air like an ornament, one black feathered arrow, very pleased in its own pure shape. She thought, if it's really hanging there, it isn't going to hang there forever. She looked down and instantly the arrow stood, waist deep in earth, trembling between her feet. Just to her right the squires were making a fire at the gate. She could hear men being wounded. Did some of them too see death hung like a slow ornament at the top of the wall?

She thought of walking along the base of the palisades with Minguet and Raymond, but there wasn't room for it, you couldn't get past the piles of faggots, the militia waiting with ladders to put up once there was a confusion of smoke.

Soon enough there was. She could scarcely see, she simply waited there with her flag and her pages. She was grateful for the fog. She thought that if anyone could have seen them they must have looked laughable and useless. As well, she still wanted to be sick.

There were a lot of Englishmen on the walls. You could hear bolts splitting armour open in the smoke. Thunk, thunk, thunk, thunk! She thought: tonight I'll remember the sound and be shocked. Now it doesn't mean much.

In this way, she and Minguet and Raymond waited for a result. Now and then the boys took a blow or two at the palisades but they were such solid timber. A few chips flew, Raymond and Minguet shrugged.

At last she could not prevent it, she leaned on the timbers and vomited. Because she had not eaten that day it was deep and painful vomit. She thought: for some reason that does it, nothing worthwhile can happen now.

She looked up. Gilles was beside her, coughing, his visor up.

Gilles: Dear lady, the militia are running back. It's useless for the moment.

She looked about. They were suddenly very alone on the scarp. She could hear foreign tongues, water sizzling down on the faggots.

Jehanne: It'll be dark soon.

266

Gilles: There's a message that Maître Jean has crossed the river with cannon and culverins. I'll ask him to blow their gate down. We mustn't stand about here.

The metal of Raymond's shoe seemed to pop. A bolt had entered his foot and stuck him to the earth. They watched him try to pull his foot away from the place and whimper. Then he raised his visor so that he could bend and withdraw the spike. In some way, he must have glanced up, for he returned to Jehanne and Gilles in slow cross-eyed protest. There was a bolt deep in his head, just above the bridge of his nose. In their last instant's vision his faulty eyes tried to focus on the missile.

All this happened in the instant it takes compassion to travel from your futile heart to your more or less useful hand.

Jehanne wanted to take the body which sat dead amongst her bile. Even Gilles got desperate. No one could carry the dead boy in his armour, no one had time to disarm him.

Gilles: Even you can't stay here charmed forever.

In the ditch were dozens of dead. Oh Jesus, were they her onus? It was very dark in there, now the sun was so low. D'Aulon dragged her along.

Fresh militia had come up and were listening to stories from the ones who'd been to the walls and back.

Jumping amongst them, what in the hell do I do now, weep, pray? Raymond, little-boy, cross-eyed.

Gilles saved her. He simply called out, off-handed, not straining to have them believe him.

Gilles: In Christ's name, we aren't going home yet. We have cannon now. I heard the English call out to Christ and then to Satan. But Satan will deceive them. They're finished.

She heard Gilles. She felt Raymond in an instant cease to be a bleeding grief. He became a stone in her belly. Portable. Gilles rejoined her.

Gilles: It's going to be *today*. Why are you limping?

Jehanne: I fell over in the pit.

They could see de Gaucourt and la Hire standing chatting. De Gaucourt did not look up till Gilles and Jehanne were feet away.

De Gaucourt: See, it isn't exactly like your Voices say.

She wouldn't answer.

267

La Hire: You're bleeding, Mademoiselle.

Her remaining page confirmed it.

Minguet: From the foot, Mademoiselle.

As soon as they all told her she felt radiant weakness in her body. She sat on the ground. Pierrolot and Jehan bent over her as of right. D'Aulon's long tranquil face came and went above her, Bertrand's long frantic one. She could see her blood drying on the weeds of the king's France. From a ridiculous little wound in the foot, a little blood.

Jehanne: At least Jacques would be pleased to know.

But Pierrolot and Jehan didn't understand the family joke she was making. D'Aulon sent Pierrolot to get water from the river to wash the wound. It was, he said, dirty.

Then Gilles bent to the wound.

Gilles: Dear lady, it's so deep, you stood on a caltrop. Those spiky things the English leave about.

She could see occult intentions forming in his eyes.

Jehanne: No Gilles, nothing fancy. For God's sake, go and talk to the master–gunner.

Minguet stood by with lard and rags. He was bare-headed and weeping and she began weeping too.

Jehanne: How old was he, Minguet?

She meant Raymond.

Minguet: I don't know. Fourteen. We weren't really friends. I suppose we were in a sort of way. Eternal rest . . .

In fact, Pasquerel and other priests had gone right up to the walls anointing the recent dead. The English did not try to stop them. She hoped one of the priests would go right up to the wall and close Raymond's awesome cross–eyes with chrism.

Partrada the Spaniard talked earnestly to d'Aulon about the wound. Those caltrops, he said, you could get a killing fever from. You could get lockjaw . . .

Minguet had bound it up tight, disciplining the pain. Some yards away the Scot Kennedy was arguing with la Hire. Partrada went out of boredom to listen. D'Aulon asked her could she stand. Yes, but she wasn't going to wear armour on that foot.

Across at the argument, Kennedy had decided against risking any of la Hire's subterranean furies. He wanted a straightforward slanging, he wanted a man who could be trusted to lose his temper and be seen to lose it. Now he had begun ranting at Partrada. La Hire played gently with the lobe of his ear and walked away.

Kennedy could be heard ranting in his weird French, Partrada answering in his. Kennedy said that the best people had been wasted all day. All that was needed was someone to go straight for the gate.

Of course, he was not being reasonable.

Partrada said the ones who'd spent all day in the rear-guard were just as brave as someone who went straight for the gate. What did a person do when he got to the gate? Knock?

Kennedy said he'd get there and if the thousands didn't follow and break the gate with mere weight then he'd rather be dead.

It was a futile chivalric sentiment and if she'd been able to walk properly she would have gone and told him.

At last, with d'Aulon's help, she stood. The wound did not hurt sharply. Minguet came up with a felt slipper for her. She meant to ask where he'd found it. But the noise of wagons distracted her. It was the gunners, preparing their arts.

If you held your arm out full length the sun was only half a hand span above Olivet hills.

D'Aulon: Maître Jean himself.

She remembered that impish master-gunner she'd seen nesting in a bridge pylon the first day she went to talk to Glasdale. The Marshal de Rais could be seen talking to Maître Jean. There were five cannon facing les Augustins from the back of wagons. On a third wagon sat culverins. Being so close to them, Jehanne began sweating. She hated the metallic stink of them, the chemical noise they would make, the random killing they were meant to do.

Jehanne was about to find that hers was not the only magic lunacy in Sologne. Looking to her front, she saw Partrada and Kennedy clasping hands. They called *make way* and began shambling forward, making good pace in all that steel.

The militia-men made way as if being attacked from behind. One of them tripped and dropped a ladder on a wounded man.

Jehanne, seeing Partrada and Kennedy running like that,

felt that through some mercy they had no right to, they were going to break down the wall. Some militia-men felt it too, and began running after them, not well deployed, but right behind, on their potent spoor.

She forgot Raymond in her furious certainty.

Jehanne: Raymond, Minguet. It's going to happen.

Gilles: There'll be a little noise . . .

The cannon noise rang horribly in the walls of her helmet.

She knew it was Maître Jean, who was breezy with knights and happened to be a new kind of gentry, would blow les Augustins open for those two ridiculous knights, Partrada and Kennedy, running beneath the echo of cannon, still holding hands. The first one to pull away was meant to be ashamed for a lifetime. What a game!

Militia-men later said they could hear the giant hold his breath. But was he as big as that, poor bastard? Was his breathing audible five hundred metres back?

One cannon shot broke a leaf of the gate of les Augustins away, when the knights were already on the mound. The second broke the parapet above the gate. The giant, it appeared, sank slow and straight amongst the broken timber. No one thought at the time he'd break his back. They all thought, that's the end of his virtue.

Partrada and Kennedy were seen entering the gap Maître Jean had made.

Jehanne: Minguet, get my flag up there fast.

Young Minguet seemed to think some code would be broken by his running ahead of her. She could see he felt he ought to explain the rites of soldiering to her.

Jehanne: For God's sake, don't waste time. I'll get up there as fast as I can.

She was in a crowd, hobbling. She looked at her feet, to see nothing new happened to them. It wasn't really an item in a great scheme—a cut foot—it was pretty mean damage. If the king heard of it he wouldn't say ah the scapegoat's blood has begun to flow. It was just a little accident and she didn't want any more little accidents.

The sun was one finger above the hills, behind her left shoulder.

She saw de Gaucourt limping forward. Was he reluctant to take the fortress?

270

On the mound ahead her big flag was standing, Minguet standing at the side of it. No one else's flag was there, and the last of the daylight gave her white and gold emblems great power. The militia went over the mound laughing. Some went in the main gate. Others set fire again to the heaped faggots. Others put ladders up and went up them easily, as if they were flights of stairs. The wind blew the smoke over the river towards St Lorent—into Talbot's eyes.

When Jehanne got to the gate she had to climb over hillocks of split timber to get inside. It was like a poor town in there. In the middle, the unroofed chapel of the monastery. The hovels ran down in streets. She could hear yowling, less than human, from the middle of the place. Militia-men ran past her to get to it. Avid to be in at the liturgy of screaming.

And the knights who should be preventing all the worst things, beginning to walk back already towards the gates with English knights as prisoners!

D'Aulon: It can't be helped, Jehanne.

She was so shocked with those others she bit at *him*.

Jehanne: Why don't you get a few prisoners yourself? Help pay the bills?

She stopped to rest the foot. She closed her eyes against the noises—axe-blows, glottal sounds, whines.

D'Aulon: Don't listen, Mademoiselle.

Jehanne: I'm not listening.

D'Aulon: That's good. Nothing can be done.

Jehanne: Did you see Raymond?

D'Aulon: Of course.

Jehanne: I want you to get some men and close his eyes if they haven't been closed. I want you to bring him back gently to the Bouchers' own chapel. All right?

D'Aulon: It'll be done.

Walking on, they moved in a bubble of their own, Jehanne, Minguet, d'Aulon. No one touched them. They met no one. They walked on the dead but saw no one dying. Ageless dead Goddams, nuzzling the ground or showing dirty faces. Too many for a tired person to feel regret for—so many they seized up the small jaws of guilt. She didn't feel guilty. They were like fallen wood, dropped gear.

In the end she had to sit amongst them. On a bench by a well. It was a busy place: the wounded were carried past, and loot.

Her brother Jehan came by carrying someone's upper armour.

He said he'd caught an Englishman sprinting for les Tourelles. The Goddams had left a gate open over there for any of their brothers from les Augustins who were quick enough. La Hire had foreseen it and diverted some men to cover the back gate.

For some reason both d'Aulon and Jehanne were angry at Jehan's mean little capture. He raised the heavy plate-armour in his hands to get the meaning across to them.

Jehan: Off an English knight!

D'Aulon: Congratulations.

Jehanne: Now you're a gentleman from the waist up.

So her brother dragged away, inadequately honoured. His eyes spun round in the dusk, expecting acclamation from some side or other.

Minguet was sent back for the horses and at last they rode out of the gates. Already militia were making camps down the road. She was cheered, she heard great bull-roars around her, terrible male acclamation. *Queen,* it said. *Mother.*

D'Aulon: I think you ought to get a night's rest in Orleans.

Jehanne: We'll see.

She didn't want to get out of touch at the wrong end of rue des Talmeliers ever again.

D'Aulon: You have to have your foot seen to as well. Lockjaw . . .

Jehanne: I won't get lockjaw.

D'Aulon: Mademoiselle, don't grieve. The dead are dead.

Jehanne: And in hell?

While she was waiting by the road, a little behind the places the militia were choosing for the night's rest, they saw a great fire rise up somewhere in les Augustins. Gilles and a Breton knight came down the road with many prisoners. He told her de Gaucourt and la Hire had decided on the fire: to clear the thousands of looting militia out. They'd feared that unless the militia organized itself and put strong pickets out to the west, Talbot would cross and eat them alive.

Jehanne: Was there time to move the bodies?

Gilles: A few. No. Hardly any.

Perhaps for the thought of stocky Raymond burning, Minguet leaned over the saddle and vomited on his horse's neck. He held Jehanne's flag at a delicate length to stop it getting fouled.

Poor damned Jesus, who died to end blood sacrifice . . .

What a fire it became. A grounded moon, that sphere of flame. A change of wind carried the smoke north-west to Talbot. No Frenchman had to cough. To them it was a bonfire.

All the knights were going back to Orleans for the night. The militia, archers, squires, and other lower ranks stayed camped in the fields of Sologne. In the bonfire light housewives from Orleans crossed the Loire from seven o'clock on, carrying brioches, meat, soup, wine for the army. The Bastard came over from Orleans and talked Jehanne into going home to Boucher's, to have her wound dressed and sleep in a soft bed.

It was better too that she didn't see what happened when women came out smiling in the light of a flaming strongpoint. To men who had spent a day as erratic and intoxicating as this one.

Nine o'clock at Boucher's: a rumour that the generals didn't want to attack les Tourelles tomorrow.

Jehanne: That can't be right.

At half past nine: the Professor of Physic at the University of Orleans looked at Jehanne's wound and said Minguet had treated it well.

At ten: d'Aulon confessed to Jehanne Raymond's body was mislaid somewhere—yes, it was taken away from les Augustins but the men hired for the work probably dumped it somewhere in Sologne and doubled back to try for loot. It lay under the moon or in the river.

A weak desperation moved in her.

Jehanne: Find those men you hired.

D'Aulon: I don't think I'd remember their faces, Jehanne.

At eleven she went to sleep upstairs, beside the child.

At two or three the child turned wildly, as children will in their dreams, and nudged the foot. Jehanne woke to pain

273

and light. She had decided she'd be angry with Messire and the ladies next time. But it wasn't possible.

Messire: My little she–soldier, my little he–nun . . .

His dazzling flattery always won.

Margaret: Their blood is on Sologne.

She meant the blood of the dead.

Catherine: And Christ's blood is on them.

Messire: It all goes forward.

But they couldn't keen for the dead this time.

She ventured an opinion.

Jehanne: They die so terribly.

Messire: Like Brother Jesus.

Margaret: Like me in my season, Jehanne, you in yours.

Catherine: Terrible, terrible, terrible!

She seemed to speak from a memory of pain.

Messire: For king and king's sister and every man, there is no consolation when the steel goes in . . .

Margaret: When the rose bleeds . . .

Messire: Jesus, your brother, lacked all consolation . . .

Margaret: As the steel went in.

Messire: This. For my little she–soldier.

He held for her a blazing wrap. She was supposed to put it on, there and at once it seemed.

She could feel her brain spin from terror.

Messire: No then. Not yet, rose.

When they went it was half past four. She felt well.

Before breakfast the Bastard came. He wrote songs, everyone said. His brown eyes looked like a singer's, half-way through a song with a funny last line none of his listeners know about.

They had a whimsical conversation: he and Jehanne.

Bastard: How's this injury of yours?

Jehanne: There's pus along the edges but it's clean inside. My boy did the dressing very well.

Bastard: With that you probably wouldn't want to go soldiering today.

Jehanne: I don't know why not.

Bastard: You might have noticed that every day you win a fortress I'm not there.

Jehanne: Yes.

274

Bastard: I'm here. Stopping Talbot taking the city. Keeping watch for Fastolf.

Jehanne: I'd forgotten about Fastolf. He's been so long coming. Like Christmas.

Bastard: You can see what a mockery it would be. If everyone was out one gate doing wonderful things in Sologne and Talbot marched in another.

Jehanne: It won't happen.

Bastard: I'm tolerant of what you know. You be tolerant of what I know.

Jehanne: It won't happen.

Bastard: No general could risk it. (He waited a few seconds.) I've spoken to la Hire.

Jehanne: I know what la Hire wants.

She hoped she did.

Bastard: He says everyone's ready to hit at les Tourelles today. However he and I know what we'd each do if we were Talbot. If I was Talbot . . .

He said that if he was Talbot he would attack the west gate, Renard, about noon, while the French were at les Tourelles. He would rightly expect to find Renard poorly defended and he'd get in as quick as he could. He'd be up rue des Talmeliers to the crossroads before anyone knew. He'd have the Burgundy Gate shut and manned. He'd burn all the French barges at Tour Neuve. He'd hang the bodies of the magistrates on the walls. He'd catapult the heads of children into the midst of the Frenchmen outside les Tourelles.

Jehanne said, *not you!*

Bastard: Yes, me! Because I would know Orleans is the navel of Royal France and I'd be monstrous for my king, the little boy, Hal Windsor. And every day I'd show the naked corpses of twenty French wives on the parapets. Just to sharpen up those locked-out French, just to make them uselessly angry. And I'd look down at them and be able to tell myself: now there's no doubt, my king is king of the heart and gut of France.

Jehanne blinked. His certainties were no mean ones.

Bastard: Yesterday I kept the west wall with a few old knights and three or four companies of militia. It won't do for today.

Jehanne: What do you want?

Bastard: I want some hundreds of knights. At least twice as many militia. Send them back to the city. Tell them you foresee too many dead amongst them, too many, but they'll be safe on the mound outside Renard. Go around some of the knights, say *I can smell your death, Monsieur, on that side of the river.* They'll pretend not to care. Keep at them. Order them. Adjure them. They'll come back in the end . . . When they're back here the assault on les Tourelles can go on.

Jehanne: I'm not a village fortune-teller, Monsieur.

Bastard: La Hire, Gilles, no one responsible will attack les Tourelles today until we have those men on the west wall and around it. Because, you see, we *know* Talbot's intentions. He moved all his troops from St Privée redoubt across to St Lorent last night. It means he'll throw full weight against Renard or Bannier.

Jehanne: They might just have been frightened in St Privée. I would be.

He could see she was angry. About the stunt that had been asked of her. To both their amazements she all at once took his beard-fringed face in her hands.

Jehanne: You're the only one I'd do it for.

Bastard: Do it for me and I'll go too. To les Tourelles. All day. There are other men who can be relied on to keep Talbot out. Maybe de Boussac, or Vendôme.

His firm bearded face was beginning to look very happy, cupped in her hands. It looked very fine on top of the black and gold braid clothes he was wearing.

Bastard: You've got big hands.

She took them away.

Bastard: I wasn't criticizing them.

Jehanne: That's all right. The bargain's made.

The day began uneasily therefore—a mad promise, his face in her hands.

Jehanne, d'Aulon, Minguet, Pasquerel left the Bouchers' front door at six. A thin rain fell over rue des Talmeliers. The magistrates were waiting in it for her, wet hands on their chains of office. The officers of the Fishmongers Hall had brought a fresh shad, at least twenty kilograms, for her to dine on that night. There were cords of blood on its gills where someone had gaffed it out of the Loire, perhaps an hour before. In its mute eyes was an acceptance of the gaff, of sharp points.

It was like a message from Messire: *Be serene*. She couldn't be. There was a sudden sweat on her cheeks. She turned to Pasquerel.

Jehanne: Bless me. I'm going to be hurt today.

Pasquerel: Hurt?

Jehanne: Hurt.

And lose the blood Jacques and Zabillet had wanted her to bleed when she was fourteen, fifteen, sixteen, but she'd held it back for the king and the king's earth.

Pasquerel looked startled. But a little excited too, to be in on a genuine prophecy. Jehanne felt lost with only such a child-priest. She hissed at him. *Bless me.*

Today her herald Ambleville rode out with her. He could add even a little more stature to the lies she was to tell for the Bastard in Sologne. Seeing Ambleville, she was reminded of Guyenne, still chained up like a heretic in St Lorent. She was reminded of Raymond's lost corpse.

Outside the city, in the vaporous morning desert where the suburb of St Aignan once stood, she would touch a knight and appeal to his friends. She would beg them to beg him to stay on the city side today, where he'd very likely be safe. Whereas, he'd die uselessly over the river. The friends would talk to each man touched. Members of the Bastard's staff would indicate where he could be of great use: amongst the earthworks outside Renard.

De Gaucourt had found so many boats and barges the day before that they were all able to cross to Ile aux Toiles very early. There was frost on the earth and, it seemed, on the river, which flowed like lightly watered, slightly green milk. On the way to where the militia were camped in Sologne, Jehanne saw city workmen coming home grey-faced with shovels over their shoulders. They had spent the night levelling les Augustins and burying the horrible dead.

The militia stood, grey-faced themselves, by their morning fires. The outer works of les Tourelles looked high and black in the haze and horribly out of scale with all else. It was a first-class background for ominous lies.

She moved round knots of hung-over militia-men telling them that on a day when a lot of people would die, their companies would lose too many for it to be profitable to anyone. They would be safe in la Beauce. They should go back to la Beauce.

Officials of the Bastard marshalled the ones she put her finger on and marched them back down the road. It was deftly done, before the rumour got to those who would be staying.

La Hire explained how les Tourelles was made:

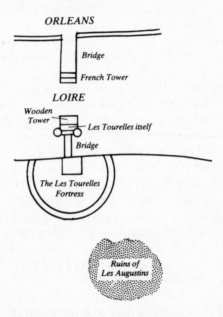

The men commanding in the fortress and the little bridge-castle of les Tourelles were Messieurs Moleyns, Glasdale, Poynings.

Jehanne went to find her flag and people. Bertrand crossed himself seeing her. Jean de Metz was sick from boozing. Jehan and Pierrolot wanted to confess to Pasquerel.

The first attack on les Tourelles was at eight o'clock. The militia sat spectating while a party of fifty knights and their men climbed the outworks, crossed the ditch, and tried to get ladders up against the palisades. No one—la Hire, Gilles, no one—doubted that you used a vast and untrustworthy army to put weight behind some single gesture by a few.

Yesterday the single gesture of Kennedy and Partrada. Everyone remembered that mad running pair. No one remembered Maître Jean. It was the duty of men-at-arms to go up to the walls and find the right symbolic act. No one managed it that morning.

Maître Jean was having troubles with his cannon, which seemed somehow to have suffered from their night in the field. Very few shots carried to the base of the palisades. Darkness must have affected the virtue of the culverins.

When the knights came back they said the ditch round les Tourelles fortress was too steep, too deep. The militia would need to fill it with bundles of brushwood. To bridge it with faggots.

The necessary vast heaps of faggots weren't ready till mid-morning. The militia made a chain up the slope and began to fill the ditch in the south-east corner. The English threw burning knots of rag at it and other missiles. The militia worked on. Tolerating a dozen deaths, a dozen damagings. It was all ready by one o'clock.

Jehanne went forward with a hundred knights. Jean d'Aulon's squire was carrying a ladder and she took it from him. It was very light because very fragile. And since she believed in symbols too . . . perhaps it would be the sight of a woman lumping a siege-ladder that would compel the army.

D'Aulon: You'll be off-balance. With your sore foot and that thing to carry.

She didn't answer.

D'Aulon: Keep your head down then.

He did some exasperated breathing, the sort of comment rare in him. But he seemed to understand what she was aiming for.

It was hard to believe this ladder would hold a man or a heavy country girl.

When they climbed the mound, her foot wound pulled, but not so on the neat bridge of faggots the militia had laid in the ditch. She felt tenderness for them, they had laid it so tidily, then carried their dead away.

Thinking of them in this way, she got across and could see the greying and yellow texture of the logs and the palisades in front of her face.

D'Aulon: Let me put it up.

Jehanne: It's all right.

She thought that if he put it up the army watchers might expect her to climb it. It was very flimsy and she didn't want to go on it first.

She lifted it upright and put its top against the wall. A man nearby screamed. She looked up: was it Jehan? She found she didn't want Jehan to be hurt. Her unfavourite brother.

The ladder sat unevenly against the wall. D'Aulon bent to adjust its base, she tried to guide its top end into level place. Someone struck her away from the ladder. She sat on the ground. Her hips felt full of the impact of being slammed into that posture. Her left hand still held the ladder, her right lay idly in the dirt. Then she remembered she had heard a metallic noise near the side of her face. An arrow was through her armour, deep in her body between her shoulder and her right neck.

D'Aulon lifted her by the armpits. The pain sharpened when she was standing. The sky yellowed for a while. All the French soldiers under the wall stood still. She heard the English up there roaring in their language and an English voice called in nearly pure French.

Voice: The witch is bleeding.

The English let themselves be happy and loud. A witch's blood was all her virtue.

Some mad French knight rode over the brush-wood in the ditch right up to the wall. He called *Gamaches*.

Gamaches had once talked about reigning over her. He'd called her a peasant and a sauce-box. Now he got down from his horse.

Gamaches (to d'Aulon): Get her up in the saddle. They're coming after her.

In fact she could hear the cross-beams being removed from inside the gate. Twenty pairs of hands lifted her up. Minguet and d'Aulon held the bridle and led the horse back over the ditch at a trot. There was no one there to hold her on, so she hoped she could hold herself.

If she fell off it would be into a blaze of English witch-hate. She kept on with her knees. Meanwhile the right side of her chest had ballooned and filled Sologne. The flesh the arrow stood in, being less rigid than the metal encasing it, shivered and jolted. The shaft rat-tatted against the rims of the hole.

Back at the militia lines, Minguet and d'Aulon lifted her to the ground. There was a press of soldiers with rabbit-feet, squares of parchment covered with magic symbols, sachets filled with God-knew-what . . . all wanting to lay them on the wound. They were so breathless and urgent she began weeping. A knight began reciting some Latin incantation. Pasquerel had come by then and told him to go away.

Minguet: It has to come out, Mademoiselle, before we can get your breast plate off. Do you want to draw it out yourself?

Jehanne: Why in the name of Jesus would I want to do that? Father Pasquerel, absolve me.

Minguet's lips moved, in a way that let you know he thought he'd got into trouble following the rules of etiquette—as if a knight *must* be given first option on drawing arrows out of his body.

Oh God. Dying amongst such tiny vanities was more than ought to be asked of a person.

Jehanne: Papa Jacques. Holy Jesus.

Gamaches took her shoulders all at once. D'Aulon's long fingers were on the shaft. She screamed as it came out. D'Aulon passed it to Minguet who stood holding it tip-forward. With his thumb the boy showed all the men around the point to which it had penetrated her body. She saw and whimpered. You couldn't stand such deep entry and live.

Jehanne: Oh lies, Messire.

The wound was so sharp and deep and had definition now. While they unbuckled her, a knight brought yet another sachet to tie round her neck. D'Aulon was furious. Of all people.

D'Aulon: Go to hell!

Knight: It stops haemorrhaging.

D'Aulon: Take it away. They already think she's a witch.

It seemed he too had felt personally wounded by that Goddam shouting about witch's blood.

D'Aulon: All of you, go away. Don't steal her air. Go on.

Jehanne: Am I dying, Jean?

D'Aulon smiled off-handedly.

D'Aulon: Not this time.

People didn't smile that way if they were lying to the dying. She encouraged him to go on in the same way.

Jehanne: Jean, you mock me all you like.

D'Aulon: We have to undress you, that's why I sent the others away.

Gamaches: Mademoiselle, would you like me to go?

Jehanne: No. I think I won't die if I've got enough friends around.

Armour came off, thin padded jacket, shirt. A rush of blood had run between her breasts and down her right side. She saw a gobbet of thick gore on the end of her right nipple. She could get an impression of the wound if she closed her left eye. It was like an eye itself and it bled but not with that surge that they called haemorrhage.

Minguet put to it a plump smear of bacon fat and olive oil. This *might* be grand blood, enriching kingship. But when it started to flow, and when it stopped, and when the linen went on it, she roared and pleaded like any animal.

The English were blowing monotones on flutes and bashing drums.

Jehanne was carried on a litter back to the Bastard. Sometimes she saw soldiers shield their eyes from the bad omen of the blood on her chest.

She lay on the litter all through the middle of the afternoon. A blanket covered her bare breasts. The Bastard came to see her but she was not aware of him. Mesdames Margaret and Catherine were nagging and not very golden presences on her right, injured side.

At les Tourelles three assaults failed and everyone stopped to eat something.

By four o'clock her head was clearing, at five she ate a little bread and said she would get up. Her legs were still in steel, but she kept wincing when the breast plate went on and chose to go forward in her padded jacket. She walked amongst the knights, smiling, then around the militia lines. They yelled for her. Then more assaults were made across the ditch to the walls. Fifty men were killed the way she had so nearly been. She climbed the mound with Minguet, d'Aulon, the flag. Lines of militia protected her with raised shields. She stood sweating and feeling remote from herself, sending the pulsations of her wound against the palisades. She was there at seven o'clock when the Bastard had Retreat blown.

Militia-men chaired her back to the Bastard's flag.

No one was going home yet. Everyone was chatting. The militia-men moved too quickly with her. She couldn't find air whichever side of her body she put her mouth, or if she painfully lifted her lips to the sky.

When she found it at last somewhere on her left, her eyes cleared. They were holding her upright in front of the Bastard. There was unreasonable hurt in his eyes, as if she'd been lying.

Jehanne: You're going home too early.

Bastard: Back to my brother's city.

Jehanne: Too early. Try again. Nothing to lose.

Bastard: Orleans, that's all.

Jehanne: You haven't lost it all day.

Bastard: I came and felt your brow while you were ill earlier. You didn't seem to notice. You're well enough now.

She brushed aside his consideration for her wound.

Jehanne: Another try!

She was as tough as Messire had been when Charlotte rolled on her foot in the small hours.

Bastard: I have a force under de Giresme on the bridge— they were to try to put a span across to les Tourelles from the city side. I have a string of barges loaded with pitch, tow, faggots, old bones, resin, sulphur, God knows what to float under the wooden bridge between les Tourelles fort there and les Tourelles itself. You can't say I haven't backed up your special vision, Jehanne. But nothing's happened and we haven't broken into the fort and it's time for everyone to go home.

Jehanne: I told lies for you this morning. At your damned begging.

Bastard: And it was just as well and thank you.

Jehanne: For Christ's sake, we'll be there in an hour!

He yelled.

Bastard: For Christ's sake, how do you know?

283

She felt sick from the wound and bit the pad of her left palm for relief.

Bastard: Forgive me.

Jehanne: Please, rest a little. Then . . .

She was aware of a movement, like a small animal shifting, between her thighs.

Bastard: One more try and that's it.

He spoke softly but still with an unfair degree of reproach. If les Tourelles did not fall this evening, he'd be very hard to manage tomorrow.

He went forward calling to both sides of him.

Bastard: One more try. Have a rest. Eat and drink.

She sent Minguet for her horse and, when he brought his own too, said no she'd go alone where she was going.

She rode a quarter of a mile south to an untended vineyard in Sologne. The vines had their spring foliage and blossoms, flat pink in the dusk. With her good arm she began to unbuckle the leg-pieces she still wore. When she got her drawers down she found she had a show of blood there. She began laughing as wildly as the wound let her. Was it a joke on Messire's part? A pat reward for bleeding from a wound?

After the laughing stopped she lay on the untilled earth. She tasted the bitter stems of weeds quite joyfully between her lips.

Jehanne: Now Brother Jesus . . . don't mess me about any more.

She realized she was lying with her drawers down and her buttocks bare to the young moon. On her haunches, she bent to wipe the blood from her legs, she urinated in the sleeping vineyard. Soon, she promised it, they'll be back with the plough. Then, left-handedly, she dressed again in drawers and leggings.

Two hours before, she'd lent her flag to one of la Hire's mercenaries, who'd taken it up on to the outer mound every time there was a storming party.

Now the man was exhausted and beginning to understand what risks he'd been taking, carrying the witch's flag. D'Aulon went to retrieve it from him. There was a Basque mercenary Jean knew who stood watching.

D'Aulon: Listen, we've got to get this flag right up under the palisades.

Basque: It was there this morning when the girl went up there.

D'Aulon: That's right. And when she was hurt, Gamaches came in to save her. And Gamaches doesn't like her. Or didn't.

Basque: So?

D'Aulon: If I go right up to the palisades, will you come with me? Carrying her flag?

Basque: Anything that lunatic Partrada can do, I can. But it's been up there already, without any bloody result.

D'Aulon: But you'll come?

Basque: All right.

D'Aulon gave him the flag and they walked up and down amongst the mercenaries and the militia, the Basque waving it and d'Aulon asking a question.

D'Aulon: Would you let this flag be lost to the English?

The English fired their cannon, and the stones lobbed hardly any further than the outer mound. The word went around that the English had no powder left.

Riding down from the vineyard she saw her flag climbing the mound. She felt irrational anger that someone had taken it without her being asked. Perhaps all that nonsense of Minguet's was taking root in her.

She galloped through the lines of the knights, then through the militia. She had no proper armour, no helmet. Her horse got its knees up high because she was so much lighter. Everyone who saw her moving along so fast after her injury remembered it all their lives. It was a divine return.

Whereas all she light-headedly wanted was her damn flag back.

At the foot of the mound she left the horse. Militia-men remembered later how it nosed the bare earth for something to nibble. Like any old farm horse. She ran up the mound— the wound wasn't even in her body's memory. She caught up with the Basque, who was weaving about amongst arrows like a sensible man. Meanwhile, d'Aulon had gone on to the faggot bridge across the ditch, his head down and shield on top of him. Lumps of stones were falling into the ditch—the English cannon couldn't carry further than the English arm, but both pitched what they could.

Just as the Basque was stepping after d'Aulon, Jehanne

caught him and grabbed the tail of her flag and wound it under her left armpit.

Jehanne: My flag please.

Basque: Let go.

Jehanne: I don't know you. My flag.

Basque: I'm taking it up for d'Aulon, you silly bitch.

This comedy on the mound didn't look funny to the army hundreds of metres back. The Basque and the girl fighting over the standard, the silk shuddering between them, looked like the right kind of sign to them.

Men began running towards it without knowing they were. Men in les Tourelles were similarly compelled by it and knew they were going to die unreasonably now, when they'd thought the day's business was over. John Reid saw it, Bill Martin, Matthew Thornton, Thomas Jolly, Geoffrey Blackwell, Walter Parker, William Vaughan, William Arnold, John Burford, George Ludlow, Patrick Hall, Thomas Sand, John Langham, Dick Hawke, Davy Johnson, Black Henry and all the other barbarously named Goddams of les Tourelles.

D'Aulon reached the palisades and looked to left and right for the Basque and then over his shoulder. He thought the Basque had given up his promise, had chosen some easy posturing with the flag on the safe side of the ditch.

D'Aulon: Is that the way you keep promises?

Basque: Oh Jesus!

He pulled so hard Jehanne had to let go out of sudden consideration for her injury. She fell hard on her spine. Alone of everyone there she sat laughing on the mound. Her laughter too worked potently on all the French and on John Reid, Matthew Thornton and others.

When she looked up Breton knights and la Hire's Gascons were all over the mound. She felt dizzy and it seemed to her her wound had begun bleeding again. The solemn visors stared at her laughter. One visor went up and she saw inside its helmet the face of the Duke of Cailly. The night she first crossed the Loire she'd slept at his house. To her mind it was a friendship that had gone on for years, yet it had only been last Wednesday week.

Jehanne: When my flag touches the palisade you can safely go in, Monsieur.

It was that know-all gut of hers told her. She let them lift her on to her feet.

Cailly: It's touching now, Jehanne.

Jehanne: It's all yours then.

So many ladders went up, the English could not push them all away. Cailly, walking over the ditch with Jehanne, chatted. A bit of an old nagger.

Cailly: I've been telling them all day the Goddams didn't have the numbers. Even the Bastard and la Hire—maybe even Monsieur de Rais—they've got a thing about the English, they've had to eat so much cow-dung at English hands. But I've been telling them all day the English don't have the numbers in there . . .

She knew she couldn't climb in, so waited for the militia to open the gate from inside. From the front gate she could see directly across the dead to the back gate where thirty English knights stood swinging at the French with axes.

Cailly: He's letting his men get away.

Glasdale's squire was beside him with the Chandos flag, a black boar's head with yellow tusks on a red ground. It all had a beautiful irrelevance, the squire and what Glasdale did amongst all these streets of strewn offal.

She began crying for him. She wanted to see his face. You want to see the face of a passionate hater almost as much as you want to see that of a passionate lover. She began yelling.

Jehanne: Glassidas, glassidas, glassidas, all give in.

He couldn't hear.

Near her feet some poor Englishman sat up to speak to her. She cocked her ear, was willing to listen. But a drench of blood ran out of his mouth and he died without having had his word.

Half-way to the back gate she ran into an execution squad of militia-men. They had a few dozen English peasants and were making them kneel one at a time and receive an axe blow across the crown of the head.

She sent the militia-men away and looked around the faces of the English. Most of them were Jehan's age. They had mute faces. You could have thought them ungrateful.

She donated them to Cailly. He wasn't delighted. They didn't look as if they'd bring much in on any market.

Next she found a little balding Englishman, knees up to

his chin. He made one begging, fluting noise over and over. With her hands she tried to hold him together—she had the idea the agony that kept him so bunched might suddenly snap him apart. He'd been piked in the stomach. She waited till Pasquerel came along. By then he was suffering less— awareness had almost gone out of his eyes.

There were stains of the Englishman's blood on her leggings. Blood, blood, blood. She was lost amongst its meanings. In Christ's garden of vengeance in Sologne.

Jehanne: Glassidas!

By the time she got near the back gate, hundreds of men stood around watching twenty or thirty Breton knights fight the twenty or thirty Englishmen. Respect for Glasdale had held up a French rush through the back gate of les Tourelles fortress to the little bridge-castle of les Tourelles itself. So there had been war all day but now it was games again, the way knights had been told, when they were little boys, it would be.

Just the same, the English detached themselves a few at a time and ran to les Tourelles by a small wooden footbridge. Hedges of flame rose each side of it—Jehanne could feel the heat many metres back in the crowd. The fire-barges the Bastard had spoken of must be in place there. It was only a small-span bridge. If you got aligned with it you could see the open gate of les Tourelles, amongst great leaps of flame, waiting for Glasdale, Moleyns, Poynings, Gifford to come home to it.

She felt her wounds blistering in the heat.

At last the Bretons simply stood back. They wanted to give Glasdale and the others the option of trying the bridge. Trial by fire, it could fancifully be called.

She knew what he'd do. She'd never seen his face. Her scream rose high above all screams.

Jehanne: Don't!

There were twenty Englishmen on the bridge, running, when it gave way, too brittle from fire. She saw steel arms waving and some flags go down flaming into the river. Not one of those men rose even once.

She was found wandering in the streets of les Tourelles fortress. She raved, something like this.

288

Darling Brother Jesus, who once thought you were the last of sacrifices, make a place in the garden of your heart not only for the rose. Make a place for the bald-headed Englishman and Raymond and glassidas. As you made a place for them in your garden of vengeance. Amen, amen.

When la Hire saw the bridge go under Glasdale and the others, he'd spoken like a professional.

La Hire: Goodbye to a fortune in ransoms.

To finish the les Tourelles story.

Les Tourelles itself, the little stone fortress Glasdale had run for, was taken from the town side. Carpenters made a light wooden frame to fling over the gap between Belle Croix and the timber outworks where the English had once called Jehanne *Ribaude!* They held it upright and lowered it like a ladder towards the far brink, but found it was a foot short. Retracting it, they hammered a few lengths of wooden guttering on the end and raised and lowered it again. It trembled over the deep green river. Stones fell either side of it and arrows studded it. The first knight to cross was a knight-priest, at the crouch, a shield carried over his face. The guttering involved two risky steps but he took them. Now it seemed easy to all the others.

From les Tourelles fortress the French threw flocks of arrows into les Tourelles themselves and Maître Jean Montesclare lobbed stone balls. Later in the evening a raving young English knight captured in les Tourelles said he had seen Sts Aignan and Euverte rising out of the flames from the fire-barges. Others had seen them too and said *Jesus we're finished.*

At ten o'clock the gap on both sides of the little castle had been bridged again with wooden spans strong enough to take horses. The Bastard, Jehanne, Gilles, la Hire rode home that way. Torches crowded the walls. Ste Croix, St Pierre Empont, the University, St Paul, Notre-Dame all rang and buffeted her brain. The canons and the regiment of priests sang *Te Deum laudamus.*

Back at Boucher's they again had the Professor of Medicine from the University to dress her wound. He approved once more of what Minguet had done.

The Bastard whispered to her.

Bastard: Talbot lost France for his king today, my love.

She put her head back, closed her eyes, breathed luxuriously. Again the Bastard whispered.

Bastard: There isn't one Goddam south of the Loire.

It was like all the significances of blood. She had not been able to contain, to assimilate them. She could not contain or assimilate his adoration. But this failure was more enjoyable than the other.

Sunday morning, so brilliant the river-flat mists had risen by eight. As soon as the lines of the earth stood out clearly, the English came out of the forts on the west of Orleans and deployed from the Forest of Orleans down as far as the river bank. Generals d'Illiers and la Hire rode out of the Renard Gate to face them, and soon the militia and the Bastard and the girl came too. The girl wore a light jacket because of her injury. Her brain and guts were gorged with fragments of many deaths. She simply postponed dealing with her brain and guts. In a dazed way, she felt very clear-headed.

Pasquerel set up a portable altar opposite some English knights who had taken a position outside Fort de Croix-Boisée. In case there was an all-out battle that day, all the French crowded round to see Pasquerel raise the consecrated host. As he was cleaning the chalice all the enemy's mounted knights formed up either side of the Blois Road.

The English army lifted swords and pikes and lances towards the sky once. Then they began to leave west by north-west. Their rear-guard stayed firm on the Blois road till after eleven, then turned its back and vanished down the plain.

The Orleanais militia couldn't stand up for joy. They fell over, embracing or singly. They clutched their thighs or knees and giggled at the sky.

Jehanne had to find the Bastard and remind him she had promised the English they could leave Orleans with their lives. Already Bretons, Scots, Gascons were saddling up to go chasing profit on the Goddam flanks.

The Bastard bent down and cried in joy on her good shoulder. He forbade any mad pursuits. But la Hire went after them to track where they were going.

He got back in mid-afternoon and said Meung, the garrison town down-river.

In the ruins of St Lorent they found Guyenne the herald lying chained amongst the English sick. He seemed hysterical and took them to the far-west corner where a heap of faggots had been piled around a stake for his burning. General Talbot himself, Guyenne said, had taken him to the stake and spoken to him. As soon as consent came from the Faculty of Paris, Guyenne was to burn.

It was a golden summer noon in spring and Orleans that day. From Solemn Mass in the Cathedral she had to ride a round-about two miles to Boucher's house. Old women touched her stirrups gently, men kissed the thews and chest of her grey war-horse. After a mile she grew terrified at how addicted she'd become to adoration. In rue des Hôteliers, leading up towards Boucher's from the Châtelet and the bridge, she began to wonder why she shouldn't enjoy it simply, the way a drunk enjoys being drunk without reference to gods of wine or any of that. Perhaps she *was* god, goddess, sibyl, sister Jesus, and her body for its own sake deserved to be touched in worship. The veins in her head creaked and expanded, the blood galloped into her chest, and she felt her kingship billow madly above the city.

This lasted only twenty seconds but afterwards she was terrified of herself in a new way.

Back at Boucher's she found Monsieur Boucher signing authorizations for payment. He let Jehanne look over his shoulder.

Forty sols for a heavy piece of wood obtained from Jean Bazin when les Tourelles was won from the English, to put across one of the broken arches of the bridge.

Authorized: J. Boucher

To Jean Poitevin, fisherman, eight sols for beaching a barge which was put under the bridge between les Tourelles fort and les Tourelles themselves to set fire to it.

Authorized: J. Boucher

To Boudon, nine sols for two S-shaped irons weighing four pounds and a half, attached to the barge which was kindled under the bridge of les Tourelles.

Authorized: J. Boucher

To Champeau—and other carpenters, sixteen sols for liquor on the day les Tourelles was taken . . .

Authorized: J. Boucher

It settled her to watch him do his books on this vast day.

At mid-afternoon the boozy city was delighted by the sight of a French knight riding an English monk piggy-back up to the walls. The monk was General Talbot's confessor and the knight had been General Talbot's prisoner. According to him, the English were in a strange insane despair about the girl. They were certain God would make her suffer some day but she was permitted certain powers first and they were unhappy grist to her power. A lot had by noon deserted Talbot to go back to their garrisons in Goddam Normandy.

She kept remembering Talbot, how fearsomely he'd threatened Guyenne. What threats would he use on her? Were there worse threats than to say to a tenor *we're going to make ashes of your song?*

Then, about ten o'clock, at the worst time of night, when she closed her eyes and jaundiced faces sped towards her out of the dark, she was told how the body of Glasdale, even in its armour, had risen to the top of the water and been gaffed and brought ashore. It had been punitively cut in four, boiled, then embalmed and laid in front of the crypt of St-Merry. The word was that it ought to be consigned to its own country. But Jehanne had little idea of how this could be done, or how it could be expected to console him for his black journey to the bottom of the Loire.

BOOK FOUR

Make Pale Charles a King

Messire: Holy Rheims, little he-nun . . .
Margaret: Holy Rheims, little she-soldier . . .
Catherine: Anointing for the king . . .
Messire: Little rose.

She was to meet Charles in Tours. It would be like the country fairs, where the magician broke an apple irreparably in two, then passed his hand over it and it was whole. So Charles and she, meeting.

But Yolande arrived before Charles in the square-walled city. She wanted to see Jehanne.

The Queen of Sicily had her usual look of unsurprised permanence. Surrounded by three sewing ladies-in-waiting and a monk reciting the Matins of the next day, she sat close to the fire. She was from some warm south and Tours was the cold north for her, even in summer.

Yolande: You made the Bastard-Royal jealous?

Jehanne didn't understand the question.

Jehanne: Jealous, my queen?

Yolande: He seems to want to outshine you. He and la Hire attacked Jargeau the other day.

Jehanne: Oh?

Yolande: The earthworks all round Jargeau were flooded by last week's rain. That's their story anyhow. They had no success.

Jehanne: Did men die?

Yolande: Men got their feet wet. But these little adventures all cost money. A lot of the Bretons went home because no cash award was made to them for what they did at Orleans. That's how short money is.

Jehanne: It doesn't matter what things cost. If you get what you're paying for.

Yolande: Peasant wisdom. What I want to talk about: everyone will start making suggestions to you now. About what ought to be done next.

Jehanne: Everyone has begun.

Yolande: Be firm for Rheims.

Jehanne: Of course.

Yolande: Has anyone told you? Bedford's written to the Privy Council in England asking them to send the boy-king to be crowned in France.

Jehanne: You don't have to stir me up. I'll be firm.

Yolande: I don't just mean against Fat Georges. I mean against your friends too. Against Alençon.

Jehanne: I know, I know.

Yolande: The Duke of Burgundy will let us through to Rheims to crown Charles. He wants to keep things balanced and it suits his idea of what the balance is if he lets our king be crowned and not Bedford's. That's my information anyhow. My information is good information.

Jehanne asked who gave her information. Fat Georges?

Yolande said people in Dijon. Machet was going off to Dijon as her ambassador. Machet would arrange it.

Yolande: The point is it *will* happen. The Rheims journey.

Jehanne: I know. It'll happen.

Yolande: My information is the English still on the Loire are sleeping poorly and having bad dreams.

Yolande had no bad dreams. Jehanne was again fascinated by the way Yolande thought the whole world was amenable to being arranged by Yolande. There were no unaccountable bolts of lightning in Yolande's world. What a different world that was from her own. What lonely strength was needed to live in it.

Yolande's last instructions to Jehanne that night were in the spirit of her picture of the universe.

Yolande: Pester Charles without stop!

They met on the road a little south-west of Tours. She had ridden out to meet him. He had heard in Chinon during the night of Tuesday to Wednesday that the English had been lifted off Orleans. He had started out to meet and review the

296

girl immediately. Some of his staff had been surprised. For at most times he moved quickly only out of some erratic need to prove he was alive by finding yet another city where people still called him king.

As soon as he met the girl he was strangely unhappy he'd come. Her eyes were full of the brightest, widest demands.

Amidst the snuffling of horses he spoke to her.

Charles: How's your wound, Jehanne?

He knew she could see it was a nothing question. She didn't answer it. She was on a palfrey with a low pommel. She took her hat off. Her forehead bent to the horse's dusty mane. So she imposed her frantic reverence on him. Seeing her brown hair he thought: that funny creature has managed it. And bled for me. He found his hand was out, caressing the line of her jaw. His glove smelt of spices. She thought: that's an improvement in manner, in style.

Jehanne: Will you come to Rheims now?

Charles: It isn't as easy as that.

Jehanne: When I went to Baudricourt and asked to be sent to you he said it isn't as easy as that. When I asked if I could see you they said it isn't as easy as that. When I asked you to send me to Orleans you said it isn't as easy as that. Yet we're here and it's all been done. What wasn't easy about any of it?

Charles: It all cost one hundred and twenty thousand livres—that's one of the things that wasn't easy.

Jehanne: You got value for cash, Dauphin.

Charles: Going to Rheims isn't the only thing available to do. Princes talk to each other through diplomats. I could talk to the Duke of Burgundy. He'd be impressed. Because now I have Orleans safe.

Jehanne: People say that won't be good enough.

Charles: People?

Jehanne: The Queen of Sicily.

The king's somnolent face tightened.

There was no rightness about this meeting. It wasn't like the magic apple. They were just bickering, no better at it than Jacques or Zabillet. She thought it was a mistake to mention Rheims straight off. What else was there to mention?

He rode right up beside her. They faced in different

directions and his left knee bumped her right. He spoke more softly still.

Charles: You've behaved royally and like a god, I know. I've had the reports. You were wounded. When les Augustins fell it was when some people had given up. Likewise at les Tourelles.

She waited to see why he was talking. It wasn't altogether praise, in fact there didn't seem to be much praise in him at all.

Charles: I applauded you in letters to all my cities. La Rochelle, Narbonne, Montpellier . . .

Jehanne: I thank my dauphin.

Charles: Châteaudun, Toulouse . . . I know you were moved by divine forces . . . I send you off with an army. Two weeks . . . just *two weeks later*, I meet you and the city of Orleans has been saved. *I've* been saved . . .

But the corners of his eyes cringed. He was faced again with all the cruel work bound up in being saved in part and never in full. All the new documentation, all the new embassies to Dijon, Rouen, Nantes, the Germans, the Pope.

Charles: You shouldn't be too influenced by my mother-in-law. She's beyond herself with happiness.

Jehanne: She's right to be. It's all going to happen.

The long face looked even more menaced. He coughed.

Charles: Is it easy to give up your blood?

Jehanne: No, I yelled a lot. I wanted to be absolved. It's as bad as for anyone, I suppose.

Charles: Why does it have to happen? Why is it *I'm* not allowed strength and sundry virtues? Eh?

Jehanne: You'd die of pride. Being king and all that as well.

He laughed, the creaky laugh she'd forgotten.

Charles: I'd risk it.

She couldn't help telling him. She hoped it was as safe as telling a husband.

Jehanne: It's terrible. I've been worshipped in the streets. Women grab my stirrup to be cured of things. Of issues of blood, that sort of thing—just like Brother Jesus. No hope of it with me, no hope of cure, but they do it. I don't blaspheme, I can't stop them.

He sounded light-headed.

Charles: Let's ride in together. You'll be adored, I'll be adored, God will be adored. There'll be enough for all parties.

That night there was a dinner in the town hall and he broke the rules of precedence to put her on his right. D'Alençon and his dark loving wife Marie were also there. Seeing her, Jehanne could not forget the occult noblewoman d'Alençon had ridden raving a month ago in this same city.

Both the duke and his wife had sought her out in the lobby.

Alençon: It's all settled. I've bought my stand-ins back from the English. Now I can certainly go to war. On the Loire. And northwards.

Marie: That part is over, you see, all the money's raised. We can even pay it back if Jean takes lots of prisoners.

Alençon: Lots of prisoners isn't the best way. The best way is to get Normandy back. Best for the king. Best for us.

She could tell they'd rehearsed the suggestion they were now making.

Jehanne: I'm sorry. My advice tells me Rheims, not Normandy.

Alençon: Normandy's where the English live. Rouen is Bedford's city.

Jehanne: My advice is Rheims.

Marie: You might think of Normandy, Jehanne.

Alençon: You will if you love us.

There was a half-bitter grin on his thin mouth. But he was also a little wary of trying that kind of pressure on her.

Jehanne: I hope that isn't the test, my handsome duke.

Marie: The *test*?

Jehanne: Of whether I love you both.

She stared at the duke, to remind him of his night of crazy adultery.

Marie: One thing we know: you do what you promise to do.

Fat Georges sat at table with the thin sensuous wife who had to bear his weight, and Regnault scurfing into the dishes. They would not speak to her except for mumbles of congratulation, but their spokesmen spoke to her. It seemed to her from the conversations at table that amongst the Council members the most admired policy for the coming

299

month was to do nothing and hold talks with the Duke of Burgundy. Next most admired was to send armies into Normandy. It was Jehanne's impression that least admired, most improbable and dangerous, was to go north–east to Rheims. For all that countryside was the Duke's. You couldn't do anything to create the risk of the Duke saying I won't parley with you any more.

All evening then Jehanne had to keep repeating it.

Jehanne: I have no advice on Normandy.

Also at the banquet was Maman Yolande. She sent a cup down the table for Jehanne to drink from and Jehanne did, sending it back. Yolande drained it, wiped her mouth and smiled slowly at Jehanne.

She spent days waiting for the king outside his apartments in Tours. Every time he came out she strolled with him to chapel or council chambers and asked him about Rheims.

Charles: Yes, yes.

He said it as if he were acknowledging something in the weather: sleet, snow, undue heat.

Jehanne: I won't be here forever.

Charles: None of us will.

Jehanne: You know what I mean, Dauphin.

He whispered fiercely.

Charles: Who will sacrifice you? No one will sacrifice you.

Jehanne: Talbot, Fat Georges . . . I could give you a list.

Charles: Rheims belongs to my cousin.

Jehanne: To you.

Charles: We're not talking the same language.

Jehanne: You say that too easily, Dauphin.

Charles: If I am king . . . kings aren't meant to be back–chatted.

Jehanne: The dauphin understands my respect for him.

Charles: You're an ingenuous girl. You don't know the forces that are working against you . . .

Jehanne: Ah!

Charles: Why the all-knowing *Ah*?

Jehanne: Forces to weaken me?

Charles: Forces to . . .

Jehanne: To?

Charles: To . . . perhaps . . . perhaps put you in danger.
Jehanne: Ah!

He stopped. For a second, hope, pity, resentment, love, envy ran down his face.

She went back singing to her apartments. She let Guyenne sing all he wanted that day.

> What shape is heaven? (he sang)
> Heaven is nearly round but has pink elbows,
> Heaven is the elbowed circle of her arms.

The dauphin returned to Chinon after a fortnight and she rode with him. Later in the month they moved to Loches, a sweet little city amongst vineyards in Touraine. In the river pastures, behind brown stone walls, stood a royal château. The Bastard was waiting there to report to his king, and the king's council. There were finance meetings every day, councils of state, reading of military reports and recommendations, supply conferences. Jehanne was invited to none of it.

On a Friday she got a pair of iron-cuffs from the armoury of St Georges's. The armourers naturally thought she wanted to chastise a servant. There was a key to each cuff and only a small length of chain connecting them. She locked her left wrist in one of the cuffs, put the key in the open right cuff, and carried the whole device hidden up the sleeve of her gown. (She had reverted briefly to women's clothing supplied by Yolande.) She talked her way past guards into the great hall of the château where a series of little wainscoted cells had been set up for the king. She told two Augustinian secretaries she'd been sent for. While they explained how she was mistaken she knocked on the panelling where she could hear Charles's voice and the Bastard's.

The king's confessor, Maître Machet, just back from an embassy to the Duke of Burgundy, answered the door. There were five men inside, all looking knowledgeable, privileged to tell and be told royal things. She walked up to Charles, knelt and kissed his knees. The old blue cloth of his gown was acrid to the lips.

When he put his hand down on her shoulders she let the

301

chain run down her sleeve and put the wristlet on him. The key turned. She removed it. She put it deep down her gown.

Charles: What's this, Jehanne?

The Bastard looked at Machet. They didn't know whether to laugh or send for a blacksmith.

Jehanne: You know damn well what it is.

Charles: I don't damn well know.

Jehanne: Your commission asked for a sign. I said Orleans will be the sign. All right. The sign's been given. Why would I say Rheims if it wasn't the advice I get. And that's the advice I get. Rheims, Rheims, Rheims.

Bastard: You make everyone very angry, Jehanne. You keep telling everyone you're the only one who wants the best for France.

Jehanne: Silence me then. Go on. Or find the key on my body.

Machet: We're not here for games.

Jehanne: Listen, Messieurs, I'll free the King when he says Rheims.

Charles: You could be . . .

Jehanne: Beheaded? Quartered? *Sacrificed?*

Charles: Don't be childish.

Jehanne: Till you say Rheims we're the one animal. We walk together, eat together, sleep together, make water together. If the idea upsets you, say yes to Rheims and you're a free king again.

He dragged at the chain wildly.

Jehanne: Please. My wound.

Charles: Holy Jesus! Tell her, Maître Machet.

Machet: You might like to hear, Mademoiselle, that I've just got back from Dijon, the capital of Burgundy. The Duke of Burgundy has sworn in writing that he will not send an army out against us if we go to Rheims. But there are a lot of strong cities in our tracks. He can't give those up without losing face with Bedford.

Jehanne: Are you going then?

The king whimpered.

Charles: Yes, I suppose I'm going. We're all going.

Jehanne: Would you all turn your backs?

Bastard: What?

Jehanne: The key is down my drawers.
Charles: Oh Jesus in Nazareth.

The army mustered at Selles in early June. Here a vast camp grew all over the river-flats of the Cher.

Sitting on a balcony with Pasquerel one day she found herself making a lunatic claim. She turned to him and said there wouldn't be an English soldier left in France by mid-summer. Before she could stop him and bind him to ethical secrecy, he went off to circulate the word.

The statement was like a rebellion in her blood; her blood was a long deep cunning animal that wanted its own voice and had found it for a moment. It wasn't the untruth that terrified her: the Franciscans were telling people even wilder things about her. It was that the blood might utterly rebel and take her voice for its own use, its insane opinions, all the time.

This terror was still with her on 6 June. On that day the widow of the venerated French general du Guesclin sent to her asking for some, *any* keepsake which she'd touched with virtue and affection. She sent a ring. The courier she gave it to didn't notice how she trembled.

Likewise she had to look grateful that afternoon when she was told the king had granted her arms. The Master of Requests read her the details.

Azure, a sword argent hilted and supporting on its point a crown or between two fleurs-de-lis. Minguet had these arms painted on a plaque and welded to the crown of her helmet. It was done in time for them to move towards Romorantin and Orleans with the army.

D'Alençon, his ransom paid off, led the army. On the night of 9 June it camped in le Portereau. The raked and levelled earth showed where les Augustins and les Tourelles bastion had been. La Hire's cavalry and Alençon's knights put up tents close by a mound on the Toulouse road which was the massed grave of English bodies burned beyond dignity the evening les Augustins was set on fire. Jehanne, d'Alençon, the Bastard, de Boussac, la Hire, and others dear to the memory of Orleans rode over the bridge to billets in the city. Stonemasons were working double-shifts under the wooden spans between les Tourelles and the town-end of the bridge. There was a salute of raised trowels.

Gilles de Rais had been in the city a week. He had mortgaged some of his Breton properties with the help of Bernardo Massimo and other Italian bankers' representatives who had rushed into Orleans as soon as the siege ended. He had taken it on himself to pay the expenses of the siege. His reasons were partly sentimental, even having to do with her. They were also that he knew the king would be generous to him with the estates of those who co-operated with the English in Normandy, Picardy, Champagne and the south. His astrolabes told him the day of delivery for those provinces was close.

Gilles: There's even a new prophecy, dear Jehanne, that there won't be one Englishman left in France by midsummer.

Jehanne: That doesn't sound very likely to me.

The war began on the Loire again. The girl in armour again, and off-hand and dominant with Alençon.

Orleans gave 1600 men, smiths, carpenters, militia-men. It also lent the municipal culverins, its biggest cannon la Bergère, and two master-gunners.

The Bastard had not been exact when he tenderly informed Jehanne a month before that there was no Goddam Englishman south of the Loire. There was Jargeau. In Jargeau were two thousand Goddam Englishmen. The Earl of Suffolk for one. And his two young brothers.

The first night of the campaign, in woods south of Checy, the French army woke up to a panic rumour that Fastolf had crossed the Loire and was hunting them. Alençon, la Hire, Jehanne went about soothing them. Pasquerel said Mass and they saw the host he raised.

The French army came in sight of Jargeau at mid-afternoon. There was a suburb, hovels for the vine-workers, from which a few flights of arrows rose.

Jehanne took her standard from Minguet and raced la Hire towards the suburb. All the French cavalry followed on. It happened to be the right thing: all the English ran for the gate of Jargeau and got there safely since they were lightly-dressed and fast as any war-horse.

304

The French were able to sleep in the hovels and houses that night. Jehanne shared one of the houses with Alençon and felt safe enough to undress and sleep sound in a camp bed.

At five o'clock on Friday morning she woke up to an argument outside the partition of her bedroom. It was Alençon and de Boussac.

De Boussac: Who in Christ's name was it supposed to be? It was supposed to be Vendôme's people wasn't it?

Alençon: It was Vendôme and he posted guards at seven o'clock. Just on dark I went round the outposts and sent them all to bed.

De Boussac: Oh bloody nice. Oh bloody nice.

Alençon: It seemed a small risk.

De Boussac: And if the English had made a raid from town—had you considered . . . ?

Alençon: A small, small risk.

De Boussac: The English were never complete bloody stupids. Never.

Alençon: I had to be certain. About the girl.

De Boussac: The girl.

Alençon: She told me I'd survive. I had to test it . . .

De Boussac: You mad bastard.

Alençon: Don't call me that.

De Boussac: If you get the urge for any more of these little experiments . . .

Alençon: Yes?

De Boussac: I'll take my forces. A man expects some bloody lunacy in the field. But . . .

Alençon said nothing. He seemed satisfied with the state of the argument. And now of course he believed he was an immortal for the duration of the war. Jehanne's blood crept at the strange way people took promises.

There were three days of lassitude and parleying. A spirit-less heat haze held Jargeau and the French in the one daze. On Friday the carpenters began a siege tower. La Bergère, the cannon, knocked occasional lumps from the Jargeau masonry. On Saturday the militia tried one small sally against the walls. In the afternoon, after a sleep that left her with a headache, she went up to the mound outside Jargeau and called on the English to give in. They didn't answer, not one voice. She felt foolish, sweating unanswered in the suburbs.

Sunday. By ten o'clock the militia had got through the ditch up to the walls. D'Alençon and Jehanne went forward together. D'Alençon halted on top of the mound and looked down into the ditch where arrows and stone cannon balls were pitching.

Alençon: We'll wait here and see how the assault on the walls goes.

Jehanne: Didn't you know you weren't going to be hurt? Don't you have promises? Don't you have signs?

She could hear her voice high and bitter. Perversely, she intended to make him go into the ditch and try out the promises and signs.

They walked down into the damp. Corpses lay in the mud.

Alençon: Look at the base of the wall.

Jehanne: I know.

But she looked at the top of the wall just the same and saw the small mouth of a culverin above her. It was a clamant throat, it screamed threats to her.

Jehanne: Come over here or that culverin is going to kill us.

D'Alençon stepped crabwise to his right. A second later a slab of stone from the culverin beheaded a knight who had come forward into the space d'Alençon had left.

At noon Jargeau had not been taken, but when the generals lunched on bread and white wine in the suburbs, d'Alençon talked endlessly, in a high key, about how Jehanne had prophetically saved him.

Alençon: It's true, you see, she was there to save me.

La Hire: She wasn't there to save my Lord de Lude.

Alençon: My Lord de Lude?

De Boussac: That's the poor Angevin bastard who had his head blown off.

Alençon: Requiescat in pace.

La Hire: Amen.

Jehanne returned to the walls with the first assaulting soldiers of the afternoon. Many ladders went up against the stonework and she began to climb one. She felt an impact from above. It was like a trapdoor falling shut on her emergent head. She found later that the helmet, loosely fitted, fell off her head and she followed it slowly, grating against the rungs. A stone fragment had hit her. The militia thought her head had been crushed. She woke very soon and very angry at the impact. They told her later that she stood bare-headed, roaring across the ditch.

Jehanne: Up you go, friends, they're finished.

Before she was clear-headed, the French were into the town and opening the main gates.

All the English made across town for the bridge over the Loire. French knights and mercenaries rushed after them through the thin over-balconied streets.

On the bridge to the north a squire caught up with Suffolk.

Squire: Stop, sir, we've got men in the woods over there.

Suffolk: Fair enough. I stop.

They stood catching their breath.

Suffolk: Are you a gentleman?

Squire: I'm a gentleman.

Suffolk: Are you a knight?

Squire: I'm sorry. I'm not.

Suffolk: I can't surrender except to at least a knight.

Farther down the bridge towards the Jargeau gate French knights had taken his brother. Militia-men had bundled another brother of his, fully entrapped in armour, into the Loire. They resented knights being able to take and sell knights.

Though Suffolk didn't know it at the time, his young brother was drowning because of the bourgeois chagrin of the militia. He would have been better able to guess what was happening inside the town: French looting, hundreds (five) of his archers dying against walls. All that was under-standable and according to pattern. But he did not know, then, about his little brother.

Beyond the south wall Jehanne sat with compresses on her head. Only d'Aulon and Minguet were with her. No one else came near them. Beyond the north wall, Suffolk and the squire. No one else came near *them.*

Squire: I can hardly help it, Monsieur, if I'm not a knight.

Suffolk: If you kneel I'll create you a knight.

Squire: It's tempting. But you might cut me down to the wishbone.

307

Suffolk: Do you think an earl of the Kingdom of England would come down to that level?

Squire: Maybe not.

Suffolk: All right then, kneel.

Suffolk created him a knight banneret of the Kingdom of England and told him to stand up.

Suffolk: Now I give you my sword and I become your prisoner. You'll get at least ten thousand livres for me. How's that?

Squire: Prodigious.

Suffolk: It's the way families get on the rise. Have you got any daughters, for example . . . ?

And they strolled back into Jargeau to meet Alençon and the Bastard.

Three days later the army began marching west through Sologne to Meung. Poton's cavalry arrived first and took the bridge across the river away from the English. The rest of the army arrived under thunderstorms during the afternoon. Alençon and Jehanne found billets in a ruined church.

Alençon was still bedazzled by her trick with the murderous culverin at Jargeau. Each solemn time he said so she laughed at him, but he had no ear for that sort of laughter. His wife didn't mock him enough. Perhaps noble wives didn't mock their husbands: perhaps that too was part of the code.

As the Marshal de Boussac had in Jargeau, la Hire now ran up against Alençon's new, fervent certainty. La Hire came up the church aisle. His shoulders stooped forward beneath light rain from the ruined vaulting. Alençon, Jehanne and their staffs were camped behind drapes in the apse.

La Hire: You haven't set pickets, Monsieur.

Alençon: I won't be setting any, general.

La Hire: I wondered why?

Alençon: Because now I know.

La Hire: That's nice for you. But . . . the knights from Dauphiné were the last to join us. They ought to . . .

Alençon: It's no use talking about it, general.

La Hire: You understand my horsemen and Poton's are the basis of everything . . . If the English crept out . . .

308

Alençon: I've had this argument with de Boussac. It won't happen.

La Hire: You sound like her.

Alençon: Good.

La Hire: You're a general, she's a sibyl. A sibyl can do what a sibyl ought to and a general has to do what a general ought to. And one of the things generals do is set pickets.

Alençon: I won't talk about it.

La Hire: The girl wouldn't want to inconvenience me.

Alençon: The girl is asleep. She had that blow on the head at Jargeau . . .

So the knights from the Dauphiné slept and la Hire had to set sentries out of his own men.

On Thursday 16 June, d'Alençon left the Meung bridge and suburbs garrisoned and marched on to Beaugency. D'Aulon, in conversation but perhaps to warn her against rash prophecy, told her that the English had been in Saintonge and Languedoc so long that French girls married them. Some of them got tenancies on farms down there, as if they intended to be there for generations . . .

Beaugency was a lovely town above the Loire. Its vineyards were still being worked. Behind its walled hill were other vineyards. Far away stood forested lines of cliff.

There was a vast tower facing the river. The English peopled the suburbs on the east, suburbs intact, not like the suburbs of Orleans. In the early afternoon, they ran back inside the walls, so that the French could catcall and feel something had been achieved.

All towns looked the same, she thought, when you considered their walls and how to get inside them. Only pilgrims see things properly. Perhaps one day she could be a pilgrim.

That afternoon two knights rode down out of the forest and found Alençon. Jehanne stood within hearing when they spoke to Alençon.

They were two Breton knights from the Constable Richemont's forces. The Constable Richemont wanted to be welcome in Alençon's army. The word *Richemont* rolled round from knight to knight. Jehanne could tell from the way they looked on hearing it that it meant different things to different people. She asked Gilles.

De Richemont was Constable of France. He'd brought a cunning cousin to court and the cousin had manoeuvred him into rebellion. Richemont had been in revolt, raiding parts of Poitou for more than a year.

Gilles: He's a great witch-hunter as well. He used to say he'd burnt out all the witchcraft in Maine and Brittany.

Jehanne: You don't like him.

Gilles: He's my uncle. So is Fat Georges.

Fat Georges was the cunning cousin Uncle Richemont brought to court.

Meanwhile Alençon was saying *no* to the two Bretons.

Alençon: Tell him if he comes near us the girl and I will fight him.

The argument grew. Generals and knights came in on d'Alençon from the flank to argue with him.

De Boussac: If you *have* to fight, there are the sodding English.

Alençon said he wouldn't be forced to let de Richemont join the army. If Richemont's friends amongst the generals wanted him then Alençon would withdraw with the Orleans militia.

The Bastard sided with Alençon. He walked about, stating his partisanship. Jehanne thought: behind all of them are secret alliances and passions I don't understand or see. There must even be alliances with women. The Bastard must have such alliances and furies behind his clean brown eyes.

The debate stretched into the evening. She thought, this Richemont already occupies the camp, even though he hasn't appeared. Fastolf himself was forgotten for the Richemont question. The English in Beaugency enjoyed a quiet evening.

At six o'clock on Saturday morning, while Pasquerel was saying Mass, a trumpet alarm was blown in the camp. Jehanne left the small church and found militia marching out of the suburbs and forming up in the vegetable gardens, unsure of what front to take.

La Hire, with a little group of knights, the sun on his neck, was peering north into the high forests.

La Hire: It's supposed to be Fastolf. He's supposed to be just up there.

Jehanne: In the forest?

La Hire: I don't believe it. I think it's Richemont who's spread the alarm.

When Alençon and the Bastard joined them la Hire told him he didn't believe Fastolf had arrived. The four of them stared at the forests where morning had not yet touched. They waited for the sun to pick out a steel surface or a silk banner. Starlings sang loudly in the undesecrated orchards of Beaugency.

Alençon: If he's there he'll roll us up into the river.

Bastard: Yes.

Jehanne: It won't happen.

Monsieur de Rais, who didn't like having his unloved witch-besotted Uncle Richemont close by, rode out of the Beaugency suburbs with the news that Richemont had come down in the night and had his army bivouacked at the north end of the town.

They all went to see.

At the foot of the vineyards stood a leper hospital, iron gates, a one-storey building around a leper's well and courtyard. In front of its gates a mass of horsemen with banners were waiting. A small man without a helmet got off his horse and advanced. He bowed slightly all the way up to Alençon's horse.

He was a dark man. When he lifted his head he had brilliant dark eyes. What strange couplings, she thought. To produce him and Gilles and Fat Georges. All in one family.

Jehanne noticed de Boussac, d'Illiers and others had politely dismounted, even Gilles. For Richemont was Constable of France. Jehanne prepared to do the same as the others, but Alençon made a preventive gesture of his hand. She obeyed him. She thought how he'd certainly got more command in his manner. But he often commanded maniac things, such as no sentries. Was this another maniac command?

Richemont: I hear you were thinking of fighting me, Jehanne?

He grinned. All his officers chuckled as if they were trying to convey *see, no guile!*

Jehanne: I've never been able to bring in armies on my side.

He laughed. His peers peered.

Richemont: It's just political. I want to join my king now Fastolf's on top of us . . .

Bastard: I don't think there's much advantage to having you with us, Monsieur.

Richemont pretended to think this too was a good tease.

Richemont: I've had good days in the field. As much as anyone.

Jehanne: They tell me you're a great witch-burner.

She received tangentially a little of the anger that was certainly there.

Richemont: There've been witches in the king's court—de Giac for one. The king might need me at court to protect him from witches.

Bastard: We don't seem to have had trouble with witches since you left last year.

Richemont: It takes a special eye.

Alençon: It seems it does.

Bastard: This rumour about Fastolf . . .

Little Richemont squinted over his left shoulder towards the forest.

Richemont: I haven't seen any sign of its being true.

Alençon: You can keep guard at the bridge on the south bank.

Richemont: That's not worthwhile employment. For a Constable. For troops like these . . .

Bastard: If you don't want it you can go away.

Richemont tolerated the insult and spent the day on the south bank.

Maître Jean the Gunner had been sent down from Orleans. All morning his bombardment ate away at the towers of Beaugency. The militia and knights, sitting in the sun on roofs and in the vegetable gardens, could tell how afraid the English and the people in Beaugency were. Soon a sort of fever would slit the walls.

In the afternoon the militia began working on the ditch outside the walled town. But a rumour grew up that Talbot would be giving up the town that night, and it seemed such a reasonable thing for the English to do that everyone sat down again in the dazzling afternoon and watched Maître Jean and his men. There were artillery barges in the river too, and in the little tributary flowing north-west called the Ru. If they did no damage they were good for scaring people and nice to behold if they belonged to your friends. In fact, there was enough light for gunners and spectators till nine o'clock.

At midnight, Monsieur Richard Gethyn, commander-in-name of Beaugency, sent two heralds to say he would give the town up, the castle and the bridge, and ride away to Meung, where the township was still in Goddam hands. The English would take with them their horse and harness and private property up to the value of one mark and no more. They would also swear not to take part in operations for another ten days. Monsieur Richard Gethyn himself and General Matt Gough would be kept as hostages.

No one slept. Everyone stayed up to watch the Beaugency garrison ride away and to whistle and call them names.

They hadn't been half an hour gone when one of Poton's scouts rode up to d'Alençon's camp in a townhouse close to Beaugency walls to say he'd sighted Fastolf about five miles north of Patay. Talbot and the Beaugency English were on a line to join him. He had a convoy of hundreds of wagons and had been marching all night, as if he knew Beaugency was in a dance of fear.

Somehow, Richemont was there, amongst de Boussac, Gilles, d'Alençon, the Bastard, as soon as the news had been given.

Jehanne: A lot of people don't want you here. But it looks as if it's just as well.

D'Alençon looked at her reproachfully beneath a high brilliant moon. Richemont took her to one side.

Richemont: I'm very interested, did your Voices warn you Fastolf was here?

Jehanne: No.

Richemont: Why, do you think, not?

Jehanne: Poton had scouts out. There wasn't any need for special counsel.

Richemont: You call it that? *Special counsel?*

Jehanne: Yes.

Richemont: How fetching.

The French knights rode off immediately to the north. Through the forests they came to the high plain above

Beaugency. Behind them the moon–dazzle lit up the pit which was the valley of the great river. Where the plain descended to the north they could see the English coming south along the Paris road. Jehanne saw first light on their pennants. She had ridden up to a hill la Hire watched from.

La Hire: That's them, Jehanne. All fitted out. Ready to fight. What do you say?

Jehanne: I don't think they're as happy as they look.

La Hire: Neither do I.

They laughed at each other.

Jehanne: Is it going to be very quick?

La Hire: If we hit them properly.

Their laughter was moist in the pristine air, the laughter of captains. It was a creation day, not a death day.

La Hire kept his cavalry on that hill and the Bastard lined out his militia either side of the Paris road and all the way up to a forest on the west. Knights and mercenaries stood between and behind the militia companies. The English stopped a mile and a half up the road and formed up similarly. La Hire wanted to go against them then.

La Hire: If we hit them now . . .

D'Alençon said there weren't enough French in position.

La Hire: But they'll dig in, they'll make a wall of pointed stakes.

Alençon: So will we.

Time burned up under the sun. Incredibly the dawn led quickly to mid-morning, mid-morning fell into afternoon, as if through a hole in the day. On the hill some of la Hire's men went to sleep.

The French army lined the ridges and put stakes in front of themselves and dug traps for horses. A mile north the English did the same.

Jehanne, tired, could not sleep. She had a bilious feeling of things not going as briskly as they ought to.

La Hire instructed her.

La Hire: For Fastolf it's just like the battle of the Herrings again. See, he's got wagons. He hasn't left them strung out on the road, he spreads them over the country for his men to shelter behind. It's already too late to deal with him.

D'Alençon again rode up for their counsel.

Alençon: What do you say, Jehanne?

Jehanne: See you've got your spurs on.

Alençon: For running away?

Jehanne: For chasing them. I think you ought to go against them now.

La Hire: It's the same as Rouvray, ask the Bastard. We can't move now.

Jehanne: This would finish them, wouldn't it? Down here, I mean? Not in Paris or Normandy, not yet. But it'd finish them here.

Alençon: Yes.

Jehanne: And it's certain they're going to be finished . . . So . . .

La Hire: You can't argue like that. This is Rouvray all over. Except we're not doing anything rash this time. This is loggerheads.

De Boussac: I don't think even the Scots will charge that line. Remembering Rouvray.

They heard the girl snorting in her annoying way.

Jehanne: Whatever's not finished today has to be done tomorrow.

Two English heralds with dragon flags rode up the hill in late afternoon to offer single combat on behalf of two English knights.

D'Alençon and the Bastard knew *that* wouldn't settle anything. They composed an answer. *For today, get to bed and rest, because it's getting late. Tomorrow, God willing, we'll come to closer quarters.*

At night Minguet tried to wrap her in her flag so that she could sleep snugly, but she wanted to walk, being drunk with exhaustion. All over the hill knights slept in little encampments with their squires and pages.

She could see the glow of English fires foreshortened by the chassis of the wagons. But the fires died as she looked, three or four vanished at a time. It was a dark fresh night. She thought for no particular reason how supremely the old oak in Boischenu would stand on such a night, remembering or not remembering St John's Gospel. She heard someone speak behind her and turned. It was the Constable. His face had a jaundiced radiance in the night.

Richemont: I said, you met the king in Chinon?

Jehanne: That's right, Monsieur.

315

Richemont: With its three great towers—remember them?

Jehanne: The Tower of St George?

Richemont: The Middle Tower.

Jehanne: The Coudray. I stayed in la Coudray with people called . . .

But the name of her host and hostess did not come easily to her. Richemont suggested it.

Richemont: The du Belliers?

Jehanne: Yes, that was their name.

Richemont: I was lord of Chinon. Of all those towers. Of those hills.

Jehanne: It must have made you very happy. I remember Chinon better than any place I've visited.

Richemont: The king cancelled my rights in Chinon. A misunderstanding . . .

Jehanne: Oh?

Richemont: Last year.

Jehanne: I'm sure his reasons were good.

Richemont: I don't deny that for a second. His reasons were excellent. It's always like that at court though. Misunderstandings. People tell the king things. About one. It might happen to you.

Jehanne: I suppose so.

Richemont: I don't want Chinon back. But I want to be welcome wherever the king is.

Jehanne: Yes.

Richemont: Will you speak to him for me? If I take an oath of fidelity in front of you? How about that?

Jehanne: What oath of fidelity?

Richemont: I swear by the spirits of the upper and lower air . . .

She thought: he's witch-hunting. The night before battle he wants me to join him in invoking suspect spirits.

Jehanne: They're not the spirits you invoke. Not for swearing faith to a king.

He jumped towards her and took her by the shoulders.

Richemont: I adjure you in the name of God the Father and his only begotten son Jesus Christ, Jesus, Jesus, Jesus . . .

She trembled.

Jehanne: Are you trying to cure me of devils?

Richemont: Why? Do you suffer from them?

316

Jehanne: No.

Richemont: Ah!

Jehanne: Do you really want me to talk to the king for you?

The yellow face wagged in the dark.

Richemont: Yes. I want to be taken back to the king's breast. I led a revolt, if you want to know. You see, devils enter all of us. I gathered a league of lords. The Counts of Clermont and Pardiac were with me. They repented early and the king accepted their repentance. I repent now. I swear . . .

Jehanne: I don't think you ought to swear any more.

Richemont: Do you always obey your Voices?

Jehanne: What else can I do?

Richemont: To be faithful to Voices is the beginning of virtue. Sleep tight.

He walked away blowing his nose into his moleskin glove. Jehanne considered if the madness, the confused talk, the begging for her intercession with Charles, was only assumed. If he wanted to arouse strange admissions in her. To protect his king from her witcheries. As he'd protected him once from de Giac's. There were always prizes for performing such services.

Minguet had made her a comfortable bed out of her saddle and a palliasse. When she lay down the radiant Voices reassured her: the king's victory, great victory in the morning. So much Goddam death. The priests must absolve all the English in the morning, they must absolve them where they stand. They won't stand long.

First light on Saturday showed the wagons were gone from behind the palisades. La Hire galloped up the road and found three sick English boys in a tent. They told him their colleagues had crept away late in the night north towards Janville.

What were the Voices doing to her?

But la Hire was delighted. *We'll catch them*, he said, *if we saddle up now. We'll catch them moving.*

There was a smell of field breakfasts—herbs, bacon—in the morning while Alençon gave his orders. Poton could scout ahead with a hundred or so horsemen. Then the Bastard and de Boussac with an experienced vanguard, all of them survivors of Rouvray and Verneuil, up to all the worst things Goddams could do. Then la Hire appointed by d'Alençon to lead the main army.

La Hire: On two conditions, my lord duke.

Alençon: What are they?

La Hire: Richemont's companies are allowed to ride with me.

Alençon: It doesn't please me. But I can't argue today. What else?

La Hire: The girl's done everything she can, she can't be of much use on a day like this, she can be a great nuisance. You can permit erratic behaviour in front of a walled town. If it goes wrong you can pull back. But that doesn't work in the open field.

Alençon: You remember Rouvray.

La Hire: By Holy Christ I do.

So Alençon had to talk Jehanne round to riding with the rear-guard. First, she was precious. Second, many fine men were riding there that day—Gilles and a grandson of du Guesclin. Third, the rear-guard might have to save the battle if the front lines were routed. Fourth, Richemont had obeyed him and she ought to. If people didn't co-operate they wouldn't catch the English on the run. And so on.

It was agreed.

That morning the French army rode twelve miles. There wasn't any cloud in the sky, Jehanne could feel sweat running between her breasts and her shoulder scar itched wildly.

The plain was screened by lines of forest. Behind such a screen Poton's scouts might run up against the English rear-guard.

Thirst. Even Gilles did not converse. The birds stopped singing before ten o'clock.

Jehanne: What's that spire over there?

Gilles: A village called St Sigismond, dear lady.

Jehanne: Why doesn't anyone ask the people here if they saw Goddams today?

Gilles: If there's anyone there, Poton's already asking them. Maybe it's a dead village.

Jehanne: The spire ahead?

Gilles: I don't know. St Peravy I suppose.

He looked at the sun.

Gilles: If it's midday—bells aren't ringing anywhere.

They had no sense that the forest and tracks ahead were full of La Hire and his thousands, and in the haze of noon dead villages kept silence. Where were births, marriages, deaths solemnized in all that countryside?

Towards two o'clock they could see rising ground a few miles away, a square tower called Lignerolles above the tree-tops. Gilles, who had travelled on this road often enough, said they couldn't see because the land lay deceptively, a mile or two beyond Lignerolles was a nice little town called Patay.

At that moment, Poton's horsemen were on the edge of the hollow in front of Lignerolles. It revealed itself without warning, a pit of forest in front of them. From Poton's left a stag jumped into the road, splendid, roan, a stallion creature. On its front hoofs it propped in front of Poton's horse and went leaping down into the hollow. Poton's horsemen stayed halted there, the lovely animal had imposed a hiatus on them.

Forty seconds passed. Below them they heard an outburst of *Hurrahs*. A Scot with Poton translated in a lowered voice.

Scot: They're saying *hurrah don't let him get away, what a big bastard damn good shot. I get the right forequarter. I spotted him, like hell you did, Jimmie spotted him before you even turned your head.*

Poton sent messengers back to Alençon and the Bastard and did not move. Within minutes la Hire rode up with thousands of knights and troopers. They spread themselves across the crest of the hollow, padded their horses' hoofs, and edged down into the woods below them. La Hire believed they would come out into an open place where the English waited.

What had meanwhile happened with the English that noon was this: an English scout had reported the French army were coming up the Paris road at a good pace. Talbot's men hadn't slept the night before and mustn't be caught moving. That was the English strength of eighty years' standing: never to be caught moving. The deceased clever King Hal had practised it.

Talbot made his vanguard stop under the slope of

Lignerolles. They made a screen of wagons, and the woods were behind them. He spoke to them briefly.

Talbot: This is a better position than the great Harry had at Agincourt. This is also as far as that Armagnac whore will ever get.

But some of them said later there must have been something lacking in the air they breathed, they knew it wasn't going to be the way Talbot promised.

Talbot told Fastolf to get the main army too up behind the wagons at Lignerolles. To give them a chance to get there he himself picked five hundred of his best archers to screen them. They were all good men, old soldiers, they knew the English drill that had won Gravelles and Verneuil. They knew how to retreat in an orderly way, section by section. They had wagon–loads of stakes with them and cut others in the woods. They were expecting the French about four and would make fools of the heavy cavalry a few times. Then they would move back to the main army, keeping to the quickset hedges that lined the road and putting up flights of arrows from behind them if the French pursued.

In all the English army these were the men who were sure about the result, who weren't convinced that the English method had lost its virtue.

They had a ditch dug for their screen of stakes. The stakes lay around in piles of fresh brown soil. An hour and a half early la Hire's terrible armoured men appeared amongst the last fronds of the wood in front of them.

It seemed that no one spoke. The English archers looked with keen interest on the weapons, the edges of steel, that la Hire's knights held. They could have been saying *those are the instruments of our death, I wonder where they came from.*

The stag hung bleeding from a triangle of stakes behind the English. It looked almost as if *this* were the just and holy thing they would die defending.

Talbot: Make a line now, make a line.

Talbot was taken prisoner but all the other English were beheaded while running, or spiked, or cut open.

La Hire took his cavalry straight on over the bodies towards Lignerolles. Through two woods they found Fastolf's column spread out on the Paris road and not yet safely in place. Only a token flank of English knights rode on its left rear.

Fastolf left the column and galloped for Lignerolles. So too anyone else with a horse.

But two thousand men were caught and all killed.

When the men behind the wagons at Lignerolles saw Fastolf and other knights riding without any pride towards them they began running themselves, up through the forests, up the Paris road.

La Hire's men caught eight hundred Goddam peasant-bowmen at Lignerolles alone and cut up every one of them.

Fifteen hundred negotiable prisoners were taken. La Hire thought that was wonderful.

All up and down the Paris road from Patay to Janville Englishmen were caught and killed.

The common militia-men even killed English knights, for reasons of class and to spite their betters and to show that the nature of the world was changing, that it was God's will.

Jehanne, in the French rear-guard, rode fast but a mile behind all the killing. The cut-open dead crowding village streets had already lost their individual features by the time she got to them. She had forgotten even in the little while since Jargeau how terrible the nameless dead were.

When she rode into the wide but unwalled town of Patay with Gilles and d'Aulon at six o'clock militia-men were slowly pole-axing a contingent of Englishmen in front of the market cross. *In the name of these severed English we O Christ adore you.* That could have been their prayer. Pasquerel anointed a few still alive and the ones still in line he sent off to a Benedictine monastery near Patay where they all swore not to fight for a year.

Jehanne was becoming an authentic general and found it possible to dine that night without thinking too much of the daily dead. She stayed with Alençon, who arranged a celebration dinner. Talbot had been invited. He was middle-aged with a firm but not humourless face. He spoke good French. He would not speak to Jehanne, but she watched him closely. Now and then she put her hand in under the shoulder of her loose shirt and slowly scratched her wound scar.

D'Alençon was dizzy with triumph. Therefore he wanted

to say memorable things for his historiographer, Cagny, to polish up for the record.

Alençon: My Lord Talbot, this morning you didn't think you'd eat with us tonight.

Talbot: It's the fortunes of war.

He was the first soldier to use the phrase and it was applauded by all around, including the Bastard who was a grammar scholar.

Bastard: Wouldn't you say that this is the worst thing that's happened to your people for many years?

My Lord Talbot looked at his hands.

Talbot: Yes. However, I think you ought to consider the means it was done by.

All at table, except Talbot, looked at Jehanne. It occurred to her the best thing was to smile vividly back at them.

A letter from Bedford to the Royal Council at Westminster. Everything prospered for Your Highness until the June when, God knows by whose advice, the siege of Orleans was instituted. It was after the tragedy that struck so unexpectedly at my cousin Salisbury that an immense mischief fell on your soldiers who gathered in large numbers in front of Orleans. This mischief was, in my opinion, the result of an intermingling of false belief with the insensate fear they had of that limb of Satan called the Girl, or the *Pucelle*, who used enchantments and spells against them. Not only have great numbers of your people been killed but also those who survived have lost their morale to a startling degree. So your opponents and enemies have plenty of encouragement to gather again in vast numbers.

She got ready to leave Patay the next morning, but so did many others, wanting to rush their picture of the battle to Charles. They lunched at Beaugency—d'Alençon, Gilles, de Richemont, Poton, la Hire, Jehanne.

Richemont cornered Jehanne.

Richemont: Do you feel no guilt for all the dead?

Jehanne: It's a fact of war: that there'll be dead. I had to understand that or go mad.

Richemont: So you feel no grief?

322

Jehanne: Now Monsieur, grief is a different question . . . a different question.

But where was the king? Like him not to show himself even to get good news!

After three days it was discovered he was staying at the Château de St Benoît, twenty miles *up river,* from Orleans.

De Boussac: Hasn't he got any consideration for us?

They began riding up river in a heat wave. All the good news went dry in their throats.

Messire: No grief for the dead. No grief, my rose.

Jehanne: Those dead? In Jesus's garden of vengeance?

Messire: Jesus died for them.

Margaret: Jesus squealed when the iron went in.

Catherine: I squealed when the iron went in.

Margaret: There is no consolation at the time.

Catherine: But *that* hell has no eternity, *that* hell ends.

Messire: No grief, my little she–soldier.

Catherine: Our little he–nun.

Margaret: Our red rose.

Yolande, of course, rode out of St Benoît to meet her on the road and talk to her. These conferences as always disturbed Jehanne, giving her the painful conviction that Council members wove patterns of self-interest she had no chance of reading. Yet some of Yolande's information was helpful.

Yolande (on Regnault): He wants to anoint Charles in his own city. That'll make a great bond between Charles and him.

Yolande (on Charles): He wants it, that sacred oil, he knows what it means to people. And he thinks he can have it. The Duke of Burgundy's forces are off, re–occupying Flanders. In any case, the Duke doesn't really want the English so strong that their six-year-old gets the double crown in Rheims.

Yolande (on the road to Rheims): Most of all, Charles has had secret delegations from citizens in Auxerre, Troyes, Rheims. Saying he's well loved, that they want to open the gates to him. They have to cover themselves by putting up resistance, but if the French army comes they'll try to talk the garrisons round from inside the walls.

Charles let her in to see him in the great hall of St Benoît. He had become more ceremonious, his chair was draped and canopied. Fat Georges was well off on the right, at a seemly distance, signing papers on an oak table. Regnault and Machet were at other tables in the room. My God, she thought, he's given up closets, he's occupying a kingly space.

Rising, Regnault got between the king and her. His sick skin snowed on her as she kissed his True–Cross ring. She could smell disease in his clothes. But he wanted to see his city before he died.

Regnault stepped back to let her go to Charles.

Charles's face recurred to her on sight, the features were like a memory planted in her womb in the days when she was in Zabillet's. She felt again the features had the force of law, and what the law was was that she must lose her blood for him.

She hugged his knobby knees.

His hand touched the tips of the basin–crop behind her ears.

Jehanne: I'm glad to see you've come out of tiny rooms.

Charles: Have I? It's just a matter of convenience.

Jehanne: Don't have any doubts, you'll get all your kingdom, you'll be crowned and anointed.

Charles: Is there anything I can do for you?

It sounded as if her promises gave him heartburn. He'd rather give her a present than listen.

Jehanne: There isn't anything. Just that the Constable de Richemont asked me to ask you to pardon him.

Charles: Oh?

Jehanne: He'll take oaths. And I think he wants Chinon back. And to prove I'm a dangerous witch.

Regnault chuckled quite roundly, like an ordinary person.

Charles: When I wrote to the good towns about the great triumph at Patay . . .

Jehanne: Yes?

Charles: I said the girl and d'Alençon were the ones who did it.

Jehanne: I was stuck right at the back with Gilles. I kept riding over terrible corpses.

Charles: It was done by your virtue.

He was always trying to buy her off by saying he'd written praising letters.

Jehanne: Dauphin?

324

He knew what she would ask.

Charles: Oh God, what?

She spoke in a small cajoling voice, a courtesan voice, foreign to her.

Jehanne: Rheims! *Rheims!*

That night she sat at her window in St Benoît. She watched the Loire viscid as lead under a vast moon rising out of the vineyards on the north. Minguet had been sent to bed, Pasquerel read by the empty fireplace and d'Aulon had gone to a finance conference with the Master of Requests.

At nine o'clock the door opened and four tall men in crimson and yellow with hands on their sword hilts stamped into her apartments.

Intruder: Mademoiselle, I am the Monsieur de Beaumont. You have to come with me to meet a friend.

Jehanne: What friend?

Intruder: Monsieur de Richemont.

Jehanne: No. I've done enough for him.

Intruder: You've got to come now. You can't knock us back.

She saw that knives had arrived in their hands somehow. Pasquerel came away from the fireplace and so was between Jehanne and Beaumont and the others.

Pasquerel: You'll be excommunicated if you touch me.

Intruder: God almighty, will we?

It worried them so little that one of them forced Pasquerel back against the hearth and put the knife-edge to his neck.

They took her downstairs and across the outer court. By the barbican gate stood a soldier minding seven or eight horses. The impassive moon lit their rumps. Jehanne was shivering and felt sick. Someone called out behind her.

The men twitched and were all at once less masterly.

Gilles and his squire walked up. D'Aulon came forward through the barbican.

Gilles: Where are you going, Jehanne?

Jehanne: To Monsieur de Richemont. That's what they tell me.

Gilles: Did you especially want to go, dear lady?

Jehanne: No.

Beaumont: Mademoiselle, you know you had an appointment.

Jehanne: Gilles, his name is Beaumont. He's a liar.

Gilles: I know of a Beaumont. One day a captain of the guards called Camus was cut to pieces on the riverbank outside Poitiers. Weren't you there then, Monsieur Beaumont?

Beaumont: You aren't properly informed.

Gilles: It must have been your putative father.

Beaumont: You can't talk like that to a knight banneret.

Gilles: Richemont wants to examine her for witchcraft, doesn't he? Doesn't he?

Beaumont: I don't know. Is it so bad to be troubled about witchcraft close to the king? Am I to report that *you* object, Monsieur de Rais?

Gilles: Richemont's been pardoned and given back his title to Parthenay. Tell him his nephew said he ought to be happy with that much, he oughn't to want burnt flesh as well.

Beaumont: You with your choirboys aren't clean.

Gilles: Who is?

Beaumont made a dismissive squeak with the corners of his mouth and went and mounted his horse. He and his party rode out of the barbican at a walk.

The girl sought about for a plinth to sit on.

Gilles: Don't ever do any more favours for my uncle de Richemont.

She admitted she wouldn't.

At Gien which Jehanne had come to in the rain with Colet and Bertrand and Jean de Metz four months ago, four lifetimes, another great army gathered quickly in the river meadows. A week after Patay there were more than twenty thousand men there. Their mounts were poor, they were self-equipped. All they got in pay was an advance of three francs a head. Grain cost twelve francs a bushel, for there wasn't much of a planting this year. In every district only areas close to the walls were being farmed. Vegetable gardens had been made in knocked-down suburbs, but even beets and beans were rich man's food in mid-summer 1429.

By 27 June another ten thousand men had come to Gien. The camp was full of whores dressed as soldiers. For a franc they let their hose down at the back and soldiers took them that way. Food was too expensive and could be stolen anyhow. The one commodity of steady price and sure satisfaction were the booted whores who dropped their hose when the priests weren't looking.

On that day the forward party left Gien. De Boussac was in command, la Hire, Poton, Gilles and the girl were with him.

They probed for nice Burgundian cities of hazy loyalty and by midday the direction they took was towards Auxerre rather than Sens.

Four days later they rode down through the vineyards and cornfields to the city of Auxerre. Jehanne had been here too in the rain of early March. On the first day of July, the breeze blowing grit from the wastelands to the west, it looked a different town.

They camped round its walls, in burnt-out suburbs and cornfields. They shot hares and rats and caught tench and shads in the Yonne. But still they were hungry, and the whores went about in jerkins and breeks.

No one told Jehanne.

The king arrived. All Auxerre, even the Burgundian and Goddam soldiers, were on the walls to see him.

Ambassadors came out from the town. Georges de la Tremoille rode in and didn't ride out again for thirty-six hours.

Gilles: They say he's been given two thousand pounds by the town council to act as mediator.

Jehanne: Two thousand?

Gilles: He'll keep it without a blush, dear lady.

Near the Gien Road they had put up a blue marquee with saffron silk fringes. Charles lived there—without his queen, for it had been decided the journey would be too harsh and risky for that sallow lady.

Jehanne dined there most nights. The meals in a hungry camp and landscape could not be too opulent. Like her, he had a delicate stomach—thin stew and sopped bread with apple were all he ate most evenings. He was fasting in any case for his coronation and a safe trip.

Charles: Jehanne, do you think it's a good thing to come to terms with the people in Auxerre?

Jehanne: Terms?

327

She knew it was a diplomacy word. Her Voices never used it.

Charles: If I take the city, and I can, there'll be terrible thieving. There'll be killing of the garrison. Women will be misused. I want to go to Rheims a merciful king.

He was in the habit now of thinking of himself, as beyond argument, king.

On terms that it victualled the army, Auxerre gave in to him. One hour its garrison rode out over the Yonne bridge, the next Charles rode in. His army made a sullen transit of the city only so that each man could receive a small measure of flour on leaving the St Pierre gate.

The note of credit the city council made out in indemnity to its king was to the sum of twenty thousand livres tournois. For royal mercy had a price. And it was high.

Jehanne visited a fresco in St Etienne she had seen when crossing rainy France in February. Jesus, dressed as well as she was now, riding in a forest with four rich friends. Knowledge was in his eyes.

On the fourth day of July St Florentin surrendered to Charles. That afternoon Jehanne was riding with the forward guard in wild hills. War had let the forests grow close in towards the road. They crossed a fast stream and rode into a grey little village, perhaps fifty people living where two hundred had ten years ago. Jehanne could see the poor cornfields on the north, movements in the stooks where the few able men and pretty women were hiding.

Above the village, on its own hill, was an ancient tower, said to be Burgundian and manned. Nothing but crows moved in slit windows. The Troyes road ran around its base into horse–chestnut and oak.

Down the road ahead a Franciscan marched with a holy water pot and sprinkler. He dipped, and sprinkled the umber landscape. When he saw riders coming out of the village he stopped and crossed himself with the knob on the end of the sprinkler.

Amongst the two hundred horsemen no one doubted what it was about: he'd come out of Troyes to drive devils out of Jehanne.

He walked on. You could see he was very frightened, but he didn't halt till he was close, no more than twenty paces.

Franciscan: Brother Richard of Paris, come to destroy the Antichrist.

He had a dark bony face, like some Spaniards. He played about with the sprinkler. Jehanne felt consecrated water land on her upper lip. If it were necessary the friar would run. He had his weight back on his left foot.

Jehanne: Come up bold as brass. I won't fly away.

After a vast sign of the cross he recited an exorcism. Down the line knights chatted about weather and war. Jehanne and General Poton tolerated the ritual. At last the priest came to its end.

Jehanne: Does that always work?

Brother Richard: Oh yes.

Jehanne: Good.

Brother Richard: Yes, you didn't spit, fit or scream. You're not Antichrist.

Jehanne: Or the devil.

Brother Richard: That's right. You're not.

Jehanne: Good.

Brother Richard: I was sent by the city council of Troyes to test you out.

He seemed pleased to have been used in such a high emergency.

Jehanne: Why you, Brother?

Brother Richard: They know I'm fortunate enough to be Christ's friend. For example, I was expelled from Paris for preaching too well.

Poton: You malign yourself, Brother.

Brother Richard: I preached at Boulogne-la-Petite one day so well that people went away and started fires that burnt a day and a night. The heads of houses threw all their vanities on the fires: gaming clothes, draught-boards, dice-boxes, billiard cues. It was spectacular. But of course the University of Paris didn't like it. They like a debased population. It's easier to fool those types of people. Women burnt their hennins and pads and whalebone hoods, by the way. A great fire. That's the sort of man I am. By Christ's grace. I'm very pleased you're from God, Mademoiselle. Everything is possible for the year 1430. The world has got at the most two years to go. Antichrist is coming in 1430. When I was in Palestine many years ago

329

I met Syrian Jews making for Babylon. I asked them why. They said *we're going to see the Messiah born*. Now *their* Messiah is *our* Antichrist, who shall be born in Babylon, brought up in Bethsaida and grow to manhood in Chorazim. You have to pardon me for thinking you might be his agent . . .

Poton: Perhaps you'd take a letter to the council of Troyes from the girl?

Richard: I would.

Poton, Jehanne, Richard turned back into St Phal village and Jehanne dictated a letter to a knight templar. She asked the people in Troyes to give up the city to Charles, because Charles was coming and would enter all the towns of the holy kingdom and make peace there no matter who tried to stop him.

The preacher stuck the letter in his belt.

Richard: Do your men have mandrake roots?

Jehanne remembered those ceremonies in Boischenu.

Jehanne: I'm not sure. Generally speaking . . . no!

Richard: No one who keeps a mandrake can be Christ's friend.

Jehanne: Perhaps not everyone who's got a mandrake knows that.

Richard: In Paris they had mandrakes dressed in silk, crowned with crowns. I preached against them and they were burnt in bonfires that raged two days in all the squares from St Honoré to the Temple.

Poton: You're a regular fire-bug.

Sallow Brother Richard at last took his water-bucket and sprinkler and walked round the St Phal tower bent towards high-lying forests and Troyes.

The next morning they themselves came down out of the hilly forests of Troyes. Here was the core of the disease. In this Judas city nine years ago Maman Isabeau, the animal-lover, had called Charles a bastard, called Hal Monmouth king. It was a fine city shaped like an oval and held in a bow of the Seine. Its inner suburbs had been levelled.

The French army arrived in groups all day in front of Troyes. They were very hungry, but all Troyes had left for them were green corn on the stalk and broad beans in beanfields. The afternoon was full of the smell of fires and bean and green corn pottage. No one had any salt and spices. It was a heavy but somehow vacant smell.

D'Alençon found a house for Jehanne in the outer suburbs.

Since riding the witch, d'Alençon had stayed chaste in a showy manner. In the summer evenings he stripped to his breeches, wrapped himself in a rug and, after praying, lay on a palliasse within sight of Jehanne. So it was that night.

Next morning soldiers started working at filling in the ditches on the western side of Troyes. At some times of the year these would be filled with water from the Seine but at high summer they were baked dry. A few flights of arrows rose from the walls and fell amongst the long lines of soldiers moving forward with hurdles and faggots. From the walls long-hatted Jews watched, far from their ghetto, which la Hire said was at the east end of the town. It was as if the city council were offering Hebrews in reparation. A patient race, the Jews scarcely moved on the high walls under hazed sky.

Jehanne and Alençon sat on portable stools in the garden of their villa. The walls of the house were tumbled and they could see the lines of sedulous infantry and the Hebrews on the wall.

Gilles de Rais, Marshal of France, found them there when at noon he rode into the suburbs with two hundred Breton knights and squires. Red dust delineated the chasing of their breastplates. Their plumes were broken, their banners stained. They broke up and looked for billets but Gilles dismounted and walked across a trampled beanfield to the garden where Alençon's flag stood limp beside Jehanne's.

Gilles: There's Israelites up there. You see them, dear lady, the wealthy Israelites of Troyes?

Alençon: They're not happy with betraying the Lord Christ . . . they've betrayed their king as well.

He yawned though. Tomorrow or the next day was the season for retribution, not this hazy noon.

Gilles: We've ridden over from Brionon this morning. The king's been there the last few days. He's considering by-passing Troyes. A king can be too merciful.

Alençon: Troyes has to be punished.

331

Gilles: My astrolabes say Troyes will be entered but not punished. What does the dear lady say?

Jehanne: The king ought to go into Troyes. He ought to show his holy body in Troyes.

Gilles: Ah!

An hour later the king and his council rode out of the forests. D'Aulon warned Jehanne and Minguet got her mounted in time for her to meet him in the cornfields on the edge of town. All the corn had been picked by the army now and the stocks bent. Troyes would need to import cornflour next autumn. Where from?

Jehanne inspected the royal face again, verifying it, looking for signs. The king wore plain white armour like her own. A crown with blue sapphires stood on his head but failed to trap the afternoon sun as brilliantly as it would on days of hard bright summer light.

Jehanne threw herself forward until her breasts hit the front-board of her saddle.

Charles: I'm going to pardon this city, Jehanne. As with Auxerre. The way Lord Christ pardons us.

Jehanne: Noël. But you must show your sacred body inside it.

Charles: I want to hold conference straight away. Come with me.

Jehanne: You don't mean I'm getting invited to a council meeting?

Charles: Yes. Doesn't it happen a lot?

Jehanne: No.

Charles: I don't believe you.

Jehanne: D'Alençon and me . . .

Charles: Monsieur Duke of Alençon?

Jehanne: Him, yes. We've got a villa. Perfect for council meetings.

Charles: All right, show us.

The upstairs apartments were cleaned up in the next half-hour. Bedding got bundled up. Minguet and Ambleville sprinkled water on the floor and swept it. All the windows were left open and a few pine boughs burnt to clear the air. Trestle tables were fitted together.

Council members began arriving—Archbishop Regnault an ill white in a mail-suit. Fat Georges rode in chased armour. Someone said, a distillery on horse-back. The legs were comic thin under a barrel weight of chest and gut. But no one laughed.

De Gaucourt: It's all going well. You must be pleased at how well it's going.

Jehanne: The king. The king must be pleased.

De Gaucourt: Oh? I thought it was your show.

When the king came in you could tell how exhilarated he was. To be in the land of his enemies and find it his land. To have people coming to him arranging for his mercy on them. For the story was that ambassadors from Troyes, sneaking out amongst the French lines, had been begging with him all night in Brionon. A fresh experience for a pale king!

He began speaking without introduction.

Charles: I want Jehanne and the Marshal de Rais to lead an attack on the south-west wall this afternoon. I want the walls broken in. You can do it, Jehanne and Marshal de Rais. Because you love me.

Jehanne stood up at table. It was the first time she had ever been ordered to go straight out and break walls down. She thought, everything's going to be simple now.

Charles: Every general, captain, knight is to tell every squire, page, archer, commoner this: that if people inside Troyes are killed or their property damaged I'll have the guilty ones hanged. I intend to break the pattern of barbarism.

Jehanne: Noël.

Maître Jean's cannon had arrived by wagon and Jehanne rode about with Gilles watching them being set in place in the open spaces facing the south-west gate, called Madeleine. The Hebrews, poor scapegoats, had left the walls. Gilles had two thousand men for the assault, which would be up the mounds, through the ditches to the Madeleine Gate. Jehanne felt elated and talked to them a great deal as she rode amidst them.

Gilles kept saying to her that they mustn't expect to do too much and had to remember mercy—as if she were the one who might forget it.

He had his Breton knights with him. One of them, visited by heat exhaustion, had seen red-scarfed knights riding across the north-west sky where Paris lay.

Maître Jean, in his lazy way, had two bombards ready to fire by half past four. He lit the fuses and his cannonballs tore two black holes in a tower west of the gate. There seemed to be no one at home there: the town had kept silent. Now a woman began wailing behind the walls.

Jehanne: Has someone been hurt?

It was a dreadful sound and ran across her clarity of purpose.

Gilles: I wouldn't say so. It's siege madness.

All at once, you could see the garrison on the walls, keeping low. They sent few arrows down. But there were cannon above the Madeleine Gate.

In the marshalling area Jehanne saw a strange brown-flavoured light isolating one of Gilles's knights. It was a young man, about twenty. He wore no helmet, had a blue scarf fashionably enhancing his throat. Over his expensive armour he wore a red silk tunic with a white ox-head on it.

Jehanne: Who's that fellow?

Gilles: That's Lavignac, my second-cousin.

The boy had lavish brown hair. It was cut military style, but didn't look severe. Like cousin Gilles he was too handsome, had over-ripe and unlikely boy-loveliness. The horrible brown light inappropriate to the lazy day hung round him. It implied the brown of decay, the brown that sets in on the petals of dying roses; it implied excreta and the skin of corpses. Marking him out as defiled and about to have his defilement confirmed.

She turned her head to talk to Gilles and saw him watching the luscious boy, a moist pride in his eyes, his lips shining with fresh saliva this dry day.

She couldn't help saying it.

Jehanne: Are you a devil?

Gilles: I beg your pardon, dear lady.

Jehanne: Tell him to go back into the suburbs.

Gilles: Him?

Jehanne: That boy.

Gilles's attention was still misted, one eye on the boy.

Gilles: Lavignac?

The name was torn out of her ears by cannon crack. Lavignac's opulent head had gone. His squire lay bleeding through a chain-meshed chest. However, Lavignac stood, though headless. Blood fell in shawls over his shoulders and he began stumbling sideways, creeping, creeping up to Gilles.

Jehanne saw Gilles's mouth open. He snorted, he gagged, his hands went out to his headless cousin. Gilles, beyond himself, offered some obscene welcome. It seemed Lavignac would walk straight between his arms. But life left the boy in a rush, he had to sit some feet short. He fell sidewise, dead. Gilles was still standing open-armed.

Gilles: Find his head if you can. His father would want his intact body.

A Franciscan was already anointing Lavignac, though the senses of his sumptuous head lay shredded in a dozen places amongst the Bretons.

The Franciscan said *a porte inferni libera eum*—snatch him from the gates of hell. But the air, Jehanne saw, was still stained with the Black One's gain of that young body.

She felt heavy. She went to d'Aulon.

Jehanne: It's no good. I've got to rest.

D'Aulon: Back at your place? It mightn't be free yet, the Council might still be . . .

Jehanne: It doesn't matter. Anywhere.

Gilles: Use my tent.

Jehanne: Marshal de Rais, will you confess to Père Pasquerel?

Gilles knelt there. They were carrying his lovely cousin off. Gilles knelt without a qualm in the middle of the stain.

Gilles: I want the pardon of the Lord Jesus, whose knight I am and will be. He knows how Satan pulls at our bowels, dear lady, because Satan pulled at his and tempted him with strange women and soft boys.

Jehanne: Soft boys, Gilles, there's no mention of soft boys.

Gilles: All the temptations of the world were suffered by the Lord Jesus. Ask the Faculties of Poitiers and Paris. They'd both say so.

Some of the Bretons watched Gilles's repentance. He began weeping gently.

Gilles: That dear boy. The waste of it. Of the richness. The cleanness of line . . .

D'Aulon: He can't have known anything. That walking— headless—he wouldn't have known he was doing that.

Jehanne thought, *the one time Charles asks me—direct—to do something, I beg off. Because I see Lavignac go to hell in front of my eyes.*

Jehanne: Just a short rest, Jean. Then back to the walls.

D'Aulon: Of course, Mademoiselle, it's a hot day.

The villa was empty, she slept very deeply. From the right of her pallet Messire sprang a new thought on her.

Messire: Little he-rose, little she-soldier, when the king is anointed . . .

Jehanne: What? What, Messire?

Messire: The steel goes in, the heat blasts, the rose bleeds.

Jehanne: Holy Jesus!

Messire: You'll never be alone.

Jehanne: But when the steel goes in . . .

Messire: There's no consolation.

She woke yelling *I deserve better!*

Amongst the beanpoles in the outer suburbs stood a temporary chapel of blue silk drapes. Here, while Lavignac lost his head under the walls, the king listened to four Augustinian monks chanting Vespers. He thought he'd never felt more royal than out there in a blue tent amongst his army, on the edge of the town that had legislated against his reality but now, this afternoon, at four, would send frightened ambassadors to explain themselves.

The ambassadors: Jean Laiguise, Lord Bishop; Monsieur Guillaume Andouillette, Master of the Knights Hospitallers; the Dean of the Chapter; the councillors of the city.

Charles had organized a throne to be put out in the beanfields. They would have to approach him over uneven ground and kneel down to him on dry lumpy earth.

At the last versicle and response, de la Tremoille came into the chapel. He genuflected heavily and with a slump of the fat head that could have been devotion or exhaustion.

De la Tremoille: Gilles and the girl have started making noises at the walls. The ambassadors have just left town by a gate on the north side.

Charles himself bowed to the bread species of the slaughtered God-man which sat in the tabernacle. He went out towards his open-air throne.

He felt *this is power.* He felt *this is her blood washing back*

336

to me from the time she's slaughtered. Her blood thickening mine.
It could be felt, blood binding his loose legs, ripening his heart.

Charles: Poor girl.

De la Tremoille: What, Lord?

Charles: The girl. I hope she doesn't get hurt up there. Near the walls.

De la Tremoille: No chance.

Gilles waited by the high chair out in the beanfield, no one had noticed his cousin's blood on the greaves at his knee, it looked like some kind of weathering.

The ambassadors crept up in capes, houpellandes, chains of office. They were uncertain how their rights to their regalia would stand by five o'clock. As was intended, their soft shoes slid off the edge of clods.

Ten yards from Charles they dropped themselves full length on the earth, all at once, a rehearsed gesture. Their forearms folded in front of their faces. They were the best-off people in France, from an affluent town. Now they were suffering for its unfortunate allegiance.

The Lord Bishop Laiguise got up on his knees. Only he.

Laiguise: Would His Majesty try to understand our problem? The bailey and the garrison won't open the gates to you. Give me time to talk the garrison around. If they can't be persuaded I think the people will take over anyhow. They'll open the gates by force and give you the obedience that's your due.

Charles: I hope you appreciate: the attack now going on in the west of the city is to help you with the argument. To make it easy for you to say no, there's no chance of holding out. If I wanted to really inconvenience your walls I would send thirty thousand men to push them down—one, two, three!

Laiguise: I know His Majesty's army is massive: I know it can swallow us at a gulp.

Charles: That's it. But it's not only your city but mine, my pleasant city. Everyone knows about the Champagne Fairs. Though St Pierre could do with a steeple.

He nodded towards the hulking but aborted cathedral of Troyes beyond the Madeleine Gate.

337

Laiguise: In His Majesty's coming peace a steeple will go up on St Pierre. I'm sure the cathedral chapter would give guarantees. But of course there are other guarantees you would want if you were to consider mercy towards us.

Yes, yes, kingship! To have one's mercy ceremoniously begged.

Charles: Indeed. Remember, my generals are at the walls. The miraculous *pucelle* . . .

But he noticed that one of his generals was there, out of place.

Charles: Gilles?

Gilles: My cousin Robert de Lavignac is dead, gentle king. A cannon on their walls went off and carried his head away. He was eighteen years.

Charles: Requiescat in pace.

Gilles: All to make it easier for his lordship the bishop to renege on his present masters.

Laiguise: Of course, the council will be happy to vote an immediate sum as damages . . .

The strange too-blue eyes snapped shut.

Gilles: He was a child.

The bishop began tugging at the neck of his alb.

Laiguise: If anyone has to pay, then I must . . .

He tried to expose his own heart. It was hard for him though to find his bare chest under all those pontificals.

Gilles: The payment ought to be in the flesh of children. Lavignac was a child.

Then they noticed the dirty blood on his hands, the stains on his knees, and his quivering shoulders. Charles shifted on his throne. He felt his new majesty a little eroded by Gilles's erratic manners.

Gilles: You ought to pray to the god of treacheries, Monsieur Bishop, that while you're talking here with my gentle king, my Bretons don't get in your walls.

He bowed to Charles and went away. It seemed to all present that he intended to get his Bretons inside Troyes and then, heigh-hay! A decapitated population!

Charles stood up at his throne.

Charles: Gilles, you know the orders. My mercy over all.

Gilles turned amongst the furrowed earth to bow to those orders. He had the grace of the high aristocracy, his manners

338

weren't rough like Fat Georges, who had begun his career as the family's poor cousin.

Charles thought: I shouldn't be standing on the balls of my feet yelling after people. He sat and kept up the hard arguing with Laiguise.

Jehanne made herself return to the wall after an hour's rest. D'Aulon, himself mounted, led her horse on a short rein. He could tell she wanted somehow to talk of Lavignac's death and that conversation would return her to the siege, the afternoon, to herself. He said it was a shame that the boy died while the Troyes delegates were actually with the king.

Jehanne: Delegates?

Immediately d'Aulon knew he'd broken up some picture she had of the event, some necessary picture.

D'Aulon: The delegation from Troyes. They've been with the king this afternoon. Everyone knows.

Jehanne: Gilles? Does Gilles know?

D'Aulon: If I know, the Marshal de Rais is sure to know.

The king had told her to break the wall down. As if it were what he really wanted done.

Jehanne: Why are we all set to run at the walls then?

D'Aulon: To make it easy for the people inside to give up.

Jehanne: Eia!

She began to fall from her saddle. He reached back and caught her arm.

D'Aulon: I was certain you knew, Mademoiselle.

Jehanne: You ought to tell me these things, Jean. I'm a simple-minded person.

Back amongst the Bretons, she got down off her horse.

She saw a dozen Franciscans come out of the Madeleine Gate and through the ditch. They carried a white flag like hers, Christ holding the earth on it. Jehanne could tell that one of them was zany Brother Richard. No one interfered with them. She walked on a line to intercept them on the road south into the suburbs. She edged round a bivouac of dozing Scots archers to confront Brother Richard.

Stop! his right hand told the others. He walked right up to her and knelt down.

In a sea of liars, she could tell he wasn't a liar. As if for company, she found herself kneeling too.

Richard: The great God is preparing his way in Troyes and beyond Troyes, and his way in Troyes is nearly accomplished.

She groaned, she didn't want perorations.

Jehanne: Does that mean they'll open the gate to their king?

Richard: On the usual corrupt conditions.

Jehanne: Corrupt?

Richard: For example: all revenues and patronage bestowed on churchmen by the late king of France should be kept by them. All revenues and patronage bestowed by the late Henry and his boy should be kept.

Jehanne: You don't care for the late Henry?

Brother Richard got incisive all at once.

Richard: Either Henry Monmouth was true heir or Charles Valois is. Both can't be. Both can't bestow revenues on fat clergy.

Jehanne: They don't think things through the way you do.

Richard: Who don't?

Jehanne: Politicians don't.

Richard: I know that.

Jehanne: What's it like in the city?

Richard: All the people are frightened there'll be a slaughter. They think you're an angel of death. They're camping in the churches and I go around reassuring them.

Jehanne: It's a work of great mercy.

Richard: I know you don't want blood from such pathetic stones.

He touched her elbow.

Richard: I tell them you're a saint unparalleled. The forerunner.

Jehanne: Let's stand up.

It was hard work kneeling in armour.

Richard got up in one angular and practised glide. His eyes glowered, in another man it would have been erotic love, and a danger to her. But erotic love wasn't one of the terms Brother Richard worked in. He had a ravishing chastity.

Richard: Let me tell you the manhood of Troyes are heckling the garrison. Cat-calling. The garrison will be let

340

go, of course. The king will agree to that. He'll let them go with their property.

Jehanne: Property?

Richard: I've come on behalf of their property.

Jehanne: I don't understand.

Richard: The garrison owns three hundred French knights and others. A good soldier isn't supposed to wriggle out of buying his ransom, that's why they couldn't write. But it seems they can tell a new dispensation will march in the gate with you. They don't want to be taken away by the Burgundians.

Jehanne: Tell them they're free, I promise . . .

Richard: But do you understand the problems, dear little saint? The king will tell the garrison yes, of course you can take them, they're yours, acquired fairly. When you ride in at the Madeleine, the garrison will be on their way out of the Comporté and over the river. On what is poetically called safe conduct.

Jehanne: I'll ride across town and catch up with them.

Richard: Ah!

Jehanne: Slip them the news. Those prisoners.

Richard: Yes.

He reached out for her shoulders.

Richard: Pax tecum, parvule virgo.

Jehanne: And with you, brother.

He began singing the *Magnificat* before he'd even taken his hands away. Turning his back then he gave the note to his brothers and led them back into the ditch. In the third verse, Maître Jean's cannon spoke, but the noise sounded lazy and equivocal to Jehanne.

She thought, I've been used. The king? Not the king. People like Regnault, people like Fat Georges. So she told herself, and for the first time did not want to ask further.

Jehanne: I've been used then. They used me.

D'Aulon: It happens with soldiers. A lot of what they do is just gestures.

Jehanne: Let me tell you, Jean. The Lord of Lavignac is in hell now. For gestures.

D'Aulon: How can you be sure, Mademoiselle?

Jehanne: Would I tell you, if I wasn't?

But she thought that if they went on talking about

Lavignac, his damnation, Charles's suspect decree that damned him, she'd be finished for the day.

Jehanne: When we go into Troyes we have to go in early. Across the town.

D'Aulon: Mademoiselle?

Jehanne: There'll be Frenchmen there being made to leave with the garrison.

D'Aulon: Prisoners, Mademoiselle. Property of the Burgundians. We can't interfere with that.

Jehanne: I see.

D'Aulon: It'd be a sort of robbery.

Too hard-up to feed captives, d'Aulon was still a man of his cast. Crime wasn't to trample harvests, crime was to take the enemy's prisoners from him.

Late on Saturday night everyone in the French army learned: the Madeleine would be opened at dawn the next morning. At the same time, the northern gates would open to let the Burgundians go. The knighthood and the girl could enter with the king. From dawn the French might line the king's path into the city with guards. But there was no one on the walls who didn't welcome him.

He knew it himself and was feverish with the gaiety of knowing it.

A little after five, Jehanne, d'Aulon, Minguet, Pasquerel, Bertrand, Jehan and Pierrolot rode in at the Madeleine and cantered across the town. From the cathedral they had to find a way north through the carts and furniture of the Burgundians.

No one seemed to notice them. Jehanne might just as well have been another decamping knight in the service of Burgundy.

The road through the centre of the city kept widening to squares. Even here her white silks drew the attention only of the early sun.

All these squares were crowded with furniture, wagons, archers, horses. You could hear laughter and songs.

Bertrand: They're happy to be going, Jehanne.

Jehanne: Everyone's happy except a few.

There were fine cloth-halls with stone-traceried fronts facing each of the squares. At the best of times it would be an elevating town to live in, a humane place.

342

With some hubris, Minguet rode through the Burgundians beating their shoulders with a knout and crying
Way! Way!

In the square inside the Comporté Gate were a clutter of
banners to show where the commandant waited for the
packing to finish. In shade against the gate the French
prisoners also waited. They wore breeches, jackets with the
panels torn and the quilting coming through. Most of them
had wristlet chains and there were a dozen on litters. Who
could tell what their ranks were? But they must have been
worth at least 500 pounds tournois.

This square was less crowded. She could rein in thirty
metres from the commandant and still be face to face.

Jehanne: I've come to tell you, Messieurs. You can't take
your French with you.

They looked up, decided who it was, decided not to
answer her, wanting her to feel foolish. But—for one thing
—there was a quiver in their shoulders, they wanted to
survey her well, the monster female, and carry their report
north.

Jehanne: I've never taken or kept a soldier for profit. I
could have. Ask your English friends. That day's gone. The
king's coming. And a new day.

Burgundian Lord: The king said we can keep them. It's fair
dealing.

Jehanne: It isn't the way things are going to be done.

Burgundian Lord: Madame, I won't discuss it. You're
embarrassing your own knights.

It was quite possible. Poulengy, d'Aulon, Minguet and
even Jacques's sons were silent behind her, no snort or
twitch of assent in them.

Jehanne: You French prisoners, refuse to go. The king
should be here by ten.

The Burgundians laughed. They muttered stag, ram,
bull brute jokes about her. They strained their laughter out.

Burgundian Lord: We'd have a right under law. We could
cut their throats here. No one could touch us, it's law. If
they wouldn't come we'd execute them. We'd have to. The
whole system would fall down otherwise.

Jehanne: Monsieur . . . ?

She was seeking for his name.

Burgundian Lord: De Rochefort.

Jehanne: Monsieur de Rochefort, if you execute them you won't get away from Troyes. You be peaceful. And understand where the power is now.

They began whistling and riding round her party in a mocking circle, taking grotesque postures in their saddle to show her how comic they thought she looked. They made the circuit only once, but she felt it was terrible, the hot walls of their contempt.

Now they sat still, waiting for her next abominable decree. She disappointed them by speaking in a hollow and feminine and almost defeated manner.

Jehanne: They're not going. In God's name they're not.

The French prisoners did not move, they didn't want to be known as breakers of the code.

De Rochefort: We've had some of these men since Verneuil. They were happy to come to us then, *don't kill us, our wives have power of attorney.* Ask your knights there how it all works.

D'Aulon: You might have to give them up freely if the lady insists.

Jehanne: Thank you, Jean.

D'Aulon made a just-visible waggle of his hand. It meant to say, *just the same, the man's absolutely right.*

The argument went on as wagons began to leave the city and form up on the north bank across the Seine bridge. Some French knights found their way to that northern square and listened. They made the debate less virulent, they transmitted a lot of brother-feeling to de Rochefort and his knights who transmitted it back. They began to despise her more genially, fear her less. It was as always: war was a jovial conspiracy by people called enemies, for the game's sake.

Jehanne: Monsieur de Rochefort, these French knights you hear . . . they didn't hoot at me at les Tourelles. They were happy enough to have a crazy girl with them then.

Someone French called out it was a treaty term. She couldn't go against her own king's treaty.

The garrison was well on their way now, the archers riding out. De Rochefort could have tried to move the prisoners across the river. Perhaps he really felt fear for her though, or perhaps he wanted to go on teasing her with them.

At seven one of them began frankly pleading with her.

Prisoner: Don't leave us. It's a bad life with them, it's a nothing life.

And the old and clownish ransom system broke apart before their eyes. French prisoners got unprofessionally down on their knees.

Soon de Rochefort knew that he would have to threaten execution to make them move, and the oddity of disposing of his property this way inside a town suddenly royal disturbed him.

At the time, Charles was robing in cloth of gold in the western suburbs with cousin d'Alençon. Someone must have reported the quarrel to him because, at eight, a herald royal arrived in the north square and let it be known Charles king would pay immediately four pounds tournois per head of French prisoner. It was twice the market price. De Rochefort called *Noël* to the French knights. They called it back in their brotherly way.

The prisoners caressed each other, half the sick sat up and called good charms at Jehanne, a dozen ran up and kissed her boots in the stirrups, kissed them open-mouthed, leaving spittle there, taking dung and dust away on their lips.

Jehanne (to prisoner): I'm the only one who cares a damn for you.

Prisoner: Mmmm.

Jehanne's party turned back through the muddle of the city. She looked at the French knights. They'd sunk back into lazy ways of thought now that they had Orleans, Patay, Auxerre, Troyes all accomplished.

Jehanne: Thank you for all your help.

But she was frightened. Now it was all nearly done. No one had any reason to be faithful to her. The time they'd sell her quick was soon.

St Pierre rang the hours. Soon, soon, soon.

For his entry the king wore no old clothes. The victories and acquired towns were all the time entering his brain, endowing his presence. His sleeves of green and gold, for example, opulent and wide-mouthed, cuffs so fantastic and wide that

345

they drooped to his boots. Making mouths of the king-hands. There was no triumph those mouths weren't willing to swallow.

The crowds raved for him, that he'd chosen mercy. The word of his mercy would get about. It would throw Bedford out of step.

On Monday the army marched in the gates and enjoyed for one night the town's brief and uneasy hospitality.

Beyond Troyes, Champagne had its worst country—yellow at high summer, a wasteland of clay. By some irony much of it was sown, poor wheat grew and there were scrawny vineyards on the slopes down to the Aube. But it was still like a desert. D'Aulon said he wouldn't be surprised to find Saracens beyond the next hill.

The little town of Arcis, deep in the country of traitors, sang *Noël* to its king on Tuesday.

On Wednesday the army camped around the forest of Lettrée and Charles sent his herald to tell Chalons its king was coming.

The Count Bishop of Chalons wrote to Rheims that he intended to resist with all his strength. So covered, he rode out to Lettrée with the keys of Chalons.

The Bishop said Chalons hoped for the same mercy as Troyes got. They were so confident of getting it that they were putting up travellers on their way to Rheims for the foregone coronation. Some of them from the girl's own town . . .

One of them she saw during the grand entry to the town. It was her godfather, Jean Morel. She spotted him quite humbly waiting to talk to her outside the cathedral. He didn't presume on their early association at the baptismal font of Domremy and in many other places on the Meuse.

Jehanne: Uncle Morel!

Morel: Your old man's coming to Rheims. Jacques.

Jehanne: Him!

Being told you'd meet Jacques now, in August, was as improbable as being told in March that you'd see the king.

Jehanne: Zabillet?

Morel: She can't come. It's harsh travel at this time of the year.

346

His eyes evaded her, pretended fresh interest in the refined stonework of the cathedral façade.

Jehanne: What's the matter, uncle?

Morel: Did you really slaughter everyone in Auxerre?

She thought, I've become a black image in people's stories.

Jehanne: Is that what's said?

Morel: Yes.

Jehanne: You shouldn't have come if you believed it. Chalons is an unfaithful city too.

He was kind enough to smile.

Morel: I'll take my risks.

She wasn't soothed so easily.

Jehanne: Then why did you ask?

Morel: When people get great . . . they're not the people they were at all.

She began sweating for terror of her legend. She remembered the la Hire legend working on her brain in childhood.

Jehanne: I'm the same person, the same person. Look at this.

She had in her saddle bag in case of rain the red cloak Alain and Durand had given her in Vaucouleurs. She unbuckled the bag and hauled out the cloak.

Jehanne: Look. Durand Lassois gave me this. He's at Burey-le-Petit, you know him. He put it on me and I still wear it. You take it.

Morel: It's all right, Jehanne. I . . .

Jehanne: No, you take it. Tell everyone. It's the same Jehanne who put it on in Vaucouleurs who's giving it to you in Chalons.

Morel: Madame Aubrit's the one who was worried.

Jehanne: Madame Aubrit?

Morel: She heard that everyone in Auxerre was killed. She said she felt to blame.

Jehanne: The stupidity of people . . .

If Aubrit had been there Jehanne would have beaten her on the lush face.

Morel made a concessive gesture.

Morel: I've really hurt you.

Jehanne: What does it matter? Show it to Aubrit and Madame de Bourlémont. Show it to Lassois and the le Royers in Vaucouleurs.

Morel: I'm sorry.

Jehanne: It isn't you.

Morel: What is it, love?

Jehanne: Listen, uncle, I'm going to be sold. Sure as Brother Jesus.

Morel: What?

Jehanne: Treachery, uncle. It's what I'm afraid of.

Morel: After all you've done.

The king and his party got down from their horses and went into the cathedral behind her back. Choirs sang *Te Deum Laudamus, Te Dominum Confitemur*.

D'Aulon and the others waited for her, some feet away. People in the crowd came up and peered at the conversing wonder-woman and Morel. Not understanding a word, they were fully satisfied.

Jehanne: Tell Jacques.

Morel: What?

Jehanne: I don't want him asking me did I kill townfuls of people.

Morel: He wouldn't. His girl? He's very proud.

Jehanne: Show them that thing.

She pointed to Lassois's best red cloak. It was nearly grey now, from all the dust of her travelling.

He was visited by some sudden pride at being endowed by a great woman.

Morel: I certainly will. Aubrit. De Bourlémont. You've got into the way of dropping their titles.

Jehanne still felt venomous towards Aubrit.

Jehanne: Titles! Aubrit hasn't got a title. From the Domremy and Greux end of things she might have. From this end she's just another girl. Like me. You ought to all call her by her first name.

Morel grinned boyishly. But Jehanne knew, when he got back to the Meuse it would be *indeed, Madame Aubrit*.

For a self-important second, in front of all those people, he let the girl's cloak, folded evenly from neck to tail, fall across his arm.

Before she left Chalons with Poton's cavalry she said goodbye to Charles. Again the Council were at work around a table in a big hall at the hôtel de ville.

348

He talked about politics as if they were his own discovery and very much his own sport.

Charles: Just like the other cities—the Rheims Council has written off to Bedford and Philip for help but they don't want it. Our informants inside the city say that the Burgundian commandant at Nogent had offered to bring them three thousand first-class troops. They've written him dense replies, as if they can't understand what he's offering.

They laughed together, king and king's strange sister.

Charles: The persistent fool's gone ahead and written again. The Rheims Council have answered and—this is really good—they've pretended that they think he's asking for supplies and cash awards for his soldiers. They said they might be able to consider his requests at the next finance meeting in July, but that funds are low and they have to spend them on fortifications.

Again they laughed amongst his heads-down secretaries and advisers. It was just their joke, hers and Charles's.

She made pace with the cavalry through the abandoned vineyards on the slopes of Rheims mountain. There were said to be a race of Champenois in the forests and caves on top of the mountain. They had been up there since the year Jean sans Peur was killed at Montereau Bridge. They lived and bred on a diet of acorns, snails and roots. If you sent heralds up there to tell them the worst part was over, the noise of trumpets would drive them deeper into their caverns.

A mauve plain of thyme-blossom ran over the chalk towards Rheims. There a letter was being read. It had come by the hand of the herald-royal.

It may have come to your attention that we have enjoyed success and victory under God over our ancient enemies the English. In front of Orleans and later at Jargeau, Beaugency, Meung-sur-Loire, our enemies have suffered severe injuries. Their leaders and others to the number of many thousand have been killed or taken prisoner. These events, having occurred, more by divine grace than human expertise, we—on the advice of our Princes of the Blood and the members of our Great Council—are

349

coming to the city of Rheims to receive our anointing and coronation. Wherefore we summon you—on the loyalty and obedience you owe us—to dispose yourselves to receive us in the accustomed manner as you have done for our predecessors.

Do not be deterred by affairs of the past or the fear that we may remember them. Accept our assurances that if you now act towards us as you ought to you shall be dealt with as suits good and loyal subjects . . . If, in order to be better informed about our intentions, certain citizens of Rheims would care to come to us with this herald whom we have sent, we should be delighted. They may come in safety and in such numbers as suits them . . .

Only later did Charles and the girl come to know what further frantic postures the Council of Rheims took up. The recurring problem: they wanted to please Charles without upsetting Philip and Bedford who might come back to Champagne with grudges in some other season.

So they convened to consider the letter but found that although each individual councillor wanted the king and the king's mercy for Rheims they unfortunately lacked a quorum to make an executive decision and send delegates out across the blue plain to Charles.

An *ad hoc* committee representing all sections of trade and the city said they would support what the councillors might decide whenever they managed to achieve a quorum.

The herald suggested that the city be searched. Three councillors were sick but five others were missing. If their names were called from street to street?

The councillors present said they were sure the herald understood . . . the councillors absent might not be in the best streets . . . discovery might be a discomfort, might ruin their reputations . . .

The herald thought it was a damned funny way for councillors to go on in an emergency. He rode alone back to Charles and told him how they were havering.

In fact the commander of Rheims was down on the Marne at Château-Thierry. His name was Monsieur de Chastillon. For his own reasons he was mobilizing to march north around the west of the Champagne hills into Rheims.

Now the Council of Rheims sent him a letter saying he must come immediately to discuss the defence of the city. Unfortunately, given the food shortage and rebelliousness in the city they could let him bring an escort of only fifty horsemen and their attendants—two hundred men.

He wrote back saying that two hundred men weren't adequate for his safety. Didn't they know a French army of thirty thousand men and a witch had left Chalons?

They wrote back and said that certainly he could bring thousands once they'd decided on the final details of the defence. But for the moment they could not permit more than an escort of fifty horsemen into the city.

On Wednesday 13 July he came with hundreds of horsemen, more than a thousand soldiers. His herald told the council that 3600 English knights and their attendant troops had landed at Calais three days before and were marching to Rheims. They had been raised to crusade against the Turks but were now assigned to the defence of Rheims. Within ten days, twenty at the outside . . .

The town council refused to let Chastillon in the gate. He'd brought more soldiers than they'd specified. Resentful, he moved away north to join up with the English.

Early on a Saturday morning the king, catching up with his forward cavalry, reached the château of Sept-Saulx in the river-meadows of the Vesle. Ten miles north-west stood holy Rheims. Monsieur de Sept-Saulx was in armour beyond the moat to receive Charles. The combined parties rode through into a sunny court of white stones, suitable to the day, the light, the triumph.

The king kissed the middle-aged lord.

Charles: Soon all your vineyards will grow again.

Lord: Despite the war, Your Majesty, they haven't entirely failed to produce.

Charles: Ah.

In the first floor hall of Sept-Saulx, the king, his councillors and *pucelle* waited to meet the councillors of Rheims. They got there before noon with broiled complexions. Monsieur de Sept-Saulx offered them no wine. Their breath remained a little short right throughout the meeting. You would have thought Charles, his council, his prophetess, had first call on the air in the hall.

351

Machet read out Charles's terms:

The Rheims garrison would go that afternoon. Any remaining after Angelus would be treated as prisoners. They could take goods to the value of two pounds tournois only. The prisoners they held would be bought back by the Council of Rheims at a German mark or its equivalent for each man. As always Rheims would pay the cost of the coronation, the coronation feast and decorations. All French peers and their staffs would enter Rheims. The French army itself would encamp in the suburbs on the south-west where they would be expected not to loot but also to find free billets if that were possible—there *were*, after all, thirty thousand and His Majesty understood the problems.

The Chief Magistrate of Rheims asked when the coronation might take place.

Machet told him the king had not decided, but the Council of Rheims must be aware that coronation day had always been a Sunday. Ever since Clovis.

The Chief Magistrate said *therefore eight or nine days* . . . ? His eyes blinked, cringed, winced. Eight days the giant army eating Rheims empty . . .

Jehanne rode ahead to Rheims after the meeting. Gilles travelled at her side. He had let his beard grow out of grief for Lavignac. Since the boy's damnation in front of Troyes, Jehanne didn't feel comfortable with him, his oddities were less amusing.

Jehanne: Have you had Masses said for the boy?

Gilles: Yes. Oh yes. But what good . . . ?

Jehanne: Some good. Who knows?

Gilles: Dear lady, the astrolabes . . .

Jehanne: Yes?

Gilles: The astrolabes say he's in hell.

Jehanne felt a gush of sweat between her breasts.

Jehanne: You ought to pitch those bloody astrolabes, Gilles!

Gilles: My eyes on the future, that's what they are. You have to pray for me, Mademoiselle!

He had stood upright in his stirrups because of the urgency that she should pray for him.

Jehanne: Why?

Gilles: At one or two in the morning demons talk to me.

352

Jehanne: What sort of demons?

Gilles: Voices. Like your Voices. Though not like yours.

Jehanne: Gilles, you can have demons driven out. At least, they tried to drive them out of me. They found the house empty—thank Jesus.

Gilles: Last night, I heard my Robert's voice, clearly as you'd want. Telling me . . .

Jehanne: What?

Gilles: I can't tell you.

Jehanne: Brother Richard. Let him drive them out.

Gilles: Perhaps.

Jehanne: Not *perhaps*. Let Richard. He's a strong personality.

Also, God help him, he belonged to the same order of humans as Gilles did, and she herself.

They rested in a pub just south of the city by the Vesle bridge. Gilles got a room for Jehanne and she rested in the suspicion that Mesdames and Messire would visit her with indications. But nothing happened. She felt it unkind of them not to speak up here, on the margins of Rheims.

At four o'clock, stretching in the upstairs window, she saw the Bastard riding up the road from Sept-Saulx with hundreds of knights, a gaudy forest of flags, plumes lighting up the heat haze, usurping for vividness and fluidity the low and sand-banked Vesle.

She ran downstairs to meet them.

Bastard: He wants to be crowned tomorrow.

Jehanne: Sunday.

Bastard: I suppose you heard it's always been a Sunday. Since Louis VIII. The ceremonial hasn't varied since Clovis for that matter . . .

Dear Jesus, it all ends tomorrow. The Voices already departed and no further instructions.

Jehanne: Shouldn't he rest a week? Go into a week's contemplation?

Boussac: There's this new English army sent out by the Archbishop of Winchester. The king thinks he ought to act while things are right.

Jehanne: The council never let him act before when things were right. I always had to wait months, except for this.

She exaggerated because of her fright. She felt Monday, the day after anointing, roaring down on her. She had not been given orders for Monday.

Rheims seemed just any other city when they crossed the lowered bridge over its narrow river. Corporation trumpeters blew blasts from above the gate. The names were roared down into the city by a basso–cryer.

Cryer: Monsieur Jean the Bastard-Royal, Mademoiselle Jehanne the girl.

The Council of Rheims was already taking ceremonial pains.

Bastard: Will you come up with me now, Jehanne?

Jehanne: Where?

Bastard: To hunt up ceremonial items. For the crowning.

Jehanne: That *would* be pleasant.

Above their heads the balconies threatened. But the city sounded and smelt good. Drums, violas, tambourines, bag-pipes, spice, fruit-mince, bacon, chicken in its own fat. *I should be happy*, she told herself.

Bastard: It's easy to forget that a lot of the ceremonial items are in the sacristy of St Denis near Paris. The Goddam English have them. The Charlemagne crown, the Charlemagne sword called Joyeuse. The sceptre . . . my secretary has the list . . . the sceptre with a golden Charlemagne on top of it. The rod of justice that ends in a hand made of unicorn horn, the clasp of St Louis's cloak, the Pontifical that's been used since Louis VIII . . .

Jehanne: My God. No one ever told me . . .

Bastard: All *that* can be substituted for. We'll find substi-tutes in the cathedral and the churches. We've got the only things that you can't afford to counterfeit. I mean, we've got Rheims and a king *and* the holy ampoule of oil . . .

The crowds in the cathedral square roared to show how well they intended to roar for the king. The Bastard and Jehanne would have been satisfied with a little less. Under high saints in the grand stone front stood a bald and ordinary little priest in a golden cope. He stood in a thicket of junior clerics, all in spectacular dalmatics and armed, as if against an enemy, with censers, aspergillums, ceremonial crosses.

He said he was the Dean.

Dean: We're waiting for our Archbishop.

Bastard: He'll be along, perhaps towards dusk.

Dean: But we've been here since noon.

Jehanne flashed her dislike at him. Letting him know she was taking in his comfortable little body as evidence against him. To be just, he *did* have a summer cold.

Jehanne: We have to see the sacristy treasures.

Dean: Mademoiselle?

Bastard: For the purposes of the coronation. My secretary has the authorization from His Grace Regnault de Chartres.

The Bastard's secretary rushed the document to the Dean's hand.

Beyond the sublime nave and the long sacristy stood a windowless treasure-hall. Three keys were necessary for entry. Inside, batteries of chests and cupboards stood about.

It was cool in there, with a deep winter smell of incense, spice, age and aged fabric. Only the Bastard, his secretary and equerry, Jehanne, Pasquerel and d'Aulon were let in there. The Dean showed them a *Liber Pontificalis* only a little younger than the St Denis books. All the coronation ceremonies were there on vellum pages too slippery for mould. He found them a blue cloak tipped with ermine and knew there were sceptres somewhere about, one of them used by Louis VI at his coronation.

Dean: Of course, I hadn't expected to have to find them in such a hurry. Our curator of treasures has phthisis.

Jehanne opened a chest at random. There was nothing inside except two small items wrapped in red silk. The silk had been dappled by mould. Her hand reached in: there was some elemental excitement as far as her armpit.

Inside one parcel was a circlet crown with sapphires around it. Inside the second some king's or prince's spurs.

Gilles lay still in the end. They took the wedge of wood from between his teeth. His nose was bleeding where the demons had left him. They'd made high-voiced female jokes, very gross, on their way out of his body. Poor Gilles's lips did not move throughout—the voices rose out of his belly and throat and nose, articulating themselves, and last of all Lavignac's voice.

Lavignac: Join me up the arse of hell, darling Gilles.

Senior Augustinians from the Rheims monastery and

Brother Richard knelt beside him, puffing. They had read the exorcism over him, but the devils' insults and the violence of the devils' departure out of Gilles had stolen their breath away.

Over-stimulated and bound to have nightmares, Pasquerel put his hand tenderly behind Gilles's ear.

Pasquerel: Welcome back, brother.

Jehanne: This is a secret. You have to understand that.

Augustinian: Of course, Mademoiselle.

Jehanne: I'll call his squire in, to put him to bed. Do you good fathers know a public house called the *Bronze Ring?*

Augustinian: The . . . ?

Jehanne: The *Bronze Ring.*

One of the Augustinians laughed.

Augustinian: Rue du Parvis. It's very fashionable. Poets. Wealthy Italians.

He didn't think much of poets or wealthy Italians.

Jehanne: My father's staying there.

The guests were in a long upstairs parlour, sitting by the front windows, checking now and then on the passage of the moon.

Jacques's voice dominated. She waited on the stairs and listened. She was wearing old clothes and had crossed the city with d'Aulon. There had been such enthusiasms for her this afternoon, when she'd left the cathedral, that she couldn't have visited Jacques in her own person.

She could hear his voice. The childish wish came over her that she could have come in velvet and with her staff.

Jacques: So a child gets born. You accept it, you start to love it. Everyone round you is a farmer or a farmer's wife and you take it for granted that the kid is going to grow up to be that. When you're given one who's not meant to be a farmer or a farmer's wife, you don't know it, no one tells you, you keep trying to force it. I mean, *you* think about *your* kids, gentlemen. Think if one of them wanted to do what my girl's done. Would you let it? You'd call it an uppity bitch. I called her an uppity bitch. Jesus Christ, often . . .

She had heard the city council was paying his hotel bill, she had expected him to be lording it and perhaps he had been lording it earlier. But she hadn't expected to walk in on such insights. In her fear of Monday, it was a high gift to have Jacques returned to her and in this self-doubting cast of mind.

She stepped up on to the floor. She saw Jacques was wearing a good gown of claret-coloured fabric.

Jehanne: Papa Jacques.

He got up, dragging his chair a little with him. For a long time he said nothing.

Jacques: My little cow.

Jehanne: Oh Jesus.

They both stood shuddering but feared to embrace. His hand stroked her collar.

Jacques: Can't they dress a good soldier better than that?

She saw her brother Jehan at the window in a very nice doublet, scarlet and yellow. He wasn't the best dressed there.

Jehan: She doesn't ask enough. She works without wages.

Jacques: Duckling, do they look after you? Tell me.

He began to hold her lightly but stiffly in his arms as you hold a person with wounds.

Jehanne: I eat with the king, I call marshals by their first name . . .

Everyone listened, plush burgesses, Italians, poets, high-coloured Jehan. The opulence of her experience seized them.

Jehanne: I always have apartments in the château with the dauphin.

Jacques: Imagine it!

Jehanne: When I'm in a field the king's cousin d'Alençon sees to my billet. Don't take any notice of Jehan.

Jacques hugged her wildly now, a glee-hug.

Jacques: All expenses paid! *All expenses paid!*

After Matins in the cathedral next morning, four notables in dazzling blue and gold rode the little way to the Abbey of St Rémy to fetch the chrism of kingship. They rode their horses up the nave of the abbey church to the chancel screen. The horses were scarcely horses at all, islands of silk drapes, their heads formalized by steel facings from which candle-light bounced. It was only when they had left and there was dung on the stones that the Grand Prior accepted their reality.

The four horsemen were the Marshals of France, St Sévère de Boussac and Gilles de Rais, the Admiral de Culant and Lord Graville who had fought at the Herrings, Orleans, Beaugency, Jargeau, Patay. They accepted from the Grand Prior a gold and enamel dove.

The dove lived in the tomb of St Rémy behind the high altar. In its belly lay the crystal phial of oil. It was the same Rémy had used at the coronation of Clovis. The story was that after each coronation the oil remained undiminished. Heaven in this way paid its compliments to the abounding kingship of the French dynasties.

Jehanne was called from her town house to the king's apartments to hear Mass with him. She found him dressed like a peasant. Charles intended to walk to the cathedral in a grey shirt and hose. On this poor kernel kingship would descend layer by layer.

Seeing him, she felt her womb kick. He took her hand and they knelt together at bare, unhassocked prie-dieux. She was delighted somehow by the self-wonderment in him.

After Mass they ate nothing—the king was fasting to undergo the mystery of kingship.

Charles: Jehanne?

Jehanne: Dauphin?

Charles: Soon to be king. But what I wanted to say, it's time to ennoble you.

Jehanne: Make me a lady?

Charles: Ennoble your family. Now that it's over.

She felt panic.

Jehanne: Over. It isn't over, Dauphin. There's a new English army. You don't have Paris. Your cousin's still a prisoner in England. It isn't anywhere near *over* . . .

Charles: A victim under Christ . . .

Jehanne: What?

Charles: You said it in Chinon. You were the victim. And I feel the strength of your sacrifice in me now. Like an advance. From a banker. (He closed his eyes.) If only a person could do something for a victim.

Jehanne: I'll try to put up with any death that's asked . . .

Charles: I'll protect you from my people. I will. From the council. From the Constable.

It was their conspiracy and it had an illicit flavour to it.

Jehanne: There are still English in Normandy . . . you don't have Paris.

She saw he knew she was finished.

Charles: Do your Voices tell you to go to Paris . . . ?

Jehanne: I . . . I dream of Paris.

Charles: Ah.

Jehanne: I hear them in dreams.

Charles: We all dream.

She had to admit it.

Jehanne: That's right. Everyone dreams.

Charles: I'm an affectionate person. And a grateful one. But a king isn't made to be affectionate or grateful the way a farmer can be. He has to dole out his affections and gratitude according to the kingdom's good. The gift to do it comes with the oil of kingship. You led me to the oil of kingship. Remember all that when I neglect you for others . . .

Jehanne: Of course, you have to do whatever . . .

He got up and kissed her on the nub of the head and went back to the chapel.

Alone in the hall she covered her face for a little while. Then she thought, I'll go home with Jacques tomorrow, I'll see Zabillet, I'll be a Domremy spinster. She knew it was a fantasy but it soothed her.

On her way downstairs she met de la Tremoille, who had never spoken to her. Today his eyes took her in and he smiled. His teeth were very bad, some of them had died and gone black in his head. His voice was soprano, as people said.

De la Tremoille: Well, we've done everything you wanted.

Jehanne: Monsieur.

She didn't have the resources to argue with him.

De la Tremoille: And such a new way of proceeding on the matter of prisoners! One would think you were trying to destroy the rules of knighthood.

Jehanne: In my tiny knowledge of the business, my lord, they look stupid without any help from me.

He did his high laugh and began climbing the stairs again.

De la Tremoille: Well, a great day for everyone. I didn't think I'd see it . . . And now it's all done I suppose you can wear skirts again.

When she put weight on the ball of her foot her whole leg trembled. She thought, that fat man would crucify me this morning if he could.

She had a place in the cathedral close to the chancel. First she held her flag herself but was feeling tired and passed it to Minguet.

The nave was thick with flags—Boussac's, la Hire's, the Bastard's, de Culant's, de la Tremoille's, Machet's, a thousand or so others. Only Jehanne's was the flag of a visitation, manifestation, something outside mere genealogies.

Charles came in in his humble clothes. The choirs sang the coronation motet hurriedly written out for them overnight and rehearsed at dawn.

Bastard: Wouldn't it be strange if they've brought the nine-year-old to Paris? If they're singing these same songs for him in Notre-Dame right now.

Jehanne: It wouldn't happen.

Regnault came out of the choir and met the king. On Regnault's back and chest were a quarter of the cathedral's treasures; he was a metallic god in cope woven of beaten gold wire. As long as one didn't look too closely at his complexion . . .

Dazzling Regnault intoned a coronation litany. He treated the words woodenly but the sweet choir took them up. Jehanne's right side glowed. Messire is coming, she thought, not too hopefully.

Messire didn't come.

The choir finished after perhaps an hour. Charles knelt on the stone all that time. No cushion. He was in awe of himself, his awe seemed to command the cathedral. No one laughed at his funny legs.

In the new silence everything sounded strange, sharp; the clack of a flag-butt, the grind of a shoe.

The king-of-arms of France came to the king's side. He called the names of the twelve peers of France who were to stand at a dauphin's side on his coronation day. Only six were present. All the others were imprisoned or senile or sitting pat with the enemy.

In their places rose:

Jean, Duke of Alençon,
The Count of Clermont,
Georges de la Tremoille,
Regnault,
and others.

A priest opened Charles's shirt to the chest and eased it down from his shoulders.

The Lord of Richemont hadn't come to hold the royal sword. He too had to be substituted for. As the Bastard said, only Rheims and the oil could not be substituted for.

Indeed there was powerful joy at the chancel screen. It had its core in Charles; it was larger than Charles. All down the nave people were getting drunk with it. Alençon turned round to take from a young knight the arms of knighthood. He put them down at the king's knees. He saw Jehanne and wagged a finger towards her. *Come up here,* the finger said. *Be in it.*

She went and stood beside and a little behind Alençon and watched him put sword, furled flag, studded scabbard, helmet at Charles's knees. Yes, it's worth any agony, she thought. Though she knew she'd change her opinion for a tiny while in the future. When—to use Messire's phrase— the steel went in.

Charles said his oath after Regnault. That took a long time. Then the irreplaceable oil went on the shoulders, eyes, forehead and wish-bone.

In the end Regnault went to the high altar and took off it the crown found the day before in the cathedral treasure-house. He raised it high above Charles's head, the brown cropped hair. Eleven other lords put their hands out to touch it. Of its own force, it seemed, pulling against them, it descended on his head.

A shocking blast of trumpets hit them all. Everyone roared and gushed congratulations. Jehanne thought, Lavignac and me, we're well-spent if we're spent on this mystery.

That night, Jehanne found, the day's exquisite clarity got clouded.

There had been a feast in the hall of Tau. Charles had eaten and been served by Alençon and Clermont. The table extended out of the archiepiscopal palace, down the stairs, into the street. In the rue du Parvis, where Jacques's pub was situated, a bronze stag, hollow, was wheeled full of wine into the street. People drank from a spout in its mouth. The wine was Charles's gift. Though the municipality paid for it.

At the *Bronze Ring*, doyen Jacques of Domremy slept against a wall with his arm round his landlady, widow Alix Morieau. Jehanne saw him there, on the first floor, on the floor. Clutching Alix for warmth in the hot night. Jehanne remembered that he'd got on well with the red-headed landlady in Neufchâteau.

She went to her apartments early and sat by the open window. There was a bonfire under her window, sparks flew perilously under the gables. It doesn't matter, she thought. Not a random fire, she thought with a little arrogance, I won't die by random fire. Pasquerel was in the other room hearing the confession of a pale and—it seemed—devout Gilles.

But in the morning people in a side street called rue Cénacle would find in a sewer the eviscerated corpse of a thirteen-year-old boy. Gilles's work? Without the close help of demons? No.

Yet she would remember the pale excessive Gilles muttering at Pasquerel.

Later on that day, Sunday night, her brother Jehan and Jean de Metz lunged in.

Jehanne: Well?

Jehan: We want to get ennobled, Jehanne.

Jehanne: You too, de Metz?

De Metz: It's safest, Jehanne. Before our luck runs out.

Jehanne: Luck?

Jehan: Fat Georges says you're a witch.

De Metz: The word catches on.

At least, even drunk, he was more ashamed than her brother.

Jehan: While we've still got some say.

De Metz: And think—a man stands more chance if he's a Monsieur. And if he's a Monsieur he can say I knew her and she was good. That'd carry weight.

Jehan: We deserve it.

Jehanne: Do you? This poor hack maybe. You're just lucky enough to come from the same womb.

Jehan: I'm going to become someone. A figure.

She yelled at him.

Jehanne: I'll arrange it. I promise.

They grinned and fell down the stairs. *After you, Monsieur,* they kept telling each other.

Pasquerel: Do you mind if I go to bed, Mademoiselle?

Jehanne: No. You sleep.

He went, the child-priest. Easy to control but no support. Now that she wanted it.

At her window towards midnight she saw Mesdames Aubrit and de Bourlémont pass down the street dressed— she would have sworn—in the exact clothes used for the Boischenu rites. She called to them and thumped downstairs. She saw them making a golden retreat around a corner and ran for that corner and for the next, for they were always at the ends of streets gliding over drainage pits. Always the streets were unlit, all the lights that were burning that night in wider places could almost be seen and all the shawms, pipes, flutes, violas, drums and jangling instruments and tenors and counter-tenors and boy-singers were always audible like a festival coming or still to come. But the coped Mesdames of Boischenu didn't want to speak to her or have her see their faces, and risked no crowds or lights. And always found the dark streets. And glided. At last she stood and begged at the top of her voice.

Jehanne: Mesdames!

Around a corner she ran into Bertrand.

Bertrand: Jehanne!

He wasn't too far gone with wine. She looked at him narrowly.

Jehanne: Where are they?

Bertrand: Who?

She hit him with the knuckles right across the face.

Jehanne: Get them!

Bertrand: Who?

She caged her eyes with spread fingers of both hands.

Jehanne: Oh Christ.

After a while choking, she told him. Mesdames Aubrit and de Bourlémont.

363

Bertrand: They're not in Rheims, Jehanne.

Jehanne: I saw them.

Bertrand: They're in Lorraine. Ask Jacques.

Jehanne: Oh God.

Bertrand: Be comforted, Jehanne. They aren't here.

She began mourning down in her throat, she fell on to her knees and felt fresh dung under them. He fell with her and had her shoulders.

Bertrand: I would swear on all my hopes they're not here.

Jehanne: In their Boischenu glory?

Bertrand: It wasn't much glory. They're not here.

He lifted her. She had to be guided home. There were two chairs set by the empty fireplace and they sat there. He kept an arm around her.

Jehanne: You ought to be out celebrating.

Bertrand: No.

But he went to sleep, his arms still round her. It was just like Jacques and the landlady three streets away.

Jehanne: Dear old Bertrand.

Jacques stayed in Rheims two months. It was a May feast for him. He never breakfasted before eleven, was fit to start on the Beaune whites with spiced poultry by two or three. Alix called him Jacquemin. Though her tenderness did not go further than that she knew a number of younger women in the city who liked figures of importance.

Meanwhile the king, his darlings and armies moved on. Sometimes in those months the king would put a gem in a cup of wine at banquets and hand it to a councillor or diplomat to whom he was grateful. But he never did it for Jehanne.

Yes, he ennobled her and her collateral family. That pleased Jehan, but Jehanne knew it was a thing done on paper by clerks.

The omens thickened around her. She was sent campaigning against mere outlaws. When Jehanne, Alençon, Gilles marched on Paris, Charles and his diplomats made arrangements with Philip behind her back. In camp in Senlis, before the king's eyes, she broke her sword Fierbois across a harlot's arse. She attacked the St Honoré Gate of Paris on a Sunday and, when wounded in the thigh by an arrow, was dragged away not begging for absolution but shouting that one more rush would give her friends the town. But the town they never got and the people of the town remembered a howling witch bleeding under their palisades on a Sunday. Alençon kept riding to Senlis to beg the king to keep up with Jehanne and the army, but Charles's darlings now were diplomats of the Fat Georges species. All the generals felt lost with the lost girl. Poton, at her side, wept, saying *there are the battlers and there are the statesmen, and the statesmen won't speak to the battlers any more*. And when Messire came, he was often silent at her side—not displeased however. More grieving for her. In the end she was pulled from her horse by a Burgundian Bastard in a skirmish outside Compiègne.

Nothing ever went right again with the old rightness that had made pale Charles a king.

Epilogue

A letter from Jacques to all his dear relatives in the region of the Meuse and in Sermaize and the surrounding districts of Champagne. This letter is written for him at his bidding by the parish-priest of Greux.

You must have heard of the reports of the death of my sweet daughter Jehanne in a Goddam fire on the last day of the month of May. Did you know that they kept her in a soldier's prison, amongst the worst of Goddam looters and rapists. But they feared her witcheries and did not touch her. I did not fear her witcheries when I took her on my knee or dealt with her with my heavy hand. But they chose to fear my duckling, and I thank Christ for that.

She would not give in and say that the Voices that led the king to Rheims were false. I saw her in Rheims and there were no false Voices in her, I swear to you, and the king that was anointed there was King of France. In Orleans and the King's France they mourn her, but imagine, friend, how Zabillet and I who made her softly from our bodies cry out for her . . . that her soft flesh has gone into unbearable fire. When the court had finished with her, the Goddams dealt appallingly with her organs, throwing her heart into the river at Rouen, where it would not sink. I curse the fire that ate the flesh away and then the bone so that my duckling's charred heart lay there for the executioner's hand to lift and hurl into unconsecrated water. I do not curse the judges and the executioner, I do not curse Bedford or that Bishop Cauchon who calls himself a Frenchman. Lord Christ will see them each and every one to their proper agonies. I leave them to him.

Pierrolot is still a prisoner in the north, but we have had word that the Burgundians will treat him as a gentleman.

When they burned my daughter they put a mitre on her head on which these words were written: Jehanne, self-styled the *pucelle*, liar, pernicious, abuser of the people, heretic, relapsed, apostate, idolater.

Be my witness, King Jesus, that her last word from the flames was your name.